Appalachian Elementals One

Rhianna, Thank you & happy reading

CLEANING HOUSE

AN APPALACHIAN CONTEMPORARY FANTASY

JEANNE G'FELLERS

Mountain Gap Books

www.mountaingapbooks.com

Published 2018 by Mountain Gap Books
Jonesborough, TN
www.mountaingapbooks.com
Copyright © 2018 by Jeanne G'Fellers
All rights reserved
Cover Design by Jeanne G'Fellers

Paperback ISBN: 978-1-7323277-0-2
eBook ISBN: 978-1-7323277-1-9

A Note from the Author

The Appalachian (properly pronounced Ap-pa-latch-un) people are a complicated mix of Scots-Irish, British, German, and Native American traditions blended with a whopping-big serving of Protestant Christian beliefs.

We're often misunderstood and commonly stereotyped by outsiders who know very little about our culture. That said, Cleaning House embraces the queer Appalachian experience, a unique blending of resistance, acceptance, and perseverance. We, like the rest of Appalachia, are as hearty as they come, and, yes, it is entirely possible to get our red on or dander up (pick your poison), though generally in the liberal sense. Again, we're unique and complicated. We're rainbow pinpoints in a red, mountainous sea, but we live here happily because we're Appalachian folk. Some of us will never leave these mountains. Some leave and never come back. But many of us, like myself, leave only to return because our lives aren't right once we leave the mountains. Something is missing. We're lost. Part of us dies when we leave because our roots run from the bottom of New River Gorge to the top of Mount Mitchell.

We're poor and middle class. We're educated and high school dropouts. We're coal miners, teachers, convenience store employees, doctors, and nurses. We're able-bodied, disabled, multi-faith, and multi-hued, but we all have one thing in common— our traditions.

Cleaning House is primarily set in Washington County, Tennessee, where I was born and raised. While Washington County rests in the Southern Appalachian foothills, I have also lived and worked in the more rural and mountainous settings of southern Carter County, Tennessee, and McDowell County, West Virginia. Neither of those locations is for the faint of heart, but the people there are amazingly resilient.

In short, I am an Appalachian woman and proud of it.

I would also like to mention the use of Appalachian Granny Magic alongside European and neopagan witchcraft in Cleaning House. While Appalachian Granny Magic has its beginnings in both European and Native American traditions, it is firmly rooted in Protestant Christian beliefs. The characters in Cleaning House embrace both Granny Magic and witchcraft in the form of paganism because their family lineage has embraced both paths, creating a unique belief system that is on the rise in Appalachia. Many, but by no means all, Appalachian witches are as likely to call on the Holy Trinity as they are to call on Gaia or the Goddess, a seeming conflict, but it isn't to the practitioners. They plant by the signs, use natural means for both medicinal and magical purposes, and practice water-witching as a means of finding a viable water source, so why wouldn't they pray to the God of their raising alongside the gods of their path? With this knowledge, the reader should also realize that the herbal remedies and medical procedures described in Cleaning House are in no way a recommendation for their usage. Medical care should be obtained from a qualified medical professional and never be based on something you read in a work of fiction.

As for the non-human characters in Cleaning House— please remember that this is a contemporary fantasy novel, a work of fiction, so the liberties are mine, the author's, to take. But if you don't believe in fae or wee people, find a quiet, wooded spot somewhere, relax, and open your eyes to the possibilities. You might be surprised by what you find.

The Cleaning House Playlist

https://www.youtube.com/watch?v=Nu55xS1TdoU&list=PLlfRTJ_vkiJfD-caJxPWts4wq_dSeqZBEe

About the Cherokee Language

A phonetic form of the Cherokee (Tsalagi) language is used in portions of *Cleaning House*. The written form of Cherokee is polysynthetic, meaning a single word may well represent several words or even an entire sentence. Written Cherokee also employs a syllabary that was first created in the early nineteenth century by Sequoyah. Each symbol represents a syllable instead of a letter sound. The written form would not be recognizable to non-Cherokee speakers, employs a unique font setting, and would generally confuse readers.

That said, the unfamiliar terms used are, indeed, the Tsalagi language, and not wholly created for the Appalachian Elementals series. The author of *Cleaning House* encourages readers to explore the history of the Cherokee people and their language through competent online and print sources.

Here are two such sources that were used for *Cleaning House*.

http://www.cherokee.org

http://www.native-languages.org

Acknowledgments

While I can safely say I am familiar with many of the cultural and magical traditions of Appalachia, I admittedly had help with a few of the finer points. As such, I would like to acknowledge the following people for their input:

1) Ian Allan, Mountain Witch, provided the information concerning snake bones and their power that I used in Chapter Thirty-Four, the tradition of blackbirds foretelling death that can be found in Chapter Thirty-Seven, and the information concerning what I call witch-nailing that appears in Chapters Thirty through Thirty-Four. All this information derives from Ian's workshop "Introduction to Appalachian Granny Magic" and the provided handout. Readers can find out more about Ian Allen, Mountain Witch, via the following source:

http://www.facebook.com/AppalachianWitchery/

2) Anne G'Fellers-Mason, my sister, historian, and the Special Projects Coordinator for The Heritage Alliance, for her contributions concerning the Civil War era in Northeast Tennessee. Readers can find out more about The Heritage Alliance via the following source:

http://www.heritageall.org/

3) Jake Richards (Dr. Henny), Conjure Doctor of Jonesborough, Tennessee, provided information concerning rolling stones for answers (a Tsalagi tradition) as used in Chapter Thirteen and dividing herb bundles and placing them in the water to see if they'll be effective as used in Chapter Thirty-Two. Readers can find out more about Jake Richards (Dr. Henny), Conjure Doctor of Jonesborough, Tennessee, through his blog: *Holy Stones and Iron Bones.*

http://littlechicagoconjure13.wordpress.com/

4) Information concerning the Cherokee presence around Embreeville Mountain and their use of mineral deposits derive from "A Historical Overview of the Bumpass Cove Landfill Controversy, 1972-2002" by Robert Clinton Marsh III available at:

http://dc.etsu.edu/cgi/viewcontent.cgi?article=1848&context=etd

Thanks, Ian, Anne, and Jake, for your vast knowledge, and an appreciative nod to Clinton Marsh III for his hard work and to East Tennessee State University for giving public access to such valuable information via its Digital Commons.

This is but the first novel in the Appalachian Elementals series, so I'll probably be referring to your wisdom again.

-Jeanne G'Fellers

Prologue

"Have you seen him?"

Wailing Woman walks Long Man's banks every night in search of her son. She asks the catfish, the bears, the Yvwitsunastiga, and the ever-watching spirits then screams up the mountainside and cries into the river, begging for answers, sending grief-filled bubbles downstream so others can hear her pain.

"Have you seen Dustu Usdi?"

"Have you seen my only child?"

"Have you seen my son?"

The catfish stare, the bears shake their heads and lumber away, but the spirits...

"Forget, Mother. It is the only way."

Wailing woman walks from Summer to Winter then back again, leaving no more tracks in the river sand than Dustu Usdi had, becoming just as lost. A shadow of what was. A cry from the past.

Have you seen him?
Have you seen my son?
Can you bring him back to me?
His life has just begun.

Chapter One

Everything You Thought You Knew
July 17, 2017

"**Fourteen**. Fifteen." Centenary Rhodes counted the bills in her hand a second time and shoved them back into the front pocket of her cargo pants. She had fifteen dollars left after she paid her rent. Fifteen dollars for food and the bus. She sighed and turned away from the hamburger joint whose door she'd darkened. "Beans and rice it is… again."

She skipped the bus— too much money— and walked the two miles back to her shabby one-room North Chicago apartment, opting for the alley that shortened the last six blocks to four, ignoring the catcalls from the construction site at the far end.

Short, dirty-blond hair styled into an undercut, black, heavy-framed glasses that hid soft blue eyes, and baggy pants that masked what little curve her large-boned frame had managed to achieve. She wore a loose t-shirt over her top-half and a ball cap with a brim bent much like her current attitude. Cent was skinny but strong nonetheless, a tough-as-nails Appalachian woman, a concept no one in North Chicago seemed able to grasp. *Those idiots will whistle at anything on two legs.*

She turned on her size twelve sneakers to jog across the street, down the block, picking up her pace the last two blocks to her apartment when it began raining, closing the progression of bolts and chains on her front door before she leaned against it to stare wearily at her dingy apartment. The marble flooring and Art Deco lighting in the corridor were still pretty, but they didn't match the cracked plaster walls. The old bank had once been grand, but now…

"What a dump." Still, it was all she could afford on two part-time jobs. Cent threw her coat over the single dinette chair and flung herself, face-down, over the sheet-draped, worn plaid couch that served as both her living space and bed. Not even a fold-out. She'd finagle one eventually, but until then she'd sleep solo. Always solo. "Who'd want to come back here, anyway?" Her romantic and job prospects had been abysmal since she'd lost her full-time accountant job in a corporate down-size. For the past year, she'd divided her time between a local bodega and a small computer repair shop. Both bosses were pricks, and the bodega owner's wife kept telling her that she'd find herself a good man if she'd try.

"You're a smart girl, too smart to attract a man, so dumb it down and pretty yourself up. Put on some makeup. Grow your hair. You can't find gold without putting a bit of polish on yourself."

Forget that. Take me as I am or not at all. Cent kicked off her shoes and rolled so she faced the cracked, plaster ceiling. She'd graduated top of her class at the University of Chicago and knew account management inside and out. Cent could do absolute magic with numbers and tell you exactly where things were going right or wrong in your financial life. But, even so, the ability to manage her own numbers now evaded her. She was in over her head and nearly bankrupt. Her monetary life was in shambles, and she knew you had to have good credit yourself to manage other people's money. "If I can't be myself then—" She startled when something struck the door four times. "What the—" Cent rolled off the couch and plodded to the door in sock-feet. "Who is it?" She peered through the peephole.

"Delivery for Centenary Rhodes." The messenger held up the envelope that'd been tucked under their arm. Ruddy-brown, almost earth-toned skin, hair that went everywhere but was short enough to go nowhere— this messenger was, well, different on so many levels. And, their, yes, their. She'd learned long ago not to make assumptions about anyone, especially those she found herself attracted to.

Interesting. "Lemme see your ID."

"Sure." The messenger held up the card tethered to their waist. "I need your signature."

"Gimme a moment." Cent opened the locks and chains slower than she'd closed them. *Another summons. It has to be.* She'd been sued three times in the last two months for debts she accrued during her good job. A ten-thousand-dollar judgment for the car. Another thousand for breaking her lease before she was evicted. She'd been forced to adopt the blood-from-a-turnip method of dealing with her debt spiral. *You can't get what I don't have to begin with.*

"Sign here." The messenger held out an old-fashioned, lined-paper signature board. "Nice neighborhood." Their voice held a muddled accent. Maybe European, but Cent couldn't be certain. "I would not want to be here after dark."

"You and me both." Cent took the envelope when the messenger held it out. "Thanks." Her heart fluttered when she peered up into their face to see piercing dark brown eyes that were inquisitive, seeking but easily humored by the way one brow over those eyes cocked.

"Make certain you lock up tight." The messenger lingered at the door to stare back at her. "Can I do anything else for you?"

Are they flirting with me? Cent looked down then back up, startling when she saw the messenger's eyes were still on her. Taller than she was, which was unusual, a bit thick at the waist, but it was clearly muscle. A puzzle, and an attractive one at that. There was something calming about this person's eyes. Something familiar Cent couldn't quite place. *They're damn-near twice my size.* The realization that such strength stood so close made her skin prickle in a way she'd come to miss. *No wonder they're on this route.* "No, um, thanks."

"Have a good day." The messenger turned down the hall, leaving Cent to watch their floor-gliding strides until they reached the stairs.

"You too."

"Cute accent, by the way." The messenger stopped at the stairhead to smile at her then descended without saying more.

"I thought you were into men." Mrs. Donright, 3J, stared at Cent from between the chains securing her door. "That was a woman, right?"

"Mind your own business." Cent slammed her door closed and turned to press her back against it. *Was that a man or a woman or...?* Hell, she didn't care. They were hot, and they'd flirted with her. That was enough. She looked out her peephole and sighed, securing every lock and chain before she turned to stare at the envelope. The messenger had left soft-dirt fingerprints along its edge. *They must work in a plant nursery or something, too.*

Maybe I should take up gardening.

Being close and sweaty, their hands touching as they worked side-by-side. Cent shivered as she scrutinized the envelope. "It's too thin to be a summons." She went to the kitchen for the scissors but couldn't find them, so she opted for a paring knife, sliding it beneath the taped flap to open the envelope, pulling out a single, handwritten page.

> *Dear Centenary,*
>
> *I need you to come home to help me clean up the homestead for sale. I'll keep you fed, and you can stay there or at my house until it's sold.*
>
> *Mr. Jones at Dryler's said he could use you ten hours a week, so that'll give you some money too.*
>
> *And some collections service man came by the other day to serve you papers. I gave him a fake address in Carter County so he'd go away.*
>
> *Never mind him or what your mama said last time you spoke to her.*
>
> *Just get yourself home. I need your help.*
>
> *Love,*
>
> *Aunt Tess*
>
> *P.S. Quit changing your phone number.*

Cent read the letter twice more, smirking when she realized she'd read it in Aunt Tess' thick, Southern Appalachian accent.

"I'm not going back to Hare Creek, Aunt Tess, but I'll give you a call just the same." Cent pulled her phone from her pocket and clicked the contact list, praying her mother or another family member didn't reach the phone before Tess did.

Chapter Two

Calling Home
July 17, 2017

"Hello?"

"Aubrey? Is that you?" Cent relaxed her grip on the phone when he confirmed her inquiry. Cousin Aubrey was not merely okay, he was the only other family in the family. The self-professed rainbow sheep, a title he'd claimed only to Cent after she'd moved away. "Is Aunt Tess around?'

"In her herb garden." Aubrey placed emphasis on the normally silent H in herb. "Hold on. I'll get her for you."

This'll take a few. Cent heard the bang of the back door and Aubrey's voice seconds later, yelling for Aunt Tess. "She's coming. So how you doin'?"

"Fine, I guess. Working. That's all."

"You and me both." Aubrey chuckled low. "Your mama's mad 'cause Tess contacted you, so watch yourself."

"I haven't talked to Mama in over three years."

"That's good, considerin'. She and that Minister Ruleman fella are getting married in three months." Aubrey sounded like he'd swallowed something midway between bitter and sour. "Nobody around here's seen her knees an' elbows in a good six months, and she's taken to wearing this scarf thing about her head. She says it's about modesty, but…"

"Geez. Okay, thanks for the info." Cent rolled her eyes. "So how are you, Aub?"

"Still driving back an' forth to K-Town on the weekends. You know how it is."

Ethan during the week. Straight on the weekends around any family besides Tess. No one should have to live two lives for their family to accept them. "Why do you think I moved away?"

"Yeah, well, maybe I won't have to be here every weekend when you— here's Aunt Tess."

"Cent? When you comin' home?" Aunt Tess, seventy-five years old and a bit hard of hearing, all but yelled into the phone.

"I…I'm not planning to anytime soon, and you know dead-to-rights why." *Damn, I slide back into the accent far too easily.*

"Your mama," Tess grumbled. "I'd tan her hide if I thought it'd do any good. I need you, girl. And you know that ain't an easy thing for me to say."

"Yeah, I know, but why are you selling the homestead?"

"Same reason you won't come home. Your fool mama. She wants to cash out her part to use for her wedding."

"Can't you buy her out?"

"The land alone is worth eighty-five thousand. Too big a poke for my little piggy."

"Yeah, mine too." Cent ran her hand down her face. She had wonderful childhood memories of the homestead. Playing jacks and marbles and shooting off caps with Aubrey and the other cousins. Spitting watermelon seeds for distance and at each other. The smell of the outhouse in the summer. Okay, so not every memory was wonderful, but she'd felt safe and comfortable there. "What about your trailer?"

"It's got too many add-ons to move. I guess I'll leave it with the property and use the money to put a new one in a park somewhere close." Each word sounded more defeated than the last. "I'll make do, I reckon."

"You mean Skibnet Land Company will snatch the place up cheap and subdivide the property for houses that'll be falling apart within a decade." The idea made Cent cringe. "I don't know what to tell you. I can't just leave my jobs and—"

"Jobs? You workin' *two* jobs up there?"

"Yeah, gotta eat, you know?"

"So, the big-city girl left her home only to struggle all alone somewhere else?" Tess grew quiet while Aubrey hee-hawed in the background.

"Tell Aubrey I said to shut up!"

"Shut up, Aub. Show your big-city cousin a little respect before I knock a knot on your head."

"Yes'm— ow! Dang it, Aunt Tess! That's not fair!"

"That'll learn-'em durn-'em. Listen, Cent. We all know you ain't got it easy up there so why not come home for a spell? I won't charge you no rent. You can eat from my pantry and garden and drive my pickup. Everyone says I shouldn't be driving anyway. And Mister Jones said he'll give you some work— cash money paid weekly that you won't have to use for that dump you're living in."

"How do you know—"

"I taught her how to use Google maps!" Aubrey chirped in the background. "Your neighborhood's crap!"

He would. Cent ran her hand down her face a second time as she looked around her apartment in the growing twilight. "I don't know. Really. Things will straighten out here sooner or—" She cursed under her breath when she flipped the living room light switch. *The electricity.* The lease's all-utilities-paid clause didn't necessarily mean that the electricity always stayed on, only that it would eventually be paid. "Give me a day or two to think about it, okay?"

"Call me back by this weekend." Aunt Tess sighed. "If you don't come, I'll be hirin' outside help. One of those junk companies, I reckon."

"There're two-hundred-year-old antiques in that house!"

"I lived in that house for four decades." Aunt Tess huffed into the phone. "So I know what's in there and what ain't." She said something to Aubrey that Cent couldn't make out. "Well, Aubrey can help some, but that ain't enough to get it done in time." Tess sighed. "All right. Call me Friday and let me know." The call ended so abruptly that Cent stared at her cell phone.

"I know you need me, Aunt Tess, but I don't think I have it in me to go back there again." Cent placed her phone on the coffee table and lay back on the couch. She had a lot to think about, but she was tired and barely remembered to set her alarm for her early shift at the bodega before she drifted to sleep.

Chapter Three

Limestone Pebbles
July 1995

Cent loved playing in Aunt Tess' garden, eating Tommy Toe tomatoes off the vine, and flicking Japanese Beetles off the leaves toward the near-full trap.

"Nasty lil' boogers," Aunt Tess said. She loathed them, but she wouldn't kill them like Mama did. No, Tess knocked them off the tomato plants or scooped them up and dumped them into the trap, where hundreds of them writhed in the bottom of the bag, trying to climb up to reach the lure that'd trapped them to begin with.

"Why don't you buy a new trap?" Mama crunched another beetle under her flip-flop. "We ain't gonna have any 'maters left if you don't replace it soon."

"I know." Aunt Tess sighed. "But I don't like killing things if I can help it. They're pretty bugs. Kinda shiny."

"And they're eating everything in the garden!" Mama flicked one from her shirt sleeve. "There won't be no 'maters or anything else to put up for winter if you don't change that trap!"

"All right!" Cent watched as Aunt Tess waded through the green peppers and tiptoed through the cucumbers toward the homestead's partially enclosed back porch.

"Cent! Pick up that poke beside the beans and start to pickin'." Mama pointed to the paper bag sitting atop the Blue Lake bush beans sprawling along the ground. Mama and Aunt Tess were both good at gardening, but they certainly weren't neat about it. "Cent!"

"Yes'm. I'm going." Cent flicked open the bag and set it beside the beans. Beans. She hated picking beans. They tasted good with potatoes and a little fatback in them and were especially yummy out of the canning jar in January, but right now, in the July heat, she hated them more than almost anything. Cent stooped over the plants, turning over leaves. One or two beans here, a handful there… "Sheesh." She swatted at the pale-yellow bug with little black dots that crawled over her hand. It resembled a ladybug but with all the wrong colors.

Almost cute, until Cent spied the little, fuzzy yellow dots on the underside of one plant's leaves. "We got bean bugs!"

"Shoot 'far!" Mama mumbled dirty words under her breath then stood up straight and arched, her hand on the small of her back as she yelled for Aunt Tess. "While you're at it, bring the dust! We got bean bugs too!"

"Dagnabit!" Tess let the screen door's creak say what she wouldn't in front of Cent. "I don't have any." She carried an old green-glass Coke bottle half-filled with water in one hand and a new beetle trap in the other.

"I left some here last week!" Mama furrowed her sharply arched brows at Tess. "Where'd it get off to?"

"How should I know?" Tess bent over the beans, plucking the bugs off the leaves and dropping them into the bottle. "Here." She held the bottle out to Cent. "Find as many as you can." She took the sack and began picking beans, turning over the leaves one by one, breaking off the ones where little yellow bean bug eggs nestled near the stem. "I'll give you a penny for each one you bring me."

"That's a lot!" Cent began picking through the beans with great care.

"Careful. Don't break any plants as you go." Aunt Tess straightened long enough to re-pin her gray-streaked hair on top of her head.

"Damn Japanese Beetles." Mama swatted one that flew near her face. "Where'd you say the dust was at?"

"I said I don't know." Aunt Tess winked at Cent when she looked at her. Tess knew exactly where the bug dust was hidden, and so did Cent, but she knew better than to say anything. Bugs ate what bugs needed to make more bugs, no more, no less. They had a right to a bite or two without being poisoned. That's what Aunt Tess had said anyway. They'd get rid of them naturally, pick them off, mush their eggs so there wouldn't be as many of them.

"Little bugs don't know when to quit, do they, Cent?" Tess dropped a stack of leaves into the sack with the beans. "Keep picking, honey. All the way to the end of the row." Tess stood and turned away. "Hey, Nida. I think the corn's tasselin' off, but the ones toward the middle are a little behind, and one of them is flat-out strange lookin'. Come see."

"I druther you'd go find the dust, but all right." Mama followed Aunt Tess into the corn. It was unusually tall this year, above either of their heads, so they soon disappeared between the stalks.

"Bugs. Bugs. Bugs." Cent followed along the row, collecting bean bugs and egg-covered leaves until she reached the end of the row and the edge of the garden. Beyond, the land turned into a steep hill, but higher up it became a mountainside and reverted to what Aunt Tess called natural. Old-growth trees, bushes of all kinds, and small patches of billowing grass with heads as tall as the corn. Cent squatted to consider the twist of blackberry cane at the garden's edge. *There're some ripe ones in there!* But snakes sometimes came with berries, so she looked carefully before she set down her bug bottle and stepped between the briars. They pricked her ankles, but the berries were purple and juicy enough to make it worth it.

She popped one into her mouth and grinned. They were good. Bursting from the July heat, sweet, and they were too far into the brush for the birds to get at. A berry patch all her own. Cent's patch.

She raised the front of her t-shirt to her midriff to make a little apron and began picking. One for her mouth, two to share with Aunt Tess and Mama. She kept picking and eating, pushing into the brush, ducking under limbs and climbing over half-rotted stumps in search of more berries until the thicket suddenly ended, placing her in a small open area amid the trees. The sunlight didn't reach much into this space, but Cent thought she saw twinkling lights darting above the ground. Lightning bugs! She thought about going back for the Coke bottle, about dumping the bean bugs to use the bottle to catch lightning bugs, but Aunt Tess didn't like it when she caught them, and she paid good money for the bean bugs.

"Dang, it's hot." Cent wiped her forehead with her berry-picking hand. She was thirsty, but not enough to go back to Aunt Tess' yet, so she moved to sit at the base of a tree in the thin spot, dropping her shirt-tail so the berries spilled onto the ground beside her. "Oh, no, my shirt! Mama's going to tan my hide!" Cent held it up to see the purple stains dotting the pink and white t-shirt's front. It was a play shirt, one she'd worn in third grade the year before, but Mama would still be mad enough to pick a switch from the willow behind their house, or, worse yet, make Cent go pick one herself. "Dang it!" Cent looked around for something to take out the stains before they set. "Water. I need…" If she listened hard she could hear the spring up the hill. That was real clean water, at least Aunt Tess said so, and better than the county water that ran down the pipes along the highway. "Yeah." Cent left the berries where they were and followed the water sound until she came to where the spring bubbled from the ground. The pipe ran to the homestead, but if Cent reached right— *yep. This'll do it.* She drank a handful of water and smeared a second one across her shirt, rubbing in earnest, but the spots only paled and spread. "Aw, come on." She put another handful of water on her shirt and rubbed harder, flicking off the berry seeds she'd knocked loose. "Mama's gonna kill me for sure!" She wrung out her shirt front and peered down, frowning when she saw the stains were still there.

"Don't be sad." A gentle voice tickled her ear. "The stains will disappear if you rub limestone pebbles over them."

"Who said that?" Cent's skin prickled as she looked around. No one. She was still alone.

"Please try." The whispering voice spoke again, this time close enough to stir the sandy-blonde hair laying over her ears.

"Aubrey? That you?" Aunt Tess had said her younger cousin was coming to play with her later in the afternoon, that he was staying over, that his mama had to work the night shift in Johnson City.

"Try the pebbles. There are two beside the pipe." The voice was strange, earthy and fresh, like how the garden smelled after it rained.

Cent knew her imagination was playing tricks on her again. It always did when she played in the woods behind the homestead. Aunt Tess called it creativity and encouraged her stories when they were together, but Mama called them fool's tales and didn't want to hear them.

"Okay." Cent would play again. She might as well. There'd be heck to pay as soon as Mama saw the shirt. "Where're the pebbles at again?"

"By your foot."

Cent startled when something landed against her sandal. Two perfectly round pebbles, shiny-white limestone, stared up at her like little eyes. "Clean them off in the water then rub them on the spots. Your mother will not be mad then, and she will let you stay the night with Tess."

"How do you know?"

"I know lots of things. Now, do as I ask."

Cent rubbed the stones over the fabric. "It ain't workin'."

"You must tell the spots to go away," the voice replied. "Command them to leave, and they will."

"Spots don't care what I say. They're just spots." Cent rubbed even harder. "Stubborn ones."

"Rubbing so hard will make a hole in your shirt, so listen close and repeat what you hear." The voice rustled Cent's hair again. "Spots. Spots. Leave my shirt. Color the leaves. Stain the dirt. Return to the earth from whence you came. So mote it be."

"Mote?" Cent had heard Aunt Tess say mote before, which gave her confidence. "Spots. Spots. Leave my shirt—"

"Color the leaves and stain the dirt," the voice encouraged. "And close your eyes, too."

"Why?"

"Because you want the spots gone." The voice sounded on the verge of laughter. "Say the words now. Color the leaves and stain the dirt."

"Color the leaves and stain the dirt."

"Return to the earth from whence you came."

"Return to the earth from whence you came."

"So mote it be."

"So mote it be. Now what?"

"Blow on your shirt really hard then open your eyes."

Cent did as she was told and cracked open one eye to see her t-shirt. "They're gone!"

"Yes, they are. Now put the pebbles back by the water pipe where they were. Gentle. You do not want to disturb the ground any more than necessary."

"Sure." Cent carefully set the pebbles back into place and leaned over the spring, drinking deep from the water again. "Thank you." Cent listened for a reply but, after a moment, she sighed. "It's gone again." Their conversations always ended this way. She turned toward the berries, determined to get them back to Mama and Tess without staining her shirt again, but when she got to them she stopped in her tracks. "Look at that." The berries were piled neatly on a mat of woven fern fronds. She picked up the mat, thanked her invisible friend again, and turned toward the garden. No lightning bugs twinkled near the ground, and the shadows surrounding the little clear spot were growing long.

"Cent? Where you at?" Mama's voice trickled through the berry cane.

Cent glanced over her shoulder, "Thank you!" and climbed through the cane, soon standing on the garden's edge. "I'm right here."

"Where you been, girl?" Mama stood beside the bean rows holding a full bag. "Wherever did you get off to? And what are you carrying?"

"Blackberries." Cent held them out for her to see.

"You filled the bug jar, picked a mess of beans, and had time to go berry picking too?" Mama rested the poke on her hip. "Good girl!" She flashed Cent one of her weary smiles. "Your cousin Aubrey's spending the night with your Aunt Tess and Uncle Kinnon. Do you want to stay too?"

"Can I?" Cent followed her mother around the pepper plants and toward the old log house.

"Yeah, you did good today." Mama reached back to steal a blackberry from the top of the pile. "I bet there's enough for both me and Tess to make a buckle tonight. Andy will like that."

Cent frowned when Mama mentioned Andy. She hated him. She always hated Mama's boyfriends, but this one seemed like he'd be around for a while, drinking beer and pinching Mama's butt every chance he got. "You sure we got enough for him too?"

"You're going to be here eating buckle, not at home."

"Oh, yeah." Cent smiled before Mama became cross again. Mama was happy and proud of her, a rare combination she'd best enjoy while she could.

"Let's double check that you can." Mama waited for Cent to catch up then they walked toward the house together, Mama's hand gentle on Cent's shoulder.

Cent still didn't know who the voice in the woods belonged to, but she knew Mama wasn't the one to ask. No, she'd ask Aunt Tess tonight after Aubrey fell asleep.

Chapter Four

Shifting Winds
July 21, 2017

After a breakfast of warmed-over rice mixed with butter and the last of the sugar, Cent placed her bag on her shoulder and headed off to the bodega. It was a quick walk to the corner, but one she dreaded whenever she had an early shift.

Spreadin' Betty, the tall prostitute who lived down the hall, sat on their apartment building's stoop. "Chupta, Cent? Early shift again?" Betty flicked ashes from her bargain-brand cigarette.

"Yeah, unfortunately." Cent stepped over Betty's splayed leg. "You're up late."

"Shit for business last night." Betty took a drag from her smoke. "I'll do a lot, but there're some things I won't do for anyone." She curled her crimson lips into a snarl. "I'm tryin' to stay clean, you know?" Betty's accent was everything Cent's wasn't— deep and New England. Her ending R sounds were more like an H, and her word choices…they'd all but needed dictionaries to understand each other when they'd met the year before.

"What is it, six months now?" Cent stood on the bottom step and peered down the street.

"Two-hundred-ten days but who's counting?" Betty tapped Cent's backside with the toe of her high heel. "Want me to walk you to work?"

"I can't afford your rate." Cent glanced back at Betty. Beneath the lacquered-on foundation, false lashes, and heavy eyeliner, Betty was actually a soft-heart, at least where Cent was concerned.

"No charge for a cute cuttah like you, and I need some smokes anyways." Betty flicked her cigarette butt onto the step below her, pulled her legs together, and pushed down her skirt to a more presentable length. "Omar hates me waltzing in there in work clothes anyhows. Always thinks I'm gonna kife something." Betty's hand landed on Cent's shoulder as they turned toward the bodega. "I'll wait outside while you open up. First lucky customah of the day."

They chatted as they walked. Betty's only customer, a sailor new out of Great Lakes Recruit Training, had been more interested in looking at her package than any delivery of goods. "You'd think he'd never seen a dick before." Betty's laugh turned bitter. "He couldn't get it up for the longest time then as soon as I got a condom on him, the cork popped. Easy money."

"Probably his first time." Cent patted Betty's hand. "Poor kid."

"He knew what he was getting into, so…" Betty's nicotine breath fanned across Cent's neck. "You off this afternoon?"

"I think. Why?" They stopped under a street light near the bodega. "Got something in mind?"

"Want to decompress?" Betty grinned down hopefully. "The electric's back on, so how about a movie, popcorn, and a glass or twelve of bubbly?"

"Sounds fun."

"Only the best for my Cent." They'd stopped outside Omar's bodega. "Got your keys?"

"Yeah, hold on." Cent dug in her pocket for the ring of keys Omar had entrusted her with. "Okay, here we… wait. Did he change the opening time without telling me?" Cent scrutinized the "now opening at eight AM" sign hanging on the gate then grabbed the paper wedged above the lock.

"What's it say?"

"Let me read it first." She swatted Betty's hand away and held the paper up to see it in the streetlight. "Damn."

"What's wrong?" Betty took the paper, holding it in her nail tips as she read. "What a jerk. The bastard could have at least told you in person." She crushed the paper in her hand.

"Yeah, you'd think." Cent ran her hand over her face. "Shit! Now what am I going to do?"

"You can't blame Omar for taking care of his family first, but his means of letting you know…" Betty grabbed Cent's hand to bring it to her chest. "You're going to be okay, baby doll."

"Not if I can't pay my rent." Cent knocked her head against Betty's shoulder. "Dammit!"

"Come on. Let's go home." Betty wrapped her arm around Cent's shoulders, guiding her back to the apartment and up the stairs to the third floor where they lived at opposite ends of the hall. "Go put your stuff away, including your phone. Put your jammies on and get to my place. I'll peel off my face and get comfy while you do." She gave Cent a nudge toward her apartment. "Go on."

"All right." Cent hung her head. "See you in a few."

"You better." Betty stood in the hall watching until Cent's door swung shut.

Without all the makeup and cheap hair extensions, Betty was quite attractive but in a high-maintenance way Cent had never preferred. The top layers were an act, a barrier to defend against the ugliness Betty faced every time she sat on the apartment steps with her skirt hiked. Spreadin' Betty didn't exist behind her apartment door, but Betty the trans woman-addict trying to keep herself clean did. She'd lost her support system, her family, most everything, but she kept plodding along.

Hope I can do the same.

"I pulled out the sofa bed and popped a bottle of bubbly, so wipe that frown off your cute little face." Betty pointed to the couch, a stained-up cast-away they'd dragged up the stairs four months earlier. With a cover, it wasn't half-bad, and Betty had refurbished the ratty-ass mattress with bleach water, a memory-foam topper, and a good cover. "Let's get comfy." Betty set the bottle and two dollar-store wine glasses on the end table.

"Not sure I'm up to this." Cent rolled her shoulders and stared at the floor. "One glass and then…"

"Play hell, you will!" Betty grabbed Cent by the back of her gray t-shirt and shoved her toward the couch. "It takes at least two, baby doll, and I'm in the mood for real company. Sit!" She crawled onto the fold-out beside Cent, grabbed the bottle, and poured two sloppy, foaming glasses, one of which she held out. "Bottoms up." She wiggled her ass and giggled.

"Why not?" Cent downed the cheap champagne in two gulps and swiped her hand across her mouth, stifling the burp that rose with the bubbles. "What movie?"

"*The Birdcage* or *Rocky Horror*, your choice."

Cliché, but why not? "No hiding ourselves today. *Rocky Horror.*"

"That-a-girl." Betty popped the DVD into the player and trotted back to the pull-out where she draped her arm over Cent's shoulders and pulled her close. "You and me. Two queers against the world."

"Yeah." Cent hiccupped and held out her glass. "Another?"

"One of my regulars gave me a whole case last week, so the sky's the limit." Betty topped Cent's glass. "I even made us a prop bag." She pointed to the paper bag sitting next to the end table. "Want popcorn yet?"

"Maybe at intermission."

"Let's get going, then." Betty set the prop bag between them. "No rice this time. The roaches love it a little too much." She pulled out a foldable sandwich bag stuffed with hand-cut confetti.

"You know those roaches could be coming from eggs mixed into the bag glue, right?" Cent shivered as she sipped more champagne.

"You serious?" Betty dropped the bag back onto the floor.

"Yeah, and keep yours here. I got enough critters of my own."

Betty laughed at this. "I love how your accent comes out when you drink." She kissed Cent on her forehead, dropped the confetti bag into her lap, and wrapped her arm around her shoulders again, pulling her even closer. "Remote's on your side."

"Okay." Cent passed Betty the remote and settled back, more than ready for the comfort of being her total self with someone who was doing the same.

Chapter Five

Go Home
July 21, 2017

Cent woke late in the afternoon to find Betty sitting in her dining nook, leaning forward in her chair as she blew smoke rings out the open window. Cent's cell phone sat on the sill.

"Why do you have my phone?" Cent rubbed her eyes as Betty turned to face her.

"I asked you to leave it at home." Betty blew another smoke ring, ground the cigarette butt against the radiator, and flicked it out the window, straddling the chair as she peered at Cent through sad eyes.

"I forgot."

"Well, Little Miss Forgetful, your Great Aunt Tess called like six times while you slept." She reached for her pack of cigarettes and lighter. "I don't know how you slept through it."

"You didn't answer, did you?"

"I thought it might be an emergency." Betty shoved a cigarette between her lips and flicked open her lighter. "And it was."

"No, it wasn't. I would have felt it." Cent rubbed her eyes. "You got something besides champagne I can drink?"

"There's some bottled water in the fridge." Betty stared unblinkingly at Cent. "And again with the feeling stuff? You're a strange woman, Cent, but I actually believe such things coming from you."

"I'm nothing special, just have a touch of empath ability is all." Cent shrugged. "Runs in my family."

"Then why do you have some of the things I've seen in your apartment? Crystals in the corners, the bag of stuff over the front door, those invisible signs you keep reading." Betty raised the corner of her mouth in a half-smile. "Witchy stuff, you know?"

"I grew up with them, that's all." Cent scratched her head as she turned toward the kitchen. Aunt Tess had taught her those things the summer before she'd left for college, after she'd turned eighteen, and Mama had gone on a wild tear, punching Cent and throwing her out of the apartment. Mama had landed in the psych ward the next day, her third time that year, but Cent hadn't bothered to visit, nor had she pressed charges. "Some of it's part of growing up in Appalachia. The rest I picked up from my aunt Tess."

"Whatever, but why didn't you tell me you had family who gives a shit?"

"They only care when they want something from me." Cent popped open the fridge to grab a tepid bottle. Betty's fridge was always slow to recover from their building's regular outages. *No wonder the champagne was room temp.* "What'd Tess say?"

"Hard to tell with her accent." Betty raised a well-plucked brow. "But I could hear the emotion clear enough." She held her lighter flame to her cigarette and sucked in until the tip glowed red. "She wants you to come home."

"Ain't happenin'." Cent opened the bottle and took a healthy swig. "My life there is done."

"Apparently not." Betty folded one arm across her seat back and lifted the other for another drag. "And who's Aubrey?"

"My cousin, why?"

"He got on the phone for a moment after your Aunt Tess." Betty waved her cigarette in Cent's direction. "Now, I could understand him some. Educated like you, but still with the same accent. Cute, I bet. Is he?"

"Oh, good grief." Cent slid down to sit in the kitchen doorway. "What'd he tell you?"

"He said the same thing your Aunt Tess did. They need you to come home." Betty stared at Cent. "They need your help."

Cent shook her head and slumped over her water bottle. "If I go home, I'll have to deal with Mama."

"Yes, Tess mentioned her, said she was the whole reason you left there to begin with."

"Her and a lot of other people in the area."

"Haters are everywhere, baby doll." Betty reached out with her toes to lift Cent's chin. "But family isn't."

"Yeah, but you're family too."

"That's nice." Betty dropped her leg and reached back to flick more ashes out the window. "But it isn't reality." She stood so fast her nightgown swirled around her calves. "We're friends because we're both queer, and that's the only reason."

"The only reason? I thought we had a connection, a—"

"If we did it ends right now." Betty tossed her cigarette out the open window and slammed it closed before spinning around to loom over Cent again. "Go home, country cuttah. This isn't the place for you, and I'm not your friend."

"But I've lived in Chicago for almost a decade. You know this." Cent sat tall when Betty drew her mouth into a snarl. "I've been to five continents. I—"

"And now your sorry ass is trying to scratch together a living outside the Great Lakes naval base." Betty jerked Cent to a stand and pressed a delicately painted fingernail into her chest. "That stink you always complain about? That's the pharmaceutical plant across the road and the fish stand next door. It's the smell of run-down, molding, festering nothing. It's a hell hole. It's Nowheresville. Go home, little girl." She pushed Cent back with the heel of her palm. "Go. Home!"

"Dammit! What're you doing?" But as Betty kept pushing, Cent realized she was being herded toward the door. "You want me to leave? Okay, I'll leave!"

"Good! Leave! Go all the way back to Tennessee!" Betty shoved her a bit harder. "Go home, country girl. Go work your educated, southern fagginess out where you should be!"

"Fagginess?" Cent knocked her hand away. "Seriously?"

"You got it, chickie." Betty kicked aside the half-used prop bag to stand over her again. "You're nothing but an over-smart, out-of-your-element, mixed-up pan cuttah who's afraid to face reality!" She spun Cent around and shoved her toward the door. "Go. Home!"

"This is my home!"

"No, baby doll, it's not." Betty's street-tough exterior dropped, and she sighed. "I can't wail on you if I try. So, listen, will you?" She grabbed Cent's hand and pulled her to the fold-out, wrapping herself around her as they both burst into tears. "Dammit. Dammit to hell." Betty squeezed her tight. "You… you've got to go home. Please. You've got something I've never had, family who takes you as-is, without question."

"But there's a lot there who don't." Cent's nose pressed hard into Betty's cleavage. "I feel out of place, out of—"

"Get your face outta there." Betty pushed her back. "You and me, we're on a downhill slide. This place isn't anything but ugly, and we're becoming ugly with it."

"You're not ugly." Cent looked up to see the mascara streaking down Betty's face.

"Your jammie pants are smoldering from that one." Betty wiped her face with her fingertips and peered down at Cent with a half-smile. "I'm an over forty, trans-woman-turned-call-girl." She sighed deeply. "And an addict."

"A former addict."

"Once an addict, always an addict." Betty kissed the top of Cent's head and scooted back to hold her hand. "Remember how I read your palm when we first met and what I told you about your lifeline?"

"Yeah, you said it ran off my hand and down my wrist and that meant I'd live forever." Cent lifted her hand to show the crease. "Why?"

"That wasn't a lie, but if you stay here, you'll make a liar out of me for certain." Betty's hold remained desperate. "I love you, Cent."

"And I love you too. That's why I don't want to leave you."

"And I don't want you to go, but— have you ever heard the saying 'if you love something, let it go'?"

"Yeah, who hasn't?" Cent lay back in Betty's arms.

"Time we both lived it, right?" Betty wrapped one arm around Cent's waist and another around her shoulder, pushing back her head with her hand until their eyes met. "Right?"

"What'll you do when I'm gone?"

"Keep doing what I'm already doing." Betty shrugged when Cent frowned at her. "I'll be okay, baby doll. Thanks for worrying."

"I can't help but." Cent grew quiet, staring at Betty's hand. "I hate it when you're right."

"It came as a surprise to me too." Betty chuckled. "Let's get on your phone and buy you a bus ticket home."

"The bus." Cent's frown deepened. "I just paid my rent, so I don't have the money. I've got a couple more checks coming, but…"

"Never fear. That's what your Betty-Boo is for." Betty reached beneath the couch to pull out the credit card she kept tucked into the frame. "My ass is worn out, but my credit's not— at least not completely."

"Your ass is fine, too."

"You've never even seen it." Betty giggled as she held out the card. "It's spectacular, by the way, but I'm not exactly your type so—" She pulled it back. "What is your type anyway?"

"I know when I see it."

"You're gonna get all smoke and mirrors mystery-like on me now?"

"Alright." *How do I best put this into words?* "I don't like too female, too male… a blending— I like tall too, but it's difficult to find someone taller than me."

"Big, androgynous, and full of surprises. Got it." Betty held out the card again. "The money's a loan. Okay? I'll need it back to keep up my hormones."

"A loan. Definitely." Cent dug her phone out of her pocket, hesitating when Betty placed the card in her hand. "I'm going to miss you."

"You're not gone yet." Betty kissed her cheek. "I've got some tuna in the cabinet. Want it and some crackers?"

"And some more bubbly?" Cent pulled the Greyhound website up on her phone's browser.

"Damn nasty combo, but you need to put some meat on you." Betty pirouetted from the couch and into the kitchen. "Make the ticket for the day-after-tomorrow so we can order Chinese and get drunk off our asses tonight."

"You're taking the night off?" Cent glanced up from her phone.

"Only for you, darling." Betty kicked back her leg as she leaned against the counter. "Only for you. Now buy that ticket and call your aunt Tess."

Chapter Six

Cheddar Crack
July 24-25, 2017

"I'll send you your last paycheck when it comes in." Betty twirled Cent's mailbox key ring around her finger. She'd paid for the cab to the bus terminal and waited with Cent until the bus had arrived... fifteen minutes late. "Your chariot awaits, baby doll." She swept Cent into her arms to kiss her on both cheeks. "Oops. I left lipstick on your face." Betty pulled a tissue from her clutch and rubbed the spots until Cent complained.

"You're acting like a mom." She pushed Betty's hand away.

"You should be so lucky." Betty caught Cent's head with one hand, spat onto the tissue, and rubbed Cent's face harder, releasing her hold only after she was satisfied. "There." She put the tissue back into her clutch and grabbed Cent again, pressing her forehead into her shoulder. "But if this is how a mom feels when her kid leaves the nest, I'm glad I'm not one." Betty dabbed her eyes. "You be careful and call me the moment you get there."

"And you take care of yourself." Cent hugged her back. "Go get your nails done or something special... a treat, just because."

"A distraction, eh?" Betty smiled down at her. "You're such a sweet cuttah."

"Whatever it takes to keep you clean." *I'll miss you.* Betty, a good six-foot-eight in heels, was a giant of a woman, but by far the kindest soul Cent had met during her Chicago years. "I'll be back as soon as I can."

"I hope not." Betty dropped her arms and stepped back. "Go on." She pulled her light-weight cardigan tighter over her chest.

"Promise you'll stay clean?"

"I'll try my best." Betty pursed her lips and batted her lashes. "Be a good girl."

"Yeah, you too." Cent glanced toward the porter who was loading her bags under the bus. Her life, her entire life. She'd boiled it down to two bags in the last two days. Not that she'd accumulated much... and most of what she once did have, she'd sold to make ends meet. She'd given Betty her entire kitchen spices, pots, pans, and CorningWare. *My bags and me. That's it.* It was as much as she'd had when she'd come to Chicago for school. *And nothing to show for it.*

"They're loading." Betty's sigh shook her chest, and her bottom lip

23

quivered. "Dammit, I told myself no tears, but now…" She dabbed her eyes with another tissue. "Go on. Make me proud."

"You *sound* like a mother." Cent hugged her one last time, finding solace in her friend's firm chest and arms. "Love you."

"Love you too." Betty stepped back. "Go."

"I am." Cent looked back twice while she waited to load. Betty smiled at her the first time and held her hand to her face the second time in a call me sign. *I'll call you, Betty. Friend. You've helped me more than I can say.* She mustered her strength and stepped onto the bus in search of an empty seat.

Crowded. Damn crowded, but she found an empty seat midway back and settled in. Cent pressed her hand against the window in hopes Betty would see, and she did, pointing from Cent's face to her own skirt pocket.

"Pocket?" Cent dug into her cargo pants as the bus's door hissed closed, pulling out a tissue wrapped around folded cash. Two twenties, two tens, two fives, and five ones, all neatly folded. Travel money. *Yep, mom.* She slipped the cash into her palm and pressed it to the window.

Betty smiled and waved harder.

"Mom." Cent spread the cash, the twenties in her pants' pocket, the tens in her shirt. She shoved the fives and ones down her sports bra beside her ID.

Betty was still standing on the platform when the bus pulled away, still watching until Cent couldn't see her any longer.

"Well, here I go." Cent pulled her earbuds from her jacket pocket and turned on her iPod, an older model no one would give her money for when she'd tried to sell it. She scrolled until she found a song befitting the occasion and sat back, watching Waukegan, Chicago, and their surroundings fade as the bus turned south and Shinedown's "Big Black Cadillac" drowned out the bus's diesel drone.

Cadillac? No. Cent pressed her forehead against the window. *But I'm going home.*

I just hope Mama ain't around when I get there.

———————⟨⟩———————

"Cent? Cent! Do you see me?" Aubrey flailed his arms like he'd stepped in a yellowjacket's nest, pulling her aside to hug her as soon as she stepped away from the bus. He was broader in the shoulders than she remembered, and taller, but still not as tall as she was. "You made it in one piece."

"And you're wearing a man bun!" She reached behind his head to tweak the twist of curly, dark-brown hair.

"I hafta for work. You've changed too." He ruffled her asymmetrical cut and lifted the right side to inspect her head. "Shaved? Your mama's gonna *love* that." Aubrey was darker skinned than her because his mother had been mixed Filipino and African-American, the daughter of a Korean War soldier and the love he'd found overseas. Aubrey's eyes were warm brown and slightly slanted, more so when he raised his brows. His looks appealed to most everyone, but he'd only been interested in men since he'd come out to Cent when he was thirteen.

"I'm not overly concerned with what Mama thinks." Betty had shaved the right side of Cent's head the night before she'd left. "Let me send someone a text to let her know I'm here." It was six in the morning, her usual work time at the bodega. But it was an hour later here, right? She checked her phone for the change. *Yep, seven.* She was back in the Eastern time zone. "Hi, cuz. Good to see you." She pointed to Aubrey's rubber-ducky-print scrub top. "You still working in pediatrics?"

"I like kids. What can I say? I managed to get off a little early to get here, but I had to come straight from the hospital." He grabbed her second bag when she pulled it from the platform.

"Can we get coffee?"

"Drinking coffee now, are we?" Aubrey wrinkled his nose.

"By the gallon." Cent turned toward the parking lot. "Which one's yours?"

"The red Camry." He flashed the car's lights to show its location.

"No more pickup?"

"Ick, no. I never got the smell of Uncle Kinnon's tobacco spit out of the upholstery." He tossed both her bags into the trunk. "Aunt Tess' car died a while back, so she was driving it until recently, and now she's saving it for you."

"Oh, joy." She buckled her seatbelt as he climbed into the driver's side. "Nice ride."

"Yeah, it is." Aubrey turned his head to see her. "You still got your license?"

"Why wouldn't I?"

"'Cause you don't own a car anymore."

I couldn't afford to keep one. "You don't need one in Chicago, but I still kept my license in case I needed a rental. We ready?"

"Coffee first?" He put the Camry into reverse.

"And Pal's for some Cheddar Rounds?"

"Ain't no Pal's 'til we reach Greeneville. You been missing Cheddar Rounds?"

"Yeah, of course. But I can wait if you can."

"Our family calls them cheddar crack for good reason." Aubrey peered over his shoulder as he backed out of the parking space.

Their conversation remained innocuous for a while. Cousins, home-cooked food, marriages, divorces, and kids. All the gossip Cent had missed during her time away but, inevitably, Mama came up.

"She ain't herself." Aubrey sipped his caramel macchiato. "And that's something, coming from me."

"Yeah, I know." Cent chewed on that knowledge as they drove along. Aubrey wasn't an atheist, but he wasn't anything else either. More of a deist, she thought, but he didn't claim any sort of faith for himself. "You walk your own path."

"Exactly. But your mama's always been easily influenced, and this Minister Ruleman…he's pushed her off the God, Jesus, and pass-the-collection-plate deep end."

"How so?" They were off Interstate 40 and on Interstate 81, heading for exit twenty-three, the Greeneville exit. Hare Creek, however, was still an hour away.

"It's like she's been possessed since they met. Driven. She talks nothing but heaven and hell, life and death, salvation and damnation." Aubrey changed lanes to pass a pickup pulling a hay baler. "She and Aunt Tess had a huge argument a while back, and Aunt Tess set protections around the property right after."

"What sort of protections?"

"Salt."

"Not so bad."

"And her herb mix."

Cent startled. "Why?"

"Aunt Tess won't directly say, but Ruleman was with your mama that last visit."

"Why on earth?"

"That ain't the half of it. Tess has put a pennyroyal plant by both doors, hung bells on the knobs, put whiskey crosses above all the trailer doors, and smudged the entire property, mumbling spell-talk the entire time."

"Something serious is going on." Everyone in Hare Creek knew Aunt Tess used her Cherokee, Scots-Irish, and Appalachian heritage in equal parts, and the neighbors came to her regularly for advice, guidance through cartomancy, and help on lots of different matters. But Mama? Aunt Tess had always been quiet with her magic around Mama. When Cent was young, Mama had claimed to have magic in her too, but Aunt Tess had always argued the point, saying it'd skipped her and she'd do better to use her energies for something more productive, like raising her only daughter.

What a shame. Cent had no magic in her either, at least none she'd ever sensed. No. It wasn't her thing. Sure, she'd talked to spirits when she was young. What kid didn't? But she remembered doing so long after her friends had forgotten all about it. None of it meant anything now, but maybe the magic was what she'd always loved best about Aunt Tess and Uncle Kinnon. They were the first ones she'd come out to, but they'd said they'd known for years, and it wasn't their place to judge or try to change her. She was family, and that was most important.

"She's even hung one of those chicken foot charms beside her front door." Aubrey tapped his fingers on the steering wheel as he glanced at her.

"Those are Hoodoo charms. Where'd she get one?"

"Same place you got the one you had hanging in your apartment in North Chicago— online. But she's made two of her own since." Aubrey slowed the Camry as the speed limit lowered. They'd reached Greeneville. "You got that charm in your bags?"

"Yeah. And how'd you know I had one in my apartment in Chicago?"

"Aunt Tess told me." He tapped his forehead. "You know how she is."

She knew though she'd never seen it. "Yeah, I do. What else did she tell you about me?"

"Couple of girlfriends. A boyfriend." His grin spanned his face. "She said he was handsome like Uncle Kinnon when he was young but not worth keeping. Got any pictures of him?"

"He got to be an ass toward the end, so I deleted them all."

"Aunt Tess said he cheated on you."

"Yeah." Cent folded her arms across her chest and sank into the Camry's seat. *Tess always knows more about me than I do myself.* "I sometimes wish she didn't have the sight." Cent sat up and reached into her pocket when her phone chimed.

> Glad you made it safe. Call me when you're settled.
> Will do. Thanks, Betty.
> For what?
> For talking me into doing this, and for the funds to do so.
> Just take care of yourself, baby doll. That's all I ask.
> You do the same. Okay?
> Sure thing. Love you, Cent.
> Love you too.

"Aunt Tess always knows too much." Aubrey shrugged. "And she's almost always right, too. So, tell me about Betty. You were texting her?"

"Yeah." Cent unfolded a bit more. "She's a friend. That's all."

"I know, but we'll have to save it for later." He flipped the turn signal as Pal's distinctive giant hamburger, hotdog, fries, and drink, all mounted on the top and front of the building, came into view. Most Pal's were drive-thru only, so stopping meant eating in the immaculate Camry.

"Welcome to Pal's. What can I get you?" The girl at the first drive-up window grinned at Aubrey.

"Two large Cheddar Rounds, a peachy tea, and..." Aubrey moved his eyes from the order window to Cent. "What do you want to drink?"

"Large Peachy Mello Yello." She sat taller in the seat. Home meant indulging in a few favorites like Mello Yello soda spiked with peach syrup because overly caffeinated, sweet-soda blood-sugar-spikes sometimes weren't enough. "Add a biscuit and gravy."

"Gotcha." Aubrey repeated her order, adding a biscuit and gravy for himself too. "I gotta have one. Ethan's vegan, so he'll have a fit if I eat something like that in front of him."

"That's fourteen eighty-two." The girl smiled at Aubrey again. "Please drive around."

"Thanks." Aubrey circled the building, stopping behind a battered Chevy Blazer bearing two Confederate flag bumper stickers. "Pricks." He rolled his eyes.

"Yeah. I haven't miss that part of here at all. And Ethan's vegan?" Cent asked as they moved forward. "No Cheddar Rounds either?"

"No nothing from anywhere that's good." Aubrey reached into the Camry's midsection for his wallet. "Damn thing makes my ass look huge, and it hurts to sit on, so I put it in here most of the time."

"Ethan needs to stop criticizing you." She raised one brow at him.

"Yeah, and—" He frowned as he flipped open his wallet. "You're as bad as Aunt Tess, you know that?"

"Maybe." She watched him pull a twenty from his wallet. "I'll pay for my part." She reached into her cargo pants for the ten she'd left there.

"Nu-uh." He pushed her money away. "Tess'll pluck me like a Sunday roaster if I let you pay for any of this."

"She won't know unless—" She put the money back in her pocket. "Yeah, right. Okay. I'm going to buy you breakfast someday soon."

"Deal, pickle." He paid for the order and passed her both bags and her drink. "I'll park then we'll feast!" Aubrey licked his lips. "Love me some cheddar crack."

"This crack ain't whack!" She shoved a straw into her Peachy Mello Yello and took a quick sip to drown the awkwardness that'd suddenly fallen between them.

"My God, Cent, I stopped saying that when I started nursing school."

"Yeah, flashback, I think. It's not exactly PC, is it?" She thought of Betty's struggle, and how she'd said it'd progressed from pain pills to heroin.

"No, it ain't." His droll expression lifted. "Now are you going to give me my cheddar crack or not?"

She passed him his biscuit and gravy instead.

"Awe, come on." He frowned at her when she hovered over the Cheddar Rounds, popping one into her mouth.

"Hot!" She pulled the Cheddar Round from her mouth and held it between her fingers to blow on it.

"Serves you right, smart ass." He grabbed the bag from her and pulled out his order, placing it on the top of the biscuit and gravy container.

Like old times. Cent smiled as she put the Cheddar Round back into her mouth, relishing the taste of cheddar and diced potatoes pressed into a circle then breaded and deep fried— the taste of home.

They ate in relative silence, savoring every bite, Cent running her finger over the gravy container's inside to make sure it was empty. "I've missed eating like this." She shoved the containers back into one of the bags.

"Can't tell you've been eating much of anything by the look of you." Aubrey squinted at her from over his Styrofoam cup. "When's the last time you weighed yourself?"

"I don't know." She tried to push out her gut, but it was too full to do so. "Why?"

"'Cause you're skinny, pasty-faced, and your hair is as flat as—"

"You know just how to make me feel welcomed." She sagged in her seat again. "It's been a long trip. I'm tired."

"Yeah, but it's more." He sucked from his straw, considering her, his gaze critical. "I'm gonna give you the once-over when we reach Aunt Tess'."

"You're a doctor now?"

"Nurse practitioner, almost the same thing." He shoved his drink into a cup holder. "So don't argue with me."

"Whatever." She couldn't think of anything else to say on the subject, so she stared out the window. "I didn't get much sun in Chicago."

"That's not it at all," he continued as they pulled back onto the highway. "Something just ain't right about you."

"You haven't seen me in years." But she knew it was pointless to argue with Aubrey once he set his mind on something. "If it'll make you happy."

"Thank you." He waited until they reached a stoplight before he spoke again. "Aunt Tess said you weren't well."

"How'd— crap— really?"

"Yep, she claims you left some of yourself behind when you left here, and the best thing you could do is come back and find it." He glanced sidelong at her. "Try arguing that point."

"I can imagine." Cent took a deep drink from her peachy Mello Yello. *Damn, but that's sweet.* "Can we stop, so I can— hey! When did they put a McDonald's in there?"

"A few years back." He changed lanes as they drove closer. "Need a potty stop?"

"And a different drink." She pointed to her cup. "Too sweet."

"That bad?" He pulled into the McDonald's lot. "You're greener than pond scum."

"Pasty, now green. Thanks for all the compliments. I think I'm not used to the food anymore." Cent tried to keep herself together until she reached the bathroom but lost it before she reached the restaurant door, vomiting her entire breakfast on the concrete walkway.

"If I had any sense in my head I wouldn't have taken you to Pal's from the get-go." Aubrey helped her step around the spot and guided her into the restaurant where he stopped her by the bathroom door. "Could you be pregnant?"

"Oh, hell no! I haven't been with anyone, even the cheater, in a good year." Cent stumbled into a bathroom stall where she finished emptying her stomach into the toilet. *Dammit!* Nerves, it had to be nerves. The idea of going back home, of maybe facing Mama.

She knelt over the toilet, making sure nothing else was coming up before she stood, exiting the stall and standing over the sink to wash her hands. She rinsed her face and checked herself in the mirror, startling when she saw an old woman with long, frizzy, white hair standing behind her.

"They know you're here." The old woman shook her head until her hair covered her face.

"Who?" When Cent spun around to confront the woman, she wasn't there. "What the…" She tore from the bathroom, running straight into Aubrey. "Where'd she go?"

"Where'd who go?" He caught Cent by the arm when she tried to pass him.

"The old woman!" Cent pushed him aside and rushed across the restaurant, turning the corner to stand in front of the counter. "Where's she at?"

"Who're you talking about?" Aubrey spun her around. "No one came out of the bathroom before you."

"Are you sure?" Cent searched the nearly empty restaurant then glanced behind the counter, but she saw no one resembling the woman she'd encountered. "I must have jet lag or something." She dug into her pants' pocket to find her money. "Large drink."

"Anything else?" The red-headed girl behind the counter batted her eyes at Aubrey.

Always him. Never me. "You want something?" She glanced over her shoulder to see him rubbing his chin.

"No, I'm good." He stepped closer to her. "A one-hour difference don't make for jet lag."

"I know." She turned back to the counter. "That's all." She waited for her change and cup, filling the latter with a little ice and lots of Diet Coke from the fountain.

"You ain't getting off so easy." Aubrey nudged her from behind. "Tell me what you saw."

"A woman." Cent placed a lid over her cup and grabbed a straw. "In the mirror. She spoke to me."

"Really?" He followed her back to the Camry, standing by the driver's side, watching her intently. "What'd she say?"

"They know I'm here." Cent shivered as she sipped her drink. "But I have no idea who *they* are."

"Aunt Tess might." He opened the doors and waited for Cent to settle in the passenger seat. "Hand me your old cup."

"Gladly." Peachy anything was off her list, but Cheddar Rounds… *I'll try them again soon without the drink.*

"You're a mess, you know it?" He dropped into the driver's seat and shoved the key into the ignition.

"I wasn't until I got here."

"So you say. Let's get you home." Aubrey exited the parking lot directly onto Highway 107, the last marked two-lane road before they reached the homestead.

Chapter Seven

Amadahy's Message
July 25, 2017

"Let's get some hot tea into you." Aunt Tess pulled the Diet Coke from Cent's hands and took it to the sink where she upended the cup.

There goes that dollar. Cent sighed but said nothing.

Aubrey pulled his cup behind his back to hide it. "I told her I'd give her a once-over when we got here."

"You do that." Tess opened her herb cabinet, took out two half-gallon Mason jars, and turned around. "But put the kettle on to heat first."

"Yes'm." He placed the cup on the table and picked up the electric kettle setting beside the stove.

"Why didn't you bring me a Pal's tea?" asked Tess as she opened the jars. She snatched Aubrey's cup to take a drink. "Nothing but ice." She scowled at him.

"I didn't know you'd want one this early!"

"Of course I do." Tess shook her head as she spooned herbs into the tea infuser. "It's good stuff." She smiled gently at Cent, who drooped in her chair. "We'll have you feeling yourself in no time."

"I was feeling fine until I ate." The unmistakable scent of chamomile wafted through the air, soothing, but it was soon supplanted by the strong odor of... "Catmint?"

"It's good for your gut." Aubrey mimicked Cent's grimace.

"No, it's horrid!" Cent reached for the infuser, but Tess knocked her hand away.

"Who's doing the doctorin' here? You, or me and Aubrey?"

"Speaking of which." Aubrey turned toward the front door. "Be right back." He patted Aunt Tess' Border Collie, Jack, on the way out.

"How old is Jack now?" asked Cent as Tess pulled the infuser from the mug.

"That's Jack number four." Tess went to another cabinet to retrieve the honey jar. "Or five. I don't quite recall."

"Four." Aubrey dropped his backpack on the table and closed the door. "Take off your over-shirt so I can check your blood pressure."

Tess handed Cent the tea mug after she'd removed her denim button-up. "Haints and hollers, girl! Look at your skinny arms." She wrapped her hand around Cent's bicep, all but circling it. "What's become of you?"

"Not much." Aubrey wrapped the cuff around her other arm, placed his stethoscope below it, and began inflating. "How much do you weigh?"

"A hundred forty."

"One twenty soaking wet, maybe. A woman your height and bone structure should be around a hundred and sixty pounds." He stopped talking to listen, deflating the cuff a moment later. "Pressure's a little low but not bad." Aubrey reached up to pull down her bottom eyelid. "Pale. You're probably anemic."

"No, I'm not." *Don't you even give Tess the notion.*

"He's right." Tess pulled down Cent's other lid. "I've got some blood tonic squirreled away."

And that's why. Cent shivered. "I'll get some vitamins next time I'm out."

"Nope. You need tonic, regular food, and fresh air." Tess pushed the tea in front of her. "But first, this."

"It's hot." *The longer I can put this off, the better.*

"Tell her about the woman while you wait." Aubrey stowed his cuff and moved his stethoscope to her chest, listening. "Hold up a minute though." He placed his free hand over her mouth when she opened it. "Lemme listen."

"My heart's still there." Cent bit at his hand when he flipped her lip.

"You ain't changed a lick." Aubrey listened, moving the stethoscope, telling her to breathe deep. "Have you always had PVCs?"

"Diagnosed with them last year. The doctor then said they're not serious. Why?" She relaxed when he put the stethoscope away too.

"I heard a couple is all. It might be due to your weight." He sat across from her at the dinette. "Now tell her."

"Wasn't anything, really," continued Cent. "I got sick at McDonald's, then when I got to the bathroom, I threw up again."

"You ain't been eatin' good at all." Tess nodded for her to continue.

Are they intentionally ganging up on me? "I went to the sink to splash my face, and when I glanced in the mirror, there was this woman standing behind me."

"What'd she look like?" Tess now sat beside her.

"Old. Her hair was going every which way."

"Could have been me, based on your tellin'." Aunt Tess pointed to her own head and the loose ponytail her long white hair was pulled back into. "What about her face?"

"I don't recollect, exactly." Cent hovered over her mug. Catmint or not, the tea smelled relaxing.

"Yeah, you do," insisted Tess. "Close your eyes. Try and see her."

"She scared the holy…" Cent stopped when Aunt Tess stared at her. "Okay, sure." She shut her eyes and breathed deep, trying to remember the old woman's features. "High cheekbones, dark eyes, her skin was kind of darker too. Native American, maybe?"

"That'd be your great-great-grandma Amadahy. Hold on. I'll be right back." She disappeared into her bedroom.

"Where's she going?" Cent turned her eyes to Aubrey who shrugged.

"I don't know, but you better drink your tea. Catmint tastes bad enough hot, but cold…" He blanched as Tess returned.

"This is Amadahy." Tess held out a faded black-and-white photograph of a young woman, her dark hair in braids. She wore a Cherokee tear dress that swept her ankles. "This is her, too." Aunt Tess held up a second picture, newer but still old by the worn edges. The same woman, this time sitting in a chair and wearing a different tear dress, her long gray hair loose around her face.

"That's her!" Cent's hands shook as she held the picture.

"Granny Amadahy doesn't come see you unless she's got a message." Tess stiffened. "What'd she say?"

"'They know you're here.'" Cent gave Tess the picture and downed her tea in three hard swallows. "Who's they?"

"Nothing good." Tess took Cent's mug to the sink where she stood with her back to them. "You need rest and regular meals to recoup your strength." She turned to face them. "We need to start clearing out the homestead as soon as possible."

"Count me out until next weekend." Aubrey yawned as he pushed away from the table. "I'm heading home." He kissed Tess on her forehead then did the same to Cent. "Nice to see you again, honey. Welcome home and get some rest." He hugged her and turned toward the door where he paused. "Something bad's brewing, ain't it?" He asked over his shoulder.

"Not if we can stop it." Tess followed him out the door where they talked in the driveway. Cent watched them for a moment before she rose, heading straight to the worn plaid recliner that dominated the living room. Uncle Kinnon's favorite chair. He'd died almost ten years ago, but the chair still smelled of his— *ick. Tobacco.*

She was too tired to think more about it, so she collapsed into the recliner and fell asleep.

Chapter Eight

Stowne
Late Spring 2003

Cent sat up in bed, almost hitting her head on the bunk above where twelve-year-old Aubrey slept. Voices. She heard voices, and they were coming from… under the bed? No, they rose from between the homestead's wide-plank pine floorboards, from the hand-dug cellar beneath. Great Aunt Tess was one voice and— *That's Stowne!* Cent leaned over the bed to listen, and their voices became clear enough to understand.

Stowne! Cent hadn't heard from her whispering friend since spring break. But why would Stowne be talking to Aunt Tess? They didn't know each other, did they? How could they? Stowne was only in her mind, in— She was certain she heard Stowne with Aunt Tess', both speaking out loud. She could hear Stowne with her ears! But why was Stowne in the house? Stowne only talked to Cent when she sat in their special place behind the blackberry cane.

She liked spending time with Stowne, liked watching the lightning bugs dance, enjoyed when Stowne suspended a little dust-cloud above her so the sun stayed out of her eyes.

Stowne was smells and shadows, there, but always unseen. Earth and rocks and… she couldn't explain Stowne besides that. No other words did Stowne justice.

Cent crept from her bunk to press her ear against the floor.

"She ain't old enough." Aunt Tess' voice verged on anger. "Not for the world we're in now."

"Her body is young, but her spirit— We have already started the bonding process, so why interrupt now?" The smell of rich summer soil rose between the floorboards to tease Cent's nose. The smell of good earth, of moss— It was how Cent knew Stowne was close.

Stowne liked fluttering dust across her shoulders and tickling her neck with grass and fallen leaves until she giggled. This always caused Stowne to laugh in deep, cheerful rumbles. Hard laughs shook the ground beneath Cent's butt, but she knew it was a good thing. Stowne was happy when she was, and Stowne always made her happy.

"You're confusing her," said Aunt Tess.

"My intentions are as clear this life as they were in her others."

"She's fifteen years old."

"Centenary has chosen to walk beside me at a younger age, and in both male and female forms." Stowne sighed. "Modern Human gender expectations are limiting and not at all natural. Your kind did not always think this way. I remember when—"

"They distress Cent too, but she shouldn't be facing such decisions yet. I need to get her away from her mama first."

"Her mother." Stowne's smell became the hard, frozen dryness of winter ground. "Since Nida cannot be allowed to access her natural magic, she has become lost to it. But Centenary…" Stowne shook in displeasure, creating the sound of rocks tumbling, of land shifting in the distance. "Humans now shield their offspring much longer than they once did."

"It keeps them alive, helps them…" Tess stopped when Stowne shook again. "Rayne will take that ground you're loosening and create a loblolly of a mudslide somewhere inside this realm if you don't quit."

"Rayne is always trying to reshape my creations." But Stowne's next shake proved quieter. "When will Centenary be old enough in the eyes of this region's humanity?"

"She must be eighteen for her mama to have no standing. It's a matter of law."

"Of law?" Stowne's smell shifted to dust that drifted up through the floorboards to tickle Cent's nose. "There are laws much older than the ones you Humans make."

"I know, but that's how it is, so you'll have to be patient."

"Can she not live with you?"

I wish I could. Bonding. Cent thought about the meaning. Bonding meant togetherness, meant being close. She and Stowne were bonding? Why hadn't she known? The idea made her feel warm inside. Kinda like when Ina Sue Jones had kissed her last summer but way better.

"I've tried to get her away from Nida for years, but she just won't let go. Closest I got was temporary custody when Nida was forced into residential treatment year before last."

"Perhaps you could use these laws in our favor?"

"Not unless Nida does something really stupid." Aunt Tess sighed. "We'll have to make do as best we can until she's old enough. Try to be patient."

"I wait for Centenary. I get a few years, maybe a few decades, then I must wait again." Stowne smelled sad, like the ground after days of rain. "The time between echoes inside me until I quake."

"Well, this time you won't have to share Cent with anyone. Male and female… Humans are relearning the old ways. We women don't have to be dependent neither. That's probably why she chose a female form again."

"Twice in a row," said Stowne. "This makes me hopeful for our future, but I still worry."

I've been a boy? Cent stared down at her body, squinting to see past her tank top and shorts in the nightlight's glow. Her once being a boy explained a lot of things. How awkward she felt. How she didn't like a lot of girly things…

"Being a woman ain't easy neither," Tess maintained. "But every Human soul should experience being a woman and the birth process at least once."

"Have you borne a child before?"

"Several times. But not this life. Not with Nida's arrival."

"It is good you have not."

"Not for Kinnon. He wanted children somethin' fierce."

"He's too young a soul to understand, unlike you… and Centenary."

"Cent's an old soul in a young body and bound by this country's laws. She belongs to Nida until she turns eighteen, so your trying to bond before she's of age only confuses her."

"But I love Centenary."

"That love has locked you harder than ever to this mountain. She's been yours before. She'll be yours again." Tess' tone verged on anger for a second time. "Three years won't be long if you think about it like that."

"But her mother…"

"My sister is the cause of that. We did the best we could after Roslyn died."

"You and Kinnon have been both mother and father to Centenary and Aubrey."

"But here Nida is nonetheless." Tess sighed. "It's all become so complicated. Maybe when Cent's finally beside you, things will ease up."

"I know it is difficult work but allowing Nida to access her magic would make her dangerous."

Mama's dangerous? Maybe when she'd had one too many beers or wasn't taking her mood stabilizers, but…

"She still hasn't accessed her abilities?"

"Thankfully, no, but she's so easily impressed that we've tried to steer her away from everything magic."

"That is for the best." Stowne's scent returned to fresh ground. "So I will wait, lest I shift things in the wrong direction, lest I do something that awakens Nida to her capabilities."

"Thank you for your…"

"Mreowr?" Aunt Tess' big gray tomcat, Vamp, butted his head against Cent's ribs. "Meow." Vamp purred and called louder, walking along Cent's side to rub her shoulder.

"Shh," whispered Cent, but the voices had already stopped, and she heard Aunt Tess climbing the cellar stairs, so she scurried into her bunk and pulled the blankets over her head. Vamp followed and climbed onto her belly, where he began making biscuits, his claws penetrating the summer-weight quilt to prick her skin as he kneaded. "Ouch." She rolled onto her side and lowered the blanket to pet Vamp. What had Stowne and Aunt Tess been talking about? How did they even know each other, and, most importantly, Aunt Tess had been talking to Stowne and that meant Stowne was *real*.

Cent pulled her hands under the blanket and kept her breathing slow and steady, encouraging Vamp to settle beside her, which he did, purring happily as Aunt Tess looked into the bedroom.

"She's sleepin'. Good." Tess came to the bunk to pat Cent's head. "Keep an eye on her, Vamp Boy." Cent saw her stand at the bed a moment more, her hands on Aubrey's bunk as she whispered one of those strange phrases she often did when she thought no one was listening.

"Are you through in the cellar?" Uncle Kinnon's shadow filled the doorway. "Everything good?"

"No, but I reckon there's nothing I can do about it right now."

"Then come on to bed. Let the youngins rest while they will." Uncle Kinnon always talked in a strange mix of local and Irish accent. His upbringing, Aunt Tess had once told her. He was a quiet man. Always watching, hardly ever speaking. Cent liked him, liked his faded overalls and flannel shirts. He'd taught her how to spit watermelon seeds farther than any boy, told her she could do anything as good as a boy could, probably better, since she was a Rhodes woman. "That's why I never asked your Aunt Tess to change her last name when we married." He'd winked at her. "There's power in that name. Remember that."

Cent loved everything about her great-uncle Kinnon except the tobacco chaw he often held in his cheek. Chaws were gross except if you had a wasp sting. Then they were good at killing the hurt, but the rest…

"I'm gonna talk to Nida tomorrow, see if she'll let Cent spend the rest of the summer with us, maybe go to school at Lamar this fall."

"I dunno, cushla machree. Nida's awful possessive. Try for the summer first. Tell her she can go on the road with Turk if she does."

"Clever man. I knew I married you for good reason."

"One of many, I hope."

Cent waited until they'd parted the bedroom door before she smiled. "Summer here," she whispered to Vamp. "That'd be funner than fun, wouldn't it?" She scratched under Vamp's chin until he purred again. "I'll get to spend more time with you and Stowne." Or would she? Cent thought back on what she'd overheard. Was Aunt Tess trying to keep them apart? No. She was more interested in getting Cent away from Mama.

"Don't worry, Vamp. Mama never wants me around when Turk's in, so she'll do what Tess wants just so she can go off with him for the summer." Cent fell asleep with that thought in mind, dreaming of Stowne's quiet presence, of their time together, of the ground, and of rocks and warm sand Stowne sometimes covered her with when she felt cold. Stowne would lay beneath the sand with her, holding her hand, radiating soft heat she snuggled into... a warm-earth body, two arms and two legs, a head she felt soft breath come into and leave from but never saw.

Chapter Nine

Reality Crisis
August 7, 2017

So you're doing okay, country girl?
Yes. Aunt Tess is good to me. Are you staying out of trouble?
Trouble is my middle name.
I mean it. Are you staying clean?
Yes. Thanks for asking.
Love you, Ms. Betty.
Love you too.

Cent had barely put down her phone when Aunt Tess burst into her room late in the morning. They'd spent the early hours in the garden but had returned to the trailer and its air conditioning before it'd gotten too hot out.

"I hired a realtor." Aunt Tess sounded excited about it, but she looked tired.

"The house isn't ready, isn't…" Cent frowned at her. "You sure you're okay?"

"I stayed up too late last night. That's all. And I know it's early, but the realtor's going to walk the house with us so we know what needs the most work." Tess rubbed her hands together. "Go do something about your hair before she gets here. It's a wreck from garden work." She creased her brow as she considered the stubble on one side of Cent's head. "Well, fix what you can. The rest— you gonna grow it or keep it shaved off?"

"I don't know." No one had given her much grief about it, and she'd seen a couple of women in Greeneville with similarly styled hair. "Shave it, I guess."

"Then we'll do so tonight before you shower. That stubble looks to be at the itchy stage."

"Yeah, I suppose." Cent grabbed clean clothes and went to the bathroom where she stared into the mirror. *Damn, I'm out of shape and sunburned.* But being back on the homestead had turned out to be good for her. If she wasn't helping Aunt Tess, she was working at Dryler's, cashiering and helping Mr.

Jones better track his inventory. The store's only computer was ancient, not even Internet-capable, so she'd borrowed Aubrey's iPad until she could afford a tablet to work from.

Aunt Tess was on the porch when Cent emerged from the bathroom. "She's here, Centenary. Come out and meet her."

"On my way." Cent smoothed down her hair, straightened her shirt, and went to the screen door where she paused to stare.

"Don't just stand there." Aunt Tess waved for her to come out. "I promise she was better taught."

"She recently returned home, so I understand." The realtor's voice was soft and bubbly, like fresh water trickling in a creek, but it was also odd in both its accent and tone. There were no inflections, no hint of either male or female in the way she spoke.

"Yeah, I was taught better." Cent squared her shoulders and stepped through the door, her hand extended. "My name is Centenary. I'm Tess' grand-niece. Nice to meet you."

"You as well. Tess speaks of you often." The woman, dressed in a loose-fitting blue pantsuit, her soft-blue hair mounded neatly on her head, took Cent's hand in hers. A damp touch, but far from cold. "I'm Rayne." Rayne released her hold and stepped back to place the same hand on Aunt Tess' shoulder. "Shall we go up to the homestead?"

"Sure." Cent trailed behind Aunt Tess and Rayne up the hill to the old house. Rayne was attractive in an odd way. Her hips— their movement was so soft and fluid that Cent could barely take her eyes from them.

"Sorry, I didn't bring my work clothes this time. I was at a showing before this." Rayne glanced over her shoulder at Cent. "I promise to bring them next time, but maybe we can find a starting place today."

"Maybe." Cent dropped her gaze when Aunt Tess elbowed her.

"Mind your manners." Tess carried three brooms in her arms: a new, store-bought one for cleaning the homestead floors, the well-worn broom she used to clean the trailer's porches, and a besom Cent had seen her craft two nights before. It had an ash-wood handle surrounded by birch twigs bound together with willow. Aunt Tess had been specific about its components and had sung as she made it.

> *I am a besom maker that lives in yonder vale*
> *Sweet pleasures that I do enjoy morning night and noon*
> *Going o'er the hills so high in gathering the green broom*
> *So it's come buy my besoms fine and new*
> *Bonny green besoms better never grew*

"Yes'm." Cent took the old broom when Tess shoved it at her.

"Clean off the porch while Rayne and I walk the house."

"Why can't I walk with you?" Cent tightened her hold on the porch broom.

"'Cause I said so." Tess stepped in front of Cent when they got to the porch, extending her hand to Rayne who helped her climb the steps. "That's what you get for looking."

"But…" Cent's stare extended to where Tess and Rayne stood on the porch.

"It's okay, Tess," soothed Rayne. "There's nothing wrong with looking." She peered over Tess to wink at Cent. "It's best to get that out of the way early in a friendship."

I know nothing about you, lady. But something about Rayne did seem familiar. Cent didn't speak as she stepped onto the porch. The view from the homestead's front porch had always been spectacular, but she'd rarely appreciated it as a child. The house was perched on the last road up the mountain, a good distance from the top, but still high enough to offer a grand view of the river-flat below. To think of it being sold off… "I'll sweep as soon as you two get inside."

"Clean the rafters and front wall before you get to the porch floor," said Tess. "And keep the broom outside. Old brooms bring old dirt in with them." She set both the new broom and besom inside the house and motioned for Rayne to follow her. "Come on. Let's get started." They both stepped through the door, and Tess turned to Cent. "Stay outside until I call you."

Cent barely got out a "Yes'm." before the homestead's heavy oak door slammed closed in her face.

She swept the rafters clean of two old birds' nests and three crumbling mud-dauber's houses then proceeded to the front porch, trying to sneak peaks in the windows every time she got close, but they were dirty and, dang it, most of the dirt seemed to be on the inside.

Cent turned her attention to the porch, cursing under her breath each time the broom straw snagged on a loose nail. The porch required more than cleaning. Several boards needed to be replaced, and the entire thing needed a hard scrubbing.

She scratched at a board with the toe of her shoe, feeling sorry for herself until she decided she'd walk around the old homestead, setting the broom by the door before she jumped from the porch, landing on the ground with a soft thud.

Ouch! That isn't as easy as it used to be. Cent rubbed her knees before she straightened and turned to look up the hill behind the house. Natural. A lot of the ground behind the house had returned to its natural state. She paused on the side of the house to peer in a window. Aunt Tess hadn't said she *couldn't* do so, and she was staying outside like Tess had insisted so… "Dang it." Cent grumbled and kept moving. This window, like the others, was too dirty to see through. She'd have a lot of scrubbing to do to help ready the house. But, she noticed as she looked up at the log walls, there were structural issues that needed to be addressed too. Some of the house's lower logs had started to decay, and the chinking had fallen out in spots, leaving the interior open to the outside. *That'll be cold come winter.* Whoever bought the property would probably tear the homestead down, a realization that angered her for reasons she couldn't understand.

She trudged up the hill to the edge of the old garden where she stared at the briars and saplings that'd taken hold. *It's always been a good place to grow things.* She glanced down the hill to the newer spot and the herb garden closer to Tess' trailer. *No, this is the best place.* But Tess hadn't used this upper garden spot since… *I left home.* Cent frowned at this, at the entire mess that'd grown-up behind the house.

We'll use the old spot next year. Cent stopped in her tracks. She was planning ahead. Planning on staying. "No, that won't work at all." Aunt Tess needed her assistance right now, not forever. She'd help get the place sold and… Her eyes drew up the hill and past the garden spot to the overgrown twist of blackberry cane edging into the woods.

She had to go there, but she didn't know why. Something pulled on her, something… She was fifteen again and it was midsummer.

Stowne.

The briars cut her hands and pulled at her clothes, but she pushed through them, blind in her determination to reach the space behind them. She'd left something there, something… She knelt then crawled through the wild purple cane full of nearly-ripe berries. One cane scratched her face and another snagged on her sleeve, but she pressed forward with only one goal, whatever that might be, on her mind.

"There." She soon stood in the clear space beyond the bramble, but it was nothing like she remembered. No lights. No green grass. No shafts of sunlight. No gentle trickle of water from the spring further up the hill. There was nothing magical at all about this place. Yes, the spring was still there, and the water appeared clean when she checked, but there were none of the cheery bubblings she remembered. This place wasn't dead, more like dormant. Saddened, though she was unsure what she'd expected, Cent sat on a patch of dry grass in the middle of the clearing and looked around, trying to feel something she knew wasn't there. *What am I doing?* She felt nothing. Nothing! But she didn't know why'd she'd expected to feel anything at all.

She touched the ground, pressing her hand against the dirt in search of the warmth she'd once felt. Cool. No, cold. "No life. No…" The ground shook under her hand, a rise then drop, almost a sigh, but it remained cold. "Where are you?"

"Stowne burrowed beneath the homestead when you left."

"What the…" Cent peered over her shoulder as Rayne stepped into the clearing. "What're you doing up here?"

"Searching for you." Rayne stooped beside Cent to place her hand on the ground too. "Stowne's gone dormant."

"Stowne?" Cent stared at the blue-haired woman. "Stowne's nothing but my imagination, so how'd you—"

"Why are you here now?"

"I guess— I reckon— I don't know." Cent moved her hand to her lap. "This is a special place for me is all. I spent a lot of time here when I was younger."

"With Stowne." Rayne sat cross-legged beside her.

"Stowne was my way of escaping reality, that's all." Cent felt the earth tremble beneath her again. Another sigh? She couldn't tell, but she saw Rayne smile when it happened. "There's a spring up the hill and when—"

"Yes, I know." Rayne's hand slipped over Cent's, pressing it against the ground. "Stowne—"

"Was imaginary!" Cent wrenched her hand from beneath Rayne's, startling when it came away wet. "Stowne was my self-defense against the haters."

"Imaginary?" Rayne rubbed the back of her neck. "Drains and dribbles. You've shoved it all aside to save yourself pain." She grabbed Cent's hand, dragging her toward the spring, her hold so strong Cent couldn't get away. Her grip was cool but steady, wrapping Cent's arm and sliding up it as she pulled her along. "Water. Water. Pure and bright. Show her so she will remember." Rayne pushed Cent to the ground beside the spring head and pointed toward the water. "Look hard. See what really is."

"Listen, lady, you don't just go around…" Cent cringed when Rayne emitted something between a gurgle and a growl. "You got no business…"

"See me!" Rayne grabbed Cent's face, pulling it up until their eyes met, but Rayne's eyes were no longer eyes. Her face, her face was…

"What the hell?" Cent tried to crawl away, but Rayne's grip was too strong, drawing her to her knees then her feet.

"Look… at… me!" Rayne's liquid lips turned up in a smile. "I am what you see, what you sense." She reached one fluid finger to Cent's face, stroking it, leaving behind a damp trail.

"What *are* you?" Cent stared unafraid. This was all familiar, but she didn't know how or why. Rayne's face had become as clear as the spring's water. Human-like features but not Human, nothing Human, something much older and…

"Think, Centenary. Remember." Rayne pulled her closer, covering her mouth… the lips were damp, warm, firm water that drenched Cent's mouth with unexpected joy. Not sexual, not… Rayne pulled Cent's hands up to touch her face. Flesh now water, curves now undulating waves. *You must remember.* Rayne wrapped her, drenched her, passed around and through her, but when Cent opened her eyes she saw a pillar of water where Rayne had stood. "Remember my true form."

"I remember." The words slipped from Cent's mouth before they registered in her mind, but she did remember, so much at once that the knowledge overwhelmed her and—

Chapter Ten

Green Corn Moon
August 7, 2017

"What'd you do to her?" Aunt Tess sounded close.

"I'm sorry. But we've little time." Rayne's voice softened. "She's awake, Tess, and staring at me."

"Cent?" Aunt Tess pushed the hair from Cent's face. "You in there, honey? You okay?"

"I'm here." But she felt as though she'd traveled in time and didn't know her way back. "Rayne? Where's Stowne? Where's my Stowne?" She stared at and through Rayne, remembering everything about their form, their preference for softer shapes, their feel and taste. "Please. Where's…" Cent gripped her head as she sat up. "I don't understand. Don't…" She scooted to rest her head against Tess' leg.

"Slow down, girl. Let it all seep in, not flood." Tess tensed as she pivoted toward Rayne. "I told you to go gentle."

Rayne's curvaceous column shook hard enough to fling water. "Forgive me. Especially you, Centenary, but I was trying to jar your memory."

"I'm fine." But she wasn't, would never be again. There were countless dreams, sensations, and memories she'd filed under imagination, under childhood fantasy— she now doubted everything. "Rayne?"

"Yes?" Rayne's column now showed a Human-like face formed from water.

"How long have I known you?"

"This lifetime, since you were eight." Rayne slid across the ground toward her, leaving a wet trail behind as they moved.

"When did we first meet?"

"Slow down, child." Tess stroked Cent's head. "Let it come back."

"It *is* back!" Cent scooted from her touch. Her magic had returned in such force she shook from the effort to contain it. "How long? How many lives? Centuries?" She peered up at Rayne whose watery form bounced.

"Over three thousand years."

So long. So many lives. So… elemental. "You're an elemental spirit."

"A water elemental, yes." Rayne's column twisted into a funnel, but their Human-like face remained stationary. "And your friend."

"You're an old soul." Tess squeezed Cent's shoulder. "Much older than me. But this lifetime, I was born first."

"Human souls come and go through time," Rayne explained. "But your soul is so old your experiences are becoming difficult to reconcile." They raised a watery arm toward the blackberry cane opening. "This place, this piece of land, the homestead, you put the house here to help yourself remember. It holds your memories."

"Why didn't I know this? Why didn't anybody tell me before now?" Cent hugged her knees to her chest, shivering as knowledge continued to reveal itself inside her. "I ran away from…" She looked at Tess when she couldn't find the words.

"You ran from yourself, from what's always been the hardest part of being reborn, making the choice." Tess flipped up Cent's hair to show the shorn side. "You've always agonized about making that choice, about all that came with it, and in the last three centuries you've become more distraught each time it came around."

Cent stared up at her without speaking.

"You chose female this time because there has to be balance." Tess smiled at her. "Our world's shifting back. It's slow, but it won't matter how you choose, or if you choose somewhere between. You can love and be who you are no matter what."

"But who am I?" Cent's eyes drew from Tess to Rayne who'd drawn closer. "I only recall flashes, most of those this life and… and Stowne."

"What do you remember about Stowne?" asked Rayne.

"Elemental, I think, but not like you." Cent shook her head.

"I'm their friend, but I wear on them." Rayne smiled ever so slightly. "And on you at times."

"I don't recollect…yet." Cent lifted her head. "This place. This spot. It's important, isn't it?"

"It's your and Stowne's favorite spot," said Tess. "But they…" She sighed. "Stowne buried deep under the homestead when you left and hasn't been heard from since."

"I hurt them." Cent placed her hand on the ground. Stowne's ground, the ground that made— Stowne was the ground and the ground was Stowne. "I'm sorry. I'm…" She lay flat to place her cheek to the dirt. "I didn't know, didn't understand."

"It's partially my fault." Tess hung her head. "I dismissed the importance of your bonding, of what'd happen if it didn't progress as it needed to."

"I left because of it." Cent pushed down her anger. Tess had only been trying to make things easier. "I think I understand why, but the result..." She squished her brows together as she sat up. "You did this because of Mama, didn't you?"

"I couldn't get you away long enough, couldn't let you develop your energies, couldn't let you bond with Stowne as long as she had hold of you. Then as soon as you turned of age, you ran and—"

I had no choice. Running had let her spread her wings, be who she thought she was, love who she— How could she have pushed Stowne aside so easily? "I'm sorry." She pressed harder against the ground. "I'm sorry."

"Me too." Tess bent to place her hand beside Cent's. "I shouldn't have gotten in the way of the natural process."

"Regrets." Rayne spread on the ground as a puddle that flowed around and under their hands, becoming fingers that grasped Cent's. "We don't have time for more. We must move ahead, try to repair the damage before it's too late."

"How do I fix things?" Cent folded her fingers into Rayne's.

"You need to remember," Aunt Tess explained. "The more you recall of Stowne, of your past, the more your energy will build, the more Stowne is likely to hear you."

"But it's late in the day." Rayne's damp fingers became as hard as flesh and bone. "You've a lot to process, so I think we should begin tomorrow."

"How?" Cent shared Tess' tear-streaked, haggard expression.

"By letting you back into the homestead." Tess let Cent pull her to a stand. "The moon is full tonight. Do you want to join us under it?"

"You're inviting me to a circle?"

"A welcome home celebration." Rayne rose from the ground to retake their Human shape. "Just wait until I tell everyone!"

"It's one of the oldest continuous circles in North America." Tess steadied Cent when her knees threatened to give. "But right now, let's get you back to the trailer for lunch and a nap."

"I'd like that." Cent glanced back at Rayne. "Are you coming with us?"

"Modern Human dwellings drain my energy, so I generally avoid them." Rayne pushed aside the blackberry cane for them to pass then followed them through the old garden and to the back of the homestead. "I'll meet you both here at dusk. Rest, Centenary. You're going to need it tonight." Rayne smiled and reached up with both arms, their entire body rising then dropping to the ground where they dispersed as droplets that dissolved into the dirt.

"Interesting." Cent hugged Tess to her. "Will you make me a peanut butter and jelly sandwich?"

"Of all the..." Tess laughed. "Like when you was a kid?"

"With chips?"

"Now those chips were your Uncle Kinnon's, so…"

"I saw a bag of Terry's Salt and Vinegar chips in the back of the pantry. Indulge me. Please?"

"You caught me." Tess grinned as they walked. "Does this mean I'm the young one?"

"No. I'm your student, at least for now." Cent looked back at the homestead. "You think I'll remember?"

"I know you will." Tess patted her shoulder. "Now about that sandwich."

———

Cent was welcomed into the circle with great ceremony, but she sat along the edge, watching in wonderment as the evening progressed. Rayne led the esbat ceremony, and it was everything Cent had hoped, magical in ways that brought up deep memories of other such nights. There was no light besides the bonfire and the rhythmic dancing of lightning bugs that'd shown up to celebrate her return. Rayne sat on her right, not too close to the fire, while Tess, dressed in a black robe that grazed the tops of her feet, sat on her left, clapping her hands along with ethereal music that seemed to come from every direction at once.

I wonder who sits there. Cent kept looking at the two sets of stacked stones standing at the circle's northern end. One was large with a broad, flat top, a sitting space that appeared more worn than carved. The other was just as tall but skinnier, with the top stone carved into a seat, a back height that'd rest comfortably on a person, and padding of purple silk. A stone with squared-off corners sat directly in front of the smaller stack, like a step. *No one's sat there for a while.* "Whose place is that?" Cent leaned toward Rayne, who was dressed in a lovely green-blue robe with a cinched waist that was part of their body. Their bare feet peaked from beneath the flowing hem, and their bluish skin reflected the firelight, giving them a gentle glow.

"Someone very special and their eternal. I hope you'll meet them soon."

Another nebulous answer. Cent had done nothing but ask questions since they'd arrived at the circle, and she had no intention of stopping. "Is this your preferred form?"

It is." Rayne smiled. "You saw my true form earlier today. I can take any form I wish, but this is by far my favorite for esbats."

"Rayne's immortal, but I'd almost kill to look so good." Tess pulled back the wrinkles on her face. "We Humans don't age well at all." She dropped her hands and nodded toward a glowing Human-like shape approaching them. "Ah, Pyre. How're you this night?"

"I'm overjoyed that Centenary has returned to us." Pyre turned their fiery eyes toward Cent. "Blessed be, Tess. Why did it take so long this time?"

"Complications of the modern world." Tess extended her right hand to Pyre, whose form condensed and reshaped, becoming a small, dark red creature that leapt into her hand. "Hello, dear friend." She stroked Pyre's back with her finger. "I'm glad Centenary has returned home too."

"I didn't know this was home until today." Cent cocked her head to better see Pyre. "Salamander?"

"A fire elemental's true form." Rayne's mouth thinned. "You're leaving soot on Tess' hand again."

"As opposed to yours?" Pyre laughed heartedly as they jumped from Tess' hand, reshaping into their Human form when they landed, this time shaking their hips toward Rayne. "Shall we dance around my bonfire?"

"You wish!" Rayne flicked their hand, showering Pyre with water droplets that evaporated before they could land. "Go play with one of my younger, more gullible siblings." They pointed to a group of blue-tinged water nymphs who stood nearby.

"You'll change your mind later tonight." Pyre stepped toward Cent, the top of their head now flickering with soft oranges and reds that resembled spikey hair. "How about you? Would you honor me with a dance?"

"Me?" Cent peered at her cargo pants and black t-shirt. "I'm not exactly known for my dancing, and I'm not dressed for—"

"Don't matter how you dance, just that you do." Tess nudged her. "Take off your shoes, roll-up your pant legs, and join them if you want. But I warn you that dancing with elementals ain't nothing like dancing with a person."

"Are you certain Pyre's the one to…" Rayne shrugged. "Better to remember now than later, I suppose. Watch yourself, Centenary. Pyre likes to heat your nethers when they dance."

Nethers? She was curious, warnings or not. "All right. Sure." Cent kicked off her shoes, rolled her pants, and slid her hand into Pyre's when they offered it. Their palm was hot but not to the extent she wanted to pull away. "So, how do fire elementals dance?"

"Like you Humans but far hotter." Pyre flashed her a white-hot grin as they moved closer to the bonfire. The only other dancing pair, a scantily-leaved dryad and a water elemental whose preferred form was overtly masculine, moved aside as soon as they touched the white sand, and the music became more upbeat. "Here we go!" Pyre laughed as they twisted around Cent's ankles, turning her as they snaked around her body, shooting up so their face hovered before hers when they stopped spinning. "I must say, your form this life is very enticing."

"You're a flirt." Cent blew out to make Pyre's white-flame smile move back a little. "I should've known."

"My kind enjoys mischief-making." They wrapped entirely around Cent, creating a cyclone of warmth that turned her, lifting her from the ground to dip her. "And flirting. We're dancing, after all." Their fingers twirled into smoke that wrapped Cent's waist. "I appreciate Human women of your size. Capable. Sturdy."

"That's not a compliment."

"Then how about strong and determined?"

"You're getting warmer." Cent cringed when she realized the double-entendre where Pyre was concerned.

"Yes, I am." The smoke around Cent's waist thickened and spread, obscuring them from view. Pyre became more direct inside the smoke, slipping their flickering hand down the front of her thigh. "I'm capable of many heated things, hot, pleasurable things, especially with Humans. Shall I show you?"

Not tonight. Cent lifted her arms and brought them down, breaking Pyre's hold before it became more invasive. "You like playing, don't you?" The smoke dissipated as she stepped back.

"No more than you, if I remember correctly." Their grin mollified into a flaming leer. "I've been yours before." Smoke seeped from between Pyre's teeth as they raised their hands, creating another cloud that encased them both. "Then your very next life, Stowne asked you to dance before I could and—"

Stowne? "Stowne!" Her heart soared at the name. Cent waved her arms to clear the smoke again. "I'm not wandering any direction right now, so—"

"Ah, well." Pyre's smile dimmed. "It was worth a try." They encased her in a soft, orange-flame hug then moved back. "Guess I'll find someone else to play with tonight." They funneled into their salamander form, crawling across the circle sands toward a mixed group of elementals who sat talking.

"Good to see you again." Cent turned back to her seat to find a waist-high creature with a long, white beard sitting in it. A dwarf? No. She'd read too many fantasy novels not to know this creature was a gnome. They nodded when she approached, laughing as they hopped from her place. They removed their red, pointed, stiffened fabric hat and bowed their head, looking up at her with a smile when she'd sat. "Hello, Centenary. Word spread quickly about your return. We hope Stowne is soon to follow." With that, they trotted off, joining a group of their own kind who kept glancing at her.

"So I've heard." She stared after the gnome until Tess offered her a pint jar filled with something sweet-smelling. "What's this— oh, mead?" She inhaled the scent of lavender, lemons, and oranges. "Summer blend?" Tess had slipped her some before she'd left home. Good stuff, and never so strong it'd made her the least bit tipsy.

"It's the wrong time of year for anything else." Tess reached up to wipe something from Cent's cheek. "Pyre left soot on you. Now you recollect why you should be wary of Pyre and the other fire elementals. It's not that they're bad, really, more like passionate about everything they do."

"I remembered fast, thank you." Cent indicated the different groups of primarily one elemental type or another. "Why do some take different forms and others don't?"

"A couple of different reasons." Tess pointed to where Rayne now stood with another water elemental dressed in similar flowing green-blue robes. "The column is a water elemental's true form, but most of them are able to wear water robes or anything else. Water, air, and fire elementals all have an easy time gaining the ability to change forms." Tess laughed. "You ain't a child no more, so I'll just say it. Elementals can't change their form, can't function like Rayne and Pyre do, until they've had sex with one of us, and they're considered soulless until they've bred a child with us."

"Us? Humans?"

"Yes, Humans, or…" Tess smiled at her. "Mostly Human."

"I'm not…" Cent stared at the soot on her hands. "I'm part one of them?"

"More than I've ever been, and this life even more so." Tess sipped from her jar. "Your grandmother, my sister, Roslyn. She made a fool of herself when she was far too young, conjuring what she shouldn't have. Exan gave Roslyn what she wanted, a memorable night and a baby." Tess shifted, unable to hide her discomfort with the discussion. "Your mother is that baby."

"Mama's half-elemental? Are you sure?" Cent stared over her jar at Tess. "Fire, water… what?"

"It don't work that way. Being part elemental makes one of us part magic."

"Mama doesn't have a bit of magic in her!"

"Yes, she does, but your great-grandmother, Sudie, and I began dampening it with spells as soon as she was born." Tess took a long draw from her jar. "That makes you quarter-blood and strong enough to handle all what comes with it."

"Wouldn't a half-blood like Mama be better?"

"Half-bloods ain't right in the head." Tess didn't apologize when Cent scowled at her. "I love your mama like my own daughter, I always have, but it don't change the fact she's touched. That's what your uncle Kinnon and me always meant when we said it about anyone. It ain't an insult but truth.

Half-bloods can't manage well between the worlds they're part of, meaning the magic must be pulled from them so they can have a semi-normal life."

"Nothing about Mama is normal."

"She's always struggled to keep stable." Tess shook her head. "But she'd be permanently institutionalized somewhere, or worse, if we hadn't pulled the magic from her."

"That's why you never practiced or discussed magic around her… or me." Cent held out her jar. "And what's with these? Shouldn't we be drinking from goblets or horns or something?"

"Everyone brings their own, and I lose or break my good mugs out here, but the jars I need for canning, so I always remember to take them home." Tess sipped from her jar.

"Sounds right." Cent chuckled. "Does Mama know I'm home?"

"She does, and so does her boyfriend, Ivan Ruleman." Tess twisted her silver and leather esbat bracelet around her wrist. "Evil name. Begone from my mouth." She spat on the ground. "That one's hiding behind the Bible and a Human form."

"Ruleman ain't Human?"

"He is, but what's got hold of him ain't."

"So he's possessed?"

"I guess that's what you'd call it." Tess sat up taller. "Whatever's got him is a powerful, dark, energy-sucking spirit that feeds off pain and fear. But we best not speak of them in the middle of such celebration." She raised her jar to Cent. "To you, sweet child. To you and your return to us."

"And here's to you and your determination to help me remember." Cent raised her jar. *Enough of this and I might be feeling something after all.* She glanced at Pyre, who smiled at her. Cent recalled dancing with them more than tonight, the energy they'd once shared. The passion that'd once burned between them. *Not going there.* She closed her eyes and tried to think about something else.

"Keep that happy feeling when we start sorting out the homestead tomorrow." Tess' voice drew Cent back to the present. "Ready to learn a bit more?" She indicated the lights flickering around them. "Them's not lightning bugs."

"Then what are they?" Cent watched in wonder as Tess chanted under her breath and held up her open palm, smiling when one of the little lights flitted over to settle in her hand. "Look closer." She lifted her arm so Cent could see.

The little light dimmed a bit when Cent bent in. Inside was a winged creature, a small, Human-shaped form clad in leaves, vine, and pieces of cast-off string and fabric. "What is it?"

"A Wee Fairy. You know the honey and biscuits I sometimes leave out at dusk?"

"Those were for them?" Cent laughed when the fairy flitted from Tess' hand to twirl around her head, slipping beneath the longer side of her hair and out to hover in front of her, its small, dark face curious. "Hello there."

The fairy chirped then flitted away, returning seconds later with a dozen of its friends, all of whom flitted around her head, picking up her hair, landing on her shoulder, hovering before her face to chirp at her.

"They're talking," said Cent.

"They're deciding whether or not they like you." Tess made a small, whistling sound and held out her finger again, encouraging two fairies to light there. "They bite, so be careful."

Cent stiffened when she recalled one of the lights biting her as a child. "They're persnickety."

"It's always best to take care of them, or they'll cause you trouble. That's why I put fairy houses around the garden and along the edge of the woods."

"I helped you make some of them."

"Yeah, you did." Tess' face crinkled with a joy that quickly subsided. "But do you remember the big fairies?"

"Big fairies? Nope, I don't recollect ever seeing one."

"They're called Hunters, and they're as tall as you, sometimes taller, and they'll be here at Samhain. That's generally the only time they show during the year, which suits me fine."

"What, are they mean?"

"Mean enough to poach deer, commit crimes, and eat Wee Fairies, but they're also tricky, so be careful with what you say to them." Tess patted Cent's leg as her smile returned. "They're a strange mix of magic and conman and as backwoods as they come anymore."

"They sound like asses."

"They are, but enough on them. I'm glad you're remembering things."

"A little at a time, but it won't be like that tomorrow, will it?"

"No." Tess' smile faded a bit. "Tomorrow and the days after will rush at you." She made sounds to the fairies again. "If they haven't bitten you by now, they like you."

"I remember them and think they remember me." She held out her hand, where one of them landed, standing, their hands on their hips as they peered up at her. "You were in my hand earlier."

"I was." Their voice was small and cheerful. "You Centenary. You come back. You stay home now?"

Stay? Yes, this place had a sense of permanence she hadn't felt before. *I'm meant to be here.* "Yes, I'm staying."

"Good!" The fairy soared up, circling her head with their friends before flying off to dance in the moonlight.

"And she speaks Wee Fairy too." Pyre flickered in front of Cent, their mouth turned up in another tempting, white-hot smile. "You quarter breeds are delightful to be around."

"Have you come back to flirt more?" Cent turned her head toward Tess. "I need time to sort this all out."

"You're doing real good, considering." Tess shook her head at Pyre whose flame immediately dampened. "Come back next esbat. Maybe she'll be more willing to play with you then."

"I should hope." Pyre bowed to them both. "Until that night, Centenary, and Stowne had best be here, or I might well burn your ties with them this lifetime."

Pyre made Cent feel things she shouldn't, but they couldn't take her mind off Stowne. She had someone, she'd had someone for lifetimes, but how did she find them again?

After Pyre had left, Rayne returned to them, saying they'd see them in the morning. "Rest, Centenary. We've a lot of work to do before the moon's full again." They smiled at Tess. "Lammas is near, and Harvest moon is approaching, so we'd best finish things up before the turn of the year."

"I'm aware." Tess nodded toward where the moon hung low in the sky. "It's getting late. The younger ones and those without business tomorrow will play all night, but not us. We should go."

"Yeah." Cent finished her mead and stood, clutching her jar so she wouldn't have to come back later.

"But don't leave before you have one of these." Rayne held out a leaf supporting two cookies. "The feast. We were in such a rush to celebrate Centenary's return we all but forgot to share."

"Who made these?" Cent took one and brought it to her nose, inhaling the aroma of fresh-baked goods.

"It's a combined effort," said Tess as she took hers. "Rayne and their kind supply the water while Pyre and their kind provide the baking heat. Earth elementals stack the oven stones, I provide most of the other ingredients, and the Wee Fairies mix."

"Wow." Cent bit into the cookie only when Tess did. It was a little bland but not too bad considering all the hands involved in their making. "I remember these. Soul cakes?"

"Yes, they are." Tess popped the rest of her cookie into her mouth and chewed, washing it down with the last of her mead. "You didn't get them often, because—"

"Mama." Cent chomped down on her last bite with consternation. "I think she kept me from a lot of things."

"Most of it wasn't her doing." Rayne filled Cent's jar with tepid water from their form. "It was to keep you both safe. That's all."

"I guess." Cent emptied her jar and nodded to Rayne. "I'll see you tomorrow."

"Bright and early." Rayne sounded too chipper for the time of night it'd grown to be.

"Neither of which I appreciate." Cent took Tess by the arm, and they turned down the hill toward the trailer.

"Look back at where we were." Tess turned back after they'd gotten half-way home. "Tell me what you see."

"Sure." Cent glanced wearily over her shoulder then stopped in her tracks, turning around to stare. "They're gone!" The bonfire, the hundred-plus revelers, all gone! "Where'd—"

"Once we're out of the circle and get some distance it disappears to our eyes, but if we stepped back where it always is, we'll see it." Tess patted Cent's arm. "It's the veil. The circle lies near the edge, and that edge grows thinner as the wheel of the year turns. Witches like me and mixed-bloods like you, we can walk into the thin spot, and we're welcome there."

"Those like Rayne and Pyre?" Cent glanced back to make certain she hadn't missed something.

"They can move on the side the living can't." Tess slowed her walk. "See, there's the world of the living, this world, and the world of spirits, of the dead. Non-human spirits are both places, but the living can only see them if they believe or have spirit blood in them."

"Aren't there human spirits on this side too? Haints?"

"Haints can be Human or nonhuman, depending on the circumstance," said Tess. "But for Human haints, for whatever reason, their soul didn't cross the veil after they died. They're lost unless someone leads them over. And the longer they're lost, the more likely they are to stay."

"I thought some stuck around for a reason."

"Oh, they do. Take Birdie up at the homestead, for example."

"Birdie?"

"She's attached to one of the wardrobes for a reason she won't say. Birdie don't speak much, but she'll sometimes stand in the corner watching. She'll take stuff too if she likes it, but if you ask her real nice, she'll most always give it back, or at least trade you for something she thinks pretty."

"Birdie. Huh. I recollect seeing a face in the homestead windows before I left, but I thought it was a trick of the light." Cent peered down at her great aunt's wrinkled face. "Was it her?"

"Maybe, maybe not. There're other haints what walk 'round the homestead, but Birdie keeps them out of the house."

"But it ain't her place."

"Isn't it?" Tess laughed. "She don't mind sharing with the living or elementals but not other haints. And she sometimes fights with the house spirit."

"I thought Birdie was the house spirit."

"Oh, no. Your Uncle Kinnon called it a brownie. I still feed it sometimes to help keep the spiders and bugs down up there, but when we start cleaning we'll have to feed it regular."

"Does it have a name?"

"Just Brownie."

"Birdie and Brownie. Huh." They'd reached the edge of the herb garden. "The homestead was occupied even when I thought it wasn't."

"Such places are never empty." Tess stopped to run her fingers through the lavender tops. "It comes with being near a veil crossing."

"Is that why the spirits congregate here?"

"Yep. You remember seeing them as a kid, don't you?"

"I recall seeing Uncle Kinnon walking up the hill late one night and seeing mists following him."

"Them mists were either Rayne, Pyre, or the dead. Sometimes a combination."

"Oh. Did Uncle Kinnon have spirit blood in him?"

"Rayne said he had a little, but Kinnon was mainly aware because of his own spiritual path."

"Druid?"

Tess scrunched her face with amusement. "And we tried so hard to hide it all."

"You hid enough." *I need to control my temper about this.* "So do you have spirit blood in you?"

"Naw, not this lifetime, but I've been a witch so many times I can see regardless."

"Can Mama see?"

"She's enough spells on her to blind her from it." Tess took Cent's hand to squeeze it. "And she's always been watched, just like you've been."

"Is that how you knew— oh, you know some intimate— well, crap." Cent dug her heels into the dirt before they reached the trailer's porch. "Is there a house spirit in here?"

"In a single-wide? Not so I've noticed. Makes the house feel empty."

"Yeah, I guess it would." Cent pulled on Tess when she turned back to the trailer. "How much do you know about me?"

"Enough to understand you like what you like and love who you love, but that's how it should be." Tess climbed the first step, bouncing gently to test the give. "These steps need replacing before Stowne returns."

"What does Stowne look like?"

"You don't remember?" Tess turned to see her.

"I recall sensations, smells, warmth." Cent shivered. "But no, I don't remember what Stowne looks like."

"Stowne is, well, Stowne. They're earth and rock and sand, but you know all that. And Stowne ain't just made of dirt. They're an earth elemental, this mountain's spirit, and that makes them older and different than the others."

"They're a gnome?" Cent knew that wasn't right the second it sprang from her mouth.

"I guess they were at one point, but not anymore. A gnome is an earth elemental's true form. I'm told it's hard for them to find a Human lover, but Stowne somehow managed where you're concerned. But above all, Stowne loves you, and they'll change their form at any given moment if it pleases you."

"They change their shape to suit me?"

"Stowne's good at readin' you and adaptin'. That's what Rayne says. I ain't been there for all those lifetimes, but from what I've seen in mine, I'm inclined to agree." Tess grumbled when the porch boards groaned under her weight. "Yep. We got work to do."

"A lot of things around here need replacing." *I guess I shouldn't be embarrassed by anything now.* But part of her… "My first kiss?"

"Ina Sue Jones behind Dryler's."

"My first—"

"Some boy up in Chicago, but you were smart about it. You always are, so I don't worry much."

"Huh. Okay." They now stood at the trailer door. "And Stowne?"

"Not yet this lifetime, but I have my hopes. A more than half-magic child or two here would be wonderful, but that's your choice to make." Tess winked at her. "Get yourself to bed. We've lots to do tomorrow." She fished out her keys and opened the door. "You need some chamomile tea to help you sleep?"

"I'm tired enough that it shouldn't be a problem." But she did have trouble sleeping and kept slipping into nightmares where a black, hulking form towered over her, lifting her between its gargantuan hands to squeeze her neck. She woke gasping each time but managed to find sleep again, only to have the process repeat. Each time, the choking lasted longer, each time it took longer for her to wake, until she finally woke screaming, bringing Aunt Tess to her room.

"What the— begone from this home before I banish you!" Tess wrapped her arms around Cent to gently rock her, chanting a protective prayer under her breath until Cent found her voice. "Shh. No need to explain. I saw the booger for myself." She rocked Cent as she spoke the prayer again. "You know the words."

"No, I don't. I—"

"Think, honey. Think real hard. You've known this prayer for lifetimes." Tess opened the small bedroom's window. "Think on it, and I'll be right back."

Cent stared after her, trying hard to recall the words to the prayer her great aunt had spoken, but Tess returned a moment later holding a Bible and a bundle of half-dried basil, both of which she tossed to Cent. "Hold them while I… now where is…, aha!" She fished an adhesive-backed plastic hook from her robe pocket. "There!" She affixed the hook to the wall above Cent's head and hung the bundle from it. "That should do the trick." She slipped the Bible between the mattress and box spring beneath Cent's head. "Now, the prayer." She sat beside Cent again. "Do you remember it?"

"Yeah, I think I do. In a couple of languages, actually."

"Show off. Let me hear it in English."

Deep peace of water come to me
Deep peace of air come to me
Deep peace of earth come to me
Deep peace of night come to me
Deep peace of dark come to me
Moon and stars grant me the light I need

Cent turned to face the window. "Begone bad dreams. Begone dark. In the name of the Holy Spirit. As I will it. So will it be."

"You do remember!" Tess hugged her then went to the window, which she closed. "There. That prayer, the good book, and the basil should keep it from coming back, but don't be too scared to ask for help if you need it." Tess kissed Cent on the forehead and left, closing the door behind her.

"In the name of the Holy Spirit. So I will it. So will it be." Cent rolled her shoulders and lay back to look at the basil above her head. It smelled of mint and anise, both smells she liked. It made her think of Tess' cooking, of her own full stomach, of eating regular meals and not constantly worrying about her basic needs. Warm and content, she finally drifted to sleep, smiling when she felt two stout, warm-earth arms wrap lovingly around her waist and soft, loamy breath spread across her neck.

That memory of Stowne helped her sleep soundly the rest of the night.

Chapter Eleven

Under the Waning Moon
August 8, 2017

"**Your** neck!" Rayne rushed to Cent's side as soon as she and Tess stepped out the trailer's back door, pulling back Cent's t-shirt collar to see her shoulders and upper chest. "What happened?"

"A booger got in and made a dark attack," blurted Tess before Cent could say anything. "I already rubbed cayenne ointment into it this morning."

"I took some ibuprofen too," Cent added but that only seemed to confuse Rayne more.

"Ibu— Is that an herb or…"

"One of those new Human medicines I told you about a few years back. Does a fair job at taking down swelling."

"I see." Rayne's water-mouth turned downward in an exaggerated frown that dripped from the corners. "Darkness is slipping in, Tess, and it risked entering the trailer to get at Centenary. It's time to renew your protections."

"I'm already renewing them weekly." Tess took Cent by the arm. "I should show you how to do them, I guess."

"Good idea." Rayne nodded. "Hers will be more powerful, but then our enemies will know she's here."

"It seems to me they already know," said Cent as they climbed the hill to the homestead. She'd awakened nauseous, and it'd only gotten worse once she'd remembered what they were going to do today. But at the same time, the notion of learning about her past lives, of who she'd been, excited her. "I don't mind helping with the protections."

"It will aid Tess." Rayne flowed past them to block their way and raised their hand to cup Tess' face. "Keeping them up is becoming difficult for anyone without spirit blood in them, so let her." They kissed Tess lightly on the forehead. "You'll need the strength later."

"We'll *all* need it later," objected Tess, but she nodded. "Y'all are going to have to help sooner or later, so I might as well let it start now." Tess pointed up the hillside. "Ready, Cent?"

"This ain't going to be easy, is it?"

"No, child." Tess shook her head. "It's gonna hurt like hell."

"I thought witches didn't believe in hell."

"It's all a mix here in Appalachia, especially these days," Tess explained. "Your Great Granny Sudie was as likely to make a witch bottle and speak a spell as she was to quote the Bible, anoint, and lay hands. It's how I was raised and how I'm going to teach you this life, if you need any teaching at all. But as for hell, seems to me it'd be the worst feeling you could imagine more than an actual place. And the Devil is a dark spirit, the darkest of them all, but even the Bible says he ain't never been a Human. He's part of the Christian threads running through our family, not the traditional witchcraft. It'll be up to you to put it all together in a way that suits you."

"This is overwhelming," said Cent. "There's so much to relearn."

"We'll be with you the entire time." Rayne wrapped their arm around Cent's until they reached the homestead's steps. "You built and filled this place, so this time you go in first, but don't touch anything until we're beside you."

"All right." Cent stepped through the door first, listening, thinking. *The kitchen.* She stopped midway across the front room to stare at the two rocking chairs in front of the fireplace. She went to the bigger rocker to sit in it, suddenly warm inside and out. *I'm coming, honey. Hold on.* Cent stood and turned toward the kitchen, reaching back to stop the rocker from moving without an occupant. *I've had enough bad luck, thank you.* She entered the kitchen and lifted her head to stare at the rafters. Dusty, dirty, and cobweb-covered. The webs didn't bother her, because they meant there weren't many other insects around, but the dust and dirt— she thought about how hard it was going to be to clean those rafters, about how easy it'd be if the dirt and dust flew away, about it being outside, and to her surprise a brown cloud rose from the rafters and flew to the window, where it hovered.

"Begone." Cent opened one of the windows and the dirt flew out, taking the window grime with it. The wavy-glass shone afterward, and light spilled into the kitchen. "Wow!" She spun around to see the whole kitchen, grinning as she used her new-found power again. "Begone dust. Begone dirt. Leave my kitchen clean. I command it!" Seconds later, the old homestead's kitchen was considerably cleaner. Not as she wanted it, but better.

"You're back," whispered a voice, and a cold breeze passed Cent, gathering in a far corner as a translucent elderly woman wearing a long white dress and an untied bonnet.

"Birdie?" Cent squinted at the corner.

"Yessirree." Birdie pulled her bonnet from her head, revealing a skeletal face holding a pair of sapphire eyes in their sockets. "You can use my wardrobe again if you're wantin'." She began to fade until only her eyes remained. "Just scrub it up good afore you do, exceptin' for that bottom drawer. It's mine, so let it be."

"Yes'm. Thanks." Cent stared into the corner after Birdie had left. *For someone quiet, she sure said a lot this time.*

"I see Birdie's already welcomed you home." Rayne clapped their hands, scattering water across the old-wood countertops and shelves. "And that you've started cleaning without us." They began to chant, agitating the water droplets so they picked up the dirt that'd refused to leave. "Begone stubborn spots. Leave this kitchen clean!" Rayne pointed to the open window, and the dirty water obeyed, flying out like the dirt had earlier. "There. Much better." Rayne rubbed their hands together and smiled.

"I-I didn't know I could…" Cent stared at her own hands then at Tess, who smiled as well. "Why'd I never see you do— Mama, I know, but this is handy." She flexed her fingers, examining the bits of dirt that'd collected under her short nails during the spell. "Huh."

"It takes a lot of energy for me to do it," said Tess. "But I've used the spell in a pinch."

"I'm going to clean this entire house and—" Cent paused when Rayne shook their head hard enough for their watery locks to slip from their tie. "Why shouldn't I?"

"It'll wear you down too fast for what you need to accomplish today," insisted Tess. "The kitchen is fine. Now follow your instincts. Where were you being drawn before you got distracted?"

"I don't know." Cent looked around the kitchen, proud of what she'd accomplished, now unable to focus on anything but that. "Something's getting in the way."

"And we all know who." Rayne glided across the floor to face Cent, their hands raised to cradle her face. "Yes, they're trying to block you from…" They stepped back with a bewildered expression. "No. It isn't them this time." Rayne spun around and pointed out the window. "Pyre! I feel your presence! I'm the elder of us, and the more powerful, so come to me now, or I'll command you to do so!"

"You would." Pyre's smoky form seeped through the window, collecting to stand between Cent and Rayne. "Hello again, my dear." Pyre flashed Cent another white-hot smile. "I see you've been doing some cleaning. Would you like my assistance?"

"You're getting in my way?" Cent waved her arm, cutting Pyre's smoke in half. "Why?"

"A part of you wishes to be mine again." Pyre moved closer, their breath hot on her neck. "You remember us. What we accomplished together. How bravely we burned."

"It was quick, and you left me singed!" Cent raised her arm to swing at Pyre again. "Get outta my way!"

"You don't mean that." Black smoke leeched from between Pyre's teeth. "The more you recall, the more you'll forget me, forget us, the power, the pleasure we shared." Pyre's form switched to flames that floated above the floor, their shape oscillating between a male and female build. "You like both. You get both. You want heat? You get heat. What does Stowne offer you? Are they here now?" Pyre held out a flickering hand. "I'll help you find your way and assist you in protecting this land. I will keep you warm and entertained like no other. This can be ours again if you'll be mine. This house and your family will be protected and—"

"You'll leave now, or I'll—"

"You'll what?" Pyre swirled into a cyclone of smoke and flame that wrapped her. "Enjoy me, Centenary. Enjoy us." Pyre's flames lapped at her ears, and their smoke slid beneath her shirt and into her pockets, becoming fingers that kneaded her.

"Enough!" Cent rushed to one of the cabinets where she grabbed a bottle topped with an aged rubber stopper. "Leave me alone!" She hurled the bottle to the floor in front of Pyre where it exploded, showering them with glass and the bottle's contents. "'Be not be overcome with evil but overcome evil with good!'"

"No! You didn't need to— All right! I'm going!" Pyre's smoke dissipated until only their Cheshire-cat smile remained. "Stowne's nowhere to be found, yet you still reject my affections. I don't understand you, Centenary." The last of Pyre disappeared in a puff of angry black smoke that slid out the window.

"You got 'em good!" Birdie's laugh drifted from the corner.

"What was in that bottle?" Cent turned to Tess and Rayne.

"Some old Four Thieves by the vinegar smell." Tess gaped at her. "It's a minor banishment spell that'll keep Pyre away for a little while. And you backed it with a strong Bible quote too. Perhaps you're recallin' more than you thought."

"Serves them right." Rayne raised their hand to their mouth to stifle a bubbling laugh. "You've used a bottle on them before. It stings, but not so long that we elementals can't forget."

"But where'd they go?"

"To their lair beneath the mountain to lick their wounds." Tess used her fingers to wipe ash from Cent's face. "Give me that shirt for rags when we get back home. Pyre burned holes in it."

"How long?" Cent drew her eyes from the shattered bottle to the window glass, which was now coated with soot. "How long will they be gone?"

"At least until the sting fades." Tess' forehead wrinkled with concern. "Why?"

"I don't want the distraction, need to..." Cent wandered across the kitchen and toward the cellar door, which she cracked open. The smell rising from the cellar was far too familiar. Cent didn't know she'd descended the stairs or taken off her shoes and socks until she felt the cellar's earthen floor beneath her toes. How connected she felt, how... *Stowne*. She had to remember, had to— She scurried into the cellar's far corner, ignoring Tess' and Rayne's worried calls as she began clawing at the dirt with her fingers.

"You'll ruin your hands."

Cent stopped raking her nails over the ground to stare at Rayne. "My flashlight." She fumbled through her pants pocket for her phone, turning on the flashlight app before handing it to Tess. "Is there something here I can—"

"We're not allowed to help you dig," said Rayne. "But there's a coal shovel by the old burner." Rayne tilted their head that direction.

"Be careful. It's rusty." Tess turned the light, exposing the short-handled shovel for the first time in decades.

"Yes, I..." Something stirred deep inside Cent, a thirst for the past, for what she'd been, for memories she'd never known. She began to dig, on a blind mission as she lifted shovel after shovel of earth. When the shovel handle broke, she threw it aside and went back to using her hands, dragging her fingers through the loosened dirt until they hit something hard. She brushed the dirt aside and reached for—

"Careful," warned Rayne, or Cent thought it might be them. She couldn't tell. All that mattered was what she'd found.

Chapter Twelve

Half Done Wrong
9th Century BCE

Cent writhed in agony, her body tight, her instincts high. She folded in on herself then flailed back, opening her eyes to peer into gentle, kind— Stowne's eyes were the color of freshly turned soil on a damp spring day. Deep brown, almost black. "You're nearly done." Their voice brought her courage, so she curled forward and repeated whatever she'd been doing, squealing at the pressure engulfing her body.

"One more." *Stowne.* She could see them. A thick shock of long dark hair hanging to one side of... *his* head? *No.* "Stowne?"

"Yes?" Stowne raised their hand to stroke her face. Their words were strange, as were her own, but she understood them nonetheless. Flesh and bone. Her Stowne was flesh and bone. There. Real. *Tsalagi?*

Cent clenched her jaw and curled forward when the pressure resumed.

"Take my hands."

She looked up to see Rayne smiling at her in the fire's low light. Native too, their hair tied back in a simple leather cord the same color as their deer-hide shirt.

"Come on. Pull!" Rayne grabbed her hands when she hesitated, pulling her forward as Stowne held her from behind, chanting under their breath. A spell, an old spell. She knew its meaning. A shield, a cover. *Male?* No, Stowne was still an elemental they, but they couldn't show this for a reason she didn't understand.

She squealed at the pain, panting and holding her breath when it intensified, engulfing her again.

"Yes. Yes!" Rayne dropped their hands between Cent's legs as something powerful exited her body. "Oh, you did it. You did it!" They held up a small, bloody, naked—

"A baby?" Cent flitted her eyes from the infant to Stowne who hugged her tighter.

"Our child. You did this for me, so I could be with you in your world." Stowne showered her with kisses and hugged her tight. "Thank you. Thank you." Such love flowed through Stowne's hands that Cent leaned back, content though she still didn't understand where or when they were. The fire flickered a bit higher, crackling. Cent held up her hand, marveling at the warm tone of her own skin. She next peered at the child Rayne cuddled against their chest. Same skin tone. Same dark hair, though matted.

The child began crying low, shaking and whining as Rayne cleaned them.

"Where are we?" She couldn't see beyond the firelight but knew they were on the ground. "Stowne?"

"Usdagalv. Remember? It is where we decided you would give birth." Stowne peered warily at Rayne, who still smiled.

"She's tired and rightfully so." Rayne extended their arms to Cent, giving her the child. "Your son."

"My, our…" Cent's stare drifted from the infant to Stowne and back. Yes, there was a resemblance. This form of Stowne could easily be the child's father, but something… she lowered her head to stare closely. Something was wrong. Not outside, she decided as she unwrapped the baby to inspect him. It was something she couldn't quite…

"We'll be careful so he never knows." Stowne leaned in. "He has your eyes."

"You think?" Within the hour Cent was sitting up, drinking herbal tea and nursing her son while Stowne held her. She stared around Usdagalv, the space where she'd met Stowne in secret before they'd married. Their first sexual encounter had given Stowne the ability to take other forms, and their child had granted them a soul, but at a price. Their child was to be denied any magic. He'd never truly know his parents.

Cent thought this over, about how much she now understood. Usdagalv was Stowne's, but they'd soon return to their community, to Cent's, yes, *her* home. She owned the land their summer and winter homes rested on. It was her mother's and her mother's before. Generations. That's how it worked. The land was high enough above the Nolichucky to be safe from floods but close enough to fish and cleanse in the river. Farming the river-flat was always a risk, but her family had been doing so for centuries. Two gardens. One high, one low. The river-flat, with its rich ground, was far more productive, but the higher garden assured her family survived the winter, flood or not.

It was early enough in the year for her not to worry about the gardens. "Unitsi will be expecting us to return tomorrow." Cent yawned and so did newborn Dustu Usdi. They'd refused to let Cent's mother come even though she understood. Unitsi liked Stowne and had said they were a good choice for a spouse, aside from the one problem.

"Take the child to the river before you bring it home so Long Man will cleanse away the effects of our world meeting Stowne's world." Unitsi had frowned at her.

"Stowne lives in this world too," Cent had argued. "And you're no medicine woman. Everyone thinks we're witches. That's why we live on the edge of town, why no one trusts us."

"Bah. Who do they turn to when they think they've heard the Raven Mocker?" Unitsi had grinned at her. "Who do they trade with for food when the low crops have failed?"

"Yes, but—"

"Take the child to the water, let Long Man cleanse him, and be content with your family. But no more children for you and Stowne. If you want more, travel. Find a town and a young man, a person, then come home."

"No, Unitsi. One baby is enough."

"We'll see." Unitsi had returned to her lap loom, weaving a red and yellow blanket for the new child. Their town always had the brightest colors, had the prettiest clothing. Stowne had shown her numerous deposits of limonite and red hematite for them to use, and this blanket was even brighter than most.

That had been the fall before, and now Unitsi's blanket wrapped their son, who stretched lazily and peered up at Cent, content against her.

"We'll go home tomorrow morning." Rayne paced the cavern. "I will leave ahead with Dustu, introduce him to Long Man, and return him to you before you reach home."

"The water is too cold." Cent wrapped around her son. "He'll become ill."

"I will warm the water first," countered Rayne. "You know I'm capable."

"Yes, but he, he should be a little older and hardier."

"You promised your mother." Rayne appealed to Stowne who shook their head and clutched Cent tighter. "Very well, as soon as the spring run-off is finished, he'll meet Long Man."

"Agreed." Stowne pulled a blanket over Cent as she slid down into the grasses mounded beneath her. More of a nest than anything else, and itchy, but warmed from beneath by Stowne's energy. They'd never let her get cold, and they'd never let their son either.

Chapter Thirteen

Half Gone Wrong
9th Century BCE / August 8, 2017

"**Etsi,** see?" Five-year-old Dustu Usdi held up his hands to show Cent the fledgling robin he'd found.

"Put it down. Its mother is nearby."

"I don't see her." Dustu bounded to his mother's side, holding out the fledgling for her to see. "It's soft."

"Put it back and come help me weed." Cent straightened, arching her back as she looked across the field they stood in. The corn was tasseling, and the beans were loaded with tiny shoots. The crops would be decent, at least Unitsi said so. Cent didn't know for certain, but she'd been uncomfortable no, wary, all spring. "Dustu, the little bird. Take it home so its mother can care for it."

"But…" Dustu's shoulders drooped as he turned away. "I want to keep it."

"It will die without its mother." Cent pointed to where he'd been. "Remember what happened last time? Go now. Go on."

"No!" The ground rumbled when Dustu stomped his foot, hard enough for Unitsi to look up from where she sat on the bench outside their summer home. "It's *my* bird!" He flexed his hand around the fledgling, squeezing as his face reddened.

"No, son." Cent rushed toward him, her hands extended. *Not again. Not another.* Half magic was worse than no magic at all. Dangerous. Unitsi had warned them twice recently, had said Stowne should stay away from their son. Cent felt Dustu's energy concentrating before she got close enough to stop him, helpless as blood-drenched feathers slipped from between his small fingers.

"Dustu." She dropped to her knees beside him and unfolded his hand, showing him the fledgling. "See what you have done?"

"I-I didn't mean to." Dustu dropped the bird to the ground. "I just wanted to keep it so badly, and…" Tears welled in his eyes. "When will Adadoda be back?"

"Soon, I hope." Cent glanced over her shoulder at Unitsi who shook her head before returning to her basket-making. "Let's wash your hands." She guided Dustu to the water skin, pouring some into a wooden bowl she plunged his hands into, reciting a prayer and another protection spell over her son while he washed. The town had become more than wary of Dustu. They were afraid and rightly so. Despite his family's efforts to hide magic, Dustu had found it on his own.

"There." Cent told Dustu to dry his hands on the grass away from their home and emptied the bowl across the ground, watching in horror as the grass withered wherever the bloody water touched it.

"I rolled stones again this morning at dawn before anyone woke, and they gave me the answer they always do. Nothing to be gained. No way to stop him. No." Unitsi shook her head again. "Raven Mocker. He has the boy in his sight." She'd stopped helping Cent with Dustu, stopped— Rayne stood at the garden's edge in Human form in case Dustu saw them. They were watching Dustu, as was Pyre in Human form along the tree line. They were a couple again, but they still clashed about most everything, especially Dustu.

Pyre shook their head like Unitsi had, then turned and walked into the tree line. Rayne waved at Cent, glanced again at Dustu, and retreated. They seldom visited anymore, nor did the ancestors or the other ghosts of the town's residents. This distressed Unitsi because Cent's father and two sisters, long gone, hadn't visited since Dustu's birth.

"Etsi?" Dustu tugged at her belt. "When's Adadoda coming home?"

"As soon as he catches enough fish for smoking." *As soon as they find the strength to regain Human form.* Rayne provided them fish from the local waters. Pyre made certain there was enough dry wood for their fire. Stowne's time away was spent re-energizing and searching for new ways of shielding their son from magic.

"Oh." Dustu followed her back to the field, kicking dirt clods as he walked, talking under his breath.

"What did you say?" Cent glanced over her shoulder at him.

"I was talking to the Yvwitsunastiga." Dustu went back to his self-talk.

"Best not disturb them." Cent began mounding dirt, readying the ground for the later crops. "Pester them too much and they'll leave you puzzled."

"They won't leave me alone!" Dustu tugged on her belt again. "See? One of them is in my pocket."

"They don't appreciate when you lie about them." Cent blinked hard when something darted across her vision. *No. No.* One didn't talk about or— Oh, how should she handle this? *Where are you, Stowne?* She needed their quick thinking right now. She closed her eyes and thought hard about her need for them. *Come home. Please. Hurry.*

Dustu was staring at her when she opened her eyes. "You miss Adadoda when he's gone too, don't you?"

70

Oh, how did— "I love your adadoda, so of course I miss him." She tried to turn back to her work, but he stepped in front of her. "Go play, son. Or, better yet, pull those weeds over there." She pointed to the sprouts projecting from the other earthen piles she'd been working on.

"Can the Yvwitsunastiga help me?"

"If they wish." The answer was easier than telling him to be quiet. Cent kept a close watch on him as they worked, and, to her dismay, brown streaks, quick moving arms and legs, joined him on the mound, making fast work of the task. *What do I do with this child?* She turned her face to the sun and prayed, hoping for an answer when there was none to be had.

———————

"No!" Dustu stomped his feet, shaking their small, winter home so hard that cracks formed in the mud and stick walls. "I want to go with Adadoda!"

"You cannot." Stowne's voice wavered in a sure sign of their utter fatigue. Winter meant being contained inside their home more days than not, meant simple tasks became harder, meant Dustu became difficult to occupy. This winter, however, he'd become destructive, tearing at the walls, setting his own blankets ablaze. Yesterday, he'd hit Cent with a stone he'd hidden in his pocket, blacking her eye.

Dustu had laughed even as his mother cried and Unitsi yelled. Unitsi had gathered her belongings and left their warm home, saying she preferred the cold of the summer house to the hatred of her only grandchild. "He'll kill us all," she'd whispered to Cent before she'd stepped out the door.

"I'll worry about you."

"No more than I will for you." Unitsi had glanced back at Dustu and sighed. "This winter. May it be short."

———————

Cent had asked the town's medicine men and women to help, but they'd refused. "Too much Raven Mocker." Their words echoed in her ears until she could hear little else.

And Stowne had become a shell, barely able to keep their Human form when Dustu was awake, almost too weak to leave by the time he fell asleep.

71

And oh, how Stowne worried about things when they had to go. "I'll ask Rayne to watch this time."

"Tell them I miss their company." Cent neatly stacked the wood Stowne had brought into the house and stood on her toes to kiss their tense lips. "A stage. He will outgrow it."

"I love him too, but I can see what you cannot." Stowne clutched her to them. "Rayne and Pyre can too." They shivered against her. "Be careful. I will be back by morning." Stowne turned from her to see their son, their face distraught. "Sometimes I wish— avaricious. I thought of nothing but myself when I convinced you..." They fled the house without saying more, setting the door so firmly in place that Cent had difficulty following them outside.

"Wait!" But Stowne had already disappeared into the driving snow.

"Go back inside." Rayne's voice rose from beneath the snow. "Feed your fire and get some sleep." They didn't say more, so Cent retreated. Where had her happiness, her drive, her... She obediently fed the fire and lay next to Dustu, watching him sleep, stroking his long, dark hair as she cried.

What have we done? What misery have we thrust onto ourselves? She refused to think more on it and soon fell asleep too.

"I do what I want!" Dustu's laugh pierced the frigid air. His hands glowed red and his eyes— Half magic had grown into full madness. Beyond puzzled. Even the Yvwitsunastiga had fled his side. An owl cried outside their small home every night, its inquiries drowned by cougar screams.

A warning. A warning.

Cent had no energy to fight.

> *Raven Mocker*
> *Raven Mocker*
> *You now possess my son*

This time Dustu had set their small home ablaze during a late-winter storm. Ice hung from the trees, weighing the branches until they broke.

"Isn't it pretty?" Dustu clapped his hands and pointed to the blaze. "Look, Etsi! Look what I did!" Cent lay curled at his small feet. Her child. She was afraid of her own child and his uncontrolled abilities. There was no balance to be had, no light flickering amid his darkness. Dustu raised his glowing hands to stare at them before pointing one finger toward Cent. "Are you cold, Etsi?"

"No." It was all Cent could muster. He'd singed off her blankets, and the fire had taken everything they owned. And Unitsi. Cent sobbed. He'd insisted Unitsi was cold, that the summer house needed warmed too. *Too much. Too—* "Stop!" She drew to her knees before him. "Stop!"

"But it's pretty." He drew out those words as his hand touched her shoulder, sending scorching heat through her body.

My son. My son! Her son belonged to the Raven Mocker. Half-magic turned full evil. She couldn't deny it, couldn't stop— Gentle water coated her body, soothing her agony. *Rayne!* They couldn't show their true form to Dustu, couldn't— *It no longer matters.*

Cent opened her eyes to see Rayne hovering over her. "I'm taking you to Stowne." They swept Cent into their arms when she couldn't stand.

"My son." The words came out garbled to her own ears.

"Pyre's taking him to Long Man."

"No! It's too cold, too…"

"Shh." Rayne placed their hand against Cent's lips to ease their burn. "Pyre and Long Man will do what they must. Let's get you to Stowne."

She lay in Stowne's arms, her body ablaze inside long after the outside flames had been doused. Stowne kept her bare flesh warmed. Rayne cooled her where it hurt most, and Pyre… they lit Usdagalv as bright as day but seldom spoke.

Cent stared at Pyre whenever they drew close enough for her to see, her eyes hollow and questioning though she knew the answer deep in her heart.

Stowne and Rayne coated her with cool damp hides and herbs, and in time, her body healed. Twisted and scarred. Disfigured. She and Stowne asked to be alone when she could finally do for herself.

They seldom spoke but often held each other, Stowne wrapping her in the silence.

Half-magic had gone full mad, taking Cent with it. She walked the river bank every night in search of her son until Stowne finally carried her to where Exan waited.

"I won't go without my son!" Cent fought Exan, beating on their black-mass form until they were forced to drag her across the veil and into Unitsi's waiting arms.

"Dustu." Cent refused to let go of the scorched pottery shard in her hand. "My son."

"I'm sorry." Rayne lay beside her, wrapping Cent to absorb her sobs as their own.

"Rayne told me what happened," said Tess from somewhere behind them. "Oh, child. What pain you've seen."

"Too much." Cent trembled in Rayne's warm hold. "I don't. No." She was too weak to speak more than a few words or remove her hand from the hole. "Help… me." She turned her head to stare at Rayne's translucent, beaming face. "Please."

"You don't need my assistance." Rayne retreated when the ground rumbled beneath them, collapsing the hole around Cent's arm as something pushed up from the bottom, becoming fingers that closed her hand around the pottery shard.

"Cen-ten-ar-y." The ground sighed beneath her, and she knew, *she knew* it'd all been real.

Chapter Fourteen

Awake and Aware
August 9, 2017

Cent woke with the side of her face pressed into the dirt. As warm as her own flesh but fine and soft. She was naked on the ground and anything but cold. The floor rumbled beneath her, reminding her of where she was.

"Good morning." Stowne's warm, loamy breath coated her with memories of the night before. "Thank you for staying with me."

"How could I not?" They'd talked all evening then enjoyed each other in ways that'd deepened Cent's understanding of who she was. Being with Stowne was in no way like being with a Human. No, using the word Human would have been an insult. Stowne was so much better, their deepest happiness deriving from her and their multi-millennia relationship.

"You missed your dinner last night. Are you hungry?"

"I'm starved." Cent rolled onto her back to stare at the bottom-side of the kitchen floorboards and their supporting beams, both of which twinkled in the light trickling through the windows. The cellar smelled nothing like a dirt basement should. Clean, like fresh ground warmed by the sun. The heavy cobwebs and dust present the night before had been cleared away.

"Brownie removed them while you slept." Stowne explained when she asked. "You have always appreciated a clean home."

"I'll have to feed them today." Cent sat up, smiling when she felt Stowne settle behind her, their arms wrapping around her waist as she leaned against them. "I want to remember more."

"You must for your power to rise where it needs to be." Stowne's breath tickled her ear until her skin prickled. "Tess is approaching with your breakfast, so you might wish to cover yourself." They held out Cent's t-shirt.

"Why?" But Cent did anyway, pulling her t-shirt over her head as the cellar door opened.

"Are you up?"

"She is." Stowne rose from behind Cent, and she could see them in the light, a Human form shaped by sand, soil, and rock, perfectly proportioned with red streaks running between. Magma? No. Cent didn't understand what the red represented, but it resembled a circulatory system.

"Careful, Tess. Let me assist you." Stowne stretched their arm up the stairs to steady Tess when she wobbled.

"Take the bowl so I can use both hands." Tess sat on the second from the bottom step, which bowed beneath her. "These steps need replacin' too. Good mornin' to you both. Cent, child, you're a mess."

"Yeah, I know." Cent ran her fingers through her hair, smiling again when she reached the stubbly side. Stowne had been infatuated with that portion of her all night, with touching, kissing, and nuzzling her there. *The hair stays.* "Rough night."

"But a happy one by your face." Tess tossed her a water bottle. "Pyre stopped by last night to apologize."

"They should," snapped Cent between swallows, and Stowne rumbled agreement.

"You handled the situation well."

"I think I've had practice." Cent glanced at Tess. "What got into them yesterday? Did they say?"

"Pyre called it a stupid, desperate, last-ditch effort and said you had every right to throw Four Thieves on them." Tess pointed to the bowl. "Eat. We've a day of cleaning to get to."

"Yes'm." Cent lifted the bowl to examine the contents. Oatmeal, but it had streaks of melted butter and brown sugar running through it.

"What are the black... oh, raisins." Stowne settled back behind Cent, arms circling her waist again. "You have always liked dried fruit."

"What's not to like?" Cent lifted a spoonful of oatmeal to her mouth, savoring the sweetness. Did Stowne eat? In a way, she supposed, but the energy they consumed would eventually return to the Earth. "I want to work in the kitchen again. There's something in the cabinets I need."

"I left most all the old dishware when I moved to the trailer," explained Tess. "I don't recall seeing anything that would—"

"Not the dishes. Something else, in the back. At least I think there is."

"Do not go too fast or try so hard, usdayvhsgi. The memories will come." Stowne drew back when she glared at them. "I know that look. What did I do wrong?"

"Don't call me your wife. I'm no more so than you are my asgayaninela. I love you. I have for ever so long, but those words indicate binary gender types, and we're way beyond that. Call me your asiule ehu. Okay?"

"Yes, asiule ehu. I like that better anyway." Stowne plucked a raisin from the bowl and held it to her mouth. "Whatever you desire. I am merely glad we are together again."

"Me too." She peered up at Tess when she laughed. "What?"

"So now you're speaking Wee Fairy *and* Tsalagi?"

"It came back to me, but Stowne's not a man, so husband doesn't fit in any language."

"It'd have been a more practical reference for your past female forms, but this life…" Tess shrugged. "Use whatever words you want."

"The word choice changes nothing." Stowne nuzzled her head again. "But do you not wish to be a woman this life?"

"No. Yes." Her skin prickled when their breath drifted across her neck. "I just— dang it. It's hard for me to explain. I feel like I'm somewhere in between most days. I was born female, and it doesn't really bother me to go by she and her, but I identify more genderqueer and definitely pansexual."

"Gender… what?" Stowne's sandy-brown brow line crinkled with curiosity. "I do not know those terms. Explain, please."

"My body is female, but I don't always feel that way in my head, nor do I consider the gender of those I find attractive to be important."

"It comes from flipping back and forth all those lifetimes." Tess nodded to show her understanding.

Stowne repeated Cent's words with great care. "So how do you feel in your head, and what do you like?"

"Some days I feel more man, some days more woman. Some days, neither, just me and the rest doesn't matter. But I know I love you. I felt that when you first touched my hand yesterday. I know you've dealt with me being either male or female for a very long time, but what about being in between?"

"As in intersex?" Stowne folded their arms around Cent's waist again. "I saw nothing regarding that last night, and you have been intersex before too."

Tess cleared her throat and stared at the kitchen floorboards.

"No. In my brain." Cent tapped her head. *Is it so hard to understand?* "Some days I feel more woman, some days more man."

"And some days neither." Stowne unknotted their brows. "Yes, I understand. I have had to present as male or female to be part of your life before, but I am unable to be either, so it always felt wrong. I am glad I do not have to hide behind those personas this time."

"We'll work on a midline appearance for when those who don't understand come around," said Tess. "Still Human-looking, but— Cent will help you."

"You will?" Stowne's smile revealed white gypsum teeth, but Cent knew those were for her and Tess' benefit. "Thank you!" They lifted the oatmeal bowl to her. "Finish your breakfast. We now have more than ever to do!"

Happy. Stowne was happy, and when Stowne was happy, Cent was happy. She finished the oatmeal in four bites and downed the rest of the water. "Where're my pants?"

"I folded them and placed them with your shoes and undergarments over there." Stowne pointed to where they were neatly stacked, Cent's white, boy-short-style underwear placed glaringly on the top.

"You two are so syrup-pie-stuck on each other it's cute." Tess laughed so hard she grabbed the handrail. "I'll wait upstairs."

"I came across you and Kinnon wearing less than Centenary more than once." Stowne raised one sandy brow at her. "Do you not remember?"

"Oh, I do." Tess grinned at them. "And that's why I'm leavin'." She laughed all the way up the stairs.

"Come here." Cent turned to face Stowne as soon as Tess closed the cellar door. "I'm sorry again for leaving you."

"I understand your reasons." Stowne lowered their face to hers, where their breath rustled her hair. "But it hurt so much I became lost until you began to remember."

"Damn hard memory." She shuddered against them.

"I know. I was there."

"Have we had any more children together?" *Please tell me no.*

"No. Children must be a conscious decision we make together." Stowne rubbed her back with both hands, soothing, absorbing the remains of the day before's pain. "Dustu soured us both."

"Half magic. No, my mother is quite enough this lifetime."

"Yes, but her existence makes you quarter-magic, and you are female, so…" Stowne drew her head up until they looked at each other. "If we make the choice this time, we are safe. The child will be more than half, so they can know the veil from both sides."

"I'm not ready to think about, much less discuss the idea." She broke from them to retrieve her clothing.

"I understand." Stowne ogled as they watched her re-dress. "I have always appreciated the lines of your body no matter the form."

"And just how many other Human bodies have you inspected as closely as mine?" She buttoned her pants and shoved her bra into her pocket. Why bother? It was a home day… their home, and she could be as comfortable as she wished.

"How many besides yours?" Stowne grinned at her. "I have walked beside you over a hundred lifetimes. Many lovers in one. That is all the variety I need."

"Wise answer, but what about before me?"

"If you remember, you are the one who allowed me to take other forms."

"Oh, so that's how— wait, you were a *virgin?*"

"That term does not apply to my kind. I had many other elemental lovers before I found you, including Rayne and Pyre."

"I'd wondered, especially about Rayne."

"Rayne is wonderful, and I do love them but differently than I do you." Stowne rose when she did, pressing against her to stroke her back again. "You are my eternal. The one I ache for every time I must wait."

"You're quite the romantic." Cent tilted her head back to kiss Stowne's warm-earth mouth, appreciating the energy she felt transfer between them. "Is this what you meant when you said I was feeding you last night?"

"Somewhat." Stowne's mouth engulfed hers, moist and tender but certainly not Human when their kiss deepened. It was enough to curl her toes, and she would have fallen if Stowne hadn't supported her weight. "I would like to remove your clothing and show you more about energy, but you should go upstairs." Stowne's smile teased her when she opened her eyes.

"Yeah, I guess— wait, you're not coming?" *But I want you beside me.*

"I cannot be above ground. Not yet. Soon, I hope. By the Ripe Corn Moon if you remember enough. I hope to dance with you that night."

"To show Pyre I'm yours?"

"To show Mother Earth, Father Eternity, and both sides of the veil that we are one again."

"Guess I should get to work." Cent kissed Stowne once more and rushed up the stairs, ignoring the bottom step's audible crack beneath her feet.

Chapter Fifteen

Play Before War
Mid-18th Century / August 9, 2017

"You're too young to play digadayosdi so stop trying." Etsi grabbed the small, round stone from Cent's hand and threw it out the cabin door where it hit the ground and rolled into the grass. "Shame. Go find your adadoda and help him. That's what a good son your age should be doing."

"But, Etsi…oh, all right." Cent ran out the door before Etsi clouted his ear, dropping to his knees amid the grasses to find his stone. It wasn't a real digadayosdi stone, more like a half-sized version. He had watched Adadoda and the town's other men play the game countless times. They took precise measurements and were careful to choose their sticks and dig the holes right. There was a lot of strategy to digadayosdi, and Cent wanted to learn it all before he ever stepped onto a full-sized field.

He tossed his stone between his hands as he walked toward where Adadoda worked reinforcing their home's walls. Cent's two older brothers were already helping, and he knew Adadoda would tell him to go away, to go help Etsi or his grandmother, but they always had lots of helpers, and one of his uncles or older cousins would inevitably shoo him away. That's what happened when you were the youngest and came later in your parents' lives.

Cent slipped to the backside of the house without being noticed and climbed the hillside behind it, looking for— *there*. He climbed into a thicket, his toes flexing against the warm ground when he reached the center. "Are you here?"

"I am." Stowne's voice rustled the leaves on the lower branches. "Have you come for another lesson?"

"Yes, please."

"Do you mind if someone joins us?" Stowne rose from the ground near Cent's feet. A slim form, darker in skin tone than his. One of the Yvwitsunastiga but not. No, Stowne was the mountain personified. No one believed Cent's stories about them and often said he was puzzled for making up such wild tales.

"Who?" Cent tossed the stone between his hands.

"A friend." Stowne waved their hand and two more stones, perfectly round and polished, rose from the ground. "They know how to play digadayosdi too."

"All right. Where is he?"

"Right here." Someone rose from the small spring that bubbled up inside the thicket. The shape of Stowne but slimmer and with a little more curve, which confused Cent.

"Girls don't play digadayosdi."

"They do in some towns, but I'm not a girl. My name is Rayne." Rayne's voice bubbled like the spring behind them. "I'm like Stowne. I'm neither."

"Oh, okay." Cent thought no more about it. Why should he? Not everyone was one or the other. Adadoda had said his brother was married to someone who was both, but they lived in another town, so Cent didn't know for certain. *Who cares.* "We have to make our field first and…"

"Done." Stowne waved their hand again, rolling one of the stones toward Rayne. "The field is set, and we have our stones. Ready?"

"Yippee!" Cent happily played scaled-down digadayosdi with his friends all afternoon, and they sat talking when they'd grown tired, discussing the rumors of outsiders, people with light skin and blue eyes who'd been seen on nearby mountains. "But not here," insisted Cent. "They'll never come here."

Stowne and Rayne traded glances but did nothing to contradict him.

"So that's what this is?" Cent held up the round, marble-like stone in her hand. She knew how to play digadayosdi, how that male form had been renowned for their skill, but something was wrong, something— "There's more." She peered pleadingly at Tess who offered no help.

"I don't know, but if you feel there is, why don't you take that marble to Stowne?" Tess turned toward the front room. "I'm going back to the trailer to put dinner in the slow cooker. Aubrey's going to be here in a few hours, so don't get lost down there."

She knows me. Cent wanted nothing more than to return to Stowne's side, to feel their form against her. She already felt like something was missing when they were apart. "Yes'm. I'll keep that in mind." She bounded down the stairs, skipping the last two to land on her feet directly in front of Stowne, who pulled her close.

"I have missed you as well." Stowne smothered her mouth with another toe-curling, energy-sharing kiss. "Did you find anything upstairs?"

"Yes, this." Cent held out her discovery.

"Ah, a digadayosdi stone. You were very good at the game."

"I was male then." Cent stared up at them. "A child, but I feel this memory is incomplete."

"There is something much more significant to that life, yes." Stowne's voice quavered. "It is not one of my favorite memories."

"Tell me." Cent's body tensed, and her side began to hurt enough for her breath to catch in her throat. "Please, I need to know."

"Your eyes are blue." Stowne wrapped her in their arms. "The same color as the eyes of your killer in that life." They returned to the thicket where they'd played digadayosdi. "Shh. It will soon be over."

"But I don't want to…" Cent blinked hard. The trees hung heavy with fall foliage, and he rested against one of them, his hand pressed against his side. "I'm injured. Please. Help me."

"I am trying." Stowne shoved energy into Cent's body but nothing seemed to help. "Those devices the outsiders carry, they kill faster than anything I have seen."

"Here." Rayne hovered over them in their true form, semi-transparent, but their Human face, twisted with worry, gave Cent no solace. "Drink." Rayne held a large leaf molded into a cup to his mouth, but he gagged on the water when it refused to go down, letting it trickle back out of his mouth.

"Blood." Rayne held Cent's face in their hands. "Calm. No fear. You're barely grown, so life is strong in you."

A battle raged outside the thicket. The outsiders' metal weapons exploded at one end, tearing open bodies. Cent's town fought hard, but the outsiders were winning the battle. He knew his people must leave, must slip deeper into the mountains, maybe try to join the towns on the other side but, but— "Stowne?"

"Yes?" Stowne lay on Cent's uninjured side to pull him close, supporting, holding. They shivered when Cent did and peered up at Rayne who pressed a stack of Lamb's Ear against Cent's side. A natural bandage, but there was too much bleeding for it to help.

"Will you walk me across the veil?"

Stowne shivered harder. "Do not speak that—"

"We both will," Rayne assured him.

"Talk to us, to me." Stowne raised Cent's head so their eyes met. "Remember our first night together and all that we did?"

"I do." Their bonding hadn't been just about sex. A good bonding never was. It'd been about sharing, teaching, and learning. Stowne had taught him most everything about the veil, what the living could and should know, and that they should never be afraid. "I love you and will miss you." Stowne appealed to Rayne who touched their head, giving them the moisture to form tears that streaked down their face. "You were a good man, a brave warrior this lifetime. I am proud, always proud to be yours."

Past. Stowne talked about me in the past. Cent gulped and nodded. "Since I'm leaving early, I'll be back faster, right?" The pain in his side increased until he almost blacked out, but he held on, clutching Stowne's arm until they both shook.

"That is what we are told." Rayne moved in to kiss Cent, their mouth cool and calming on his. "You're not the only one crossing the veil today."

"Your father," said Stowne. "He says he's waiting for you. And so is your father's father."

"I never met Ududu. He died before Adadoda was born."

"He was a good man. And so was your adadoda." Stowne wiped more tears from their eyes. "Your ududu has refused to go to his next life until you've safely crossed. Two of your brothers are crossing today as well, and your sister."

"No, Etsi will be alone, and—"

"She is already with your father," Stowne explained. "They are all waiting for you or will soon join you."

This hurt Cent more than his injury. *So many of us.* There was no fighting the outsiders. A few early ones wearing metal on their heads had seemed harmless enough, but they had been allowed to stay only if they married a land-owning woman. Their descendants had been killed by these invaders too. "Everyone?"

"All who cannot escape." Stowne kissed the side of Cent's face and held him tighter. "Look at me, adageyudi. Know I am here with you. Know I... shh. Yes. You cannot fight the inevitable." Stowne's face hovered above Cent's, keeping him from turning away. Words of love, of devotion. They'd begin again. Time. It was only time. Cent would come back to this place, live here again. That's the way it worked between them. And Stowne would wait. They always waited. "Steady. Let go. Do not fight. Remain calm." Stowne held Cent closer, shielding him when another presence entered the thicket.

"Leave us, Exan." Rayne rose to block this form from Cent's view. "You've plenty of others to guide today. This one's ours."

"Let me assist." Exan's voice boomed deeper than Stowne's and was distressed in ways Cent had never heard before. "It is my purpose and the natural order of things."

"In times such as this, we can replace you." Rayne's voice churned and dropped like water over tall falls, becoming even deeper than Exan's. "*That* is the natural order."

"You take significant risks for this one, but you both love him enough to warrant my indulgence." Exan's shadow backed away. "Very well. You may cross him yourselves. I have more than enough to accomplish today."

"Call off your lessers as you go," commanded Stowne as Exan faded. "We do not need their interference."

"Done."

"We'd best get moving." Rayne turned to face them, their voice bubblier than when they'd first met, but it held an urgent undercurrent. "Come on." They held their hand out to Cent. "You can stand now."

"I don't think…"

"You must, adageyudi." Stowne let go of Cent to rise, their form changing into the one Cent knew most intimately. Not Human in any way but a column of rock and soil where white energy circulated. "Come. The veil will not remain open long."

Cent nodded and began to rise, finding it much easier than he'd thought. His pain was gone, his steps light. "I'm fine, really, I'm— see, I can move again. Your energies, they healed me!" Cent spun to prove his point, stopping on his heels when he saw his own body lying in the dirt, Rayne's Lamb's Ear stack-bandage soaked through with his blood. "Oh, no." He fell to his knees to stare at himself, at what had been, then lifted his hands to stare at the translucence he now shared with Stowne and Rayne. "Will I be buried with honor?"

"We'll see you are," said Rayne.

"I guarantee it." Stowne gently pulled Cent to his knees and turned him around, pointing to where the thicket thinned into a narrow opening. "Come with us." Stowne placed their hand on Cent's shoulder to guide him.

"Don't worry about the bushes or trees. You can pass through them like we do." Rayne held Cent's hand, urging him along when he slowed.

"So many dead, so…" Cent shuddered when he saw one of his cousins, younger than himself, among the dead.

"Do not look back. Exan and his lessers have already led them across. There is nothing left for you here."

Cent closed his eyes to the carnage. The pale men were searching the town, searching for— Whatever it was, they weren't finding it. "I won't come back to you as one of them. Not blue-eyed. Never. I swear."

Stowne clutched Cent's hand in theirs. "Just come back to me again. That is all I ask."

"Like you could keep your eternal from it." Rayne pointed ahead. "Do you see the thinning?"

"I do." Cent's insides twisted with equal amounts of joy and fear. The way before them had grown thicker than river fog on a damp morning, and other forms walked ahead of them. "The veil?"

"Yes, we are crossing through it now." Stowne's hold on Cent tightened, reluctant, as was Cent, for what must be. "Kiss me, adageyudi. This is goodbye… for now. I will wait for your return."

"I'll be back as soon as possible." Cent stared up at his eternal love, his thoughts muddled but knowing Stowne would always be there, waiting, happy when they finally reunited. "I love you."

"And I love you." The white-hot glow within Stowne had eased to a soft orange-red. "This mountain. Remember, it is where I will always be."

"I…will." The white light ahead proved almost blinding to Cent's eyes. He drew Stowne down to kiss them before he forgot, but he felt none of the energy they'd come to share in the last two years. *Two years. Not enough. Not…* "Goodbye, Rayne."

"I'll see you again soon. Remember your way back. Remember your way home."

"I… will." Cent kissed Stowne again, pressing his head against their powerful column until Stowne moved back.

"Go. Adadoda and Ududu are waiting for you." Stowne pointed toward the light where two shadowy forms stood.

"I don't…" Cent surged forward, drawn. Family waited. His feet were not his own.

"Welcome, son." Adadoda hugged him to his chest. "Come. Your mother and sister have just arrived."

"Our family." Ududu hugged him too. "We'll show you the way from here."

"But, I've left something behind that I…" Cent turned to see two columns, one liquid smooth and softly curved, the other broader and burning a soft, sad red, moving away. *Who are they?* Cent couldn't remember, but he knew he'd left someone important behind and that the same someone was anxious for him to return.

———

Cent sobbed uncontrollably against Stowne until they raised her head to see her face, their eyes sad even though the red inside them burned brighter. "All is well. We are together again. That is what matters." They cleared Cent's eyes and leaned back to press their hand against hers. "This is your memory."

She held the small, dented metal ball up to the light trickling through the basement window. "A musket ball. Is it the one that—"

"It is." Stowne wrapped her hand around the ball and gently squeezed. "What once took your life now brings us closer."

"But every time I leave, it hurts you." She buried her head in Stowne's shoulder and cried harder, shedding pain she'd never known she possessed, crying for Stowne's pain every time she had to leave their side.

"Shh. Now is not the time to mourn. It is the time to celebrate. To enjoy each other and fall even deeper in love." Stowne rose, dragging her up so her head grazed the kitchen floorboards. "The balls, the pottery. They mean we are inseparable no matter the pain." They dropped her into their arms, hugging her to the point of nearly smothering her. "I need to practice my form for this current world we find ourselves in. Can you help me?"

"Of course! Does this mean you can leave the cellar?"

"Not yet, but soon." Stowne bent to kiss her, shooting incredible energy through her that left her taut and teased in their arms. "I hope to share myself with you again tonight."

"Even more than last night?"

"That was merely the beginning." Stowne's laugh shook the cellar. "It is but a taste of what we can accomplish together." They placed her gently on the floor. "That kiss left you wobbling, so we will have to practice often to build your strength."

"Yeah, you left my spidey senses tingling with that one."

"Your what?" Stowne furrowed their brow at her again.

"A modern reference. I'll explain it someday soon. Right now, let's work on your presentation. Show me what you got."

"This new semantics is going to take time for me to learn."

"It's called a learning curve, and you're doing fine." Cent broke from Stowne to sit on the floor. "Show me what you got means that you should share what you've been working on."

"I understand now." Stowne turned away from her, moving and mumbling as they used their energy to carefully reform. "Does this work?" They turned around smiling.

"Oh, bless your eternal heart." Cent raised her hand to her mouth to quell her laugh. "We've got a lot of work to do before you come out of this cellar and into the modern world."

Chapter Sixteen

Wee Fairies in the Honey
August 9, 2017

"**Wow,** Cent, you look great!" Aubrey leaned in to hug her then drew back frowning. "But you smell like a dirty ol' cellar. What gives?"

"I've been working up at the homestead." She'd changed clothes and fixed her hair, however, a shower had been out of the question. She and Stowne had spent far too much time working on their appearance, on updating them to modern ways and linguistical nuances. It'd proven more tiring than she'd expected, but thoughts of the upcoming night kept her energized. Stowne had made her promises, and she wasn't about to let them go unfulfilled. "There's a lot to get done."

"Yeah, I bet. So, how's work, I mean your paying job?" Aubrey filled his bowl with chicken and dumplings from the slow cooker. It was nothing more than stewed chicken with canned biscuits plumped across the top, but it was good, especially since Cent had skipped lunch to be with Stowne.

"Fine." *Crap, I'm scheduled tomorrow morning.* She wouldn't let it get in the way, but she'd have to let Stowne know. "How's Ethan?"

"Fine, I guess." Aubrey shrugged. "We're ships passing in the night anymore."

"That makes it hard." Cent glanced at her phone. Betty hadn't returned her last text, so she'd sent it twice more. *Still no answer.*

"How's your friend up in Chicago?" Aubrey pointed to her phone.

"I don't know. She hasn't replied to my last few texts."

"Have you tried calling her?"

"Yeah, but she didn't pick up."

"Work?" asked Tess as she joined them at the table.

"She works nights and relies on her phone to reach her customers."

"Customers want what they want, no matter the hour." Tess cast her a knowing look. "Maybe she's been busy."

"Or maybe her phone's broke," suggested Aubrey. "It happens."

"Yeah, I suppose. I want to know if she got my last two paychecks, so I can e-deposit them and pay her back for my bus ticket." Cent put her phone aside to hover over her bowl. "What're you and Ethan doing to combat your ships-in-the-night problem?"

"God, how I love your chicken and dumplings, Aunt Tess." Aubrey shoved a heaping spoonful into his mouth.

"You're meat hungry, that's all." Tess waved her spoon at Cent. "Did you hear how fast he changed the subject?"

"Yeah, I did." Cent held up her spoonful so it could cool. "Trouble in paradise, cuz?"

"No. Not exactly. There's nothing happening in paradise, to be honest. Ethan does his thing. I do mine. We hardly ever see each other anymore."

"That's sad," said Cent as soon as she swallowed. "Have you two talked about it?"

"No, and since when do you give relationship advice?" Aubrey narrowed his eyes. "You've found someone, haven't you? Less than a month back home and— damn, girl. Tell me all about him or her or them. Come on. Let me live vicariously."

"They, um, aren't your type."

"No, they ain't," confirmed Tess. "But you'll get to meet them and a few of their friends if you're lucky." Tess finished her bowl and took it to the sink. "Since you're both here tonight, I'd like you to help me reset the property protections."

"Sure," said Cent. "But the moon's waning. Won't that make them less effective?"

"Yeah, but we forgot them last night. We were celebrating too hard and—" She glanced at Aubrey, who was listening. "They need refreshing, so let's get it done tonight. Between the three of us, we've enough energy to make good wards."

"There ain't no magic in me, Tess. You know that." Aubrey poked at a dumpling with his spoon. "I'm not like you and— since when've *you* been into magic, Cent?"

"I'm learning, why?"

"It seems weird is all. What's that?" He pointed to a white ceramic ramekin sitting on the counter beside the sink, more importantly to the fact it was moving. "You got a mouse again?"

"I don't think so." Tess rose to see the ramekin, cursing under her breath when she peered into it. "I forgot to feed the Wee Fairies on the moon too, and now they've come inside looking for something to eat."

"Sheesh. Stop. Just stop." Aubrey dismissed her with a wave. "That story worked when I was six, but now..." He took a slice of bread from the plate on the table, nearly dropping it when something swooped in to break off a crumb. "You got some serious moths this year."

"That ain't no moth." Tess brought the ramekin to the table, placing it before him. "Whatcha see in there?"

"A big honkin' moth. No, *two* moths." He swatted at the hovering fairy when they swooped to gather another crumb. "You need to call an exterminator." Aubrey covered the butter with his hand as soon as he opened the dish.

"They don't like butter." Cent watched him spread some across his bread and cover the dish again, watching the fairy that now hovered over his head. "They want your bread though." She held out her finger to one of the stuck fairies. "Do you want some help?"

"Yes." The fairy grabbed onto her finger, holding tight as she slowly lifted them out of the honey.

"There." She lowered the fairy to the table. "Let me get you something to clean off with." Cent lifted the other fairy out, sat them on the table, and went to the sink to wet a paper towel.

"Awe, come on!" Aubrey swatted at the fairy above his head when it dove at him. "This ain't no game. Where's the flyswatter?"

"Don't you dare!" Tess whistled to the fairy, and it came to her, alighting on her finger. "They're hanging around because they're hungry, and they like Cent. That's all. And if I'd fed them like I usually do, they wouldn't be in the house. I'll get them out as soon as Cent cleans those two up."

"Dear Lord, seriously?" Aubrey shoved his piece of bread into his mouth and pushed away from the table, chewing then swallowing before he spoke again. "I'm all for your magic, Tess, and you can believe whatever you want, but you, Cent? Really? I thought you were like me."

"I thought I was too." Cent returned to the table and tore off two tiny pieces of damp towel that she held out to the fairies. "Here's something to start with." She tore off more pieces she piled beside the fairies, watching with amusement as they scrubbed their arms, legs, and worked on their delicate wings. "Look, Aub. Would a bug do that?"

"I don't..." He lifted his glass to peer at the bottom. "Did you two doctor my tea?" He rubbed his eyes and blinked.

"I fixed that tea, Aub. And there ain't nothin' special in it." Cent held more damp towels out to the fairies. "You're seeing this for real."

"But that ain't possible." He drew his eyes from Cent to Tess, who was keeping the cleaner fairy occupied by feeding them bits of bread dipped in honey. "Okay, if this is real, how come I haven't seen it happen before?"

"Because I hid it from you," said Tess. "It's a long story, but I hid it from Cent too until she'd come of age, and then she shoved it away and left, so I went back to hiding it." She laughed when a third fairy landed beside their sticky friends to help them clean their wings. "Now that Cent's back and learning magic, I ain't gonna hide it from either of you. You can see because you're an empath and a strong one at that."

"Me? An empath?" Aubrey stared at her. "Not possible."

"Sure you are." Cent sat back to consider the fairies. The clean one was helping the sticky ones with their wings, wiping gently, twice leaning in to lick honey off their shoulders. "I think you can open the door. All but one of them is ready to go."

"Let me pour some more honey. They like my homemade biscuits better, but store-bought bread's all I got right now." Tess broke two slices into small pieces, placing them and a fresh ramekin of honey on a plate she carried to the back door. "Out you go." She opened the door, shooing back the multitude of fairies that flitted about on the other side. "Calm down, you hungry critters." She placed the plate on the porch railing and stepped back into the house, frowning when she saw that a fairy still stood on the table. "They're gonna miss their dinner."

"Not yet." Cent held out a crumb to the fairy who accepted it with a bow. "You still not believin', Aubrey?"

"You mean to tell me you're a witch like Aunt Tess?"

"I am, and you're an empath like she says. I feel it in my bones."

"That's total BS." Aubrey rubbed his eyes and stared at the fairy. "We're sharing a group hallucination. There's a gas leak or something, and we're all suffering from oxygen deprivation."

"There ain't no gas line running to this trailer or even up this road," said Tess. "I'm a witch. Cent's a witch. You're an empath. Your Uncle Kinnon was a druid too, since we're goin' there."

"Now that, I believe." Aubrey wagged his finger at her. "I recollect playing in his closet and finding these green-trimmed white robes. They had hoods attached and— I thought it was a Halloween costume because I knew beyond a doubt you wouldn't have married a klansman."

"Lord, no. Those were Kinnon's ceremonial robes." Tess returned to the table. "He had his robes, and I went naked under the moon until I got too old and the ground got cold. I don't rightly recall which came first."

"TMI." Aubrey grimaced. "This is going to take some processing." He leaned in to watch the fairy, clearly intrigued though he still looked confused. "Cent?"

"Yeah?" She grinned when the fairy took flight, hovering in front of her to dance a quick display of gratitude. "You're welcome. Are you ready to go?"

"Please." The fairy flew to the door, where it hovered until Tess opened it enough for them to pass.

"Holy— it's speaking to you?" Aubrey rubbed his eyes.

"Yes." Cent gathered the used napkin bits into a pile. "Wee Fairies are feisty, so be careful around them, especially if Tess or I aren't around."

"Damn, Cent. You talk like you've been around them for decades." Aubrey stared at her again.

"Only recently this lifetime but hundreds of years overall, I think. And—"

"Wait. Wait! *Wait!*" Aubrey slammed his hands onto the table and pushed back, rising before Cent or Tess could say more. "I've heard lots of strange stuff over dinner tonight. I was going to sleep on the couch, but I think I'll grab a hotel room in Greeneville instead."

"That won't be necessary." Cent rose as well. "I'm sleeping up at the homestead now, so you can take the extra bedroom."

"You're sleeping up *there*?" He glanced out the window at the old house. "Is the power even on?"

"Not yet." Cent looked that direction too. "I've got a solar lantern."

"Yeah, but it's still hot this time of the evenin' and— sure, whatever. I'll stay, but you two need to quit with the weird shit."

"Deal, pickle." Cent shrugged. "But think about things, will you?"

"Yeah, I guess. But I'm too creeped out to help with the protections tonight."

"We can renew them without you." Tess motioned to Cent. "Let's go do it before it gets any later."

"Yes'm." She and Aubrey stayed quiet while Tess gathered the supplies, but he kept looking at her like she had two heads, snaky ones at that.

"I'll clean up while you're gone," said Aubrey when Tess returned.

"Thanks. Let's go, Cent." Tess sighed as soon as the door closed behind them. "That boy has an incredible gift, but he don't recognize it or the ways he already uses it in his nursing."

"I wondered about that."

Tess passed Cent the cotton sack. "Dig out the white salt."

"Do you want me to follow it with the herb blend?" Cent could smell the aromatic mix, Lavender, bay, star anise, and rosemary, Tess' unique blend. *Mine includes rose petals too.* She startled at her own knowledge and dug into the bag, as confident about Tess' mix as she was her own.

"Yes." Tess stepped from the porch and rounded the trailer, Cent following until they reached the end of the gravel driveway and the property line, where Tess opened the plastic gallon bag and began dropping the sea salt in a line, moving to the right. Cent walked beside her, a canning-jar-turned-herb-shaker in one hand and the solar lantern in the other. Tess chanted as she moved, and for the first time, Cent did too, repeating her words, a prayer to the creators, telling the spirits and fairies and elementals that this was to keep out evil, that they were welcome as long as their intentions were good.

"Show off." Tess turned her head.

"What?"

"You're chanting in Tsalagi." Tess returned to her work, repeating the prayer before walking clockwise along the property line, Cent moving with her until they reached the corner where a grand old oak stood. "Beautiful tree. Kinnon prayed at its base most every day."

"I recall it being here when…" Cent shook her head. "It's still cloudy, but I remember deciding not to cut it down when I made room for the house and garden."

"Really?" Tess placed her hand on the tree, thanking it for its continued presence, for its protection from the wind, rain, and snow. "Deep roots." She turned the corner and kept moving along the northern property line.

Did she mean the tree or me?

They followed the fence, walking up the mountain and into the forest in the dark. Rayne joined them along the way, following behind, and Pyre watched from a distance.

A ghost fire. The old Jack Tale made more sense. *Walking the earth because neither heaven nor hell wants you. That'd be a lonely way of being.* As Pyre drew closer she could see their hands folded at their waist, their body circulating deep oranges and reds. A gentle, almost censured flame. *They're embarrassed.* This made Cent stop. *Embarrassment is such a Human emotion. Do elementals feel it too?* Yes, she surmised as she thought back on her limited time with Stowne. Maybe they hadn't expressed embarrassment to her yet, but she'd seen almost every other emotion flow through them, so why not embarrassment too?

"Come on. We ain't got all night." Tess looked down the hill at her. Wee Fairies fluttered around her, lighting the way better than the solar lantern, so Cent turned it off, laughing as a fairy landed on her shoulder, crossing their legs primly as they settled their back against her neck.

"Don't get any more distracted than you are," Tess grumbled as she stared at the fairy. "We've got half the property left."

"I'd help you if that salt was in a natural container." Rayne drew closer to Tess. "But plastic…"

"I know," Tess replied. "Don't know what I was thinking. I'll switch containers for next time."

"How about assisting me?" Cent glanced at Rayne.

"Only if you help Tess. She's growing tired."

"No, I'm…" Tess stumbled over a Maple's protruding root. "Go ahead and let them take over the jar, Cent. I could use your help after all. Here, hold the salt bag."

"No, I'll do it." Aubrey approached at a trot, pausing only when he saw Rayne, who'd already changed into their Human female form. "You're the realtor, right?" Aubrey stepped back to better see Rayne. "I don't mean to sound rude, but what're you doing here this time of night?"

"I was driving by when I saw Tess and Cent outside, so I, um, thought I'd stop to see if they needed any assistance." Rayne bit their bottom lip, a decidedly Human habit they must have acquired somewhere along the way.

"O-kay." Aubrey glanced down the hill at the driveway before he took the salt bag from Tess. "Let's finish this up so you can get back inside. It's going to rain overnight."

"I know." Tess pulled her summer-weight jacket higher on her shoulders. "Let's stop a moment so I can warm by the fire." She moved out of the trees and toward where Pyre, now a small, cheery fire, crackled and smoked in small black puffs.

"Sounds good." Aubrey led her to an old stump near the fire. "I came outside because I had a question for you both, but now that I'm here, I have a bunch."

"So what are they?" Cent appreciated how the fairies had settled, appearing more like lightning bugs than some breed of alien moth, save for the one still sitting contentedly against her neck.

"First, why are the moths making light?" Aubrey moved his eyes from Tess to Cent. "And don't tell me they're lightning bugs, cause they ain't." He held up his hand for quiet when Tess tried to answer. "Let me get them all out before you say anything. Second, Aunt Tess, why is your realtor lying to me? Unless she walked in, she didn't just *drop* by. And third and fourth, Cent, maybe you can answer these two."

Oh, boy. "And they are?"

"Why is one of those moths snuggled up on your neck all cozy-like, and why in the world am I seeing a face in the fire? I know it's not fumes in the house 'cause I'm outside. It's not a gas leak or food poisoning, and there was nothing weird in my drink." Aubrey dropped to the ground beside Tess, his legs crossed, his hands to his face. "Damnation, I'm losing my pea-pickin' mind!"

"No, child, you're not." Tess patted his shoulder. "Pyre, come on out."

"Are you certain he's ready for that?" Rayne held their finger to Cent's neck so the fairy would take flight, fluttering around Aubrey's head before they flew into the woods behind the homestead, the other fairies following them until their lights faded.

"I've been seeing all manner of stuff as of late." Aubrey rubbed his eyes with the heel of his hands, shuddering as he peered over to Rayne. "This tall-ass, stick-man green thing walking across the road the other night, a face in my sink water. Like you, lady." He pointed to Rayne. "Are you a spirit? A haint? I ain't seen one since Birdie when I was a little kid, but I know Tess sees them and…"

"Rayne ain't no haint," explained Tess. "At least in the way I know you're meanin'. They're an elemental."

"An el-e-men-tal? Like fire and water and— okay, she's water, right?"

"That's correct." Rayne kept their voice soft. "And you see me because I will it and because you're an empath."

"There y'all go again with the empath stuff." Aubrey jerked both his arms above his head, palms up, to stall their explanations. "I can almost get the empath line of thinking, but I know a couple of people who claim to be one and they've never said word one to me about no spirits."

"That's because they ain't real empaths." Cent peered around Aubrey to Tess who nodded. If he wanted the whole truth, he'd have it. "You are." She took a deep breath. "And you're a caul healer too. You were born that way."

"Bullshit!" He blurted. "My mom said the same thing before she died year-before-last, but— healers aren't real, aren't…" Aubrey stopped to stare at his hands, holding them level, palms facing each other, leaving about six inches between them. "We're taught they don't exist in nursing school, and it ain't even mentioned in grad school so…" His mouth tightened as he gulped. "But, damn. What if you're right? Is my career over, is…" He turned his palms up to stare at them. "One of my kids at the hospital died on me last night. Just up and…" Aubrey sniffled and looked at Cent. "What kind of healer am I if I can't help kids?"

"It was her time," explained Rayne. "All biological creations have a lifespan. Some are simply shorter than others."

"How'd you know the kid was a girl?" Aubrey's eyes brimmed with tears.

"Girl. Age six. Her name was Charline, but she went by Charley. She had something wrong with her blood." Rayne closed their eyes, head back as if picturing a scene in their mind. "Her maternal grandmother met her at the veil. Charley says she'll see you at Samhain, that she wants to thank you for being so kind to her and her family."

"Wow." Aubrey sagged against Tess when she stooped to wrap her arms around him. "I can see her then?"

"She doesn't want to be reborn until you do." Rayne pointed to Pyre whose face was becoming more apparent by the second. "Get out here and show the man he's not losing his mind."

"You expect me to reveal myself so easily?" Pyre raised their flames until they spun into a heat-blasting funnel that lapped the nearby trees.

"Stop being dramatic." Cent glowered at them. "Shame on you for trying to frighten Aub when he's learning to see you."

"Can he really see elementals, or is it because you and Tess are both here?" Pyre's funnel slowed, allowing them to see a well-defined face amid the flames.

"Is he an elemental too?" Aubrey stared at Pyre. "Let me guess, a fire one."

"Yes, they are." Tess knuckle-scrubbed Aubrey's head. "High time you woke up to it."

"I knew, I think, but I didn't want to see, so I wouldn't let myself. But when Cent came home…" He craned his neck to see her. "So you knew you had magic in you?"

"Not until I got home, but I do, some old magic at that." Cent turned her face to the rising moon. "I promise I'll explain later, but we need to finish the wards first so that booger doesn't return. Pyre, will you light the way for us?"

"I thought you'd never ask." Pyre slid into the form they'd presented when they'd first met Cent, complete with red hair and white-hot smile. That smile faded when they moved closer to her. "I owe you an apology, Centenary. My behavior yesterday…I don't know what happened. And Four Thieves? That mix stings, but I'm more hurt that you had cause to use it." They extended their hands, palm-up, to her. "I am truly sorry."

"All right." She nodded but wouldn't take their hands. "Apology accepted, but don't expect me to dance with you again this lifetime."

"I know that won't happen, but…" Pyre leaned toward her. "Your cousin? Does he dance?"

"Don't even try." Cent flicked her hands so they'd back away. "Let's finish the wards. Aunt Tess needs rest, Aubrey acts like he's got a headache, and I've other things to do tonight." She glanced toward the homestead to see Stowne's face in the cellar window. Cent pushed warm energy toward her elemental love, then turned back to see Aubrey helping Tess to a stand. "Are we ready?"

"As we can be." Tess used Aubrey for support as they moved along the property boundary, especially on the uneven, steep surface that formed the forested southern line, but they finished before midnight. Tess and Aubrey turned to the house after saying goodnight to Rayne and Pyre.

"Are you really sleeping at the homestead, Cent?" Aubrey looked past Rayne and Pyre to the old house.

"Yeah, I am. Someone's waiting for me there." She turned that direction, eager—

"Whoa." He caught her by the shoulder. "That someone lives up there with you?"

"Someone wonderful. You'll meet them tomorrow if you stay."

"I'm going to." Aubrey turned back to help Tess up the steps, spinning around to see Cent again as soon as their great aunt was inside the trailer. "I think I'll stay a week or two, take some sick days. Tess isn't feeling good, and—"

"Yeah, I know, but are you sure Ethan will understand?"

"I moved out yesterday. Most of my stuff is in storage or in the Camry." Aubrey's shoulders sagged. "Just as well. His design firm's grown so popular that he practically lives at his office." He ran his hand through his hair, which had fallen from its band to hang loosely around his shoulders. "He's having an affair with his assistant."

I knew it! "Oh, Aub, I'm so sorry."

"Don't be. I knew it'd happen before it did, same as you. But what could I do to stop it?" He tapped his forehead. "This empath feels things he wishes he couldn't."

"Runs in the family."

"Yeah, sure, but this magic shit. All of it. Ethan wouldn't understand it no matter how I explained. I'm not certain I do either."

"Lots of it's still weird to me too, so give it time." She turned back to the homestead. "Night. Sleep tight."

"Yeah, you too— hey!"

Cent glanced over her shoulder at him. "Yeah?"

"What's their name?"

"Stowne. And all elementals are they. They take whatever form they— it's more complicated stuff. We'll talk about it later, okay?"

"Sure, but how long have you known Stowne to be setting up housekeeping with them?"

"Lifetimes, and we're cleaning the homestead, not setting up housekeeping." *Not yet, leastways.* "Have a good night." Cent ignored his inquiries after that, jogging up the hill to where Stowne, her past and her future in one, waited.

Chapter Seventeen

A Man Possessed
August 10, 2017

"Hey, Cent! Get up!" Aubrey opened the cellar door and bounded down the stairs before she could wake up enough to cover herself, so Stowne did, draping one arm and leg over her body. "Tess said you had work this morning, so I…" Aubrey skidded to a stop at the bottom of the stairs. "I got mushmelon, eggs, bacon, coffee and— whoa, Nelly!" He gaped at Stowne when they wrapped further around Cent. "I'll let you get dressed." He turned to gaze up the stairs.

"Yeah, thanks." She reached for the clothing Stowne had once again folded while she slept.

"Do you mind introducing me to your, um, friend?" Aubrey chuckled under his breath.

"Aubrey, meet Stowne." *I smell coffee.* "Stowne, this is Aubrey Rhodes, my cousin who doesn't know to knock first. All right, I'm dressed."

"Centenary speaks highly of you." Stowne watched Aubrey turn back around and pass Cent a plate and a cup of coffee.

"Extra cream." He stepped back to scrutinize Stowne. "Earth elemental?"

"I am, as well as Centenary's companion for most of her lives." They wrapped their arm around Cent's waist as she ate. "I see bacon is still a favored food."

"Love it." Cent lifted a piece to her mouth. "But Tess always overcooks it." She sighed when the piece shattered across the plate, leaving her holding a fragment that she put in her mouth.

"I like it just fine." Aubrey sat on the bottom stair. "Tess and I talked for a bit last night then I went to the back porch to think after she went to bed. Rayne came to sit with me, and I talked to her, I mean them, most of the night." He yawned and stretched his arms above his head.

"Did they answer more of those questions you had?" Cent sipped her coffee. What Tess lacked in bacon-cooking skills she made up for in coffee-making. It was a good cup, and she'd used real cream too, not the powdered stuff.

"Yeah, they did. They said you have to find your memories and that as you find them, your power will grow." He peered up at Stowne. "You're gearing up to fight for the homestead, ain't you?"

"Yeah, this has been my land for centuries, and Stowne's for much, much longer, so I'll be damned if Mama is going to yank it out from under us." She swallowed a mouthful of eggs before she spoke again, pulling out a piece of shell when it caught between her teeth. "That's why I'm here, I think, why I came back."

"It's a hell of a reason to." Aubrey's eyes were still on Stowne. "Rayne explained all about the elemental they and about Humans living more than one life. It made me wonder how many I've lived."

"I have known you before," said Stowne. "As a healer, a Cherokee medicine woman. You were Centenary's younger sister that lifetime. There were other times as well, but you will eventually remember them."

"It doesn't surprise me that we've all crossed paths before." Aubrey fished his phone out of his pants pocket when it chimed. "What time do you need to be at work, Cent?"

"Nine, why?" She glanced out the window.

"It's eight-thirty."

"Crap!" She shoveled the rest of her crunchy eggs and shattered bacon into her mouth, washed it down with coffee, and turned to straddle Stowne's waist, kissing them soundly on their mouth. "I'll be back late this afternoon. Promise."

"I miss the era when you worked the land, so we could stay close." They hugged her tight, returning the kiss with one that lasted until Aubrey again reminded her of the time. "I will be here when you return." They slipped their hand into her pocket, depositing something small and hard into it. "Let them protect you when you leave the wards."

"You're sweet." Cent patted her pocket. "Love you." She pressed her head against Stowne's shoulder and turned around to face Aubrey. "Shower?"

"Tess has it all set up for you." Aubrey followed her up the stairs. "Dang, girl. You're filthy beneath those clothes. What'd you and Stowne do all night in that cellar?"

"What do you think?" Cent grinned at him.

"So you and they… huh." Aubrey shrugged. "Whatever gets you there, I suppose."

"We talk a lot too, and Stowne's helping me remember my past lives." They'd reached the trailer door. "Ain't all of it good, neither, but I need to know."

"Make sure you tell me it all later." He shoved her toward the bathroom door.

"I put a towel over the rod," said Tess as Cent passed her. "And rinse the dadblamed shower out afterward this time!"

"Yes'm." Cent began stripping off her clothing the second the bathroom door closed.

———————⊙⊰⊱⊙———————

"Have you finished entering that new stock into the system?" Ephrem Jones, a lanky, overall-wearing man in his early sixties, stood in the doorway of Dryler's stockroom.

"Almost. Give me a… there." Cent looked up from her iPad. "Whatcha need me to do?"

"Can you watch the front while I go down the road for lunch?"

"Sure, just let me finish up here and…" Cent drummed her fingers on the desk top and squared her shoulders. "Mr. Jones, your inventory. Can we talk about it for a minute?"

"What's wrong this time?" He looped his thumbs into his pockets and stood straighter.

"The Marlboro count is off again. Two whole cartons. And there's two gallons of milk, four loaves of bread, and three cases of beer missing this week. And that's up and over the petty stuff that disappears. I know some of it's normal, but those first items I mentioned…"

"That'd be Ina Sue again." His face reddened. "She promised me she'd quit smoking for real this time. The rest, well, she's got four kids and no job."

"How do you want me to label the shortage in the system?"

"Can you create a category with her name on it?

"Yes, I can. Should I file all she takes under that heading?"

"Until I get up the nerve to face her about it, yeah." He shook his head. "Twenty-nine years old and…" He sighed. "You went to school with Ina Sue, graduated the class behind her, right?"

"Yes, sir."

"Why'd you grow up, and she didn't?"

That's a tricky question. "I'm living with my great-aunt and only working part-time, so I'm not certain I'm a good example."

"You've a decent head on your shoulders, went to college, and… dang it!"

He ripped his ball cap from his head to throw it on the floor, kicking it so it skidded across the stockroom. "I need to change the locks again."

"I'm sorry." Cent considered the numbers and the weight the missing items had on the store's bottom line. "Can I make a suggestion?"

"I'm up for anything." He retrieved his ball cap from the floor and dusted it on the front of his overalls.

"I know Ina Sue is on SNAP, and the store takes SNAP, but this isn't the best place to use the benefits, economically speaking."

"It's a convenience store." He frowned at her. "Nothing here is as cheap as it would be at the Walmart or one of them big grocery chains."

"I know that, but I also know she doesn't drive, so—"

"Three DUIs, the fool kid. Last one they took her car for." His shoulders drooped. "DHS got hot on her tail about the kids after that too. They're threatening to take them away from her if she don't clean herself up."

"I know, but what if you took her to one of those larger stores once a week after you take away the keys? Shop with her. See what she's buying. You'll get to spend time with her, this store won't lose inventory, and even if you have to buy some of those things, you'll save money overall."

"That's— you know, that's a real good idea." He managed a little smile. "It's time I set some boundaries with her, I guess, and stop supportin' her. It's the grandbabies, you know? I'd do anything for them, especially little Emmy."

"I know, sir, but please don't let on that any of this was my idea. Ina Sue's got a temper and…"

"Oh, no, I wouldn't do that. You're good help, and Ina Sue tends to drive off the good ones with her BS."

"Yeah, I was told that." Cent glanced out the front door to see Ina Sue's trailer, Mr. Jones' rental, sitting alongside the parking lot. "She's only been in a few times when I was here, but I saw what she took and wrote it down for you."

"She didn't even bother to buy something to cover it up?"

"Sometimes she does but not usually."

"I swear I'm gonna— well, hell. Ol' Scratch has got that girl more days than not." He grumbled but kept his smile. "If you can take over up front for a while, I'm fixin' to grab some lunch at that diner up the road. Can I get you something? My treat for keeping such good track of things."

"A BLT would be nice if they have one." The peanut butter and jelly sandwich Tess had sent with her could stay in her bag.

"They do. Want a sweet tea with it?"

"That'd be great." She stored the iPad in her bag and followed Mr. Jones up front, waving to him as he pulled out of the parking lot.

He'll be gone a bit. The diner was popular, so they were always busy this time of day, even for carryout.

Cent tended the customers as they came and went. Dryler's was never overly busy, but a steady stream of customers made the time pass faster, so she focused on her work, carding two beer sales, ringing up a pair of regulars. "Have a good day."

"You too, Cent. See you soon."

"Yes, ma'am."

She had time to text Betty again and was happy when she replied.

> Sorry, baby doll. Dropped my phone down a toilet. What a crapper of a mess. It took me a few days to get the money to buy a new one.

Crapper… toilet. That's funny. Glad you're okay.

> Yeah fine. You?

I'm at work and it's boring.

> At least you got a job.

Part-time, but you're right. Did you send that check?

> I sent it day before yesterday.

Good. I'll send you back the money when it clears.

> Thank you.

Love you, Ms. Betty.

> You too Country Girl. Gotta go. Customer calling. Bye.

Bye.

Cent stowed her phone in her pocket then broke a roll of quarters into the cash drawer, feeling good about things as she looked up, ready for the next— *oh, no.*

"Centenary. I thought by now you'd have done right by me, but here you stand, peddling legalized sin." Nida Rhodes, squat and round and dressed ultra-conservatively, her arms folded across her abdomen, stood inside the store's double doors. "And *what* have you done to your hair?"

"Mama." Cent made every effort to keep her voice calm. "Imagine meeting you here. I'm an adult, so my hair is my own. Now, what can I do for you?"

"Ivan wants gas." Mama set a can of creamed corn on the counter. "Twenty dollars on pump two and this." She nudged the can toward Cent.

Ivan? New boyfriend, new… Cent glanced out the window to see a balding man, wearing a white shirt and necktie, standing on the far side of a black Cadillac Escalade, and he was staring straight at her. *Ruleman.* "Yeah, okay.

That and the corn together will be…" She rang up the amount, cursing low when her fingers shook hard enough to necessitate that she do it twice.

"Don't take the Lord's name in vain!" Mama stiffened. "Sinful when you were a child. Sinful now. Why don't you go back to where you were?"

"I *have* come back to where I was." Cent waited for her to swipe her bank card, which she'd noticed was in Ruleman's name, through the reader. *Geez.* She cringed when the card was rejected. "Try it again, please."

"I am!" Mama ran the card a second time and, again, it was rejected. "I'll have to get Ivan." She opened the door to call for him, giving Cent the opportunity to see her mother from behind. Mama had grown her graying hair long and was wearing it pulled back in a loose ponytail further contained by an oversized white headscarf. Her black skirt lapped the bottom of her calves, her legs were covered by black stockings, and she wore simple black flats.

Great. Just great. My mother's turned into a religious wingnut, and I'm fixin' to meet the tool what turns her.

"What's the problem?" Ruleman pushed past Mama and into the store, leaning over the counter to stare at Cent through dark, hardened eyes. He wasn't an especially tall man, not even her height for that matter, and he was almost as round as Mama, but he possessed a holier-than-thou expression that made her doubt he ever uttered a kind word to anyone unless it suited his purposes.

"Your card's not working." Cent stared back at him, noting when a slight smirk formed in the corner of his mouth. "Sorry, but you'll either have to use cash or another valid form of payment, and we don't take checks."

"Cash." He opened his wallet to pull out a hundred-dollar bill, one of who knows how many that made his wallet difficult to bend. "There." He threw the money onto the counter.

"Thank you." Cent reached for the Dri-Mark, a requirement for any bill twenty dollars or larger.

"How dare you insult a man of God!" Now Mama stood at the counter too, up on her toes to lean over it.

"Store policy." Cent ran the Dri-Mark over the bill, capped the marker, and counted the change. "Seventy-Seven twenty-two." She slid the hundred into the large-bill deposit box beneath the counter and shoved the change at Ruleman whose smirk had morphed into a scowl. "Have a good day."

Ruleman raked the money into his hand and dropped it into his pants pocket. "Come along, Nida." He took two steps toward the door before turning back, his expression now twisted into full disgust. "Wait. Aren't you…" He peered over at Mama who took several back-steps under his scrutiny. "Well, I'll be. Nida, why didn't you tell me your ingrate, faggot-whore of a daughter was in town?" He grabbed Mama by the arm, dragging her forward again. "Do you see what became of your young sin?" He turned his eyes to Cent. "Your mother will spend the rest of her life atoning for the sin your birth cast on her!"

"First off, I'm neither a bundle of sticks nor the British English slang term for a cigarette. Second— no, we're done here." *Even the local Mennonites can keep their opinions to themselves long enough to pump some gas.* Cent pointed to the door. "Have a nice day."

"For the fear of the Lord is the beginning of knowledge; fools despise wisdom and instruction." Ruleman's eyes narrowed as he returned to the counter, pulling Mama along behind him. "You, girl, were bred and born out of wedlock. You're the regrettable product of sin, so the only way for you to save yourself from the pits of hell is to repent your disgusting ways." He shook his finger in her face. "Faggot, fornicator, and disobedient woman. You spit in God's eye with your very existence!"

"Sinners, angry God. Hell-fire and damnation." Cent feigned shock then raised one side of her mouth in a sneer. She'd faced tougher haters than this over the years and had heard enough to know listening did no good whatsoever. "My goodness, Mister Ruleman, Jonathon Edward's got nothing on you, does he? Tell you what, why don't you have a rainbow-hued, chocked-full-of-pride-'til-you-pop, first-gay-kiss kind of day. In other words, kiss my queer Appalachian ass." Cent looked past him to see Mama, who wouldn't make eye contact with her. "Nice seeing you, Mama. You know where to find me if you want to talk without *him* tagging along."

"Can I go to the car, Ivan?" Mama rubbed her arm as soon as Ruleman released it.

What the… Cent rolled her eyes. Mama hadn't even said something stupid like she usually did. Meek and deferring. Mama was everything Aunt Tess had taught Cent not to be.

"Stay where you are, Nida. Don't move." Ruleman lashed out to grab Cent by her wrist. "You're going to apologize to my fiancé, you ungodly whore. Now!" His hold tightened until her hand began to throb.

"For what?" Cent tried to wrench from his hold, but he was stronger, increasing the pressure on her wrist. There was a heat to his grasp, a white-hot burn that shot up her arm and into her neck. "Let go!" Her eyes blurred as panic engulfed her. *This man's hiding something dark inside him.* Her free hand found her pocket to pull out the protections Stowne had given her, and she opened her palm to press them into the back of Ruleman's gripping hand, nearly screaming when smoke rose from between her fingers.

"Witch!" Ruleman jerked back his hand to examine it, growling low when he saw two round blisters rising on his flesh. "Tess' apprentice!" He shook his hand three times before peering at it again. "Leave now, Centenary Rhodes, before it's too late." Ruleman backed toward the door, his hand landing on Mama's shoulder as he went. "Repent!"

Cent watched them drive away before she peered at the two small rocks in her palm. They stuck together when she turned them. Magnetite. Stowne had slipped lodestones in her pocket. Had they known she'd run into Ruleman and Mama or—?

"What the hell happened?" Mr. Jones stood in the doorway holding a brown paper bag and two Styrofoam cups tucked into a cardboard tray. "A customer just tore outta the lot like you'd took a shot at them!"

Might've been easier. "He— he got mad when his card wouldn't work." Cent pulled down her sleeve to cover the blisters and bruises forming on her wrist. "He didn't get his gas even though he paid cash." She slid the lodestones back into her pocket. "I'll make him out a prepaid slip, so he can pump later."

"Yeah, that's fine, but what an ass. He slung gravel all over my parking lot. It's a wonder he didn't break a window." Mr. Jones took the bag and tray to one of the store's two diner booths, a throwback to the days there had been a lunch counter inside the store. "I'll check the recording to see if I know him."

"It was Ivan Ruleman." While the run-in with Ruleman had rattled her, seeing Mama so complacent and controlled by another hurt deeply. But that was Mama, always searching for someone to take care of her, to tell her what to think and feel.

"Come over here and sit." He unpacked their lunch as she settled into the opposite side of the booth. "Take a deep breath. Ruleman's become a plumb-out, hate-filled holy roller as of late, but he's gone now."

Yeah, but for how long? Cent sipped from her drink, savoring the tea's fresh-brew taste. "Thanks for lunch, but I don't think I'm hungry anymore."

"Can you at least try? That'd be a bad waste of good, thick-cut bacon." He took a big bite from his bacon cheeseburger and began to chew.

"Sure, I guess." She lifted the edge of her sandwich to see the contents. There was too much mayonnaise, but the rest didn't look half-bad, and the bread was toasted right. Determined to get past what'd happened, she lifted the sandwich— A customer pulled up to the gas pumps. *Figures.* She set her sandwich aside.

"I got this one." Mr. Jones wiped his mouth on his sleeve as he rose.

Cent relaxed when he'd left the booth. The lodestones pulsed in her pocket, so she pulled them out, setting them on the table to examine them while she ate. So much power in a tiny package, and they'd protected her, but at what price? Now Ruleman was furious, and she was certain he'd take that anger out on Mama.

"You are injured!" Stowne cradled Cent's arm in their hands. "What happened to cause this?" The energy inside Stowne burned whiter and brighter. They were growing stronger.

"Ivan Ruleman. That's what happened." Cent couldn't say more without her nausea returning.

"Aside from those two blisters, it's a minor burn and a sprain from him twisting, but he could of broke your arm." Aubrey stood on the cellar stairs. "She's shaken, Stowne. Don't let her fool you."

"I feel her fear as my own." Stowne wrapped their hands around Cent's waist, pulling her to the floor and into their warm lap. "Tell me what happened."

"I need a moment first." She burst into tears as soon as she turned to face Stowne, pressing her face into their shoulder, shaking and quivering like some… "Dammit!" She raised her good hand to grab their shoulder, clinging until her tears abated enough that she could talk again. "I left here because of people like him."

"You have every right to be upset." Stowne hugged her to them. "But I am glad you made the choice to return. Otherwise—"

"Oh, honey. I don't regret it one bit *because* of you." Cent managed a little smile against Stowne before she burst into louder tears. "It's— she— she just stood there like— like she wasn't there at all and—"

"Who?" Stowne lifted her head so their eyes met. "Share with me."

"Mama." Cent gulped to contain another round of sobs. "She wasn't herself, wasn't— That ain't my mama. She always has something to say, mostly dumb or off-the-wall stuff, but she still speaks up."

"He's got control of her." Aubrey, who'd come downstairs to sit behind her, placed his hand on her back, absorbing some of her pain. "I tried to warn you."

"I didn't want to believe it." The spells placed on Mama when she was born had accomplished the exact opposite of what they had with Dustu. While he'd been impossible to control, Mama was easy to manipulate. "Half-magic." Cent pushed her forehead against Stowne's chest, trying to understand.

"Half-magic?" Aubrey leaned in to see her face. "What's that mean?"

"I will explain." Stowne cuddled and rocked Cent as they told Aubrey about Dustu and the events surrounding his death.

"Aw, geez. Cent, honey, I'm so sorry you went through that." Aubrey slipped his hands under her arms to pull her to him. "Damn."

He kissed her head. "Was I there?"

"You had yet to be born for the first time," said Stowne. "Your soul is maybe a thousand years old if that. Rayne, Pyre, or even I can help you if you decide to search for your memories, but right now—"

"It's not the time." Aubrey turned Cent to see her face. "You're quarter magic? That explains a lot about you. Ain't nothing about you ever been normal. And I ain't talking the whole bi-pan thing neither. That makes sense given who Stowne is." He hugged her to him and laughed. "No damn wonder Tess was slow to teach either of us who we were, what with your mama and all."

"Yeah." She slid back to Stowne's side on her knees to press her face against theirs. "Thank you for protecting me."

"The lodestones worked this time, but they will not again." Stowne took the magnetite when she held it out. "We must continue with the memories, so you will be able to better defend yourself."

"I already know self-defense." She spoke with a sudden fierceness that startled them all. "He just caught me off guard."

"Physical defenses are not going to aid you where Ivan Ruleman is concerned." Stowne squeezed their left hand then opened it to show the lodestones had disappeared. "We are not dealing with parlor tricks or a pseudo-magic practitioner." They pointed to their arm, showing where the lodestones trailed up as small lumps until they disappeared into their shoulder. "No sleight of hand." Stowne squeezed their right hand, turned it palm-down, and placed it in Cent's injured hand, pulling back to show she now held the lodestones. "This is all very real. Evil exists, Centenary, and Amadahy is correct. They know you have returned. Ruleman will only become more aggressive as your power grows."

"Impressive demonstration, and I get it." Aubrey rose to pace the cellar. "You're saying that Cent's dangerous to Ruleman's agenda, whatever that is. So what now, and how much longer do you need to be down here, Stowne?"

"I must remain here until Centenary's memories are more complete."

"The sooner you're out of here, the better." Cent tucked the lodestones into her pocket, cleared her eyes, and extended her good hand to Aubrey, who pulled her up beside him.

"So where do you go to find these memories?" he asked.

"Instinct," she replied. "I rely on instinct, and right now it's telling me to go upstairs."

"Can I come with you?" Aubrey tilted his head and smiled. "Please?"

Cent glanced back at Stowne who nodded. "I know you are still wary of what lies ahead, but you do not need my blessing to do whatever you wish.

You have always had a good head on your shoulders." Stowne smirked. "Is that saying still in use?"

"Sure is." Cent looked up the stairs. "And thanks for the vote of confidence. I'll be in the front room."

"And so will I." Aubrey turned when she did.

"I am asking Rayne to come assist if they are available." Stowne held up their hand and closed their eyes. "Yes. They'll be here in a moment. I feel more comfortable having another elemental alongside you if I cannot be there myself."

"Rayne?" Aubrey whistled low. "Now Rayne, I like. All smooth and fluid and—"

"They're really made of water, you know." Cent paused on the stairs to look back at him.

"Humans are primarily water too, so what's wrong with that?"

"Just saying." Cent blew Stowne a kiss and turned back around. "You'll find out all on your own if you keep thinking that way. Come on."

Chapter Eighteen

Cold Wounds Healed
May 1816/ August 2017

"She's gone." Cent hammered the carved wooden plaque into the frozen ground above his wife's grave. "They're both gone." He'd chiseled into the dirt alone until Stowne had interceded, helping him to hollow out the hole they'd lined with small rocks. No one had been there to help with the birth. No one else had been there to help lay Aggie or her baby to rest.

No Human, that is.

Cent and Rayne had tried to help Aggie when the time had come, and Stowne had been there for them both to lean on afterward. But Pyre— they'd been beyond consoling. Aggie had been theirs. She'd been locally born but quarter-magic and even more of a witch than Cent had been when he'd first arrived from Ireland. And she'd been better versed in the local traditions than anyone Cent knew. They'd become the best of friends, and that friendship had resulted in a marriage of mutual convenience. Cent had Stowne. Aggie had— Cent wiped his blue eyes and turned them toward Pyre. "I'm sorry."

Pyre nodded but said nothing, their flames a weak pinkish-red. They'd all but extinguished while feeding Aggie energy, and everyone had tried with the baby, but it'd changed nothing. Aggie and her more-than-half-magic child both resided behind the veil. They'd all been too tired to escort them, so Exan had helped Pyre lead them across, unusually gentle in their guidance.

"Go inside." Rayne's hand stuck to Cent's coat when they touched it. Cold. Ever so cold. "I already made a fire for you."

We're all doing things against our nature. "Thank you." Cent trudged wearily down the mountainside through knee-deep snow, stopping only long enough to watch it fall across the river flat below. *Such a strange year.* Spring was unusually late, and it was quiet. Too quiet. They should be celebrating, Pyre beaming one of their white-hot smiles as they sang their daughter a lullaby. But instead, they shivered when they passed Cent on their way to the cabin.

"I don't want to be a woman ever again." Cent leaned into Stowne when they wrapped their arm around his shoulders. "Never again."

"Remember the Balance, asgayaninela." Stowne pulled Cent up when he stumbled. "Remember what must be."

"Aren't any of these memories happy ones?" Cent clutched the baby rattle she'd found beneath one of the front room's hearthstones. The rattle was covered with carefully carved leaves and tied to a mother-of-pearl teething ring— it was a true piece of Colonial-era art, one she wanted to throw away and forget. "That was a hard year." She sobbed against Aubrey's shoulder. She missed Aggie, missed... "You." She lifted her head to stare at him. "You were Aggie."

"Me?" Aubrey pushed away from her. "Naw, not me." His jaw went slack when Rayne nodded.

"You've been a woman more than once. And been mine more than once too." Rayne slid closer to them. "Aggie's full name was Agnes Aubrey O'Sullivan. She was named—"

"After my, I mean her father." Aubrey gulped.

"You've only been mine once." Pyre slid down the front room's chimney to flicker inside the firebox. "I so loved you that life. I do now too, but time has tempered that flame. Our child. Our daughter. Gone too soon. Gone as soon as she lived. One breath. One small cry. She was a redhead just like me." Their sigh sent a tiny puff of white smoke drifting up the chimney. "That life was the last time I let myself love someone so completely." Pyre's gaze fixed on Aubrey. "But not this time. Not you. I know that for certain."

"You deserve happiness." Rayne cast a rare smile to their fiery companion.

"Until then, there's you, dear Rayne." Pyre released another puff of smoke, darker than the last. "But you've found Aubrey this time, haven't you?"

"I hope so." Rayne moved around Aubrey to look him in the eyes. "Will you consider what you've learned? Will you think about it?"

"Whoa." Aubrey rocked back hard enough to land on his ass. "You and me? How does this even work?"

"Like every other relationship." Cent scooted back to clear the way between Aubrey and Rayne. "It's nothing you haven't done before." She peered through the kitchen to the cellar door, anxious to share her newest memory with Stowne.

"Yeah, but I don't remember doing it before." Aubrey retreated to the homestead's front door. "I need time to think about this." He glanced back at Rayne. "I ain't attracted to women this time around, and—"

"Just because I prefer the graceful shapes and garb Human women often wear doesn't mean I'm a woman." Rayne shaped into their columnar form, followed by a decidedly masculine Human build, and back to their preferred shape, flouncing the bottom of their water robes hard enough to throw droplets across the room. "If you cannot understand then perhaps we aren't meant to be together this time after all."

"My memory's beginning to return." Aubrey crossed the room to take the rattle from Cent, examining it closely. "Stowne provided the ore, Pyre forged the shape with Cent's help, and you, Rayne, polished it to the sheen it once had."

"You do remember." Cent scooted closer to Pyre in search of their heat to warm her injured wrist, which now throbbed. "That rattle was a trigger for us both."

"He'll rediscover more over time, just like you will." Pyre's flicker brightened when Cent extended her arm to them. "Do you trust me again?" They rose from the fireplace to stand beside her.

"I sometimes believe in second chances." She relaxed when Pyre pushed a funnel of heat over her, twisting it around her wrist until the bandage warmed. "Thank you."

"I am strong enough to hear what is happening up there, Pyre." Stowne's voice rose through the floorboards. "Behave yourself."

"Always." Pyre winked one glowing eye at Cent. "At least for now."

"Pyre!" This time the floorboards shook.

"They're fine, Stowne." Cent laughed as she winked back at Pyre. "I'm on my way down."

"Wait a minute before you go." Aubrey motioned her to him. "If I'm a healer then let me do my thing." He pointed to her arm.

"But you wrapped it so prettily." Cent sat beside him again.

"Smart ass. You want a bow on it when I'm done this time?"

"That'd be nice." Cent quieted when he began unwrapping the Ace bandage, which he rolled before he moved to the gauze squares he'd placed over the blisters.

"Now this part's not going to feel nice but bear with me. I think I need to see the entire injury for it to work." He lifted the squares and passed them to Rayne, who held them suspended so they'd stay clean.

"The air on it burns." Cent gritted her teeth.

"Hold on, asiule ehu. Let him work." Stowne sounded like they were immediately beneath her, and she felt their energy pierce her from beneath to dull the pain.

"Don't use up—"

"You can return it to me later."

"Well, then." Cent settled firmly on the floor to enjoy the sensation. "Do your thing, Aub. I'm ready."

"You two definitely act like newlyweds." Aubrey raised his hands, placing one on each side of her wrist without touching it. He adjusted them, seeming to balance, spacing them evenly… "There." He closed his eyes and breathed deep. "If you tense, it will disrupt the— no, wait." Aubrey popped open one eye to see her. "Relax."

"Do you even know what you're doing?"

"It feels right, so shut up and let me work." Aubrey closed his eyes again, pursing his lips as he blew softly over the burn.

"Close your eyes too, Centenary." Rayne moved behind Aubrey, pressing against him to hold him steady when his hands began shaking. "You're trying too hard. Gentle. Recall how it all works. Feel the energy, the blockage caused by the injury, then blow it away."

"Yep, he's Rayne's." Pyre crackled.

"Not helping." Cent tried to sit still though her entire body tingled. Both Stowne's and Aubrey's energy pulsed through her now, Aubrey's moving through her wrist as he blew over it again.

"There. There… yes." Aubrey's energy began to shake inside her, oscillating between heat and cold until— "I can't!" He fell back into Rayne's arms as Cent opened her eyes. "I'm sorry, Cent. I can't."

"But you did." Aunt Tess stood in the front doorway. "See for yourself, Aub. The blisters are gone."

"Naw, I didn't do nothing to help, didn't…" He opened one eye when Rayne encouraged him. "I did that?"

"Yeah, cuz, you did." Cent turned her wrist to examine it. The blisters were mostly gone, the worst now in the post-fluidic, loose-top period before they dried and the dead skin peeled off. And the bruises that'd been rising when Aubrey had wrapped her were now a dull yellow-brown. "Thank you!" She turned her wrist to show him that the swelling and pain had eased.

"I did it?" He pulled her arm close to examine it for himself. "I did it!" But he shook against Rayne.

"You're tired." Rayne pressed their cheek to his forehead. "You helped her, now let me help you."

"Why, you're as warm as a person." He reached up to touch Rayne's face, pulling back to see the damp on his fingers before reaching again, this time with a smile on his face. "Yes, I remember you." He sagged against Rayne. "But I'm dadblamed tired."

"Shh." Rayne wrapped him much like Stowne did Cent when she was fatigued. "Let me feed you a while. You'll sleep better then."

"Feed?" Aubrey looked at Cent who nodded. "Are we talking vampire stuff?"

"It's what they call an energy transfer."

"So I fed you?" Aubrey could barely lift his head.

"No." Tess went to the cedar chest sitting in the living room corner. "Healing and energy-feeding are different things." She pulled out a quilt that she spread over Aubrey and Rayne.

"It smells musty." He peered down at the patchwork. "Is this the crazy quilt that used to be on my bunk?"

"It sure is. Your great-granny Sudie made it when I was a kid. It'd do her heart good to see it in use again." Tess leaned in to pat his head. "Let Rayne help you to the bunkroom after they finish feeding you, and you take a nap. Supper should be ready by the time you wake." She lifted her head to see Cent. "Wrap your wrist and go see Stowne. Take a nap too, and I'll see you later." Tess turned toward the door but stopped, turning back to see Pyre. "Can we talk outside?"

"Certainly." Pyre floated with their feet a good three inches above the floor. "There's too much touchy-feely in here anyway."

"Supper's at seven." Tess led the way out the door. "Touchy-feely, Pyre? You're how old again?" Their voices faded as soon as the door swung shut.

Cent found the rattle and left Aubrey and Rayne to themselves, moving wearily down the cellar stairs, becoming overjoyed when she found Stowne waiting for her halfway up.

"Almost free." Stowne led her to where they'd prepared a bed of soft sand. They set the rattle aside and stripped her of everything but her bandage, easing her onto the sand, wrapping around her to feed her, share with her, and tell her more about the life where Aggie had been so important to them all. "Feeling better?" Stowne moved to lay beside her.

"Much better. Thank you." She smiled when they moved again, this time to hover over her. They pushed her legs apart and settled their lower half between them, propping on their arms above her.

"I have something more to show you before you sleep. Something we have done together many times but I have been unable to sustain the energy for in your current life until now."

"Don't waste your..." Her eyes widened as Stowne's form changed, becoming semi-transparent then clear except for a waiver of distorted light that descended on her, pressing against her. "Let me share what makes us who we are. This is our truth."

"What... you're..." She felt Stowne everywhere inside her at once, sampling, experimenting, and learning what pleased her, what she responded to, what— Stowne possessed her in true spirit fashion.

Forgive me, but this is the best means I have found to quickly share our history. Stowne flooded her mind with joyous memories, with lifetimes of love and laughter that soon became laced with sadness and anger until she thought she'd burst. Only then did Stowne pull from her, quivering above her as she compartmentalized what they'd shared. "Now that I have shown you some of our past, we have something to begin building upon."

"That wasn't all good." She shivered when Stowne lowered to press against her again. "You've cheated on me three different lives." Cent snarled when old anger flitted through her. "You can be an absolute son-of-a-bitch when you take a mind to be."

"So can you, and you have been unfaithful to me as well. I shared not to hurt you but to show that neither of us is beyond fault. It is part of who we are, and we have found the strength to forgive because we love each other." Stowne pushed into her again, sharing darker memories. Deaths. Bitter arguments. Elemental feuds she'd been drawn into. Memories flooded her until they seethed together, staring daggers and cursing each other's existence until Cent could no longer bear it.

"Stop!" The memories turned to a careful mix of sweet that ascended into the sensual. Midnight promises became hard sex, tangled energies, sometimes with Rayne, Pyre, or both involved, and possession for the sheer pleasure Stowne could bring her through that means. What she liked each life might change, but her need for Stowne never faded.

"That suffices for now." Stowne floated over her again.

"That wasn't all?" She shivered when their form solidified and pressed against her.

"No. Delivering it all at once would madden you. I have made that mistake in the past." They drifted down to nuzzle her neck. "I want to share more joys of a physical nature, but you have reminded me that you are unable to remain silent." Stowne pushed against her to prove their point. "You have always been vocal when we share like this, and while I enjoy the sounds, others are trying to sleep above us, so may I help you contain your voice?" Stowne pushed the slightest of energies into her throat, showing her how gently the quiet came, how it felt. "Is this acceptable to you?"

Cent nodded, trying to control the joy she felt building throughout her body.

"Do not resist what you feel. Trust that I can remind you how well we work together." Stowne balled their energy and pushed it into hers, tightening until they swirled together, lifting above their sand bed. "Push your energy back into mine."

I don't know how to do this. Her energy danced around theirs.

"Perhaps not, but you do recall how to tease me. Do you remember what happens every time you do so?"

Show me. She wanted the reminder, longed for whatever happened next, but Stowne held back, teasing her in return, sharing knowledge of temptations she'd never imagined possible but had experienced countless times before.

"We will relive them together, but you— It is time I show you where we start this life." Stowne pulled her energy deep inside theirs, shattering every concept of pleasure Cent knew. They rolled in the air, twisting in and out of each other, rolling inside, alongside, and through each other until they were more one than two. *Look down.* Stowne's voice had become hers. *See what we have become.*

Stowne lay over her— sand, rock, and dirt with white-hot energy flowing between them, a column she wrapped her arms and legs around, holding, embracing, but there was more. Parts of her were rock, sand, and dirt too, while parts of Stowne— a strip of flesh ran down the center of their column. *This is us, what we become, what we are, where we begin this life.* Stowne's energy slowed, but she also felt it building, concentrating even tighter. *And this is where we go now.* They split a thousand directions inside her, exploding in such joyous pleasure her physical form threw back her head in a noiseless scream. Blended energies, blended bodies. *Over three thousand years of practice. Over one hundred lives. Almost infinite joy has built between us, and it will continue building.*

Cent woke to the reds and oranges of a setting sun.

Tess will be expecting you soon. Stowne's voice rang gently inside her.

Already? She stretched and rolled into their warmth. *I don't want to—* "Wait!" She sat up to stare at Stowne's naked Human form sprawled across their sand bed. "Why can I still hear you in my head?"

We mastered the technique several lifetimes ago, and I am pleased that we returned so readily to it this one. You may speak to me whenever you wish, and I to you. It is a valuable skill, and with practice, you will be able to contact others using it.

But I don't want so many in my head at once.

Others will come and go as you welcome them, but me— I am always here, as you are inside of me. Stowne opened their eyes. *It is a most satisfying place to begin things, I believe, and highly indicative of our possibilities this life.*

It seems you have plans for us. Cent rolled against Stowne, happy when they wrapped around her again.

Tess roasted one of her chickens and a basket of garden vegetables for you and Aubrey. Breathe deep. Can you smell it? Stowne moved energy to her olfactory senses, helping her to smell Tess' herb-roasted chicken, potatoes, onions, carrots, and— Cent's mouth watered— wild mushrooms.

Biscuits too?

114

Yes. Stowne chuckled. *I am glad you prefer simple foods to the highly processed, chemical-laden, unnatural, unhealthy—*

Tell me how you really feel about modern American foods. Cent sat up again. Listening. *Aubrey's up too. Guess I should get dressed.* She looked for the neatly folded stack Stowne always made of her clothes.

We are on top of them. Stowne pulled her pants from under them. *Your undergarments are beneath you and your shirt…* They pointed to the floor joist where Cent's t-shirt hung from a loose peg. *I was anxious to share when you arrived this afternoon.*

I noticed. She couldn't reach the shirt until Stowne lifted her, dropping her back into their arms to hug her.

Humans require both grounding energy and food to survive, so go eat. They kissed her mouth.

I wish you could go with me.

Tess' current home is not suitable and—

Rayne said that too.

Bring a blanket back with you. Please. One you are not afraid to get stained.

"But you keep me warm enough without one." Cent pursed her lips when she realized she'd used her voice.

"Yes." Stowne changed their communication too. "But this is to keep the sand from irritating your skin."

"Okay then." She blew them a kiss and trotted up the stairs, nearly running into Aubrey when he came out of the bunkroom.

"Hey there." He scrubbed the sleep from his eyes. "Did you get a nap?"

"A short one. You?"

"He slept very well." Rayne skipped through the house, leaving tiny puddles in their wake. "Enjoy your meal." They touched Aubrey on the shoulder as they went into the kitchen. "I'll be with Stowne should you need me."

"Sure thing." He watched them before he turned back to Cent. "How's the wrist?"

"Better. Thanks." She caught his arm when he pivoted toward the front door. "Hold on. Rayne sure is happy."

"I slept. Rayne was there, right beside me. They held me, and we talked. That's all." Aubrey shrugged, but his smile suggested more. "I like Rayne a lot. But I just broke up with Ethan and— I dunno. I don't think I'm ready yet."

"I can understand that." Cent looped her arm through his as they walked toward the trailer. "And I'm sure Rayne does too."

"They said it wasn't the first time I've been hesitant." Aubrey pulled on her arm, spinning her around to face him. "Not like you at all from what drifted up from the cellar earlier."

She felt a blush rise on her face. "Stowne tried to help me be quiet."

"I didn't hear anything but your voices, then even that went away. It's more what I felt. Love and energy. What you two share is old and powerful and doesn't have much at all to do with sex, does it?"

"Not really. It's something more. Better, I think."

"Better than sex? Now that's something." He spun her back around and began to walk, pulling her along this time. "I'm half-past hungry and on to hangry, so that chicken smells real good."

"Not half as good as those homemade biscuits."

"Aunt Tess made real biscuits?" He picked up his pace, passing her in what suddenly became a race to the trailer. "I hope she made enough for the fairies. Come on, slowpoke!" Cent let him take the lead, more content in her new life than she'd thought possible, but she knew they were far from safe and that whatever Ruleman wanted, he'd try to get at any expense, even Mama's.

Chapter Nineteen

Ganolesgi Blowing
August 23, 2017

Cent woke to the sound of heavy equipment tearing up the land beyond the homestead's fence.

"I do not… no!" Stowne shook with rage, moving back-and-forth between their Human and columnar forms. "This is our land, our…" The entire house shook with their distress.

"That land isn't part of the homestead anymore." Cent stood beside them at the window. "Aunt Tess said it wasn't when she and grandma Roslyn inherited the property." She gasped when the sound of a chainsaw echoed through the house. *That's near the property line.*

"It and everything to the Nolichucky is part of me!" Stowne backed from the window to sit cross-legged on the floor, their head in their hands. "They are destroying our home!" They rushed to the cellar stairs and climbed them. Four steps from the top something knocked them to the ground, and they sprawled on the floor in their Human shape, groaning.

"Careful!" Cent rushed to Stowne's side to cradle their head in her lap. "Is there a wall I can't see that's keeping you down here?"

"Of sorts." Stowne resembled the messenger who'd struck her curiosity back in North Chicago. Another earth elemental who'd wanted to help, Stowne had told her, and one accustomed to navigating inside humanity's modern complexities. "For me to cross it, you must find more memories than what you have and what we have shared." They closed their eyes, pushing out energy that vibrated through Cent's body as sound. *Rayne! Pyre! Come help! Stop the destruction!*

Pyre already is. The cellar door flew open, and Rayne descended the stairs in Human form, holding a paper bag in their hands that they thrust at Cent. "Clean clothes." They turned to the basement window, their expression now mimicking Stowne's. "Tess and Aubrey are talking to the one in charge of whatever is going on, but I don't know how to stop these monstrosities." Rayne peered over their shoulder at Cent. "Pyre's pushing energy into the bigger pieces to burn their insides, but the small thing making the horrid sound and eating the tree— tell me how to stop it!"

"It's a chainsaw." Cent quickly explained how it ran on a similar concept to the bulldozers, but she didn't know how to... "The cutting chain is lubricated with oil. Adding water should increase the friction when it bites in, and that might stop it from working."

"Let's hope." Rayne raised their arms, chanting words Cent couldn't understand, but she felt their intention. Water flowed up the center of the old Maple and poured from its leaves, cascading over the worker and his saw, drenching both until the saw ceased its horrible noise.

"Dammit!" The cutter wiped the water from his face and looked up, only to be hit by another soaking gush. "That's it!" He backed away from the tree when a sudden breeze threw more water from the leaves, dousing him again.

"What's the holdup?" A man in a blue hard hat, the apparent supervisor, approached at a trot. "We've only got a week to clear this property so... the hell?" He lifted his hard hat to scratch his head. "What happened to you?"

"That tree pissed all over me, that's what!" The cutter held out his saw. "It's gotta be dried, cleaned, and reoiled before I can use it."

"Shake yourself off while I get the other saw." The supervisor scratched his head again. "Damnedest thing I've ever seen. Must be from the rain the other night." He took the ruined saw and turned back, cursing even louder when he saw white smoke billowing from beneath the hood of his truck. "Jesus H. Christ!" He dropped the saw and raced to the pickup, stopping long enough to slip on his work gloves before he opened the hood. "How'd it overheat when it wasn't running?" The supervisor launched into a long string of curses, kicking the truck's left front tire, which hissed disapproval as it deflated.

"Gan's here!" Rayne couldn't contain their delight. "I called to them when things first started happening."

"And Gan is..." Cent smiled when she saw another tire go flat. "Air elemental?"

"They are." But Stowne didn't seem enthused about Gan's presence. "Their name is Ganolesgi."

"Gan." Rayne laughed. "They like to be called Gan."

"By their friends," rumbled Stowne.

Rayne leaned in to speak in Cent's ear. "The two of them had a falling out a few centuries ago. I'm surprised you don't remember."

"Was I involved?"

"No, but you were affected. Gan foolishly allowed an unfamiliar air elemental through the realm, and they dropped a powerful winter storm, an attack from one of Stowne's enemies at the time, as they crossed. It destroyed the winter home you and Stowne shared, and you were forced to live out the rest of the season at Usdagalv."

"You lost four toes and two fingers to frostbite." Stowne glowered at Rayne. "Ganolesgi was never to return, so what did you say that convinced them they could?"

"That you forgave them," Rayne spoke without hesitation. "that they were welcome in your realm. And then I told them what was happening, so they made considerable effort to get here quickly."

"All bluff and blow." Stowne's eyes narrowed. "If they are going to help, they should be mindful of others."

"Especially me?" Cent leaned against Stowne, nudging them until they placed their arm around her. "The past is the past. I'm here again, with my fingers and toes." She wiggled them to prove her point, realizing as she did that she was still naked. "I'm getting far too comfortable with my ass hanging out around you two."

"Then don't get dressed on my account." A stiff breeze descended the stairs, congregating next to Rayne as a semi-translucent, white-haired Human form dressed in a billowing, white robe cut to their hip on both sides. Cellar dirt swirled around their feet, giving them an odd, pink tint. "I've already admired you from afar, Centenary, but you're most definitely Stowne's again." Gan opened their sky-blue eyes to reveal cloudy bits that moved within the blue. "Long time, Stowne. Thank you for allowing me back into your realm." They bowed, one funnel arm across their swirling waist.

"I did not *allow* you," Stowne boomed. "Rayne lured you here under false pretenses."

"Now, Stowne." Rayne slipped between them, muddying the ground with a combination of water and earth that rippled from Gan's constant movements. "We need Gan in this fight."

"I've stopped equipment heavier than what's out there." Gan stepped forward to stand beside Rayne. "Let me help, Stowne. Please, at least until you're better able to do so yourself."

"I am managing quite well." Stowne folded their arms over their chest.

"Stop it." Cent smacked their solid arm with her open hand. "You can't leave the cellar yet, so how are you able to help with this?"

"This is an elemental matter, not Human so—"

"So what? My opinion doesn't count?" Cent stood by the cellar steps to dress. "Then, by all means, hash this out in the cellar of the home *I* built, without me having *any* say-so." She picked up her shoes and turned. "I'll be upstairs talking to other Humans unworthy of having input."

"Centenary, I did not mean to…" Stowne's angry voice immediately changed into one of keen distress. "I am sorry." They moved to stand at the bottom of the stairs. "I apologize."

"For what?" She gripped the railing as she glanced over her shoulder at them.

"For my harsh words. You have every right to be a part of this discussion." Stowne changed to the Human-like form they'd been practicing and, while it'd made her swoon the night before, it did anything but now. "It is only that—"

"Don't think for a second that I can't see what you're trying to do! I'm not a child, and I'm not easily persuaded, so stop discounting my opinions now or you'll never get outta this goddamn cellar!"

"Hold on." Rayne tried to move between them, but Cent didn't stay to listen, rushing up the stairs and closing the cellar door to lean against it.

What a total ass. What a— she saw something gray peeking over one of the kitchen rafters. She wanted to flee the house, to discuss her rage with another *person*, but she was also curious, no, drawn to whatever sat on that rafter, so drawn that she forgot her anger, dropped her shoes, and moved a bench to stand on it. *Too short. Where's a ladder when you need one?*

"Let me help you." Gan rose from between the floorboards to stand beside her, their expression sad, their wind-blown hair flicking softly back-and-forth.

"I don't think that's a good idea," said Cent, but Gan was already lifting her, rising with her until she could almost reach the rafter. "Where's Stowne?"

"Lecturing Rayne. Stowne's far more upset by your current anger than anything I've done in the past." Gan's mouth curled into a subdued smile. "Stowne has every right to be upset with me. I've been far from reliable, but it's difficult for one of my kind to settle, to be there every time they're needed." They supported Cent on a cushion of swirling air. "I never intended to hurt you back then."

"I believe you, and I can also see why you would have difficulty settling. Your nature is to move." Cent couldn't quite reach whatever rested on the rafter. "Can you lift me a little higher?"

"Certainly." Gan raised their air cushion.

"Got it!" Cent slid back as her world began to spin. She was falling, tumbling head-first down the homestead's hillside to land against a line of trees near the bottom.

Chapter Twenty

Bluebellies, Corncrackers, and Gallinippers
Fall 1863

"Stop! You're hurting me!"

"Not as much as we're gonna, old man!" The voice, slow in its southern drawl, came from up the hillside. "Damn bluebelly lover!"

"Scalawag!" cried another voice. Both were male. Both…

"You're hidin' contraband. Where're they at?"

"I ain't hidin' nothin'!" Cent rose despite the ache in his side. Broken ribs. He knew the feeling. This wasn't his first run-in with Confederate soldiers, especially with the Confederate Iron Works' furnaces just over the mountain at the mouth of Bumpass Cove, but this group of boys was meaner than the others. They'd walked in half-starved and wanting liquor, but when Cent told them he had none, that he hadn't drunk since Aggie, his wife, had died decades before, they'd turned ugly, holding a pistol to his head as they accused him of hiding the escaped slave they'd been pursuing.

But it wasn't one slave. It was two— a woman and her ten-year-old daughter, and they were hiding in the root cellar Stowne had dug for the potatoes and carrots Cent grew every summer. They'd been wary of an old man like Cent, but he'd felt an odd kinship with them. Outsiders. Rather like he and Stowne were to most of the world. "Take whatever you want outta the house and git. I don't mean you no harm!"

"You ain't no corncracker, old man. We heard you got money." One of them descended the hill again, sliding part of the way on his ass until he found where Cent lay beneath the trees, grabbing him by the arm to pull him out into the moonlight. "We heard that you found gold up in a mountainside cave and that you roll in it every night!"

"Do I look like I got any greenbacks?" Cent stared up at them, watching on the sly when he saw movement between the trees. Not the runaways but Stowne, silent as settled dust, and Pyre muted down to a lightning bug's twinkle.

"Where's your bark juice?" squeaked the youngest of them, a boy age fourteen if that. He'd been the one with the pistol, but his hand had trembled when he'd held it to Cent's temple.

They ain't killers… yet. "I don't imbibe," explained Cent, and the boys frowned, unsure what to do next. "Go on up to the house and take whatever you want. I ain't got much, but you can have it all if'n you leave me in peace afterward." They tied him to one of the trees and went to the house to ransack it. *Go now.* Cent smelled Stowne's warm-earth scent when they slipped behind him to remove the rope from his arms.

You are injured, adageyudi. Stowne nuzzled Cent's neck, rumbling softly with anger until Cent assured them he was okay.

Ain't nothin' that ain't happened to me before. Cent cringed when the sound of breaking glass drifted down the hillside.

Those boys need a lesson in being mannerable. Pyre flickered in front of Cent, showing white-burning eyes curled with concern.

They're yahoos, that's for sure. I got them off me without using a spell, but can you two do something to get them outta the house? I'm too hurt to use my energy, and they're gonna tear it apart. If they find the root cellar— Cent had neither the strength nor will to say the rest.

Do not worry. Rayne is watching over them. Stowne lifted their gaze from Cent long enough to view the house. *Wait here.*

Gladly, but don't burn the house down, Pyre. Promise me you won't.

I promise, mumbled Pyre when Stowne nudged their clear-heat outline. "But I might well set those boys' britches on fire."

"You're welcome to do that, but don't hurt them, and for God's sake don't kill them. We don't need any new haints 'round here."

"No." Stowne shook their head. "This situation does not warrant that. Remember to move your hands behind your back when they come out."

"You mean when they *run* out." Pyre crackled with anticipation. "Let's get to it."

"Stay here." Stowne placed their hand on Cent's shoulder and gently squeezed, their sign that they were taking charge of a situation, so Cent scooted back, resting against a tree's base, ready for a show of the type only elementals could manage.

Stowne went first, shaping into a crystalline Human form as they stomped across the homestead's front porch hard enough for Cent to feel the shake. *Careful. You'll have to help me replace every board you break.*

You know I will.

Voices rose from inside the house, and the door flung open. "Who's out here?"

That bummer's wearing my checked tablecloth 'round his neck! Cent drew to his knees, ready to knock the towheaded boy off the porch.

Sit down, Centenary. We've got this. Pyre touched their hand to Towhead's hat, setting it to burning.

"Hell 'far!" Towhead threw the hat onto the porch and stomped on it, smothering the flames.

"Hey, Art!" One of the other boys stepped onto the porch holding an open jar of apple butter. "The old man's either a bully-good cooker or…" He stopped to stare at the hat, which still smoked. "What'd you go and set your hat on 'far for?"

"I didn't!" Towhead stomped it harder. "Dammit, Amos! This place ain't right!"

The house descended into chaos after that. Pyre slipped inside to hide Cent's muzzle-loader and set another boy's hat ablaze. Stowne, now in their largest possible Human form, grabbed Amos off the porch, ripping his gun from his hand as they turned him upside down to shake him. Stowne then held him up by one leg to give him their most sulfurous smile, the one that always made Cent double over in laughter, but to someone who didn't know better…

"Holy…" Amos' mouth opened for a scream that wouldn't come.

"Best go home, boy. Bluebellies are on your tail." Stowne's smile broadened as they righted Amos to sit him on the ground beside the porch. "Go on now and never come back to this mountain. You hear me?"

"Yes… sir?" Amos moved like a back-walking crawdad until he was some distance from Stowne, then he turned and ran, tumbling down the hill to the wagon trail at the bottom, where he picked himself up and ran harder.

"That's it. Run!" Cent clutched his side when his laughter made it hurt worse.

Towhead ran after him, and one of the other boys, now disarmed, followed with his shirttail on fire, but the last, a great big teen with greasy, black hair and a missing top-front tooth, was sizing up Stowne who towered over him. "I don't know where you came from, mister, but you ain't got nothin' on me!" He swung at Stowne who didn't try to dodge. Rather, their form tightened, deflecting the blow like it was nothing but a gnat.

"What the…" This last Confederate boy shook out his hand and drew it back again, but this time Stowne caught his arm, holding it in theirs when he tried to pull away.

"Run, Gallinipper, before I swat you." Another smile leeched onto Stowne's face. "Or I let Jack here bite you." They pointed to Cent's half-blind, floppy-eared Blue Tick Coonhound. "Jack likes biting you rebel boys on their backsides."

"Go boil yer' shirt!" Reb reached for his absent muzzle-loader before he pulled his arm back harder, bellowing at Stowne to let go even as they lifted him from the porch. He reached above his head to punch Stowne's gripping hand, but Stowne reached out with their other, holding Reb by the wrist so tight his hand began to pale.

Careful, said Cent.

He will be fine. Stowne glanced Cent's direction then turned back to Reb, who kicked and hollered and— Reb foolishly kicked Stowne in the abdomen, squealing when his boot toe turned upward and split from the sole. *That was not me.*

I know. He caused his own hurt. Can we get rid of him, please?

I am weary of this foolishness as well. Stowne growled, shaking the land all the way to where Cent sat, as a third arm, this one more muscled than the others, emerged from their side, catching Reb by the ankle before Jack could sink his teeth into it.

One, two… Cent could all but hear Reb counting Stowne's arms.

"What *are* you?" Reb's eyes grew wider when Stowne smiled again, but their grin wasn't the least bit malicious. No, Stowne was trying hard not to laugh at Pyre as they sneaked up behind Reb.

Turn him around. Pyre floated above the porch boards on a cushion of heat, their white-flame eyes and smile hidden as Stowne lifted Reb to blow dust into his face.

"Go home, boy." Stowne shook Reb hard. "Tell your mama about this dangerous place. Tell everyone that earth rose to stop you, that rock lifted you from the ground with three hands, and that fire ate your boots until they fell off. They will all think you mad." Stowne whipped Reb around to see Pyre.

"Boo!" Pyre opened their eyes and leered, illuminating Reb and the entire porch, including Jack, who bounced up and down with excitement.

Reb wailed something unintelligible and fainted, his boots dropping from his feet as he fell limp in Stowne's grasp. Jack grabbed one of the boots and trotted to the end of the porch where he began chewing on the leather. "Good." Stowne pulled back all but the arm that held Reb by his collar. "You fool. Why are so many of your kind so willfully ignorant?" They dropped Reb off the porch and called for Rayne's assistance. "Remove him from the property but do no harm to him."

"Do I ever?" Rayne approached at a gliding trot to stand over Reb, nudging him with their foot. "He's unconscious."

"I scared the jackanapes half out of his skin." Pyre's grin lit the night like a toothy jack o' lantern.

"Seems you have things under control, so why do you need me?" Rayne smiled when Stowne made a whooshing sound. "Ah, I understand." They clasped their hands, raised them, and released, dropping a load of water over Reb's head.

"What the…" Reb jumped up, his eyes wide as they drifted from Rayne to Pyre and finally to Stowne.

"You are where you should not be!" Stowne's voice boomed down the hill to shake the tree Cent rested against. "Leave this mountain, you vile little man, and never come back. Evil has no place here, and you will not be allowed to ravage our home."

"I'm goin'! Lord Jesus help me! I'm goin'!" Reb tripped over himself in his haste to get away, tumbling down the hill, rolling past Cent to the bottom of the property and landing in the wagon ruts below, running in terror as Jack, barking and growling, pursued him down the road.

Stowne followed Reb to the property's edge, watching him limp into the night, turning back only when they were certain Reb and his friends were long gone. "Come here, Centenary." Stowne extended their arms to Cent, who rose slowly to stand beside them.

"They ain't comin' back, but there'll be lots of others. The river's gettin' more dangerous by the day." Cent stared at where the Nolichucky flowed in the dark, pressing his arm against his side, wincing as he thought of the obstacles the war had placed in their path. "Maybe I should go stay a spell in Jonesboro with my nephew and his family like y'all want."

"I will miss you, but yes, go as soon as you are healed enough for Rayne and Pyre to fly you there." Stowne carried him back to the homestead, where Pyre burned in the bedroom fireplace and Rayne brewed willow bark tea. "We will clean everything up." Stowne undressed Cent to the waist and covered his worst bruises with an Englishman's foot poultice to further reduce the pain. "And we will tend the chickens and horses."

"Or I will," said Rayne. "You and Pyre spook them."

"But not ol' Jack." Pyre called for the hound to return home. "That dog loves you, Rayne."

"He's a good boy." Rayne patted Jack's head when he trotted inside carrying the upper from Reb's boot. "Aren't you?"

"He sure is. Did you see him try to bite that last boy right on his ass?" Cent shared Stowne's rocker while he drank his tea then lay back against them. "Looks like you got nothin' left to do tonight but sit here with me."

"You should be in bed. I will energy feed you there." Stowne carried Cent to their hand-carved bed and crawled in beside him.

"Rayne, will you take some cornbread and beans up to that woman and her daughter?" Cent groaned when Stowne's hand warmed against his side.

"After they eat, tell them to get as far from here as they can before daylight." He looked over his shoulder to peer at Stowne through tear-filled eyes. "I don't mend so fast these days." He patted Jack's head when he placed his front paw on the bed.

"That is the order of things, adageyudi. Sleep, please. You will heal faster if you do." Stowne reached past him to pat Jack's head.

"I know." Cent placed his head on Stowne's shoulder. "But only if you aim to keep an eye on things for…me…while…"

Chapter Twenty-One

Legal Troubles
August 23, 2017

"Get down from there before you get hurt!" Tess yelled up to where Cent and Gan hovered.

Yeah, there is that. Cent stared at the scorched Confederate cap in her hand then at Gan, whose windblown face hovered close. "Down, please?" Her head spun from the sudden shift in time and place.

"Certainly." Gan lowered her slowly, taking great care as they set her on the floor, turning to bow before Tess and Aubrey as soon as she was steady. "You can both see me without my willing it to happen. Therefore, you must be friends." Gan cocked their head and smiled, their eyes now solely on Tess. "Or magical enemies, in which case my senses are off, and I'm lucky to still be upright."

"Friends." Tess extended her hand. "You must be Gan. This realm's former air elemental."

Aubrey did nothing but stare, his eyes darting between what Cent held and Gan, who slowed their perpetual swirl to stare back.

"Indeed I am." Gan kissed the back of Tess' hand. "There's multi-generational Human magic inside the realm again? It's been a long time since that's happened, but it's good, very good, especially since Rayne was desperate enough to lie so I'd return."

"Dear Lord!" Tess drew her hand back to cover her mouth. "How's Stowne handling it?"

"Not well at all." Stowne's voice rose from between the floorboards. "I have addressed the issue with Rayne. Ganolesgi, I would like to speak with you now."

"Why am I starting to believe Stowne's in charge here?" Aubrey thawed enough to take the cap from Cent. "New memory?"

"Yeah." She raised her head to see Rayne glide up the stairs, passing Gan.

"How is Stowne?" Gan looked hopefully at Rayne, but they shook their head.

"I am not happy! Get down here!" called Stowne. "Centenary?" Their tone softened. "Will you please come talk to me when Ganolesgi and I are finished with our discussion?"

I'm not yours to command. But they had said please. "Yeah, sure. I guess."

"The more recent memories will be harder on you." Rayne closed the cellar door behind Gan and wiped their brow. "And you're right, Aubrey. Stowne is in charge. They are the eldest of us, the first to—"

"The earth elemental is the spirit attached to the land. It's part of them, and they're part of it." Tess snatched the cap from Aubrey and handed it back to Cent. "Stowne's possessive of you, child, because they love you. That don't make their jealousy right, but it explains it."

"You should've taken me up on my offer at the last full moon celebration." Pyre whizzed through the homestead door in their clear-heat form to stand with them.

"Stop!" Tess pointed to the porch.

"I was joking, Tess, and—"

"You're burning too hot to be in here, so scooch right back outside. Cool and calm down before you come back in."

"Sorry." Pyre retreated to the doorway, where they stood as their form softened to oranges and reds. "I came in to tell you that the workers left, but their equipment's still here except for the truck, and they had another truck, one with a flat back, carry that away."

"They'll return soon enough." Tess loosened her shirt collar when her face reddened. "Pyre overheated the entire house. I heard one of the workers say they're on a deadline."

"Did the Nelson kids up and sell the land?" asked Aubrey, "I thought they'd promised to sell to you if they decided on it."

"They had." Tess put her head on her chest and frowned. "I've been savin' for it for years. The plot's smaller than the homestead, so I thought— Let me make a phone call."

"I got my cell with me." Aubrey pulled his iPhone from his pocket. "If you wanna—"

"I don't know the number off the top of my head." Tess wobbled as she turned for the door. "Some of us still have landlines and paper address books with numbers written in them."

"At least it ain't a party line anymore." Aubrey shoved his phone back into his pocket when she'd left. "Okay, Cent, tell me all about that Confederate cap."

"All my memories have been bad until this one. I don't understand."

"The memory associated with that cap is sad for us rather than for you." Rayne's mouth corners pulled down. "That night. You were with Stowne and... oh, oh." Rayne dabbed at the water trickling from their eyes. "Calm. Slow. If I don't contain myself, I'll flood the entire homestead."

"Then I'll finish." Pyre stepped back into the house wearing a soft red glow. "You died in your sleep that night, Centenary. You had more wrong than a few broken ribs."

"I was an old man, so it could've been one of a thousand issues."

"It could have," said Pyre. "But Stowne— you'd been together for five decades that life, so they buried deep when they lost you. It took you a long time to pull them out your next life, and this time when you left..." They peered toward the cellar door. "Isolation is an elemental's punishment for loving a Human across so many lifetimes. You see, every time you die, Stowne buries deeper to cover their pain, and it becomes harder for you to find each other again."

"These items I leave behind, they're part of a system?"

"Your system," Pyre explained. "You leave them behind to trigger your memories, but each time there's more to remember."

"Stowne relies on you to find them." Rayne sniffled. "Pyre and I have been fortunate enough to be yours before, but Stowne—"

"You've been Stowne's one hundred and two times." Pyre let out a heavy sigh. "I know when I flirt with you that it's in vain, but it's always fun to see your expression when you remember Stowne's the only one you want."

"Stowne has loved you since Humans first arrived here," added Rayne. "It took you a few lifetimes to find them, but now they worry and wait while you're behind the veil then watch for you the next life, ever hopeful that you'll remember."

"They've been my childhood friend many of those lives, my guide." Cent fingered the Confederate cap's rim. "Just like this life."

"They were terribly disappointed when Tess said they had to wait, that your mother had control of you until you were old enough." Pyre's color intensified. "And then you left. No reasons. No goodbyes."

"Tess kept magic from me because of Mama until I turned eighteen, and by then, I was too mad at the universe to see what was. Oh, Stowne."

"Yes?" They stood just inside the cellar door, their eyes transfixed on her. "I am sorry that I became jealous, that I let Gan's return anger me, that— Tess is correct. My saying I love you is no excuse, but it is that love that drives me. However you come back to me each time, I embrace it. I always have, but this time..." Stowne shook their head. "I thought you would never return, that I had lost you this life and perhaps forever, so I had prepared for a long wait. It has always been decades, and twice it has been over a century."

"But I'm here now, and I'm yours." She rushed into Stowne's arms. "I want you upstairs. With me. In *our* home. How much more do I have to endure, how many more memories do I need to find?"

"Only one more, asiule ehu, though not today. We need to gather together and plan. Whatever Ruleman is attempting to do, he is investing a lot into it."

"Yeah, he is. Enormous amounts to be a small-time preacher." Aubrey pulled out the bench from the kitchen table to sit facing them. "If Aunt Tess can't come up with anything, I'll go digging at the county courthouse later today to see who bought the property."

"That's a great idea." Cent asked Stowne to sit in the doorway so she could be with them, but before she sat, she pointed to the table, which looked more familiar than ever. "Did I build that?"

"In 1830," said Stowne. "You were hoping to adopt several children, but you could not find any with magic in them who needed us."

"I was a single man, so it wouldn't have been allowed anyway." Cent went to the table to inspect it, happy to see that everything was held together with tight-fitting wooden pegs. "It needs sanding and oiling to renew the wood, but otherwise…" She looked up with a smile.

"You've always been an artist with your woodworking." Pyre's tone became admiring. "And I've appreciated when you allowed me to heat your forge for metalsmithing."

"I've done that too?"

"Far more than the rattle," said Stowne. "Especially since my mountain contains a variety of ores. I assisted you in laying the rock for this home's foundation, dug the cellar with you, and built the chimney beside you, but the rest…" They nodded to Rayne, Pyre, and to Cent's surprise, Gan, who now wore gray pants and a flowing blue shirt as they stood in the homestead's front doorway.

"Come in, Gan. Please. I was telling Centenary—"

"How I helped keep the homestead cool in the summer, and how I provided fresh air during the winter when Pyre burned in the fireplace? Sounds nice, but, unfortunately, I wasn't here then." Gan sat beside Aubrey. "It's no one's fault but my own." They nodded to Stowne. "I overheard Tess talking on the telephone. She found out some information and is now madder than a— what's the expression?"

"Madder than a wet hen?" Aubrey offered.

"Or a hornet caught in a Coke can? Neither one's good." Cent returned to Stowne's side to sit against them in the cellar doorway. "And let me guess. Rayne, you provided water to the home?"

"No, you did that yourself by piping it in from my spring," they explained. "Tess and Kinnon replaced the piping a couple of decades back. I contributed to this house by planing all the interior wooden surfaces smooth." Rayne ran their hand across the table's top. "Nearly two hundred years and there's still not a splinter to be found."

"This home is yours, Centenary, but we can stay with you in it because the materials are natural." Stowne nudged her. "That is also why none of us can enter Tess' trailer for long."

"Yes." Gan tilted their head to one side. "I was meaning to ask about that structure."

"We'll eventually move it off the property," said Cent. "I want to fix the homestead, make it livable again without ruining the feel." Her home crafted by her hands over lifetimes, she didn't want to change it any more than necessary.

"That'll take a whole lot of effort, and even more cash." Aubrey pressed his lips together in a small grimace. "You sure you're up to that?"

"Yeah, I am, but I've lived here alone, at least Human-wise, most of the time." She peered back at Stowne who nodded. *You know what I'm thinking even before I do.* "What do you say, Aub? Wanna help me?"

"I'm anything but a carpenter, but, yeah, I need the change. There'll be a job for me around here. It won't pay as much as working in K-Town, but…" His eyes drifted to Rayne.

"The rent's cheap here, but the accommodations will suck until we fix things up." Cent sighed when she thought about the volume of work ahead. "You might not be much of a carpenter, Aub, but you're one mean-ass cook."

"So you want me here for my fried chicken and bibingka?"

"Your cornbread and blackberry cobbler ain't half-bad either. Ooh, and I love your kutsinta."

"Least you're honest about it." He grinned at her. "Okay, but can we redo the bunk room into something more adult?"

He didn't mention staying in the trailer. And Rayne was up here too. "How about we plan for two master suites?"

"No hiking down to the trailer?" Aubrey's expression brightened. "Even better, but aren't we jumping the gun a bit? I mean—"

"We can dream." Cent settled further into Stowne's presence, at ease, loved and wanted, though she knew they were anything but clear of the danger Ruleman presented. "What about Aunt Tess?"

"Give her that suite, if you want." Aubrey shrugged. "I'll sleep wherever as long as there's a functioning bathroom up here. Tess loves this house and deserves to be here too."

"There'll be room for all of us. We'll make certain of it." Cent nearly laughed when she saw a smile creep across Rayne's face.

"All-natural materials but modern conveniences." Aubrey scratched his head. "That'll be pricey."

"The bones are already here, and if we do it one step at—"

"Centenary Rhodes!" A woman's voice rolled up the hill and through the homestead's open front door.

"What the..." She broke from Stowne to peer down the hillside. "Shit. That's a sheriff's deputy." Cent tensed as Aubrey came to stand behind her. "Yes, ma'am? What can I do for you?"

"We need to talk." The deputy held up a thick stack of papers.

"I'll go down with you." Aubrey placed his hand on her shoulder.

"Who is that?" asked Stowne. "Rayne, go with—"

"Be right there." Cent spun around. "Non-Humans stay here. We'll be fine. It's a little, um, legal trouble."

Aubrey followed her down the hill, tucking his hair into a knot at the base of his neck as they walked. "Bad debt?"

"From when I lost my job up in Chicago." She gritted her teeth and kept moving forward, trying not to focus on the stack of folded papers in the deputy's hand. "I lost pretty much everything."

"I'd wondered, given how little you came home with."

Cent smoothed her hair, pushed up her glasses, and straightened her shirt, blowing out as they neared the bottom of the hill.

"Miss Rhodes?" The deputy pointed to Cent.

"Yes, ma'am. What can I do for you?"

The deputy set the papers on the hood of her cruiser and whipped out a pen. "I've got, I mean, *you've* got twelve summonses here."

"Twelve." Aubrey whistled low.

"Shut up, Aub." Cent grinned sheepishly at the deputy. "I lost my job a while back, you know how it goes."

"I spend way too much time delivering these to want to know the reasons." The deputy held the pen out to Cent. "Do you know where to sign them?"

"Yes'm." Cent spent several moments bent over the car, passing the summonses one by one to the deputy, who countersigned, tore off the top page, and handed her back the rest.

"Good luck to you." The deputy took her pen and returned to her cruiser, backing from the driveway and onto the road while Cent watched.

"Dammit to hell and back." Cent's eyes moved from the summonses to Aubrey who grimaced.

"I'm sorry."

"Yeah, me too." Her eyes shifted up the hill to the trailer where Aunt Tess sat on the front porch in a folding chair.

"Guess Carter County didn't work after all." Tess glowered at the papers when Cent stepped onto the porch. "Want me to hold them down here? You don't need such negativity up at the homestead."

"I've got to read through them for the dates first." Cent sat on the steps with Aubrey, thumbing through each summons to find the appearance date. Four separate dates with six hearings on the same day.

"Blood from a turnip," Tess told her. "When's the first one?"

"Tomorrow." Cent hung her head. Almost all the joy of living on the homestead had fled from her. "I can't even consider owning this place with this hanging over my head."

"How much?" Aubrey sat on the step below her. "How much do you owe?"

"Forty, fifty thousand, but I can't be exact without knowing all the court costs and attorney fees. I paid off my student loans right before the job went, so that's something."

"Something good." He leaned forward to drape his arm over her shoulders. "What's the biggest one?"

"The car." She stared at her hands. "I already got a judgment against me for it."

"That's right." Aubrey tilted his head toward her. "You had what? An Aston Martin?"

"Prius, you jerk." She managed a laugh. "I almost had it paid off too, but after the legal fees and other stuff, it's an almost ten-thousand-dollar judgment."

"I was going to give you a wet-willy to distract you but, damn, honey." Aubrey smooched the side of her head instead. "You've only just moved back here, are only working part-time at this point, and you're living with family. The judge won't bark at you, but they'll tell you to get your shit together and slap judgments on you."

"And that'll garnish all my money above minimum wage when I get a decent job." Cent hung her head even more. "It compounds itself. I have two other judgments against me up in Illinois too."

"Credit's great until you can't afford it." Aubrey pulled her to him so her head rested on his shoulder. "The homestead comes first, right?"

"Yeah, it does."

"Then this is what we'll do. I'm going to ask for a year's deferment on my student loan. I ain't never asked for one before, so they'll give it to me easy, what with the job change, and you file bankruptcy while I'm not paying. Between us, we'll be fine financially no matter how things land."

"You'd do that for me?" She turned her head to look sidelong at him.

"Do chiggers bite?"

"It'll give you both time to work out your finances," said Tess. "Family helping family." She sat back smiling, her eyes closed. "It's going to take all of us to beat Ruleman off the property."

"What's his beef with us anyway?" asked Aubrey as Cent sat up. "He's already got Aunt Nida."

"Ruleman wants something here," Tess explained.

"What could he possibly want?" Cent wiped her eyes.

"Somethin' important enough that he's running through money like water through a sieve to get at it." Tess folded her hands in her lap. "I found out that much on the phone today. The Nelsons gave him a sky-high price in writing like he'd asked, but he accepted, so they were bound by it. He trapped them in legalese. Their land ain't worth a quarter what he paid." She popped open one eye to regard them. "He bought the property on the other side of us too, just so y'all know."

"Shit." Cent turned her head to the afternoon sky to ask why, though she expected no reply. "I don't understand. Why'd he attack me at Dryler's if he only wants the land?"

"You tell me." Tess' gaze was fully on Cent. "How'd he feel when you faced him?"

"Strong and mean." Cent raised her injured hand to look at it. "I'd have called 911 on him if I'd thought anyone would've believed me."

"I met Ivan Ruleman when he was about your age," Tess continued. "Good soul. A true Christian. He did more than talk the talk. He lived the life. He was quiet, a working type so you'd never know he came from money, and his church congregation adored him."

"You attended his church?" Aubrey wrinkled his brow.

"Why not? Just because he and I don't share all the same beliefs doesn't mean we haven't got a lot in common. He talked about helping, of loving your neighbor, about how a person should not judge another. He even visited me after your Uncle Kinnon died, brought me a Bible and a stack of casseroles his congregation had made. Those meals are long gone, but I've still got that Bible and have read it cover-to-cover several times." Tess stroked the porch rail with her weathered hand. "It's like every other religious text. It can be used for good or bad, dependin' on how you take the words. But this ain't about the Bible.

This is about Ivan Ruleman. He changed a few years ago, suddenly got mean. His congregation split soon after. Most of them moved to other churches, but a handful stayed, and they've turned mean too. Ugly. Full of piss and bile. Negative. Genuine hypocrites. They're every bit as hate-filled as he is."

"He has minions, great." Aubrey sighed. "But that doesn't explain why he wants us off this property so bad."

"I think it does," said Tess. "He wants it sold so he can have it for himself, but he don't want the house nor the land. Ivan Ruleman wants other things here, things much more important."

"He's a preacher, so why would he…" Cent gasped as the reason behind Ruleman's powerful grip on her arm became clear. The problem wasn't Ruleman himself. No, he was merely a puppet, a conduit for something in search of— "Energy. He's being controlled by the same force I felt directing Mama."

"Exactly." Tess dropped her arm into her lap. "We're gatekeepers, Cent. We watch over this land so others can cross the veil to rest before their next lives. The elementals here are bound to this place to help protect it." She opened her eyes wide and leaned forward to stare at Cent. "And something dark wants what we're guarding."

———

I tried to call you earlier, but you didn't pick up.
Sorry. I've been busy getting the homestead ready.
OK. I really miss you.
I miss you too, Betty Boo. It's 3 AM here. Rough night?
One of several in a row.
What can I do to help?
Can we talk? I mean for real?
Sure. When?
Right now.
So call me.
You're a saint, baby doll. Thanks.

"I'm going upstairs to use my phone."

"Is something wrong?" Stowne touched Cent's back when she sat up.

"I don't know yet." But she did know and hoped a phone call was enough to stop the motion.

Chapter Twenty-Two

The Woes of an American Diet
August 24, 2017

Cent woke the next morning knowing that she and every other creature on the homestead had a purpose. They protected the veil crossing. Stowne was the oldest of them, and she was their eternal companion.

Good morning. Stowne pulled her closer. *You have one more memory to work through. Do you believe you are up to it today?*

Maybe after court. She went to Tess' to shower and change into her best clothing, trying to figure out how she'd explain herself, how a woman who'd once had a good job had returned home with almost nothing to her name. Mister Jones paid in cash, so there was no record of her doing anything to remedy the situation since she'd been home.

She left the courtroom much like she'd entered it, her head down, her hands in her empty pockets.

"Find a job, Miss Rhodes, and repay your debts. I know you're taking care of your Great Aunt, but there's no reason you can't work as well." The judge hadn't been hateful. No, the judges she'd faced had never been mean, but they were always direct. She had an advanced degree but no prospects, nothing— She had magic and that meant a lot, but it didn't pay the bills.

Cent picked at her lunch then returned to the homestead for the night with a paper plate holding a half-bag of Tess' precious potato chips and a potted-meat sandwich. She held a big glass of Pal's sweet tea in her other hand that she dropped on the homestead's porch when her pant leg snagged on a loose nail.

"Aw, dammit." She pulled out her phone to call Aubrey, who helped her clean the mess.

"Try not to break this one, okay?" He handed her another tea in a quart canning jar. "Tess wants the jar back in the morning."

"I'm glad you bought a gallon jug of tea this time." She thanked him twice more before stepping into the house. It was absent of everyone but Stowne, who sat on the cellar stairs waiting for her.

Such a bad day for you. Stowne carried the tea down the stairs. *I see you do partake in some poorer food choices after all.* They frowned at her.

It's comfort food, so lay off me. She set the plate on the blanket covering their sand bed.

I was merely commenting. Stowne patted the space between the plate and where they sat. *Such emotion always proves draining. Would you like—*

Leave me alone for a while, will you? Just don't say anything. Cent set the plate on the floor and lay on her side facing away from Stowne, silent in her sense of utter failure. She pulled her knees to her chest and began to softly cry. This was the first of four court dates in the next two weeks, the first...

Cent didn't realize Stowne pressed against her until evening light trickled through the cellar windows. *I do not understand many events that occur in the Human world, but I do know sadness, especially when it rises from you.* They said nothing else but wrapped their arms around her, their breath warm against her neck.

She didn't want Stowne to understand, to worry, so she rolled into their hold, pulling their hands up to her waist, breathing slower until Stowne turned her onto her back, their face hovering over hers as they dried her tears. "I cannot stop what has saddened you, but I can help you push the pain aside for now." They held her face to kiss her then draped over her body, trying to absorb what caused her pain.

You can't diffuse what you don't understand, but thanks for trying. She reached up to touch their face.

Then help me understand. This is financial? Monetary? I do have some knowledge of these matters from your past lives.

Yes, but... I'll tell you a little, but I don't want to discuss the details.

I am listening. And Stowne did listen, even with interest, but she couldn't effectively explain.

I do not understand this credit you keep speaking of. Stowne slid back to sit beside her.

Neither do I, not anymore. Cent sat up to eye her sandwich. *I'm tired of trying to explain. Maybe I should eat.*

I kept your tea chilled. Stowne pointed to where the quart jar sat partially buried in the cellar floor. *Cold or hot, you like nothing in between, if I remember correctly.*

You're so good to me. Cent took a swallow from the jar and bit into her sandwich, frowning when Stowne took it from her to examine the contents.

Bread made with whole grains but with considerable filler and unnecessary ingredients. They placed their finger on the edge to sample the potted meat. *What is that? There is little actual meat in there, no quality meats at all, and too many chemicals. Roast chicken or venison would be much better for you. Even egg.* They passed her back the sandwich.

Yeah, whatever. Cent pushed Stowne's hand away when they reached for a chip. *If you don't like potted meat, these ain't gonna suit you either.*

I am familiar with fried potatoes. Stowne snatched a large chip with their other hand, sniffing along its edge. *A vegetable-based oil, potato, and salt. I would not refer to the oil as quality, but it is better than animal fat. However, the rest…* They held the chip to Cent's mouth, so she'd take a bite.

No wonder you approve. She took the rest of the chip. *It's plain.*

No, there is salt on it.

That's all there is. Still, it was good, so Cent chewed and swallowed. *Are you going to scrutinize everything I eat for the rest of my life?*

Of course not, but I claim the right to examine what you bring into our home.

So no Vienna sausages?

Vienna? Imported food? Those are surely expensive.

They're anything but. I ate them all the time in Chicago. What about cheese puffs?

You used to make excellent cheese if memory serves. It was something you used for bartering.

I don't think there's much if any cheese in cheese puffs. Tell you what, I'll eat that sort of stuff at Tess' or off the property from now on, okay?

If that is what you wish. Your energy is stronger now that you are speaking to me.

I needed to talk about something besides what happened today. Her head was now abuzz with possibilities. *Tell me about other things I used to make for barter.*

Cent fell asleep late but woke earlier than she should, her bladder full of tea. She rolled into Stowne's chest, reluctant to move though she knew she had to. Stowne's body was neither rock nor soil against her, more like the soft, fine sand they lay on but firmer. She didn't have a word for it but being beside them made her feel good both inside and out, somehow powerful.

You are awake early.

Full bladder.

Ah, now that, I cannot assist with. Stowne kissed the top of her head. *Be careful. It is still dark out.*

I'll grab something for breakfast while I'm down at the trailer. She peeled away from them to sit up.

Something that exists in nature?

Tess has some apples and granola bars.

Granola?

If it doesn't pass inspection, I'll eat it on the porch. She crossed her legs as soon as she stood.

Very well. And, since you are awake, how is your friend in Chicago?

I'm worried about her.

Would you like me to ask my elemental acquaintance in that area to check on her?

Yes. Thank you. That would help a lot. Now, I really gotta go pee. She turned toward the stairs.

Certainly. Get yourself something to hydrate with while you are at the trailer.

With any luck, there'll still be tea in the fridge.

Yes, you do like your tea. Be careful on your walk. Stowne's form fragmented into a million bits that sank into the soil, leaving her alone.

"And they disappear before I get a goodbye kiss." Cent's voice echoed in the emptiness. She climbed the steps two at a time to the kitchen, grabbed the flashlight, and trudged out the door, her need increasing with every step. She looked at the old outhouse. *Ramshackle thing. We'll have to use the trailer until we get something more than a handpump for plumbing installed.* At least then she'd have a means to— She stopped to ponder the outhouse again. It was still a long, dark walk to the trailer and too early to be bothering Tess and Aubrey, so why not?

Cent cracked open the door to shine the flashlight inside. It was dusty, some of the boards were loose, but she didn't see any bugs, and it didn't smell anymore. Too bad she hadn't— She remembered she'd shoved tissue into her pocket yesterday when she'd been crying in the trailer's bathroom. She'd dried her eyes with it, but other than that...

"Lucky me." She now had time to settle in, to think like she did when she was occupied by her morning routine. *Elementals have it so good. No need to do this, no— What's that?* She reached out to pull an old paper, a flyer of some kind from between the boards. No, it was a magazine ad and far too old and brittle to be used for the reason it had originally landed in the outhouse, but as soon as she touched the paper her world began to spin again.

Not now. Please.

Chapter Twenty-Three

Cheating Death
Summer-Fall 1952

"So there's nothing to be done?" Cent stared at the x-ray the doctor pointed to. Lung cancer. Advanced. Terminal.

"Go home. Set your affairs in order," he told her.

"Yeah." She'd driven to Knoxville by herself to get a second opinion, and that opinion had matched Doc's back home. No hope. No— "Guess I'll be going then."

"We could do a biopsy to make certain, but I confirm the diagnosis." At least he'd tried to sound helpful.

"Then what's the point of a biopsy?"

"There's really not much of one, considering."

"That mass is as big as my fist." She held her hand up to show him.

"Yes, it is." He shoved another x-ray into the viewer. "There's a second mass on your liver that's half the size of a baseball."

"Now, my doctor mentioned nothing about that." Cent bit her bottom lip so hard she tasted lipstick then blood. "Why not?"

"The machine at your local hospital isn't as powerful as the newer ones we have here." The doctor sat back to consider her. "Like I said, go home and get your affairs in order. Do you have a family?"

"Yes, of course." *You don't need to know they're not Human.*

"Are they close enough to help you?"

"They'll do everything they can." Cent tensed when he raised one brow at her. She'd seen that expression a million times. Every independent woman in her fifties had. *Here it comes.*

"Does your husband know you're here?"

"I'm not married." *At least not in a way you'd understand.* Cent looked toward the door. "Guess we're through then?"

"I'll phone your doctor with the results. My nurse will see you out." He pressed the button on his desk, and a young blonde woman wearing a crisp, white apron pinned over her blue uniform escorted Cent out of the office, leaving her at the reception desk to make payment.

She dug into her purse for the six dollars and fifty cents and fled the building, stopping as soon as she reached the parking lot to pull out a Lucky Strike that she shoved into the tip of her black cigarette holder, her hands trembling so hard it took her three attempts. Cent brought the holder to her mouth, clenching it between her lips as she lit up. "Cancer. Fucking cancer." She found her way to the pickup, threw her purse in, and dropped into the seat beside it, pulling her skirt just right so she could drive. A three-on-the-tree, and she knew how to drive the shit out of it on or off the homestead.

Pyre had told her she was ill before she'd known herself. Rayne had offered to come to Knoxville with her despite the drain on their energy. And Stowne— they were speaking less and often sat watching her with sad eyes. They didn't want her out of their sight and had shaken the entire homestead with their longing to go with her, but they knew, Cent knew, Stowne couldn't.

"I'm sorry, baby." Cent coughed, hard and raspy, before taking another puff from her smoke, settling into the small calming rush the nicotine brought. Good stuff, nicotine. It made her cough, bringing up all the bad things that'd built in her lungs, that's what Doc had said. Pyre disagreed and had claimed there was nothing clean about cigarette smoke, but they were neither a physician nor a Human.

Cent traveled the two-lane roads a good hundred miles back home, practically crawling from the truck when she got home, wobbling on her heels as Stowne helped her out.

"Kick off those ridiculous shoes, usdayvhsgi. Let my soil slip between your toes and feed you."

"Help me take off my stockings." Cent leaned against the truck while Stowne did so for her, loosening them from her girdle and slipping them from beneath her dress to ball them in their hand.

"These are not natural." Stowne threw the nylons to Cent's terrier mix, Jack, who growled as she trotted off with them in her mouth. "So much of this world—"

"Stop her, honey. That's my last decent pair."

"She's already burying them behind the house." Stowne smirked. "You have a perfectly good silken pair in the back of your dresser if you feel inclined to wear stockings."

"Those have a run, and you ain't got to pay for— sure. I'm home most of the time, so who needs them? Help me inside so I can put on my overalls." She ignored the catch in her side to stand straight, her hand extended to Stowne.

"Gladly." Stowne practically carried her inside, propping her against the post of their quilt-draped bed to help her change clothes. "The doctor said you would recover, correct?" Stowne's tone revealed how much they doubted their own words.

I wish I could— "No, I'm afraid not. Not only did he say Doc Leonard was right, but he claims it's spread to my liver too." She placed her hand on Stowne's shoulder, squeezing until they rose. "I'm dying, baby, and ain't nothing gonna stop it."

"No. You are *not* dying." Stowne helped her pull up her overalls and button them, but their hands trembled as much as hers. "You are a strong woman."

"One with cancer." Cent caught Stowne's hand and brought it up to kiss it. "I am sorry I found you late this time. I am sorry we only got a decade. I—"

"We still have many years left together." Stowne pulled her into the bed to wrap around her. "Many years."

"Six months, maybe less." Cent stared at the rafters. "I'm sorry, baby. I'm—"

"Hush." Stowne wrapped tighter around her. "Be quiet for a moment." They shushed her every time she tried to speak, still against her as she breathed, their hand to her chest to feel its rise and fall. "You must quit smoking," Stowne finally said. "It will help."

"It won't stop things, so why bother? Besides, most doctors say—"

"Modern technology. Modern medicine. They fail to use sense, to see the real problem even when it is directly before them. It is related to the cigarettes, to— Promise me, Centenary. No more."

"I can't." Cent looked to where her clutch sat on the dresser. "I need them to feel right."

Then I will banish them from the property." Stowne stretched their arm to knock the clutch to the floor. "No more. I insist."

"It's not that easy, baby, but I'll try." Stowne fed her as they lay together, giving her body the energy she needed to work the homestead. It was only mid-summer. There were tomatoes to can, beans to pick, and the hog she'd bought from the Nelsons was gaining weight snout-over-hoof. It'd be ready to butcher and smoke by early fall. Stowne and the others would help for much of it, but the idea of so much work when she felt so bad... "I need a nap."

"Rest. I will feed you more while you do."

"Save some for yourself." She fell asleep in Stowne's arms.

"Put it out and give me the rest of the pack."

"Of all the— here!" Cent dropped her pack of Lucky Strikes onto the floor and kicked them under the outhouse door to Pyre. *They're almost gone anyway.* It was the middle of the night, and she'd gone to the outhouse to sneak a smoke. One, that was all, and the rush felt so good. It was the best she'd felt in days, and—

"Drop that lit cigarette down the hole. Stowne's on their way."

"Dammit." Cent took a long drag, exhaling as she rose. She couldn't hide that she'd been smoking again, and—

"Centenary, please come out." Stowne knocked on the outhouse door.

"I'm busy."

"We must discuss this."

"I was just going," Pyre's light drifted away.

Coward. Cent tied her robe and stepped out the door. Fall had rolled in early and wet, setting her up for a rough bout of bronchitis that wouldn't go away. "Fancy meeting you here at two in the morning." She cleared her throat to stifle its perpetual tickle.

"Centenary." Stowne folded their arms across their chest. "You should not be out here this time of night, especially in these cooler temperatures." Stowne held out the quilt from their bed. "You should be inside where it is warm and dry."

"I had to pee. It's something Humans need to do regular."

"There is a night bucket beneath our bed for you to use when the weather is bad." Stowne caught her before she moved away, wrapping her in the blanket. "You gave Pyre the cigarettes, but where are the matches?"

"You already took my lighter."

"And I am removing every pack of matches from the homestead."

"But what if we need to light a new fire?"

"Centenary!" Stowne pointed to where Pyre hovered on the porch. "That is not a legitimate argument." They lifted her into their arms.

"Put me down."

"Please see reason." They turned toward the house.

"Put. Me. Down!" Cent all but fell from Stowne's arms before they turned her straight. "You and me, we gotta talk about this."

"About what?" Stowne towered over her. "Your refusal to care for yourself?"

"About the elephant in the damn room!"

"El-e-phant?" Water ran off Stowne's head as they stared at her. "Those large gray mammals you told me about? There is one in the house? Brownie or Birdie surely would have sounded the alarm if—"

"No, honey. I…" Cent shivered as the rain began falling harder. "Let's go inside and talk."

"That is what I wanted when we began this elephant-filled argument." Stowne walked beside her up the hill, helping her at the slick spots until she was inside the door. "There. Safe and warm." Stowne unwrapped her blanket and pulled off her rain boots. "Sit. I will stoke the fire and heat water for your tea."

"Chamomile, please." Nothing else agreed with her stomach anymore. "And do it over the fire so I can watch. Pretty please?"

"Such simple things bring you pleasure." Stowne set her favorite earthenware mug on the table beside her chair and another blanket across her lap.

"Tell me a story from our past lives together." She watched as Stowne talked and worked, admiring the ever-changing lines of their body. Larger or smaller depending on what was needed, delicate as they poured water over the tea strainer but strong in the way they held the steaming cast-iron kettle without using a potholder.

"Cream and sugar?" Stowne peered up at her.

"Sugar, yes. But cream?" Cent blanched. "But I used to like it, didn't I?"

"Until this life, yes. And you like it in your coffee now, along with lots of sugar." Stowne slipped into the kitchen to get the sugar bowl and a spoon from the table, dropping three heaping teaspoons into Cent's mug and stirring. "There. Now we discuss this elephant."

"Sit down first, honey. You're pacing."

"I cannot help it. I worry." Stowne turned their rocker to face her. "Tell me why you do not care for yourself like you should."

"It's hit the point of why bother." Cent pointed to the medication bottles beside her. "I take something to sleep. Something for pain. Something for my stomach. Something for— Smoking calms me, all right? It helps with the— I'm afraid."

"What are you afraid of?" Stowne seemed genuinely puzzled.

"This ain't about dying if that's what you're thinking." She pulled the blanket higher on her chest and reached for her tea, cursing softly when her hands shook too hard to lift it without spilling it. "I'm afraid of hurting more, of leaving you with horrid memories before I go. Lung cancer is an ugly death."

"What about the radiation your doctor spoke about?"

"It'll only delay the inevitable and make me nasty-sick until then." Cent smiled when Stowne lifted the mug to her mouth. "Thank you."

"That is why I am here. Never forget that." Stowne knelt before her. "I will be here the entire time."

"You've never seen me like this."

"I have watched you die from battle wounds, from Small Pox, and countless other ways. None were attractive, but I have been there every time to walk you across the veil. This will be no different."

"But I don't want to leave you alone." She reached out to stroke Stowne's face.

"I will wait for your return, same as always."

"But this land…"

"Yes, there is that." Stowne kissed her palm. "It must be handed down correctly."

"I have been thinking about that. What about Tess and Roslyn Rhodes?"

"Sudie's daughters?"

"Yes. I saw Tess dancing with Kinnon Byrne under the last full moon, outside the circle sands. They would take good care of the property. Roslyn too, but I cannot see her future enough to know where she will land."

"Tess and Kinnon?" Cent's laugh strangled beneath a cough that left her gasping. "She's a wild doe, and he ain't much of a hunter."

"I see Kinnon in Tess' future. Opposites often make the best pairings, and until that time, she has Roslyn to help her." Stowne scooted closer. "Yes, Tess and Roslyn. They will know best how to care for it and will work with Rayne and Pyre to protect things."

"I know." Cent took Stowne's face into her hands, pulling them up to kiss them firmly on the mouth. "All right. Tess and Roslyn it is. I'll have the documents drawn up and made legal before things get worse."

"Thank you. Does this mean the elephant is gone?"

"Not gone, but it certainly shrank. Take me to bed, baby. Make love to me while I'm still able. Remind me why I'll be coming back as soon as I can."

Stowne scooped her into their arms and rose, turning toward their bed. "You are weak, so I must feed you first."

"It's sexier when you call it foreplay."

"I was thinking about feeding followed by foreplay." Stowne rumbled against her, a sweet reminder of their power. "Whatever you wish, usdayvhsgi, as often as you wish. I will be here for all that comes."

"Damn useless." Cent didn't have the strength to throw her breathing medication across the room like she wanted. Doc had come to see her, had driven all the way from Johnson City and up the muddy road leading to the homestead, just to check on her. Rayne, in their most feminine, humanlike, appropriately dressed form, had met him at the door. He'd briefly stared at Rayne, then shrugged and entered, mumbling something under his breath about Rayne being one of the Blue Kentucky Fugates.

"I want you in the hospital, Miss Washburn." He wrapped his stethoscope around his neck and shook his head.

"Ain't happenin'." Cent wheezed. "I'm stayin' home." She was propped against Stowne on the bed. They'd refused to leave, so she'd told them to look like pillows. It was improper for a single woman to have a man in her bedroom, and rumors about her ungodly nature already ran rampant in Hare Creek.

"Centenary Washburn, you're one stubborn woman." Doc glanced at Rayne who nodded. "I'd argue with you, but I've been living in these hills too long to be fool enough to argue with anyone past my own age. As long as you have someone with you, I'll let you be. I've raised your morphine again, but I can't raise it any higher."

"It don't matter anyway." Cent's breath caught in her side again, throwing her frail body into another round of coughing so hard she vomited. It was a vicious cycle, but there was nothing to do except wait for it to be over.

"Nice old place." Doc peered around the homestead. "But I wish you had better heating."

"There's a coal burner in the cellar," said Rayne. "But it's broken right now."

"And the fireplace in here…needs a new damper," mumbled Cent.

"That's why this bedroom always seems cold." Doc sighed. "I can give you the number for my repairman."

"I'll have her bed moved to the front room." Rayne took the pan from Cent's lap and wiped a damp cloth over her forehead and across her mouth. "We'll see she stays comfortable."

"I'll be fine." Cent lay back on the pillows, ready for Doc to leave so Stowne could reshape to keep her warm. "Go home, Doc. You're interruptin'…my rest."

"I'll be back the day-after-tomorrow, Miss Washburn." Doc hooked his arm through Rayne's, pulling them toward the door where he spoke in such a low tone Cent couldn't hear. Not that she cared to. Doc could say what he wanted. They all knew she wouldn't make it to his next visit. The veil would soon thin. Her mother had already come for a visit, her father too, and they'd both said they'd be waiting for her. But Mamaw… Cent had sat bolt-upright in the bed when she'd stopped by to visit.

"Signs are all around you, child, so be ready." Mamaw Jett had stood all pretty and young in her best Sunday dress, her hands folded at her waist like she always did when she was serious about something. "Have them bury you next to me beneath that big Oak at the top of the ridge."

"Next to Usdagalv?"

"Yes, child. Stowne should cross you. Rayne should tend your body and set up with it. Them and Pyre are the closest to family you got left."

"They *are* my family."

"I know. It was your turn to watch over the veil crossing. What about the homestead? Have you seen to it?

"Yes'm. Two fine neighbor girls named Tess and Roslyn Rhodes. I'm willing it to them. They'll be the next keepers."

"I remember the family. Good choice since you didn't see fit to have a child."

"Stowne and me… No children."

"Half-magic's brewing here with or without your input, but that's not your worry this life." Mamaw's form began to flicker like one of those old silent films. "Remind Stowne to cover the mirrors once you've crossed so you won't get sucked back, and remember that we'll be waitin'. Have Rayne put you in somethin' nice, cause that's what you'll be wearin' the whole time you're waitin' to begin again."

"I'll be in my overalls. Thank you much."

"You would." Mamaw's chuckle had faded with her.

———⟨◦⟩———

I can't breathe. Cent was ready for Exan, but they hadn't come. She'd been lingering for days, Stowne holding her tight while Rayne eased her pain as best they could with the morphine. Pyre had gone in search of Exan but had come back alone twice.

"They're nowhere around." Pyre's column tightened with worry.

"What about their lessers?" Stowne eased Cent's head back to help her breathe.

"I didn't find them, but I asked Gan to send one from where they're at."

"Demis?" Rayne worried their hands until they dripped.

"As long as Ganolesgi does not attempt to— No. Not Demis." Stowne tightened even more around Cent. "I sent them from this realm because they are anything but gentle." They rolled so they supported Cent from behind, craning their neck to look at her. "Please, usdayvhsgi. Let us help you begin the transition instead."

She didn't want them to feel guilty, didn't want them— It took all her strength to take her next breath. "No." She lifted her hand to touch Stowne's face. "No."

"Then I'll feed you to give you strength until we find Exan." Stowne's strength was all she could ingest now. No water. Not even broth. Nothing stayed down but Stowne's offerings. She breathed easier afterward, but they all knew it was temporary.

"I'm weakening you." She reached up to stroke their face again. "Let me go…baby. I'll go it…alone—" She took a ragged breath. "— if Exan doesn't… come soon."

"I will not let you!" Stowne's anguished roar shook the entire house. "No!"

"We should take you, all three of us, together." Rayne settled onto the bed's edge and motioned Pyre over. "Yes, we'll all go together."

But then who'll watch over my body? Someone always sat with the dead, someone… a wake, a celebration but no mourning. Sudie, Tess, Roslyn, Kinnon and a handful of neighbors would come, and Rayne would be there too, in their most Humanlike form, trying not to gush tears. But Stowne— *Please, baby, don't bury yourself this time. Come to my funeral. Let yourself mourn.* She had no strength to argue when they all surrounded her, speaking softly in turn, reminding her of their love. Afterward, Pyre retreated to the doorway, and Rayne picked up the morphine bottle, pouring five times Cent's usual amount into the dosage cup.

"Doc said this would help when you were ready." Rayne's hand trembled when they held the cup out to Stowne. "As easy as sleep, and we'll be there to help." They retreated too, leaning against Pyre so hard that steam rose between them.

"They'll be back before we know it." Pyre's color faded to a soft, flickering orange-red as they pulled Rayne's head to their shoulder.

"As easy as sleep." Stowne lifted Cent from the bed, carrying her to the front room and the huge rocker an earlier version of her had made during the 19th century. "Are you ready, usdayvhsgi?"

No. But she was, and… Cent gulped and nodded. *As easy as sleep.*

"They're always brave about it," mumbled Pyre. "Braver than any of us left behind."

"Brave enough to be reborn and return." Tears streamed from beneath Rayne's robes. "We admire you more each time."

"You are our inspiration." Stowne cuddled her before they brought the medicine cup to her lips. "I will fly beside you a final—"

"You'll not take her from me!" Demis' black-mass form flew in to knock the cup from Stowne's hand. "The great Centenary Rhodes. This one's mine!"

Their icy hands snatched Cent away from safety, from peace, from dignity, clutching her as a ghastly, yellow-toothed grin rose amid their smoke.

"She is my eternal!" Stowne reached for her, tried to pull her from Demis' heavy, dark hands but let go when Demis wrenched her away. "You would rather have her body ripped in half while she still breathes than give her to me?" Stowne stared at Demis, their shoulders rounded by defeat, their voice now pleading. "I will remember this far longer than she will be gone from this world, so let her go peacefully. Let her fall asleep and let me lead her across."

"My way is the *natural* order." Demis turned Cent up to stare into her eyes. "You'll not cheat me. You'll go as intended." They pushed their hand into her chest to capture her energy inside theirs. Jack lunged at them when they did, but Demis deflected her with a wave, sending Jack rolling with such force she didn't move afterward.

My dog! Cent tried to catch her breath, but Demis had already stolen Stowne's feeding from her, leaving her to suffocate in her own fluid. She reached for Stowne, but Demis jerked her arm down with such force that she felt the bones crack.

"Beyond cruel! Give her to me!" Stowne rushed forward with such force that their steps bent the floorboards, but Demis' lessers rose from between the gaps, gray wisps with long, slender arms that grabbed Stowne, pulling them down until they became trapped between the boards. "Centenary!" Stowne reached for her, but Demis only laughed and stepped away.

"You cruel, abysmal—" Rayne struggled when Demis' lessers covered their mouth with gray webbing.

"I should've heeded the warnings." Pyre burned through the webbing and lunged forward, but Demis' lessers used the soaked webs Rayne had removed to pull Pyre back, filling the homestead with smoke and steam.

"She's mine!" Demis wrapped Cent in their black smoke and flew from the homestead with their lessers, Rayne, Pyre, and Stowne in pursuit. "Feed me, woman. Feed me, and you may cross." They thrust their hand inside her chest again, pulling the last of her energy, her breath, her— "Where's the rest? You're so ill that there's not enough left to justify my journey here!" Demis threw her body aside, but Cent's spirit, the last bit of her existence, remained trapped in their grasp. "Go on!" They shook their hand toward the open veil, but Cent clung to them, unwilling, determined. "I said go!"

Not before I say goodbye. Cent ignored the thinning veil, launching toward Stowne and the others, but Demis pulled her back to shove her toward the veil again.

"You go, or I lose my feed!"

149

Then lose. But the veil was calling her, singing to her. She could see her family. Mom extended her hand, but Mamaw swatted at it.

Show them, girl! You've got the strength in you! Remember!

And Cent did remember, at least long enough to earn her goodbyes. She screamed a powerful spell then flew through Demis, turning back to push through them again, retaking her energy and stripping theirs away. Demis' lessers rushed forward, but Cent held them off with thoughts of shredding them one by one. *It'll take you centuries to recover.* They trembled as they fled, leaving Demis alone and shivering on the cold ground.

"You'll pay for this indiscretion." Demis crawled away, a dark fog hugging the ground until they reached the road below the property where they shot upward, fending off Rayne and Pyre's stinging energy lashes until they faded from sight.

Centenary. Stowne's call brought her to their side, and she hovered before them, pure energy in mid-fade. *I love you and will be waiting for your return.*

I don't want to go. But Mamaw was calling her to come along, and the veil was beginning to thicken.

Go so you do not become a trapped spirit for Demis to take revenge on. Stowne pointed to the crossing point. *It has grown too thick for me to walk you through. Please. Go now.*

I love you. Cent circled Stowne's head then dropped lower, pressing against their chest before she darted through the veil that kept the spirit and the living worlds separated. *I will remember…* But she was already forgetting what she'd left behind. *Mamaw. Mom. I've so much to tell you!* Cent now stood between them, and Jack turned happy circles at their feet. She didn't know where she was going, but she was with family, and they had lots of catching up to do.

Chapter Twenty-Four

Dark and Light
August 25, 2017

"**Breathe,** Cent! For fuck's sake, breathe!" Aubrey forced something hard between her clenched teeth. "Come on!"

What? Wait! Alright! All— she opened her mouth to gasp and something with an abhorrent taste coated her tongue then slid down her throat to make her cough. "What the… stop!" She pushed Aubrey away and fell sideways, finding the ground was right where she'd left it.

"Thank goodness!" Aubrey snatched her up to shove an inhaler into her mouth. "Hold your breath this time so it'll take." He clamped her jaw shut before she could object, and Tess reached down to pinch her nose closed, telling her that she had to inhale before they'd let go.

"All right!" Cent crawled away, coughing, to rest face-down on the ground. *My pants.* She pulled them up and curled in on herself, crying, shaking. Cent opened her hand to see the old ad and cigarette holder she'd been clutching. "Stowne."

"I'm here, asiule ehu. I'm here!" Stowne rose from the ground beside her, hanging over her to deliver kiss upon kiss. "You did it! Thank you! Thank you!" They kissed her more, their mouth on hers until she gasped for air again.

"Let her breathe, Stowne. You have the rest of her life to thank her." Tess rolled Cent onto her back so the morning sunlight flooded her face. "You did it! You set them free!"

"And damn near killed yourself in the process, you big twit." Aubrey smacked her upside the head with his open hand. "You owe Rayne and Pyre a whoppin' big thanks for waking us. Jack too. He wouldn't quit barking."

"Yeah, you do," said Tess. "Pyre came into my dream to say you were outside and not breathing."

"Rayne woke me the same way." Aubrey knocked Cent's shoulder with his palm. "You scared the hell out of us!"

"Do you remember?" asked Rayne. "Do you recall what you had to do to say goodbye to us the last time?"

I fought a pissed-off death elemental and won." She shivered when Stowne lifted her upright and slid behind her, hugging her to them. "That bastard, Demis, killed my dog."

"You made an enemy of them," said Stowne. "You stripped them of energy so completely that their lessers fled. And you carried enough energy with you across the veil to remember. That is rare." Their eyes softened, taking her in. "And powerful."

"Very powerful." Rayne nodded to Pyre, and they both moved toward the old house, talking low as they went.

"It means you're a witch to contend with this life," explained Tess when Cent said she didn't understand. "You have the strength of generations behind you."

"I thought elementals didn't kill." Cent peered at Tess and Aubrey in turn then at Stowne, whose earthen form had solidified back into a humanoid shape. Sun-kissed, ruddy-brown skin and a thick, dark shock of straight hair that spilled over their shoulders. *They look even better than the messenger in North Chicago.* And Dockers? Someone had remembered what she'd worn to court the day before.

"Elementals ain't supposed to kill." Tess grinned at Cent. "That was Demis' downfall. They ain't been seen nor heard from since. How 'bout Stowne takes you up to bed for some rest? I'll be up later with some breakfast for your lunch."

"And I'm coming up with my backpack to check you out when she does." Aubrey placed his fingers on her wrist. "Your pulse is high, but I think it'll calm if you don't exert yourself in that bed." He raised one brow at her.

"I ain't got the energy." She turned to Stowne. "I don't want to go back to the cellar. I loved being down there with you, but now that we don't have to— please?"

"Rayne and Pyre are making us a pallet in the larger bedroom." Stowne didn't sound disappointed. "Even earth enjoys a soft bed." They scooped her into their arms and walked up the hill, helping her into her long t-shirt as soon as they were alone.

"Take me to your chair."

"You remember sharing with me." Stowne settled into the rocker with her, kissing her temple as they sat back. "Is this what you wanted?"

"More than anything." She now recalled a good portion of her lives and everything she and Stowne had built together and fought to maintain. The good far outweighed the bad. "Are my books still in the trunk?"

"Tess has them at the trailer in a box with some other items you wanted to keep."

"The trailer?" Cent frowned. "My books need to breathe, need—"

"And they will. Quiet, please. You are weak. Reliving Demis' attack took almost as much of your energy as it did the first time." Stowne fed her as they rocked, wrapping her in a quilt when she began to doze, waking her in the bed later that morning by caressing her abdomen with their fingertips. "Centenary." Their breath spread across her shoulder, causing her skin to prickle.

"You know how to wake me up just right." Cent smiled when Stowne's mouth covered hers to transfer even more energy.

"You need me soft against you," they mumbled. "Caressing, loving…" Stowne lay atop her to slide down her body. "Tasting."

"Aubrey said—"

"He does not know how gentle I can be, and, apparently, you do not recall. So here is a reminder."

"Wait a minute." Cent peered into the bedroom's far corner. "Birdie, do you mind?"

"My house too." A self-lit orb appeared and moved toward the doorway. "You two, always kissin' and going at it like…"

Cent watched until Birdie was gone before she looked down at Stowne. "Please continue."

"My pleasure." Stowne pushed up her shirt.

Energy, Cent soon remembered, could be intertwined with their love-making. Feeding and satisfying, done right, were almost identical.

We've had more than enough time to learn this about each other. Stowne pressed against her thigh. Hot, but soft and gentle, they gave her what she appreciated best about being with a woman and let her reciprocate, sharing their favored feminine form with her. Afterward, Stowne moved their body somewhere between genders as they lay together.

"The full moon is in two days." Stowne stretched their arms toward the rafters, smiling, happy with their freedom. "And that night, I am going to dance with you beneath it."

"I don't even get asked?" Cent rolled on top of them, straddling their bare, brown form, admiring her lover's shape and the power she knew resided within it.

"I always make great ceremony of the request." Stowne placed their finger between her breasts, drawing along her ribs then down her side to trace her shape. "Ancient traditions remain where that is concerned. And it is expected of me as the land spirit."

"Now that, I don't recall." Cent raised her brows when she noticed Stowne had left smudges across her abdomen. "Will our bed always be this messy?"

"We have always preferred browns and reds to hide the inevitable stains." Stowne lay their hand on her thigh to leave a perfect brown handprint behind.

"Well, that won't keep me clean." Cent rubbed the corner of the print. "You left your mark most everywhere on me."

"I enjoy seeing myself coating your body." Stowne backtracked when she raised her brows higher. "Only where it should be. Your most sacred spaces should always remain clean."

"I dunno about clean, but—"

"Then natural and deserving of my perpetual worship." Stowne lowered their hand to stroke her thigh. "And as damp as a puddle on a stormy day."

Bad similes during playtime. What a perfectly human thing for you to be doing. "You talk dirty, too."

"I *am* dirt. Rock, soil, roots, tremors, and quakes. The hottest of magma. And *always* longing for you. I promise you as much as you wish, whenever you wish, however you wish." Stowne drew their hand up to walk their fingers across her abdomen. "You enjoy me most when I vary forms in our bed." They proved this by taking a more masculine shape that pressed into her in all the right places.

"Wow. Just— no wonder no one else seemed to be able to— the things we do…" She arched when Stowne ran their hand down her thigh. "Show me both ways, one by one then together, and after that—"

"I will have you in whatever manner I wish because you appreciate the unexpected joys that come with it." Stowne made her theirs again, wild and consuming, feeding her energy afterward so they could begin again. Pinning her. Holding her. Clutching her. Lifting her. Turning her to hold her from the front then the back. Wearing her. Worshipping. Yes, worship. That was the right word, and worshipped was exactly how Cent felt when she fell, trembling, onto the bed.

"There. What you wished." Stowne sounded proud, if not smug, about what they'd accomplished together.

"I couldn't have found the words to tell you all I wanted, so how…" She smiled when Stowne slid back on top of her, not a strand of that dark shock of hair out of place, though she felt her own hair stand on end. "You're beautiful no matter the form you take. It makes me feel undeserving."

"But you are beautiful as well. Do you not realize your own— Why does this happen every time?" Stowne rose from the bed to grab her hand, pulling her until she stood before Birdie's wardrobe. "Look." They stood behind her, their hands around her waist. "Look at yourself in the mirror. You are beautiful, Centenary. Deeply so, but every time we find each other, I must convince you again to appreciate yourself." They placed her glasses on her face and pointed to the mirror. "Look."

"You're sweet but biased and…" She turned her eyes away, embarrassed to see herself so knock-kneed, ruffled, and red-thighed. "I'm nothin' special, just a big-boned, glasses-needin' mountain girl. I got moles, a scar on my thigh from when I fell from a crabapple tree when I was ten, a wart that keeps coming back on my ankle." She lifted her arm to see the pit. "I need to shave." She dropped her arm and frowned. "And shower."

"You. Are. Beautiful." Stowne trapped her head with their hands so she couldn't turn away. "Look!"

"I don't—"

"Look!" Stowne's voice became commanding. "See past the glass to witness what we spirits do whenever you are near." They stared into the mirror too but solely at her. "You are more than flesh. More than bone. You are energy. Pure, beautiful, desirable, eternal energy."

"There ain't nothing about me pure." But as Cent stared, she saw her external layers slip away. Skin. Muscle. Bone. They fell aside to reveal the pulsating white energy that symbolized her existence. *My soul, my very spirit.* This was the part of her that existed on both sides of the veil, the part most Humans couldn't understand or remember.

This is what I make love to. This is what I crave. You hold the energy and the knowledge of the ages inside you. There are precious few like you. Your kind is sought after, hated by those who wish to possess your power, and that makes you more precious than anything rising from the earth. Magic burns strong inside you. Stowne's energy pierced hers, becoming warm hands that wrapped and held her spirit. *This is why Rayne and Pyre love you, and why I protect you with such ferocity I appear jealous. You are much more than your wrappings, just as we elementals are, and you will change your form just as readily once you remember the spells and teachings inside your books.* They turned their hands to hold her from the inside out.

More and more are returning to me. Cent placed her hands over Stowne's, squeezing them as the brilliance they stood inside faded.

Remember that for there to be light, there must be dark. Stowne's hands exited her body to hold her from the outside, rising to force her eyes open when she filled with unexplainable dread. *Balance in everything. Everything in balance.* Black mist rose from the mirror to consume her. She was a dark hole, neither alive nor dead, clinging to the mirror's interior, slipping between the glass and the silver behind it. She was Stowne's shadow on the floor, her lover's darkest thoughts and willing fulfiller of their most carnal needs. Cent laughed at this as she came to understand, knowing Stowne served the same purpose for her.

Thief in the moonless night. Taker of bloodless revenge. Mad lover when she thought she desired solitude. She now understood why Demis despised her, why she'd been able to pierce their form to retrieve her energy and why she'd stripped theirs away.

Balance. Balance.

Cent turned herself inside out to face Stowne, kissing them, tasting their dirt, their power, holding it within her and returning it because that was what eternal lovers did. Beauty came with dark too, but it should be used only when needed and then used well. Stowne was both light and dark, neutral because equal energy existed within every land spirit.

And I can be both as well, a switch on a dimmer. The lighter outside, the darker it must be within. I choose balance because I can. She raised her arms to break the dark, shattering it in her mind until only light remained. *I remember.*

You always do once I show you. Stowne still stood behind her when she opened her eyes, larger, stronger, warmer, now a shaft of white sand and dark soil that swirled together. *Your body is disposable. It holds you here for this life only. It is imperfect because life is not perfect, but there is beauty in imperfection that human eyes rarely see.* They turned her around and slid her glasses from her face to kiss her eyes. *Use your magic to better understand your true form so that you see what I do, to see what I love most about you.*

Beauty in dark. Beauty in light. Beauty in imperfection, in being different. In love. In anger. In rage. In adoration, envy, sympathy, and scorn. She saw herself now as Stowne did, in variations of dark and light and color and muscle and— "Aubrey."

"What?" Stowne's columnar form crumbled at her feet.

"He's walking up the hill with Tess. Or they will be in a moment. I smell biscuits and gravy."

"Oh." Stowne became a pillar of fine white sand that wrapped her, telling her to raise her arms above her head so they could cleanse her. "You are presentable." They cleansed the bed in the same manner while she pulled on a t-shirt and shorts.

"Back to reality." Cent glanced in the mirror before she climbed back into the bed. She was beautiful in her own unique manner. The knowledge was empowering, but such knowledge brought with it a responsibility she'd never known she had.

Chapter Twenty-Five

In the Company of Good Books
September 1, 2017

Ivan Ruleman wanted energy. That's why he wanted the homestead. At least that's what Cent had decided by her next shift at Dryler's. Okay, maybe Ruleman himself didn't want the homestead, but whatever controlled him and Mama wanted energy and power over the veil crossing, but no one knew exactly why.

She'd gotten her books back, and they were even more than she'd imagined. How they had fit in the bottom of a trunk she'd never understand because it'd take an entire bookcase to hold them. *I'll have to build one.*

We will build it together. Stowne stayed with her almost every moment she was on the homestead, and she found their ever-presence endearing, but she sometimes welcomed being alone inside her own head.

Thanks, but I don't know where to start reading. She stared down at their pallet bed where the books were spread. Beaten covers, yellow paper, and dog-eared pages. She loved them all, but where should she begin?

"Which one is calling to you?" Stowne stood beside her, rubbing their chin as they stared down at the selection. "If more than one is speaking, then which one calls to you the loudest? Which one's song do you hear above the others?"

"Are you saying that my books sing?"

"Not in the conventional sense, but yes. You have said that they do, that the one which calls to you is the one that holds exactly what you need. Bibliomancy is one of your strongest skills."

"Bibliomancy. Huh." The word didn't sound half as strange as it should. "A Bible? How'd that get in there?" It was the second largest book on the bed and the most worn of them all. The black leather cover was split and curled, the spine was broken, and the pages were tucked full of folded papers and old photographs.

"It has its place among your other texts and has long been your favored one for bibliomancy," explained Stowne when she picked it up. "Are you hearing its song?"

"More of a bookish duet, but I heard this one first." She closed her eyes and thumbed through the pages, thinking hard about what puzzled her most.

Ruleman. Who controls him? Her hand stopped on a page and her ring-finger scanned the text until she felt compelled to stop. She opened her eyes to see where she'd landed. "Matthew nineteen, verse twenty-six, 'But Jesus beheld them, and said unto them, with men this is impossible; but with God all things are possible.' Now, what does that mean?"

"We shall eventually find out." Stowne told her to close the Bible. "Do you have another question for it?"

"Yeah, I do." She shut her eyes again. *Betty. Is she okay?* Stowne's acquaintance had yet to report on her wellbeing. Cent thumbed through the text, finding a page, and pointing. "Job forty-two, verse six, 'Wherefore, I abhor myself, and repent in dust and ashes.' Oh, wow." Cent peered up at Stowne through tear-filled eyes. "I need to call her." She fished out her phone, dialing, waiting, and dialing again. "Come on, pick up."

"Perhaps she is busy with a client."

"Then I'd get her 'call you back as soon as I can' autoreply." Cent stared at her phone. "Can your spirit friend in Chicago get into her apartment?"

"If I ask, yes."

"Please do. I need to know that she's okay." Cent set her phone aside and shook her head to refocus. "I'm still hearing a song."

"That means you need to read from more than one text."

"Have you made that request?"

"Yes, but the reply will take time to arrive."

"Thank you. Let me... yes, there." She chose a small, cloth-bound book held together with worn leather cords. A prayer book, she knew the moment she touched it, and it sang so strongly that it vibrated in her hand. "What should I ask?"

"That is up to you."

"Let me think." She freed the book from its cords, and it fell open in her hands, signaling that what she needed was on the facing pages. "Who controls Ruleman and Mama?" She ran her finger over the text until it seemed to stick to the page. "'I accept the power of Earth, for the strength to know and walk my path. I accept that I must sometimes walk blind, that I sometimes must wait." The vibrations ceased, and the book flipped closed, knotting its own cords before she could do so. "Well, this one's certainly opinionated."

"Your own words written in your own hand." Stowne placed the book back among the others. "Earth prayers, my favorite of your poetic texts."

"I wonder why." Cent leaned against them. "My question about Betty aside, the answers don't make sense. One says patience, and the other says I need strength." She peered up at Stowne. "What do you think they mean?"

"Only you can interpret the meaning. It has always been that way." They kissed the top of her head and returned to the books, choosing one housed in its own wooden box. "This is your oldest text." Stowne placed the box in her arms.

"It's heavy. Help me carry it to the kitchen table."

"The weight of knowledge within it should make it even heavier." Stowne lifted the box as if it were empty, balancing it in one hand as they took her arm in their other, leading her to the kitchen table. "It is written by your hand as well but done across lifetimes, so the text changes." They brought her the solar lantern that'd been charging on the porch all day, holding it by the braided-twine handle Aubrey had put on it to make it spirit-friendly.

"It's beautiful!" She lifted the book from its case and placed it on the table. "And even more chocked full of stuff than my Bible."

"You brought this with you from Ireland. You said it and a change of clothing were all you managed to carry."

"Given the book's size, it's no wonder." She stared at the cover, at the triple-moon goddess etched across the top, wondering why she recognized the symbol when she'd never… *There're lots of things I remember though I never saw them before.*

She opened the cover, and her nose was immediately inundated by the odor of old ink, aged paper, and stale herbs, a rich mix she inhaled as if it was one of Tess' apple pies. "Hello, old friend." She thumbed through the pages, staring at the writing, at the detailed drawings. Herbs and their uses. Spells to help. Spells to— "Balance." She nodded and kept reading, noting how the language shifted from Gaelic to English to— "A typewritten page?"

"The means do not matter nearly as much as the intention you put behind the words." Stowne ran their finger along the faded paper glued to the heavy parchment. "But it hasn't aged as well as some of the pages."

"I'll have to redo it." She could feel the energy coming from each page. Dark. Light. Positive. Negative. Some books were arranged in opposites to keep an overall balance but not hers. Everything was arranged in sections she'd created. Herbs. Rites. Prayers. Recipes. Spells. The wheel of the year. There was a sizable section concerning her personal struggle with Christianity. Dark and light magic mingled within all the sections, not competing but working together to keep the Balance. "Why are there blank pages?" Cent showed Stowne one in the Herbs section.

"Your book is alive. Growing. Changing. You add and remove material each life. We have recovered it twice over the centuries and redone most of the pages." Stowne turned the page to show a carefully rendered drawing of poisonous Foxglove. "I have come to enjoy delicate artistic endeavors."

"Now that makes sense, because I can't draw a lick."

"No, that has never been among your skills, but you have many other talents." Stowne stroked the back of her hand with their finger when she closed the book. "Sometimes beautiful writing. Woodworking. This home. Sometimes you have had a talent for singing or writing poetry. Others…" Their fingertips drew up her arm to rest on her neck. "You are multitalented in every life." Stowne sent a careful pulse of energy into her that shot from her abdomen to her thighs, where it spiraled inward.

"Did you just call me good in bed?"

"Ever so whenever you learn to let go of your inhibitions." Stowne lifted her into their lap. "Aubrey and Birdie are correct. We do act like newlyweds."

"Yeah, but have we ever been married?" She twisted her finger where a ring would be on her left hand.

"Yes, but we must renew our promises every time you return."

"Interesting." *But I'm not ready for that yet.* "Do elementals marry each other?"

"No. Spirits might linger together eternally, but they do not marry each other. That is a convention of mortals."

"My body makes me mortal?"

"Any creature reliant on a fleshy form for survival is mortal." Stowne lifted her hand to kiss it. "That flesh keeps you earth-bound."

"Tell that to the astronauts on the International Space Station."

Stowne considered her for a moment, their brows furrowed. "I do not understand."

"Let me…" Cent pulled her phone from her pocket. "Crap. My phone battery's too low to show you any video." She took a moment to explain the basics of Human space exploration, that technology had rapidly changed since her last life, and that it kept moving faster.

"So now Humans not only fly in airplanes, but they fly to other worlds as well?" Stowne looked out one of the house's wavy-glass windows to see the setting sun. "Do you wish to travel to one of these worlds?"

"Don't matter," she replied. "Space travel won't be accessible to most Humans in my lifetime."

"But if it were?"

"Maybe, but only if you could go with me."

"It would be most interesting to meet a spirit or a living creature from another world."

Yeah, it would be. "I'm going to rig something up to show you a video of people on the Moon and on the International Space Station."

"Humans have visited the Moon?"

"The United States has had six manned landings."

"I wonder…" Stowne chuckled. "Mother Earth is not always happy with the Humans living on her, so I am quite certain Lady Moon is not thrilled with their presence either."

"Well, we don't live there yet. We've only visited."

"That is good." Stowne tilted their head toward where the sunlight streamed through the window. "I am confident Humans have not ventured to Lord Sun's surface."

"Too hot," Cent confirmed. "Hotter than anything on this world as far as I know."

"That does not surprise me. We should put the books beside our bed. You have enjoyed reading them across several lifetimes, and I do not expect that to change." They helped her move the books from the bed, using a kitchen bench to stack them on when Cent insisted they shouldn't rest on the floor. Stowne placed the largest book in the wooden case on the bench's center with no other books stacked upon it. They placed the Bible beside that.

"What do you do while I read?" asked Cent as they finished up. "For that matter, what do you do when I'm asleep?"

"Meditate, talk with other elementals while their human lovers sleep, listen to the radio until the stations shut down for the night. Is there still radio?"

"Yeah, but…" Cent brought her hands to her mouth. "Oh, good grief, honey, we're *so* past radio these days. I've got to get some proper technology up here for you to explore."

"Until then, I suppose I can engage in one of my favorite activities while you sleep."

"What's that?"

"Watching you."

"That's just creepy." Cent stepped away from them.

"I am teasing you." Stowne's happy laugh shook the room. "You taught me to read some two hundred years ago, and I quite enjoy the activity."

"Where're your books?" She peered around their room.

"The bunkroom held my collection during your last life, but many are still in here." Stowne tapped their forehead. "I would greatly appreciate some newer titles to pour over."

"Tess likes Zane Grey, so I'm certain I can find you some westerns down at the trailer."

"Those copies are likely mine, but they are worthy of rereading." Stowne drew her into their arms for a lingering kiss. "Are we to meet everyone on the trailer's porch this evening?"

"Yeah, Tess wants us to help her make smudges from what she harvested this morning."

"And I believe she said she would have a bean bur-rito for your dinner. What is a bur-rito?"

"Thin bread wrapped around mashed beans and cheese. All warm and soft and delicious in your mouth. It's good stuff."

"Obviously, by your hungry expression." Stowne slid their hand into hers. "We should make a smudge to burn together tomorrow night."

"You sure are focused on tomorrow."

"It is the full moon, a night filled with energy and togetherness." Stowne lifted their head toward the rising moon and smiled. "Tess is already on the trailer's porch, so we should join her."

Chapter Twenty-Six

A Quart of Good Peach Moonshine
September 6, 2017

The celebration over Cent's return paled next to the one for Stowne's. The bonfire burned high and laughter rang throughout the circle. Cent sat with Tess, who clapped and sang along with music that seemed to come from every direction at once.

"Gan's providing it to say thanks to Stowne for allowing them back in the realm." Tess held a half-pint jar out to her. "Summer's at an end, and it's a corn moon, so be careful. We ain't drinking mead this time."

"Did we use up all the pints and quarts that last run of tomatoes?" Cent's smile faded when she brought her jar to her nose to sniff. "Holy hell, this is moonshine!"

"With just enough peach added to cut the burn. Rayne and Pyre run two or three batches for me every summer up at Usdagalv." Tess grinned at her. "For ceremonial and medicinal purposes, of course."

"Aunt Tess, you're a moonshiner!" Cent took a tentative sip from her jar. "Ooh, and you're a good one."

"That's your Uncle Kinnon's recipe," she said with pride. "But it's got a whoppin' kick so mind yourself." Tess poured some of the moonshine into a chipped saucer that she sat on the stump beside her. "The Wee Fairies like it too, and it keeps them from getting too annoying on nights like this."

"Drunk fairies. Now that's something special." Cent took another sip and looked around the circle in hopes of seeing Stowne, but the flames obscured the view of them sitting on their stacked throne.

"You ain't supposed to see them until the dance," insisted Tess. "There's a bunch of ritual here tonight. I've seen it before between lesser elementals and their Human lovers but to see one of my own blood and the realm's land spirit…" She held her jar up to Cent. "Enjoy what's to come."

"It's our first dance." Cent shrugged. "It's sweet. That's all."

"That's all?" Tess spat out her mouthful of moonshine. "Did Stowne not— Didn't anyone *tell* you?" She downed the rest of her drink in a single swallow.

"Tell me what?"

"Why, it's your weddin' night! Oh, no. I was so certain someone had said something that I didn't bother to. I didn't want to make you even more nervous."

"Wedding?" *Me and Stowne?* Cent was dressed in the same ripped-knee jeans and stained t-shirt she'd been working in all day. "You're messing with me."

"No, I swear I ain't." Tess set her empty half-pint jar aside to drink directly from the quart, holding it out to Cent, who did the same. "You and Stowne. Tonight's your night. You're coming together represents the joining of our worlds. It's all about— it's symbolic. That's it." Tess wiped her mouth on the back of her hand. "But you look ready to turn tail."

I might well be. "Stowne didn't say it was a wedding, just a dance."

"For two Humans or a Human and elemental to dance together within the circle in their land spirit's presence is to be wed, and for a Human to dance *with* that land spirit, like you with Stowne…" Tess took another swallow of liquor. "Stowne's both an earth elemental and this mountain's land spirit and—"

"No one told me!" She snatched the quart jar from Tess to take three quick swallows, shivering as the moonshine scorched down her throat, landing on her stomach with a thud that set it to churning. "No one!"

"Stowne never mentioned marriage?"

"We discussed that Humans and elementals sometimes married and that elementals don't marry each other, but that's all." Cent stared into the flames, pushing questions toward Stowne on the other side.

You can't do that. Rayne's voice rang in Cent's head. *Not until after your dance.*

Why didn't any of you tell me? Cent returned to her seat with her arms crossed.

We all thought you knew, that you'd remember after doing it so many times! Rayne materialized beside Cent. "Oh, my. I'm sorry. I'm…" They disappeared again, materializing beside Pyre to speak with them.

Cent kept sipping from the quart while she watched. They both seemed as upset as Tess. *Damn.* She pulled from the quart again. *Let me think this out. I've been with Stowne for centuries. We've been married countless times, and it always seems to have worked so—* "All right. I'll take the leap." Cent took another swig to bolster her courage. "But I need to change into something nicer."

"No, you don't." Rayne materialized beside her faster than before.

"Don't do that when I'm so nervous!" Cent clutched the quart to her chest.

"Sorry. We have a surprise for you." Rayne reached for the jar. "Why don't you leave that with Tess and come with me?"

"No. I'll keep hold of it, thanks. I think I'm gonna need it." But she still passed the half-filled quart to Tess. "What surprise?" She glanced over at her great aunt, who shrugged.

"Guess you'll see."

"Come with us, Tess." Rayne held their hand out to her. "You are part of this too."

"Only if I can bring the jar along like Cent wants," said Tess. "I think we're *both* going to need it tonight."

"You perhaps, but Centenary needs a clear— Yes, certainly. Otherwise it would break what's become a tradition." Rayne pulled them close. "Off we go."

⁂

"I ain't wearing no dress." *I'm so drunk my own God-given accent irritates me.* Cent shook her head and tried to focus on what happened in front of her. Usdagalv was a limestone cavern with multiple chambers and countless formations. It was Stowne's personal art gallery, a natural, multi-chambered space, and it'd been used for— she couldn't remember how long. The fire pit was located deep enough inside that it couldn't be seen from outside, and a small fire, more for light than warmth, flickered in the center. Not Pyre, Cent soon realized, but another fire elemental, one with a soft dance to their flame. Torches burned inside too, their pulsing flames indicating that they were fire elementals, but ones still bound inside their original salamander forms.

"It's not a dress." Rayne waved their hands. "More of a— oh, see for yourself." They held up the result as soon as the lesser elementals moved away. "Wear it however you'd like."

"A flower sheet? How do I wear that?" Cent scratched her head then smiled and poked her fingers through the sheet, working open a hole large enough for her head. "Is there something I can wear for a belt?"

"Well, that ain't a dress, that's for certain." Tess sat on a bench made from a flat rock. "It's so short it shows most everything from your waist down."

"Yeah, it's short." Cent appealed to Gan, who was instructing the lesser water elementals on how to weave a vine belt. "I don't want a dress, but—"

"How about a piece under the top part that hangs down. You've done so before." Gan glanced at Rayne, who nodded.

"It won't be a skirt?" asked Cent.

"No. Wait." Rayne disappeared, returning seconds later holding a piece of old deer hide cut just the way Cent had tried to describe, complete with strings. "I recalled that this was in one of the deeper caves. You've worn it to dance before. You were younger and a man, but I don't believe that matters." They soaked the deer hide between their hands and shook it out, the leather

165

now soft enough to hang straight as they bent before Cent to tie the strings at her hips.

"Oh, for Christ's sake, take off those sneakers." Tess laughed so hard that she began hiccupping. "And the socks. They don't work with the more natural stuff you're wearing."

"My shoes are leather, and the socks are cotton-ish." But Cent didn't mind being bare-footed, so she held out her feet, one at a time, when Rayne said they'd remove her shoes for her.

"We'll put them and the rest of your clothing where you'll find them tomorrow." Rayne called the water elementals in their charge to do so, then turned back, now focused on Cent's hair. "You wear yours short so there's no need for a complicated style or— no, wait. Yes, we'll braid the longer side back and—" Rayne swept over to Gan, speaking low as they moved their hands around Gan's head.

"Yes, that would work well." Gan stood before Cent. "May I?"

"What're you gonna do to my hair?" Cent took a healthy swig from the jar. "You already blew it sidelong and—"

"Close your eyes, and I'll show you."

"I don't know if..." Cent stumbled back a pace. "That shine has a kick and a half to it."

"Sit down." Tess sat on a stump beside her, keeping the moonshine more to herself than she offered it, watching Gan work, but Cent saw nothing but a blur of hands moving over her. There was a quick brush of something against both sides of her head, and the tug of braiding followed by something being shoved into the braid.

"There." Gan clapped their hands. "Yes. That's most satisfactory. Rayne! Come see!"

"Why do I still feel air up under my longer side?" Cent raised her hand to that side of her head. "What the... where's my hair?" She was bald save for a strip to one side that'd been braided back.

"It's a very old cut, Centenary, a modified warrior's style." Rayne sounded delighted. "Stowne has always appreciated it on you."

"Is that a feather sticking out of my braid?" Her hair, or what was left of it, was braided partially back and tied off with deer hide. Beyond that, it stood up straight with a section falling to the side and the feather was tied in, hanging so it covered her ear.

"Wish I had a picture to show Aubrey." Tess gave a lopsided grin. "It ain't bad, just different than what I've seen." She motioned to Rayne, whispering in their ear.

"Yes, we were planning to do so."

166

"Planning to what?" asked Cent, but Rayne was already holding her face. "Be still, please. Gan, bring me the paint."

"I ain't wearing no makeup." Cent stomped her bare foot on the cavern's stone floor before she considered the probable result. *Good thing I'm drunk.*

"This isn't the chemically-based cosmetics some modern women wear," said Gan. "It's natural, traditional, and it'll thrill Stowne."

"All right." Cent relaxed when Rayne told her to, letting the alcohol have its way with her until she almost draped over her boulder.

"I've helped you many times on this night." Rayne stirred the clay paint pot they held. "And it's always been an honor to— no, sit straight so I— no. Tess, can you prop her up?"

"Tess can't hold herself straight, so allow me." Gan stood behind Cent to steady her. "She's going to be unable to dance."

"No more liquor for either of you!" Rayne called to her lessers, giving them a list of ingredients. "Take what's left in that jar to the homestead's porch as you go."

"I ain't that drunk!" cried Tess.

"Yes, you are," said Rayne. "You both are."

"It's too late to fix it." Cent laughed so hard she nearly fell from her perch. "We're going to hate ourselves come morning."

"Forget morning, we're going to fix the problem right now," Gan insisted. "Rayne, have your lessers bring me what they gather, and I'll do the grinding."

"Be quick with it, because Pyre says they're ready." Rayne turned with their hands on their hips to consider Cent and Tess. "What are we going to do with you two?" Moments later, Cent sat with her nearly-bald head in her hands, wishing she hadn't drank a single drop of moonshine.

"That was disgusting!"

"Bitters." Tess stuck out her tongue. "Dandelion, milk thistle, and peppermint. I made it for Kinnon now and again, and he always said it was horrid, but it never worked this fast. What else did you put in it?"

"Bitterwort, ginger-root, and a double shot of concentrated energy." Rayne handed them mugs filled with tepid water. "Drink this, then Gan is going to give you each another spoonful."

"Oh, God, do I have to?" Cent stared at her earthenware mug.

"Stowne's waiting, child." Tess turned her mug up to empty it, belching and groaning as soon as she swallowed. "I'm too old to be drinking so much. Whatever got into me?"

"Celebration." Gan softened their voice. "And nerves. Drink, Centenary. I'm ready with your next dose."

"Dang it." Cent did as she was told and opened her mouth for Gan's wooden spoon, swallowing the bitter mix before she was tempted to spit it out. "I'm sober!" The night's importance came rushing back to her. *Damn, am I ever sober.*

"I wouldn't call you sober, but maybe you'll remember things for next time." Rayne stood Cent up to tweak her outfit. "You were simply too drunk to dance like you'll need too."

"I'm not much of a dancer anyway." Cent turned when Rayne told her to. "And will this be anything like with Pyre?"

"You danced with *Pyre?*" Gan dropped the spoon but caught it in a breeze before it hit the ground, bringing it back to their hand.

"It was before Stowne woke." Rayne spoke before Cent could. "And she quickly remembered why she shouldn't." They stepped back to look Cent up and down. "Pyre was only flirting with you, Centenary. What happens tonight is much more serious."

"Are we ready?" Gan spun into the form Cent had first met them in. "Shall we, my dear?" They held their hand out to Tess.

"Why not?" Tess took Gan's hand, and they disappeared in a blast of wind.

"Are you ready?" Rayne held out their hand as all their lessers disappeared along with most of the fire elementals.

"I want to see myself first."

The remaining fire elementals mumbled between themselves and drew closer, gathering to light Cent's body from the ground up.

"I thought you might." Rayne shaped into a water pillar then a vertical puddle so still that Cent could see her reflection.

"I'm… geez. Okay, that's enough. Thanks." She turned away.

"Are you upset?" asked Rayne.

"No. I'm just not— I'm about to— what am I doing?" Cent let something between a wail and a shriek. *I'm not going to cry, not going to…* She burst into short, gasping, desperate sobs. "I look like something from *The Last of the Mohicans* crossed with a wrist corsage and—"

"Is it the hair or clothing or— No, you're genuinely frightened." Rayne wrapped Cent to absorb her tears into their form. "This has all come fast, hasn't it?"

"Two months ago, I was up in Chicago just trying to get by, and now, now…" Cent clutched Rayne by their robes. "Yeah, I'm scared. This isn't anything like I had planned for my life, wasn't— I don't know if I'm doing anything right."

"No one knows their path for certain until they've walked it." Rayne's cool hand rested on the back of Cent's neck. "But you love Stowne?"

"Yeah, that I do know. I felt it deep in me when we first met then again when my memories began returning." Complete was such a cliché, but it was true. Stowne did complete her. She'd never felt any more right living in Chicago than she had living with Mama in a second story apartment in Kingsport. She'd felt detached, separated from the earth and from herself. But with Stowne she felt, for lack of a better word, grounded, like she was part of something bigger, and she felt loved for who she was, though she still didn't know exactly *who* that might entirely be.

"What about the homestead?" Rayne leaned closer.

"Absolutely. It's part of me in ways I never thought possible." This was her land, Stowne's land, their home and responsibility, but it was so much more to so many others. "I want to fight for it, to protect the veil crossing, and—"

"Tonight is part of that protection." Rayne wrapped Cent in their arms, rocking, swaying. "You do this every time."

"What? Get cold feet?" Cent crinkled her toes against the cavern floor.

"I've heard it called that, so yes. I think it's natural for Humans facing major change." Rayne held her at arm's length. "This is your next step on your path. You found your way home. You've found Stowne, and in them, you're finding yourself."

"Yeah." Cent raised her hand to wipe her eyes but stopped when she remembered her face paint. "You and Gan made me look old Cherokee."

"You were Tsalagi when Stowne first met you. They've loved you as both male and female, so blending the two this time seemed the right thing to do."

"It is," said Cent. "I'd have died if you'd brought out a wedding dress."

"That would have been cruel considering who you are." Rayne repaired the streaks in Cent's face paint and took her by the arm. "Are we ready?"

"Are you sure I can't have another swig or two from that jar to steady myself before we go?"

"It's not here." Rayne swept her into a hug. "We all love you, and your sense of humor. And we're glad you're back. Hold on. Away we go." Things swirled, water flowed, and they landed right where they'd been, Cent standing near the bonfire, which now burned low enough she could see Stowne's eyes on her.

Chapter Twenty-Seven

First Dance on the Full Moon
September 6, 2017

This *is the first of many dances, asiule ehu.* Stowne smiled down at her. They were in the form they knew Cent found most physically appealing. Tall, broad shouldered, a hint of curve at the hip, and— They danced slowly as everything except their touch and the music seemed to disappear.

You don't have to take this form for me to love you. She stood on Stowne's feet as they moved together. *I know it takes energy to maintain.*

I've been reserving for this occasion since you freed me. Stowne turned for another pass around the fire. *But the same applies to the way you have worn your hair tonight. While I find it appealing, I love you no matter how you choose to wear it.*

Blame Rayne and Gan. It was their idea. She shivered when Stowne lifted the feather to kiss beneath the braid and just above her ear.

They know my likes well. Stowne turned again, keeping pace with the music. Dust rose around them as they moved, creating a cloud that obscured their feet. *You are mine, and I am yours. Pairing. Bonding. This is how it should always be.*

Then why is it harder each time?

I believe it keeps us from becoming lackadaisical in our drive for each other. The gods have been building us for centuries. Stowne slowed as the music changed from common to three-quarter time. *We are warriors, and together we are stronger.*

Warriors for what purpose? She stared up at Stowne, but their eyes were closed, feeling the music, feeling her against them, swaying softly as they took another turn around the bonfire.

Against whatever is coming. Stowne pulled her up to kiss her long and hard, their mouths combining as they almost slowed to a stop. *Not yet.* Stowne's hold on her tightened even more. *I heard Rayne took you to Usdagalv to prepare for this evening.*

Both Tess and me, yes. I know I've been there before, but we have a deeper tie at Usdagalv, don't we?

Indeed, we do. There were other dancers around them now. A couple of people Cent recognized from Dryler's rounded the fire with their elemental loves. Rayne danced with Gan, creating a gentle swirl of wind-blown rain that twisted around them. Tess sat in a carved stump-chair just her size, tapping along to the music, petting Jack's head, and laughing at the Wee Fairies who swayed in twos and threes above her head.

I wish Aubrey could've been here.

He is not ready, but Rayne says he is learning fast so maybe the next moon. Where has he gone? His car is not beside Tess' trailer.

He's gone back to Knoxville to get the rest of his stuff.

Yes, Rayne told me about him parting ways with his boyfriend. While I do not wish Aubrey pain, I am glad he will be joining us. He and Rayne will be good together.

Cent shook her head. *He isn't ready for that either.*

Ah, but he will be. We will soon be watching them dance like we are now.

Aubrey's like me. Can't dance a lick.

I find you to be an excellent dancer. Stowne laughed.

I'm standing on your feet.

Yes, you have done so every time we have wed. I have come to both expect and appreciate it.

You like me letting you do all the work? Cent squinted at her new spouse.

Sometimes. Other times I appreciate when you take charge, but I mostly appreciate when we work together.

The Balance.

Yes. Stowne stopped moving to lift Cent again, kissing her like before, but the joy behind the kiss… She didn't realize that the music had stopped and the dust had settled until their mouths parted. *We must finish the ceremony.*

Then get back to the homestead. Cent didn't know whether to bow or not when Stowne called all the elementals forward by their designation, so she followed Stowne's lead. Each leader stood before them. Rayne grinned at her. Pyre's flames danced merrily. Gan shared space with another air elemental whose chosen form was a perpetual swirl of leaves. Sonos. Stowne said Sonos had taken power during Gan's absence but had agreed to step aside.

Sonos moved back as Gan moved forward, bending to touch the ground when Stowne nodded to them.

Natural order. They were bowing before their leader. *Where do I fit into all this?*

You are my consort. My eternal. My partner and equal. You have their respect. Stowne returned Gan's bow and nodded to the lesser earth elemental who'd taken charge in Stowne's absence. *That is Quar.*

Quar was still trapped in gnome form, but all the other earth elementals in attendance were too. *It is difficult for my kind to find a willing Human.*

Then why did I?

You were able to see beneath my limited form even then. You saw me as I truly am. That is why I fell so madly in love with you. Stowne turned to bow to her, and she returned their bow, looking up smiling as she accepted their hand again.

"Thank you all for coming this night." Stowne's voice vibrated across the circle. "My blessings to you all." Stowne opened their hand to reveal the smudge they and Cent had made together the night before. *Pyre spent much of the day drying it.*

An extra blessing to them for doing so.

I agree. "Fire powers this blessing." Stowne lit the smudge from the bonfire. "Earth softens our path." They tossed a handful of dirt into the air so it fell through the smudge's smoke. "Wind cools our backs." Stowne fanned the smudge so it burned brighter. "Water eases our way." They dipped their fingers into the water bowl beside their stack-stone throne, flicking their fingers so the smudge steamed.

> *Light the way*
> *Soften our path*
> *Cool our journey*
> *Ease the way*
> *We ask of thee, Mother and Father.*

Cent found herself reciting the prayer with everyone else in attendance.

"And you, Centenary." Stowne dropped to their knees to kiss her feet. "A special blessing for you this night and every night hereafter." They smudged her from her toes upward, repeating a version of the prayer in Tsalagi as they rose.

> *You light my way*
> *You soften my path*
> *You cool my journey*
> *You ease my way*

"I thank Mother and Father for you each day we are together and plead for your return every day you are not beside me.

"Bless you, Centenary. Bless you for choosing to be mine again, for coming back to me so we can continue."

What do I— I remember. Cent pressed against Stowne, kissing their smiling mouth as she took the smudge from their hand. She knelt at Stowne's feet, kissing them, rising slowly as she swung the smudge before them.

We light our way together
We soften our common path
We cool each other on our journey
Togetherness eases the way
I thank God for you each day
And can hardly wait for my return
I am yours. I walk beside you
Through rising flame
Through thickening earth
Through howling wind
Through raging water
Two become one tonight again
Because together we are stronger

She raised the smudge to the top of Stowne's head, completing the blessing. "I love you, you big hunk of rock."

"And I love you as well." Stowne placed their hand over hers, and together they tossed the smudge into the fire, letting the sage bless the entire circle. "The ceremony is finished." Stowne leaned down to kiss her cheek. "You should tell Tess goodbye for tonight."

"Should we say something to everyone else?"

"I will." Stowne turned to the crowd. "Please, carry on for as long as you wish without us."

The crowd of elementals and Humans cheered as Cent rushed to Tess, hugging her tight. "Thank you! Thank you!"

"Thank you for coming home, for embracing who you truly are." Tess smiled as she pushed Cent back. "Go on, child. This is your night. Enjoy it."

"Come, Centenary." Stowne took her hand when she stepped back. "It is time for us to go home. Hold on tight." The air around them swirled much like it had when Rayne transported her. *Close your eyes!* The swirling air filled with churning dust. Stowne pressed against her until the movement stopped and the dust settled.

"Achoo!" Cent covered her nose with her arm before the next sneeze happened. "Dang it, I—" She sneezed twice more. "Now, dammit."

"You are apparently more sensitive to my stirrings this life, so I will do my best to keep them to a minimum." Stowne chuckled when she sneezed again. "Welcome to your second home and my first."

"Thank you, I—" Cent stared between sniffles, trying to take it all in, but there was so much! What she'd seen of Usdagalv with Rayne had been only the beginning. "What are…" She blinked twice when three gnomes ran across the space, one of them carrying a canvas backpack she recognized. "That's—"

"Your bag. Inside is a quart jar of water and a peanut butter sandwich for you," said Stowne as the gnome placed her bag on a stone table flanked by two wooden chairs. "Tess packed it. I thought you might be hungry later, especially since you have been drinking."

"Is it that apparent?"

"You are tipsy."

"I *was* flat-out drunk, but Rayne and Gan undid most of it before I made my appearance."

"I must remember to thank them for intervening." Stowne called to the lesser earth elementals in the space, thanking them for their hard work. "You may leave us now and join the celebration."

They winked out of the room one at a time until only a gnome taller than the others remained. "Your table and bed are ready, Stowne. Prepared just as you directed."

"Thank you for heading the project, Ori." Stowne gripped Ori's hand in theirs. "Meet my Centenary this time around."

"Charmed." Ori's grin spanned their bearded face. "She knows just what you like by the look of her."

"Now, Ori. We have discussed that tongue of yours."

"I'm teasing." Ori twisted the end of their white beard around a finger. "You know this. I've been around you, what is it? Five, six hundred thousand years?"

"Twelve if it is a day."

"You don't have any siblings do you, Centenary?" Ori extended their hand to her. "One who, say, prefers old and gray and…"

Twelve hundred— that's over a million years! No, they're kidding around. "Only child, sorry." She squeezed Ori's hand, revelling in how different in texture it was from Stowne's.

"Should I tell your Roc you asked such a question?" Stowne crossed their arms over their chest to drum their fingers on their bicep.

"Please don't. You know I'm joking, but Roc— they're jealous of such suggestions even when I make them in jest." Ori bowed deeply before them. "Ever at your service, Stowne. Yours too, Centenary. Welcome home."

"Please call me Cent, and didn't I see you at my first circle?" She laughed, happy that her eternal had such a caring friend of their own kind.

"Yes, you did. I was talking to Tess. And might I call you Cent?" Ori's grin returned when Stowne nodded. "I'm delighted to do so. Again, if you should need me—"

"We are well equipped, I am certain of that." Stowne motioned Ori toward the entrance. "Good night."

"Same to you both. Especially you, Cent, though I know it will be." Ori's laugh followed them out.

"They're a card." Cent pulled the feather from her hair. "Are those the solar lanterns from the porch?"

"Two are, but the other four are gifts." Stowne pulled her close to nuzzle beneath her braid again. "Some of our Human helpers make technology useful to us like Aubrey has the lanterns at the homestead." They held out a warm, damp cloth. "For your face."

"Thank you." Cent scrubbed off her face paint as she peered around the cave. "This place is smaller than the one I was in before, almost cozy. And not one bit damp either." She flexed her toes. "Is the floor heated?"

"Geothermal energy. Fire still runs deep here." Stowne ran their fingers through her hair to loosen the braid. "Let me help you with what's left." They took the cloth from her, scrubbed at her face, then tossed the cloth aside to lift her hair, kissing beneath it as they whispered Tsalagi promises into her ear.

Cent shivered and turned to see Stowne, her face tensed with concern she couldn't mask. "You're really something special down here, aren't you?"

"As much as your memories have returned, apparently there are some wider concepts you have not fully recovered." They held her at arm's length, their hands wrapping her shoulders. "I am who I have been since I emerged from the ground when this mountain was born. I am as old as it is."

"Oh, dear gods!" Cent backed from Stowne to stare at them. "You've been here this long, and *I'm* the one you want? The one you— I just married eternity itself!" But she couldn't, wouldn't deny what she felt, so she returned to Stowne's side, shaking within their hold.

"I am but a minuscule portion of the Earth and one of a long line of siblings that make this mountain chain." Stowne lifted her head until their eyes met. "My full name is Agayvli Itseiyusdi Nvya Odalv."

"We're on Embreeville Mountain." *Or inside it, I think.*

"Yes, those are both geographical names." They bent to kiss her nose. "My sibling, Ayoli Invigati Saquu Odalv, said their eternal reacts much the same every time they return, and they have been together for nearly as long as we have."

"Ayoli Invigati Saquu Odalv." Cent smirked. "Your sibling is named Young Tall One Mountain? Interesting. Which mountain does Ayoli Invigati Saquu Odalv protect?"

"You call it Mount Mitchell."

"That's the biggest mountain anywhere around— the tallest in the entire Appalachian range!" This made her laugh. "Now the name makes sense."

"They are younger and more than twice my size." Stowne ran their finger beneath the edge of her flower shirt. "This is not a discussion I wished to delve into at present."

"See what happens when I'm sober on our wedding night?" Cent placed her head on their chest. "Give me the short version then I want to…" She wrapped her leg around theirs and pressed into their hip.

"If I did not I certainly do now." Stowne removed her shirt, untied the deer hide from her hips but left the vine belt, grasping it as they led her to a boulder that'd been carefully carved to fit a Human shape and lined with soft padding like her seat at the circle. "Like you, I have an energy form and a physical form. I can manipulate my energy into what you see before you, but we are within my physical form."

"You're truly this mountain?" Cent raised her hand to her mouth. "And your given name is Agay-yvli It-itseiyusdi Nvy-a Odalv?"

"Old Green Stone Mountain." Stowne smiled at her. "Yes, that is my name, Centenary Irene Rhodes, but unlike your name, mine is so difficult to pronounce that even you are having trouble saying it. I go by Stowne because it is easier to pronounce. You added a W to the English spelling during your last life to make it more visually appealing."

"Does your sibling have a shortened name?"

"Their eternal calls them Younger."

"That works, but…" Her head swam with the importance of everything she now remembered. "Dear Lord. I thought your saying you were the mountain was a metaphor!" Her eyes widened when Stowne pushed her legs apart and dropped to the floor between them. "The you I see is this mountain's spirit, its soul?"

"It is." Stowne grasped her hips and pulled her forward then up until her legs draped over their shoulders. "No more discussion. You are my temple this night, and I am exceptionally physical in my offerings."

I married and am now being worshipped by a four-hundred-million-year-old god. Cent became lost in the knowledge, within Stowne, but knew her own power had somehow earned Stowne's respect and adoration. It was lifetimes of magic, lifetimes of— *trust. I love them eternally.*

One never asks anything from a witch without offering something valuable in return. News, food, herbs, and sex were all acceptable offerings, but Cent preferred the last, though only where Stowne was concerned.

Chapter Twenty-Eight

Four Corners of the Realm
September 7, 2017

"**Is** it morning already?" Cent woke to Stowne's kisses on her shoulder.

"Not quite." Stowne rolled her onto her back to straddle her, their body glowing soft reds and whites whose light spilled across her. "As much pleasure as we have shared, I still ache for you in a way I cannot find here." They shushed her questions with their finger. "Do you trust me?"

"Of course, but—"

"Close your eyes when I say and do not open them again until I say you should." They lowered to kiss her mouth, balancing on two hands while others stretched from them to push back her blanket and caress her. Those come-and-go appendages were easily the most disquieting part of having an elemental lover, but she was becoming accustomed to them. "You are exactly as I remembered, as I hoped, as I needed." The light emanating from Stowne intensified, pulsing with her increasing heartbeat. "I am going to show you the entirety of our realm. Four corners. Four directions. The four endpoints of my physical existence. This will seal our bond for this life and will keep others from doubting or intruding on what is rightfully ours."

"There are some in doubt?" Cent wrapped her arms around Stowne's neck, pulling them in for another kiss. "No. Not possible. You and me, we're—"

"Bound by magic to share the great rite in our truest forms in every corner of our realm." Stowne wrapped their mouth around hers. *Bound by magic.* Their eyes drew her in as they kissed, and they pressed their tongue hard into her mouth until she groaned. Bound. Gripping. *I will not hurt you, but you must trust me and obey my every word without hesitation.*

You're frightening me. But she'd been here before, bound, limited in Stowne's world just as they were in hers. This was part of the process, part of what made it work. When they shared the great rite before dawn they strengthened everything including their realm's borders and each other. She relaxed as Stowne raised their head to stare at her with dark, consuming eyes. *I understand now. I remember.*

Then say yes.

Yes.

This is how we begin. Stowne turned her, one hand cupping her breast as the other gripped her where her hip and leg joined. A new appendage grabbed her by the belt, as warm as flesh against her front, a part of Stowne she couldn't understand that supported her as other tentacle-like projections locked her hard against Stowne's form. *We are going to travel. I cannot effectively explain the means, but trust that we are going to do so. I will tell you to open your eyes after we reach our first destination. Nod to show me your understanding.* As soon as Cent nodded, a projection wrapped around her forehead, holding it firm as another stretched over her mouth. *Close your eyes.* Cent heard the ground tear and felt Stowne drag her inside the opening. She could barely breathe, couldn't—

What choice have I made in this? They landed with a such force it vibrated through her body.

Open your eyes. She could see nothing outside Stowne's glow, but she felt their form change, becoming something greater and eternally stronger. This Stowne represented power, energy, and they clutched her hard against them, declaring their ownership of her with a roar that shook the void they stood within. No opening. No outlet. No escape. Cent tried to scream, but Stowne hushed her by tightening the projection over her mouth.

Calm, Centenary. I was restating our bond to the ages, an ancient custom. This is the northern corner of our realm. It is where I was created from the love between Mother Earth and Father Eternity. It is where my physical form came into being, and this is how the conception took place. Stowne made love to her, as rough and taking as it was giving and considerate.

So much. So much. She was drenched in sweat and nearly smothered when it ended but fulfilled in a way she hadn't anticipated. Together, they were something greater. *Get us out of here, please. There isn't much air.*

Stowne tilted her head back, breathing into her mouth until the pain in her chest eased. *Close your eyes again.* The ground parted to their right as they sped that direction, Stowne's body so warm against her that the sweat evaporated. *Open your eyes.* This space glowed from Stowne's energy, revealing a cave filled with yellow crystals.

A geode.

Yes. Citrine. This sets at the eastern corner of our realm. It is a space of solitude, of sacred reflection. It is where I gestated into awareness while listening to the wind blow. Stowne declared their ownership then made love to her again, slow and rhythmic and as restrained as a gentle breeze until she begged them not to be. They then turned her so they faced, still holding her bound, her middle to their mouth to pleasure her, a hurricane of energy she thrashed inside until she shattered into a million pieces that would have blown away if Stowne hadn't held her together and turned her upright.

Close your eyes.

Cent did so without hesitation, clenching them tight when the heat between them became burning cold. Being so deep in the earth and so cold at once didn't make sense, didn't...

This is the southern border of our realm. It is where I learned that suffering is part of existence. Cold heat. The fire of renewal. Without suffering there would be nothing to celebrate. Stowne's declaration hung in the air as fog, becoming ice that fell at their feet. Their lovemaking stung, a thousand tiny bees that swelled her until she felt almost nothing, but the cold soon took that swelling away, leaving Stowne frozen against her until she pled for warmth.

I am with you. They were a single ice block that began thawing when Stowne reached through her, warming her with their magic, their heat hers as they combined, melting as one across the ice, flowing over, under, and through each other. Grinding like glaciers over the frozen ground until it thawed, dried, and burst into flames.

Suffering to celebration, and they celebrated together, cold and ice becoming fire and heat. To burn, to be so wildly impassioned, meant life.

Close your eyes one more time. This time they landed beneath water, and Stowne's declaration rose as bubbles from their mouth. Stowne pulled her up, their mouth over hers as they sank. *Open your eyes.* Cent managed to open them despite the increasing pressure, finding Stowne staring into her as they breathed together. *This is the western corner of our realm. It is where I was cleansed before I rose from beneath Mother Earth to begin my existence. It is now where you are cleansed too.* They continued to sink, clenched together, Cent dependent, aware, and relaxed, knowing Stowne would be there, knowing nothing besides their love and interconnectedness. Stowne made love to her there as well, loving her mind, caressing her insides, worshipping her past forms alongside her current one. *Witches follow nature, and I follow you.* Stowne's hold on her loosened, but their mouth stayed clamped around hers until they broke the water's surface. They pulled her from the water to rest beside her, watching with her as the sun rose at their feet.

We're not where we were when we entered the water. "Is this Rayne's pool behind the blackberry cane?" Cent wriggled her toes to say hello to the day.

"It is." Stowne flicked their hand and two perfectly round limestone pebbles, glistening white, landed against her side. "These will serve as your memory for this lifetime. I love you. Welcome home."

"I love you too and— What's that noise?" She raised her head from the soft moss to listen. "Heavy equipment! They're back!" Cent grabbed the white pebbles and crawled to the thicket's edge, staring out. "Son of a—"

"They're destroying my mountain!" Stowne tore aside the berry cane to stand in the sunshine as Cent scrambled to stand beside them, both naked and soaking wet. Stowne's form changed to show clothing as they wrapped around Cent.

"It's about time you two showed!" Aubrey called to them from the homestead's back porch. "You need to quit playing Adam and Eve, Amy and Eva, Rock-Paper-Scissors, or whatever it is you've been doin'. We got big trouble!"

Chapter Twenty-Nine

Devil on the Fence
September 7, 2017

Ivan Ruleman walked along the property's edge, spreading something along the fence line as he repeated fractured scripture in his loudest fire-and-brimstone voice. "A witch should not be allowed to breathe!"

"Exodus twenty-two, verse seventeen." Tess curled her upper lip then breathed deep. "He ain't even saying it right." She walked along the fence opposite Ruleman, matching his hateful words with peaceful quotes from the New Testament. "First Peter three, verse eleven. 'Let him eschew evil, and do good; let him seek peace, and ensue it.' Proverbs twelve, verse twenty. 'Deceit is in the heart of them that imagine evil: but to the counselors of peace is joy.'"

"Any fool can speak the words." Ruleman turned to face her as he reached into his pocket and pulled out another handful of salt. "You pervert the meaning and twist it into lies."

"No, Mister Ruleman, that'd be you." Tess raised her hand to deflect the salt he flicked at her face. "You'll not harm my land. You'll not harm my family. You'll not harm what's right and good." She raised her hand in a hex sign. "You shall suffer for your—"

"Get back, old woman!" Ruleman resumed his walk up the hillside, his book closed and to his chest. "I know the word and the word—"

"You ain't fooling no one. That ain't no Bible you're holding. It's an old Sears catalog wrapped inside the good book's cover." She motioned for Cent to join her along the fence line. "He don't like witches none, child. Whatever are we gonna do about it?"

"Why, nothing." Cent kicked the salt aside the moment it hit the ground. "Touching black salt don't harm the living, so why're you wearing gloves?" She peered down the hill as dark smoke gathered above Ruleman's helpers. "Are you afraid of something?"

"It's to bind and imprison your evil assistants." Ruleman flung salt at her too. "Begone, faggot witch. Your mother has seen the error of her loose ways and is devoted to our Lord and Savior."

"Mama's not right, just like you." Cent flicked bits of salt from her arm, tossing it over her left shoulder for luck, amused when Ruleman rubbed his eyes like something was in them. "Begone, dark spirit!" She glanced down the hill to see where Mama stood among Ruleman's followers, but the smoke she thought she'd seen earlier had grown into a dark mass that moved among them, twisting, undulating. It reared up every time Ruleman lifted his hand. "I see his puppeteer," she whispered to Tess.

"I see them too." Tess lifted her hand, walking her fingers at a downward angle away from her body. "Help me. They're too strong for me to fend off alone."

"Help us!" She peered up at the homestead porch where Stowne and Rayne stood watching. Pyre and Gan were outside the fence, disabling the heavy equipment one piece at a time.

"They can stop the equipment, but they can't do nothin' to stop Ruleman. That's for us to do." Tess lagged behind Ruleman to speak low to Cent. "Black salt will bind Gan and Pyre outside the property if he finishes. We have to stop him."

"Yes'm, I'll help you walk him all the way home." Cent moved her fingers like her great aunt's. The simple motion took tremendous effort but, after a moment, Ruleman turned and walked down the hill.

"Tell your followers to get in their cars and go home." Tess' fingers slowed. "The energy… it's…"

"Let me finish." Cent found she could push harder without Tess' energy mixing with hers, and she all but shoved Ruleman from the property. *I can do this, but I can't help Mama yet.* "Go with him, Mama. I'll come for you soon. I promise."

"Don't make promises you can't keep." Ruleman's voice rang up the hillside as he motioned to his followers. "Get in the car, Nida." He lowered his voice but not so much that Cent couldn't hear. "We need to discuss your daughter."

"But I…" Mama stared up the hill, and Cent thought she saw tears in her eyes. "Yes, Ivan." She marched to the black Cadillac Escalade, sitting in the back seat when one of Ruleman's cronies held open the door.

The black mass hovered above them the entire time, so thick it darkened the ground where Ruleman walked. He paused long enough to dump the black salt from his pocket and climbed into the Escalade's driver's seat, tearing off his gloves to hold his hand out the window, the index and pinky fingers of his right hand extended while the others folded in, palm-down. Cent couldn't hear his words, but she felt an energy shift as a piece of the dark mass broke off, taking residence at the end of the driveway.

"He's trying to curse us, but it's not powerful enough to pass our wards." Tess raised her hand, but it tremored so hard she had to lower it. "You'll have to get rid of it before it causes chaos somewhere else. Do you recall how?"

"I think so." Cent balled her energy and pushed it toward the smaller mass. "I command you not to return. I command you to leave. You will dissipate and leave us free. Because I say, so it will be." The smaller mass immediately absorbed back into the larger one, which screamed in a high pitch and flew away. Ruleman and his followers left soon after, taking Mama with them.

"What just happened?" Aubrey dashed from the porch to support Tess, who leaned heavily on his arm.

"The fool tried to curse us, but Cent deflected it."

"She did *what*?" Aubrey peered up at Cent. "Are those my sweatpants and t-shirt?"

"It's the first thing I found." She held out the shirt to better see it. "A rainbow unicorn? Seriously?" She was too tired to say something more smart-assy. "Good grief, that fight took a lot out of me."

"Me too, but we've got to clear the black salt and reset the wards this evening." Tess pointed down the hill to where the equipment operators were climbing into their trucks. "Seems they're leaving."

"How much could they see?" asked Aubrey. "I saw Ruleman walking, and you, and Cent on the other side of the fence, and all the other people, even Aunt Nida, but what was with that dark cloud?"

"You ain't got magic in you, Aub, but you got a good eye." Tess hugged his arm. "I'll explain inside. Make me some catmint tea, will you?"

"Yeah, sure. Are you coming, Cent?"

"No, I'm going up to the house to rest." She glanced up the hill to see Stowne motioning to her. "I need fed."

"If I didn't know better I'd say that's code for sex." Aubrey glanced up the hill to see Rayne decked in a pastel blue shirt and what looked like jeans. "They sure look nice today."

"They're learning what you like." Cent chuckled at his puzzled expression. "You take good care of Tess down there."

"You know I will." Aubrey glanced at Rayne again, smiling as he turned with Tess.

Come along, Centenary. Stowne motioned to her again. *You need more than a feeding after that.*

Like what? But she heard nothing enticing in their tone.

Walk with me. Stowne met her at the bottom step. "You need to be cleansed again. That black salt will blister your skin." They lifted her arms so she could see the welts rising on them.

"Why'd it hurt me if it doesn't hurt the living?" Cent pulled back her arm. "It's the quarter-magic, isn't it?"

"It is." Stowne tried to pull her closer, but she swatted their hand away.

"Don't touch me until we know it's all gone."

"I'll bring you up some fresh clothing," called Rayne. "Do you want anything special?"

"My overall shorts and a tank top. Thank you!" Cent walked up the hill beside Stowne, knocking their sympathetic hand aside twice before they reached the springhead where she'd awakened only two hours earlier. "This is starting to hurt."

"A curse is meant to hurt."

"He tried to curse us after the salt happened."

"Evil uses black salt to curse, not protect." Stowne spun her around. "This entity is old and powerful."

"So are we." Cent peeled off her shirt before she even reached the thicket but was thankful to see Stowne had cleared away most of the cane in their earlier haste. *Just as well. We've got more than enough blackberries in the freezer.* But it'd take years for the cane to grow back.

"Strip and submerge." Stowne stood behind her. "I'll join you when Rayne arrives." They watched her undress with more than casual interest, audibly admiring her shape.

"I can't say that I'm in the mood to hear it right now." Cent slipped into the pool, shivering as she submerged to her shoulders. It felt good, but— "Cold!" *Why didn't I feel it earlier?*

"Your head too." Rayne materialized at the pool's edge, holding clothing and a handful of fresh rosemary sprigs. "Clean it all." They tossed the rosemary into the pool as soon as Cent submerged, and the water began to bubble. Not hotter or colder than it'd been but…

Cent floated to the surface when the bubbling ceased. "That's better." She slipped off her underwear and tossed them out of the water, stopping to quickly examine her arm before she dropped it into the water again. "Ill intent."

"He was testing the strength of your magic," said Rayne. "I think I'll join you."

"Won't the salt hurt you?"

"Not after the rosemary, and you need more than Stowne feeding you to recover enough to reset the property protections tonight." Rayne peered over to Stowne, who nodded.

"Help me help her." Stowne slid into the water to press against Cent. "Join us." They extended their hand to Rayne.

"What?" Cent stared as Rayne joined them in the water. "Feeding is so intimate, so…"

"I've fed you thousands of times, Centenary." Rayne pressed against her other side. "First when you were mine and later alongside Stowne when you needed a quick recovery." Rayne kissed her cheek then leaned over to kiss Stowne's. "I've been Stowne's too, long before you came to this realm, but we were only together for a few centuries."

"Should I be worried?" Cent nearly melted within the comfort they offered.

"Hardly," said Stowne. "We did not part on the best of terms, and it took another century afterward before I would let Rayne return to my realm."

"Wow." They both held her now, offering her energy, helping her heal. Rayne pulled one of the rosemary sprigs from the water to place it over Cent's worst blister. "This is going to put me to sleep."

"It is supposed to." Stowne stretched their arm behind her head to support it. "We have you, Centenary. You are loved and safe and—"

"Stowne?"

"Yes?" Their hold on her tightened.

"Did your friend check on Betty?"

"Shh, *asiule ehu*. Later."

"No, now."

Stowne sighed. "Yes, I heard just before I brought you up here. Betty is in the hospital. My acquaintance found her unconscious in her apartment and contacted a Human friend who called for help. It was an… I do not remember…"

"She overdosed." Cent tried to crawl from the pool. "I need to call her, need to…" She slid back into the water to knock her forehead against Stowne's shoulder. "Dammit! Betty! What the hell?"

"She's going to undo the healing waters if she doesn't calm down," said Rayne.

"You need to care for yourself first." Stowne pulled her back into the water when she tried to crawl out again. "Stay here."

"Goddammit! I gotta call her."

"Not right now." Stowne held her tight. "Stay here. Be calm. Relax. Heal."

"But…" She drew her head up to stare at Stowne when Rayne entered her mind alongside them, pushing away her worry. *You're both jackasses for doing this.*

Betty will recover, but you will not unless you take care of yourself. Stowne shushed her before she could reply, taking parts of her energy until she sagged between them.

You can be a better friend if you're well. Rayne took a share of her energy too. *We will return it as you sleep.*

I can't believe…you did this. Cent fought to keep her eyes open.

You can be angry at us later. Stowne and Rayne worked together, cradling and comforting but reserved in their refeeding, and it was soon enough to render her unconscious.

Chapter Thirty

Devil in a Big Black Truck
September 8, 2017

Clank! Cent woke to the sound of metal striking metal. Pain came with the sound, and she grabbed her head, curling into herself and moaning low. *Not right. Not right.*

"Centenary?" Stowne sat up beside her, touching her shoulder to roll her onto her back. "What is—"

Clank! While this noise didn't cause her pain, she could feel the ill intent behind it. "Aunt Tess!" Cent crawled from the bed, trying to stand, but she grabbed her head and dropped to her knees before Stowne could catch her, rolling to her side on the floor to pull her knees to her chest.

"What is happening?" Stowne went to the window when a vehicle peeled out of the driveway. "Who owns a black pickup truck? Jack is chasing it down the road."

"No one I know." Her voice rattled in her head so hard she moved back to all fours to vomit on the floor.

Stowne pulled her from the spot before she fell into it and cradled her against their body, moving slowly and carefully to the bed where they placed her, setting the night bucket beside her before they stepped back. "What can I do?"

"Can you check on Tess for me, please?" She pulled her pillow over her head and moaned, trying to interpret the similar pain she felt rising from the trailer. *What's it mean?*

"I do not want to leave you." Stowne contacted Rayne who flew down the hill and called for Aubrey outside the trailer until he came to the back door. "Yes, she is ill as well."

"This doesn't feel like a bug or food poisoning. Does Aubrey know what it is?'

"No, he does not." Stowne returned to her side to stroke her head.

"Don't. Please. It makes things worse." She rolled into Stowne as soon as she felt able, her head to their chest, listening as they mumbled healing and protection prayers over her. *You're being so damn tender right now that I can almost forgive you for yesterday.*

I do apologize, but I will do it again if necessary. This morning would be infinitely worse for you if Rayne and I had allowed you to undo the healing waters. Stowne lay beside her, still and silent until Rayne entered the bedroom, wringing their hands like a sopping dishrag.

"Pyre's helping Aubrey bring Tess up here." They levitated a bundle of fresh sage before them that they tossed into the front room's fireplace. "There is something dark afoot."

"We all feel it." Stowne sat up beside Cent. "I am going to lift you, asiule ehu, and Rayne is going to move our sleeping pallet to the front room, so you and Tess can share until we make a second one."

Cent grumbled when Stowne moved her and glared at Rayne as they entered the bedroom.

"Are you still mad at me?" Rayne cocked one brow when Cent nodded. "You're just like Stowne in that regard, always holding onto your anger longer than you should. I suppose I should be accustomed to it."

"Huh." *Good thing I'm too sick to say what I really want.* But Cent supposed she should let go of her rage. Stowne was right. She'd be worse if they hadn't calmed her before she undid the healing waters.

"She and Tess should stay together until we know what's going on." Rayne grabbed the bedding, dragging it into the front room. "Pyre's bringing smudges."

"I brought my bag up with me." Aubrey carried a bundle of blankets and his backpack into the house. "Tess wants me to get all her magical doings too." Pyre followed him in, carrying Tess, who was curled much like Cent. "Put her on the bed."

"Two at once, same pain." Pyre deposited Tess on the bedding and lingered to stroke her face. "She's crying."

"I ain't." Tess rolled to face Cent, and their eyes met, sharing their pain. "You okay, child?"

"No, but you aren't neither, so we'll lie here miserable together."

"Seems we ain't got no choice."

"You two hush and try to sleep." Aubrey turned toward the front door. "Any of you non-Humans know what's going on?"

"No." Stowne stared out the door. "I heard the thuds and saw a black truck driving away."

"Black truck. That's a start," said Aubrey.

"It is." Stowne followed Aubrey to the porch, where they stood talking, but Cent couldn't hear them, so she watched Pyre dry then burn the sage in the fireplace and light a dried bundle that they fanned until it smoldered.

"Some of last summer's," mumbled Tess. "Morning of a full moon, so it's strong. I put sprigs of lavender and rosemary in the middle of each one too."

"Hush, Tess. Please, rest." Pyre stood over them, using a gentle wave of heat to fan the smoke across them. "Peaceful thoughts. Peaceful rest." They moved around the house then walked outside and had smudged the entire perimeter by the time Stowne and Aubrey returned carrying boxes of supplies.

"Stowne gave me some ideas, but I need to go shopping for a few things." Aubrey dropped his box inside the doorway. "Anything I can get our invalids while I'm out?"

"Chicken noodle soup," mumbled Tess.

"I brought three cans up from the trailer," said Aubrey. "But I'll make a homemade pot tonight over the fire."

"Since when have you been any good at cooking over an open flame?" Cent squinted at him.

"I've been camping and was an Eagle Scout too if you recall." His expression turned sour. "But that was before the organization became so— water under the bridge. I'll be back."

"I'd go with you if Gan were here." Rayne batted their eyes at Aubrey. "But they're meeting with this realm's other air elementals and—"

"We're finished." Gan burst through the door and spun to the pallet where they hovered beside Tess with an anguished expression half-hidden by their swinging hair. "What has happened?"

"Some sort of dark attack." Rayne caught Aubrey by the arm when he turned toward the kitchen. "I'd like to go with you."

"But you're an— Okay, but how?"

"I can ride in your car if you place a natural material in the seat."

"You can do that?" Aubrey dug two mugs from his box and set them on the mantle, pouring water from a bottle into each.

"I can. Concrete, metal, stone, and brick contain natural ingredients, but I do have issues with some of the modern floorings. Tess gave me shoes constructed of natural materials so I don't touch them."

"Solid leather huaraches with natural rubber soles," explained Tess. "I've been meaning to take Rayne out in them for a while."

"Won't someone see you?" asked Aubrey.

"We can be seen if we choose to, and if I go out with you, I will be choosing to. But I need you to carry a natural material container so I have a place to retreat to if I run into a problem."

"I've got an empty metal boot-flask in my glove box." Aubrey scratched his head and grinned. "I can slide it into my sock. Would that work?"

"Rinse it out, leave the top off, and take Rayne shopping with you." Cent's voice still echoed in her head. "There's some money in my cargo pants hanging in Birdie's wardrobe."

"Ethan and I divided the bank account equally when I left K-Town." Aubrey's smile faded a little. "The man's good at business, so money ain't an issue right now."

"Lucky you." Cent closed her eyes as the morning sun stretched toward the bed.

"Guess I have been really lucky in that regard." Aubrey scratched the floor with the toe of his shoe. "Where's the paperwork for your hearing tomorrow? I'll go see if I can get the date changed."

"You can't do that. I'd have to be in the hospital and—"

"It's worth a shot." He shrugged. "So, where is it?"

"On top of my books in the bedroom."

"I will get it for you." Stowne returned a few seconds later with the entire stack of papers. "This weighs heavily on her."

"I know." Aubrey tucked the papers into his back pocket and took Rayne by the arm. "You remember those jeans and shirt you were wearin' yesterday?"

"I do." A smile stretched across Rayne's face. "Would you like me to wear them again?"

"Yeah, they looked nice. And we'll work on pinking up your skin-tone a bit along the way so you can pass."

"Don't use that term." Cent would have screamed at him if she'd been able. Passing. Making yourself fit into someone else's box. Cent had found out the hard way that it caused nothing but trouble. "Just help them appear a bit more Human and go for an androgynous appearance. Who cares what others think?"

"Yeah, passing wasn't the best word choice." Aubrey turned Rayne toward the door.

"Should I work on my hair color too?" Rayne bounced as they walked. "I do like blue, but…"

"Wear it back in a ponytail but leave the color alone. You're going to fit right in with what's out there now." He left the door open behind them.

———◦⟨⟩◦———

Rayne returned to the homestead tired but full of new experiences that they wanted to share. "There's a shop in Johnson City called Atlantis that sells spiritual supplies. The energy in there is strong and positive!" They held up a paper sack for Stowne to see. "It's full of wonderful things, and I can handle almost all of them!"

"It took all I had to get them out of there." Aubrey set two cotton canvas sacks on the kitchen table and began to unload them. "How're Cent and Tess feeling?"

"Alive." But Tess sounded weaker than Cent, who'd recovered enough to sit up without her head threatening to explode.

"Did you two get any sleep?" Aubrey emptied the sacks and returned to kneel beside Tess, checking her for fever.

"That's all we got done." Tess reached up to pat his face. "And no fever."

"You're right." Aubrey moved to kneel beside Cent. "You look a little better too."

"Stowne made us some good tea." Cent leaned back in her eternal's arms.

"Your brewing preferences have remained the same across lifetimes, that is all." Stowne hugged her to them. "Do you need assistance with the supplies, Aubrey?"

"I'm helping." Gan carried in a cardboard box bearing a Walmart logo. "Aubrey is filling containers, so I can carry in the supplies."

"Where *haven't* you been today?" asked Cent. "It's four in the afternoon."

"A couple of outfitter stores, the courthouse." He took a breath. "We went to The Willow Tree Coffeehouse and Music Room for lunch. You ever been there, Cent?"

"No. Are they new?"

"They've been around a few years, I think. We'll have to go after this blows over. They've got a good ol' peanut butter and banana sandwich on the menu."

"Okay." *I think I'd rather have tea right now.* "Where else did you go?"

"Atlantis since it's down the street from Willow Tree, the Walmart, and Earthfare. I gave Rayne the full tour." Aubrey lifted a bag from the box Gan held. "I brought back the last one's chicken and rice soup for you."

"Never had it before." *I must be feeling better or it wouldn't smell good.*

"There are two locations in K-Town. Ethan…" Aubrey frowned. "Ain't no Ethan. Just me. But I love the soup and the store regardless. I'm glad there's one in JC too." His eyes trailed to Rayne, who was sharing the contents of the Atlantis bag with Stowne and Pyre. "Come on, Gan. Let's get the rest."

"Gladly." Gan followed him out the door.

"Bring back my manual can opener," said Tess.

"I bought a new one, all metal so everyone can use it," Aubrey called. "We'll be back."

Rayne seems to have enjoyed their time with Aubrey." Tess sat up with Stowne's help, but her hands shook when she lifted her mug to her mouth.

"Sounds like it." Cent watched Aubrey and Gan from inside. The Camry's trunk was loaded, and she could see the back seat was filled as well. "How much money did he say he got when he and Ethan split their bank account?"

"He was not specific." Stowne rubbed their chin. "I will be happier when we need not rely on money for your needs."

"Money is a requirement these days." Cent set her mug on the floor. "We should bring more furniture up here."

"What do you need?" Aubrey stepped back inside the house.

"I was thinking on bringing up Tess' recliner and a few other things, that's all," said Cent. "Nothing fancy. Just comfort stuff if we're all going to be hanging together."

"We might be over this by tomorrow," added Tess. "So let's not talk about house-sharing just yet."

"And here I was thinking about going furniture shopping tomorrow." Aubrey stacked canned goods to make room on the dining table. "The bed in my room is tiny."

"That bunkroom's meant for kids," Cent held her head at an angle to still its ache. "Are those my court papers in your back pocket?"

"Yep." He returned to the front room to give them to her. "Taken care of."

"When's my next date?"

"Never. I paid them off."

"Uh-uh." She thumbed through the pages, reading every receipt. "You even called Illinois to pay off the car lien and the others?"

"Weren't you listening when I told everyone that Ethan and I split the money in our account? My share was in the mid-six figures before the decimal point." His smile faded when she glared at him. "I screwed up, didn't I?"

"You said you were gonna change the date, not this." Cent rounded her shoulders as she stared at the papers. "I don't want charity."

"It ain't charity. It's family taking care of family. I had the means for once in my life. Consider it rent paid forward."

"I wasn't wanting this." She rose, unsteady as she walked to the back porch where she sat with her head in her hands.

"I can't unpay it." Aubrey joined her a moment later. "I'm sorry if I— No, I'm not. You're in a tight spot. That's all. If you want to repay me, we'll work something out, but we're going to balance that out with rent payment, okay?"

"I don't own this place. Aunt Tess and Mama do." She wiped her eyes and looked up, squinting at him until he came into focus. "And Tess is having to sell it because—"

"I talked to the realtor today." He grasped her arm when she reeled away from him. "Don't tell Tess, but I'm putting in an offer tomorrow."

"I didn't know it was actually up for sale."

"Tess had to before you came home, and the realtor contract runs through the end of October. The property's listed at some hundred and twenty thousand dollars."

"It's not worth that much."

"No, it isn't, but that's the asking price, so I'm offering it. Cash money. No inspections or stipulations. Quick closing."

"That should do it." She sighed. "It'll be yours. Tess'll have a nice cushion, Mama will be happy, and it'll all be over."

"No, it's *our* land. Yours, mine, Tess', Stowne's..." He squeezed her arm. "I wouldn't dream of taking away what you've built here."

"All right." She heaved another sigh. "But, just so you know, I'm going to buy in as soon as I can figure this all out."

"I'd hoped you'd say that." He leaned into her. "You look like shit, honey. Do you want to take a shower down at the trailer?"

"Yeah, I think that'd help." She leaned into him too. "What have you got hidden in the back seat of your car?"

"Stuff to help us be more tech-savvy up here in the old house. I'll show you after you shower."

"Sounds good." They went back inside to tell everyone what they were doing, but Cent tempered her joy. She didn't mind that Aubrey had the money to buy the homestead or that he wanted to live there too, but to pay off her debts without asking first? *I'm going to pay you back, Aub. Just wait. I'm going to figure it out.*

She wouldn't be beholden to anyone. No, being so served no good purpose, even with family.

Chapter Thirty-One

Nailed During the Waning Moon
September 9, 2017

Clank! The pain returned in spades the next morning, immediately followed by the sounds of heavy equipment.

"Dear… help me." Cent vomited as soon as she turned onto her side. So much for good chicken soup, so much for— she vomited again before Stowne could put the bucket beside her. Aunt Tess was doing much the same on the other side of the bed. She couldn't lift her head either, couldn't— Cent was too caught up in her own pain to think more about anyone else.

"Aubrey!" Stowne's bellow shook the house, causing both Cent and Tess to cover their heads with their arms.

"I'm coming!" Aubrey trotted out of the bunkroom, still in his boxers and pulling his unicorn t-shirt over his head. "Aw, geez. Help me get them off the bedding." He glanced out the window. "They're back with the equipment. And on both sides of the property!"

Cent gripped the bed in hopes it'd quit spinning. She gripped Stowne too as they moved her, trying to turn her head in a half-attempt to escape their arms when her stomach tightened again. "Bucket." But she'd already said too much. "Sorry. So, sorry…"

"One of the many complexities of having a Human mate, that is all." Stowne forced her head around before she did so again. "Rayne, a little help, please."

"As soon as— oh, my." Rayne lifted Tess from the bed while Aubrey removed the top covers.

"I'll drop this into the wash, and—"

"Hang it over the clothesline behind the trailer," Rayne told him. "I'll take care of it after I help stop the equipment." They peered out the window. "You should help this time, Stowne."

"I am staying here."

"Go," whispered Cent. "They need you."

"I'll be here," added Aubrey. "Go stop the idjits."

"Very well, I will return shortly, Centenary. Rest." Stowne reshaped into a plume of dust that drifted out the door with Rayne, as a low cloud, immediately behind them.

"Now, you two…" Aubrey turned to face the bed. "Off with those clothes. They need to be washed too."

"Get me some clean ones first." Tess waved him away. "And you ain't undressing me, boy. I'll do for myself." She glanced at Cent. "All I want to do is sleep."

"Yeah, me too." Cent tried to cover her head with her pillow, but Aubrey jerked it from her hands.

"You puked on that too, honey."

"Aw, hell." Cent rolled to the edge of the bed and grabbed the bucket. "Just leave me be for a while. It'll go away like yesterday."

"Let's hope." Aubrey said something else, but Cent was too preoccupied to hear.

"Ruleman's walking the fence line again." Rayne paced in front of the window, each step leaving behind a wet footprint.

"Has he got black salt with him?" It'd taken Cent longer to sit up this time, and Tess was still asleep.

"Yes, he does." Rayne turned to see her. "We have to stop him before— Get back into that bed!"

"Help me to the window." She held her hand out to Rayne. "At least Mama isn't here this time." But the Escalade was, and two burly men were walking the fence line with Ruleman.

"Is Aubrey back yet?"

"No, but he should be soon."

"Fetch me the besom, will you?" Cent leaned against the window frame. "We're going to handle this ourselves."

"But you're sick and—"

"We ain't got no choice." Cent looked to where Stowne, Gan, and Pyre were attacking the heavy equipment. Stowne had broken the tracks on one of the excavators, and Pyre had overheated two backhoes. Gan, to Cent's joy, had overturned a dead tree onto a small track hoe, crushing the cab soon after the driver had climbed out. "Put on your Human face. I'm going to need your help."

"Do you need any of your books?" Rayne held out the besom Tess had made.

"Yep, the Bible."

"Fire with fire." Rayne retrieved that too, holding it and the besom in one hand while they supported Cent with the other. Cent's head hurt more with every step, and she had to stop twice to still her stomach's churn, but she made it to the fence line to stand directly across from Ruleman.

"Back for more?" Cent took the Bible from Rayne. "I got a good book too, a real one."

"Devil's Bible. No Satan's spawn can handle the Lord's word without being burned." Ruleman went back to his recitation.

"Oh, so *that's* why you're wearing gloves again." She traded Rayne the Bible for the besom.

"But I suffer not a woman to usurp authority over the man, but to be in silence!" preached Ruleman.

"First Timothy two, verse twelve." Cent startled at her own knowledge. "Are you still using a King James' version? That's so outdated."

"Wording changes nothing." Ruleman tossed salt at Rayne who deflected it with a flick of water. "I see you brought an assistant this time."

"And you brought two." Cent ignored her throbbing head to smile at him. "Are you scared?" Ruleman's men wore black jackets with raised hoods that hid their faces.

"I have righteousness on my side." Ruleman threw salt at Cent, but Rayne deflected that as well. "What do you have with you? A pathetic water nymph you conjured?"

"Oh, no. They're much, much more." Cent raised the besom to clear the space between them. "You are not allowed to seal this land from the spirits that live here."

"I own the surrounding ground and will soon own yours too." Ruleman's reaching hand bounced off the wards.

"You don't own the road or what's on the other side of the mountain," said Cent. "That's government land, national forest, and it's Stowne's too."

"I don't need legal status to take possession of what's mine." Ruleman spread black salt as he returned to his walk, mumbling as he moved.

He isn't saying anything from the Bible. That's Latin. A curse. Cent walked directly across the fence from him, swinging the besom in gentle movements to negate his words. "Rayne, please open to the thirty-seventh Psalm."

"Good choice." Rayne flipped open the Bible and held it up for Cent to read.

"Ugh. King James here too. I need an updated copy." Cent recited as she walked, reading from the text only when she needed the reminder, grinning when Ruleman rocked on his heels and raised his hand to his mouth to bite his knuckle.

"Enough!" He turned to face her. "If words won't work, perhaps actions will." He waved his hand and the men walking with him turned, lunging over the fence but they, too, bounced off the ward. "So, you know how to maintain your wards and can use that book too. But you are looking rather ill, girl. Is something making you sick? Perhaps you should come to one of my services for a laying of hands." He lifted his balding head to sneer at her. "I lay hands on your mama quite regular."

"You bastard!" Cent dropped the besom to lunge with her hands extended. Ruleman's men caught her by the arms as soon as she crossed the ward, trying to pull her over the fence. But their hands weren't hands, not in the Human sense. They were red clay in color, veiny, long, and clawed. Their cold touch burned her flesh. *These things aren't alive.*

Help! Rayne grabbed her by the waist, pulling her the other direction, but they were quickly losing the battle. Cent used all her energy to pull herself back, but she was weak and— Ruleman growled when Stowne lifted the men gripping Cent's arms, turning them so they were forced to release their hold. Pyre set their clothing ablaze at the same time, and Gan slid in front of Cent to blow the men back.

"Golems." Cent fell back into Rayne's arms. "Take your— No, Stowne. They're earthen. And yours to control now that we know what they're made of." She winced when the burning spread up her arms and into her neck. *His touch. Ruleman's magic. It'll go away just like before.*

"They are mine to destroy." Stowne raised the golems above their head, bashing them together then throwing them to the ground where they crumbled into dust. "You will not use natural means for your unnatural gain!" They grabbed Ruleman by the scruff of his neck and turned him to blow dust in his face. "You have too many spells on you to reveal your identity without harming your host, but whoever you are, begone and never return here." Stowne set Ruleman on his feet and nudged him down the hillside. "I will not harm an innocent body no matter how vile the possession."

"Possession?" Ruleman's laugh turned bitter. "I own this body!" He glanced over the fence to where Cent lay in Rayne's arms. "Just as I do one gullible, magical Nida Rhodes." Ruleman picked up his worthless book, dusted it off, and trudged down the hill, mumbling under his breath as he passed Aubrey, who'd driven up as the chaos had ended.

"I'm buying this property, you son-of-a-bitch! I signed the offer contract! You hear me?" Ruleman hissed at him but said nothing, retreating to his

Escalade and pulling away. "What the hell just happened?" Aubrey knelt beside Cent who sat on the ground cradling her arms. "Let me see."

I've nothing left in me. Her head hurt so much that her nausea had returned. "Will someone help me to the healing pool? Tess too? She's still sick."

"Let me see your arms first." Aubrey gritted his teeth when he looked. Two skeletal-handprint-shaped marks stretched up Cent's arms. What wasn't bruised below her elbows was either burned or covered in deep scratches. "Damn. I go for a bit and— How'd this all start?"

"He tried to seal the property lines again." Cent relaxed when Stowne replaced Rayne behind her.

"I should have intervened earlier, asiule ehu. I am sorry."

"No, you did right keeping back until you did, but those golems were vicious."

"They're meant to be." Pyre nudged the golems' dust with their toe. "They crumbled faster than they should've, considering."

"They weren't fully formed." Rayne drenched the piles until they faded into the soil. "Whoever's controlling Ruleman has spent so much energy concealing themselves that they don't have power for much else."

"But they've got hold of Mama." Cent tried hard not to cry, but it spilled from her anyway. "My arms. Please help me to the pool."

"You lie." Stowne lifted her into their arms. "You fear for your mother as much as you ache."

"We both do." Tess sat on the homestead's front steps with her hands over her face to shield it from the sun. "Now, are we going up to the pool or not? 'Cause I'm too weak to get there by myself."

"You don't have to turn around, Aubrey. I don't give a hoot if you see me naked. I just didn't want you takin' my clothes off me this mornin'." Tess sighed when Rayne sat her in the water. "It's a bit cold. Pyre, can you be a dear and do somethin' about it?"

"It's that temperature when it bubbles up from the ground." Pyre glanced at the water.

"They're too weak to get chilled." Aubrey turned around when Tess told him to.

"So you want me—" Pyre sighed. "Sure."

"I would appreciate it," said Stowne as they slid into the water to press against Cent. "And I have no desire to command someone I consider a friend."

"Ever the diplomatist. Yeah, I'm on it." Pyre steamed as they dove into the water, which immediately began to heat.

"I should try calling Betty when I get back home." Betty had contacted Cent the evening before to say she was back in rehab, that she'd no option, and insisted that Cent should call her as often as she could, but they'd already slid back into texting during the few hours Betty had access to her phone. The facility restricted their usage to reduce outside influences that could draw their patients back into the world they were trying to escape.

"You sure do worry about her," observed Aubrey. "She must be one hell of a friend."

"She was the only real friend I had up there that last year. We took care of each other."

"Is she getting her hormones in that rehab facility?" Aubrey rolled up his pant-legs and sat so his feet dangled in the water.

"She said she is, why?"

"I know that when Ethan didn't get his for a couple of weeks last year, he had a hell of a time with headaches and mood swings." Aubrey shrugged. "Doesn't excuse Sir Grumpy Pants for the things he did, but it explains his asinine mouth."

"He cheated on you before his assistant?" Cent grumbled low. "That wasn't hormones."

"Yeah, he cheated, and I know it wasn't because of the hormones." Aubrey stared into the water. "Ethan was a real dickwad sometimes, but I still loved him."

"That makes for an unhealthy environment," said Tess. "You're better off without him."

"I know." But Aubrey didn't sound convinced.

Gan spun into the thicket holding a jar, their arms laden with rosemary. "As requested." They dropped the rosemary into the water and held out the jar. "I'll blow it out as soon as I light it."

"Then let me." Stowne rose from the water and stooped, opening the jar and upending it onto a rock that they heated with their energy until it glowed soft red.

"Whoa." Aubrey's eyes drifted to where Cent sat. "You two got married while I was in K-Town? Impressive." The curve of Stowne's body had taken a decidedly male form as they bent over the rock to fan the smoldering incense. "I might be jealous."

"They're all mine." Cent flashed a tired grin. "But when are you going to get it through your head that appearances mean zip to elementals once they're free of their initial form? They present however they want."

"Form means little to us aside from what our Human companions enjoy." Rayne changed to a more masculine form, though leaner and softer in line than earth elementals could manage. "Stowne moves between forms without thinking because they know Centenary is attracted to both males and females."

"And forms between. This is but one form I take for her benefit." Stowne's lines reformed into a more feminine shape without their looking up. "I have merely had more time to perfect my ability." They blew softly on the burning incense once more and stood to face Aubrey with a bare body smooth and genderless in appearance. "To expect an elemental lover to retain a singular appearance denotes a lack of acceptance of our capabilities."

"And a lack of imagination," added Gan with a soft smile to Tess.

"Okay, I get it." Aubrey held out his hands. "I didn't mean to step where I shouldn't or question why any of you do what you do. I was just commenting on— can't I admire?"

"Oh, so you were admiring." Stowne glanced at Cent who shrugged. "Thank you?"

"You need to see what's beneath, see the truest form, the light beneath any and all coverings." Rayne eyed Aubrey up and down. "Only then can you understand our purpose and—"

"He doesn't recall his past lives," Cent reminded them. "So lay off him." She raised her brows at Aubrey. "At least for now."

"Guess you're right. I don't remember." Aubrey ran his fingers through his hair to loosen the back. "Maybe I should just keep my observations to myself until I better understand."

"Might be a good idea." Cent sniffed. "Now that incense smells good."

"It contains frankincense," said Stowne. "However did you afford that, Tess? Last I knew the price was exorbitant."

"You can purchase it locally now." Rayne followed Aubrey with their eyes.

"And online. It's not that costly these days." Tess laid her head on Rayne's shoulder. "I'm feelin' a might better."

"That's good to hear." Rayne extended her hand to Cent. "I've enough in me for you both."

"I'll be all right."

"No, that battle left you weak." Stowne motioned to Gan. "Come into the pool so Rayne does not drain their stores."

"I'll take Tess." Gan changed into an almost translucent Human form, their body defined by air ripples that turned into bubbles when they stepped into the water.

"You've got yourselves a regular spa going there." Aubrey watched with interest as Rayne moved beside Cent.

"You can help them best if you join us." Stowne motioned to him too. "You can release your healing energy into the water. We will not absorb it, but Tess and Centenary will."

"I'm still getting used to this healer-man thing." Aubrey scratched his head as he stared at the water. "Okay, I'm in, if it'll help them, but I'm sitting between Gan and Rayne. Anywhere else is too close to, um… personal space-ish."

"Just shut up and get in here." Cent held her arms above the water. "They're still stinging somethin' fierce."

"That is what his energy is needed for." Rayne peered up with the slightest of smiles. "But he needs to undress first."

"Not even my shorts?" Aubrey frowned.

"The energy travels best through the water if you are unencumbered," said Gan.

"Dadgummit. All right. But Cent and Aunt Tess, you two close your eyes. You too, Rayne."

"I don't need eyes to see you, Aubrey, so—"

"Humor me."

"As you wish." Rayne shut their eyes, but they smiled while doing so.

"I changed your diapers, boy." But Tess closed hers as well.

"And you used to piss in the bushes while I stood right beside you. Always hated that you could do that, and I couldn't. Still do." Cent shrugged and closed her eyes too. "Prude."

"That's Healer Prude, thank you very little." He stepped into the water.

"Rayne, your pool is crowded." Pyre popped their steaming head from beneath the water. "I can keep it warm without submerging and— hello there." They showed their flickering smile to Aubrey. "No wonder I felt the energy rise again after Gan climbed in."

"Yeah, it's a regular energy-fest in here." Aubrey settled beside Rayne and looked around Gan to see Tess. "She's almost asleep."

"Just relaxing. It's been so long that I'd forgotten how good this feels." Tess' mouth trembled. "Not since Kinnon…" She sighed and leaned into Gan. "Getting old ain't for the weak."

"That's why you do it so nicely." Gan kissed her cheek. "Some meditative quiet would be most helpful, I believe."

"So would some closeness." Cent moved so she sat in Stowne's lap. "Sink down a bit, please. It feels better when I'm up to my shoulders."

"You need to submerge," replied Stowne. "Hold onto me." They dropped beneath the water to emerge a good five minutes later.

"I couldn't see you down there. This pool ain't that deep." Aubrey stuck his face into the water to see for himself then looked up even more confused. "Is it?"

"It depends on how you see it." Rayne held out their hand to him. "This is my home, so I can show you better than anyone."

"Go on." Cent settled back into Stowne's arms. "It feels great."

"That it does," mumbled Tess. "I've dunked with Pyre and Rayne many times." She sighed as Gan pulled her into their arms. "But right now, I'm fine where I am."

"I could take you down for a moment," said Gan. "I've never had the honor of doing so with you before."

"Thank you, but no. Maybe when I'm feeling better. You go, Aubrey. It's beautiful."

"You've got me curious." He accepted Rayne's hand when they held it out again. "Let's go."

"Neither of you bothered to mention the breathing method," mentioned Pyre when they'd disappeared below the water.

"Oops." Cent smiled as Stowne wrapped around her. "Some things are best left to discovery."

"You are pushing them together." Stowne held Cent out to consider her. "Are you also a matchmaker this lifetime?"

"No, I just know what Aubrey likes. And he'll like Rayne if he'll give them a chance."

"I ain't never had an elemental lover," said Tess. "And I ain't lookin' for one now, but I'll remember those underwater liplocks forever."

"I'm the one who first took her down." Pyre sounded proud. "Much to Kinnon's chagrin."

"He got over it." Tess chuckled. "It's him I married, after all."

"Intimacy doesn't always mean being lovers." Gan held her closer. "You're a good soul, Tessa Jo Rhodes. I'd like to spend time getting to know you."

"My full name?" She couldn't hide her blush. "Why, Ganolesgi, I'm seventy-five years old!"

"And I'm over twelve million years in age. Your point?"

"I guess there ain't one after all." Tess raised her hand to her mouth when she yawned. "Kinnon would hee-haw if he heard me. He insisted that Pyre was trying to steal me away, and that's why he had to marry me."

"I *was* trying until you accepted his proposal." Pyre sat on the pool's edge to dangle their legs in the water, sufficient contact to keep it warm. "I had too much respect for you both to interfere afterward. And now, you're a friend, so I don't want to complicate things"

"Such honesty," Stowne smirked. "And you have not made a try for Aubrey either, Pyre. What has gotten into you?"

"Eh, he's Rayne's. We all see it."

"All of us except for Aubrey," said Cent.

"Oh, he does." Tess yawned again as she relaxed against Gan. "He just doesn't want to fess up to it."

"Here they come." Cent smiled as Aubrey emerged. "How was it down there?"

Aubrey glared at her and climbed from the pool, stopping just long enough to gather his clothing before he left the thicket.

"Aubrey?" Cent tried to follow him, but Stowne pulled her back into the water.

"Let him go."

"But—"

"Stowne's right." Rayne emerged from the water. "Let him go." They climbed from the pool to sit beside Pyre. "That didn't go well at all."

"What happened?" Cent asked.

"He took to the mouth lock nicely and had the initiative to turn it into a kiss, and it was a good one, too. But then his expression changed, and he broke off to swim to the surface." Rayne glanced to where he stood pulling on his clothing. "Is it too soon?"

"Probably." Cent watched him too. *Get past it, cuz. See what's really going on here. Rayne'll be the best thing that's ever happened to you.* "Ethan broke his heart and then some."

"Bad relationships take time to heal from," added Gan. "Don't let this discourage you, Rayne, but I do suggest being his friend for now."

"Yes, I— I'm trying too hard." Rayne stared into the water. "I should wait for him to decide he's ready."

"Good idea." Gan stroked Tess' hair. "Such a kind woman. Does she have children?"

"Is she asleep?" Cent squinted at her great aunt. "Guess so. No, she doesn't have any children. I don't think she and Uncle Kinnon could."

"She would have been a wonderful mother." Gan wrapped their arms around Tess' shoulders.

"She was certainly a mother to me and Aubrey when ours couldn't or wouldn't be there." Cent sat up in Stowne's lap. "Is she really doing better?"

"Some, I believe." Gan kissed Tess' head right on the top part. "I've been feeding her heavily since she let me hold her."

"What about you, asiule ehu?" Stowne sat up behind her. "You seem some better."

"I am, thanks, and hungry enough to eat— I dunno." Nothing sounded good, especially soup. "Maybe a sandwich."

"Peanut butter?" asked Stowne.

"Yeah, I think so." Cent stood so the water dripped from her. "Brr. It's getting cool."

"The blankets should be dry," said Rayne. "I'll go get them." They slid from the thicket and moved down the hill, saying nothing to Aubrey as they passed him on the back porch.

"Hand me my shirt, Pyre." Cent held out her hand, but Stowne grabbed it, pulling her toward them. "Not now, baby. I'm trying to get dressed."

"Your abdomen." Stowne rose higher in the pool. "Where did that bruise come from?"

"What bruise?" Cent looked down to see a black, circular mark midway between her rib cage and navel. "I dunno. Maybe the golems?"

"Perhaps." Stowne touched the spot with one finger, but that was enough to make Cent whimper. "The golem marks have mostly faded since we have been in the pool, but this one— no, it is not that at all." Their upper body stiffened with worry. "This is not in any way right." Stowne kissed her abdomen above the mark and climbed from the water, lifting her out behind them. "Does the pain increase with movement?"

"Yeah, and my nausea's returning too." Cent leaned against Stowne for warmth until Rayne returned with the blankets. Rayne passed one to Stowne and draped the other over their arms.

"Gan, hand me Tess so you can get out."

"Thank you." Gan's energy rotation had reduced to a breeze when they rose from the water. "She required a significant portion of my energy."

"Older Humans take more energy to heal," said Stowne. "Go up to Usdagalv and recharge. I will send word for my lessers to assist you."

"Thank you." Gan placed Tess in Rayne's arms and exited the thicket, moving slowly between the trees until their form faded.

"They barely had the strength to stir the leaves." Pyre moved to help Rayne with Tess but stopped, pushing aside the blanket before Rayne could fully wrap her. "Did you see this?"

"No, I— Mother Earth, please protect this woman." Rayne kissed Tess' forehead. "This isn't good."

"What?" Cent tore away from Stowne to see for herself, dropping her blanket to her ankles when she saw Tess had an angry black circle on her abdomen too.

Chapter Thirty-Two

Ode to Cricket Jameson
September 10, 2017

The third morning proved worse than the last two combined. Two clanks meant more pain, more violent vomiting, more…

Jack howled at the door then tore outside when Rayne opened it.

"You're both dehydrated." Aubrey held a cup to Cent's mouth, but she choked instead of swallowed, spewing the water from her mouth.

"I can't," she whispered when she'd found her breath. "Just, please."

"You should both be in the hospital." Aubrey laid her against Stowne, who raised her t-shirt to see her abdomen.

"It is growing."

"And they're both fevered." Aubrey knelt to examine the spot. "Let me get my bag, and I'll take a better look." He'd examined the spots on both Tess and Cent the night before and determined they weren't bruises.

"An abscess?" offered Pyre.

"That is no abscess," Stowne moved their hands to toward the spot. "Observe how her skin crawls away from the wound."

"I don't care, just make it stop." Cent pushed them away, turning on her side to pull her knees up.

"Aubrey is putting on gloves, asiule ehu. Try to be patient."

"Tess' skin is crawling too," said Gan. "Illness typically doesn't do this."

"We should not make conclusions until Aubrey finishes his examination." Stowne paced beside the bed, stopping every few turns to reach for Cent, pulling back when she cringed and shook her head.

"All right, let me see." Aubrey returned holding a magnifying glass and wearing a mask and nitrile gloves. "Come on, Cent. You gotta lay flat so I can see."

"I'm trying." But her body refused to cooperate.

"Then we're going to have to pull you straight, honey. I'm sorry." He motioned to Pyre. "Come help us."

"I hate to cause her pain." But Pyre grabbed her feet regardless, helping Stowne hold and turn her straight when she tried to pull away.

"I know it hurts, but you must." Stowne stared into Cent's eyes the entire time, speaking softly to her, kissing away her tears. "Calm." They blew in and out, asking her to breathe with them, their touch careful but firm.

"I'm going to swab the opening," said Aubrey. Cent screamed when he did, panting, crying harder. She turned her head to vomit across the bedding they'd just changed. "Black?" Aubrey stared at the swab. "It's identical to what she just threw up."

"The same?" Rayne turned on their heels. "I might know what it is, but I need Cent's books to make certain."

"Then get them." Aubrey's eyes darted from the swab to the bed. "Not blood. Not puss. This ain't like anything I've ever seen come out of a body. It's like tar." He set the swab on one gauze square and covered Cent's wound with another. "I don't have any clue how to get rid of this, but I need to examine Tess to make certain that we're dealing with the same thing."

"Do you need my assistance?" Stowne lifted Cent enough to pull the sheet from under her. "Rest, asiule ehu. I will soon return to feed you."

"Just let me sleep." Cent rolled onto her side as soon as they tucked a towel under her head.

<hr />

Cent woke, sweat-drenched and dry-mouthed, to see Aubrey placing a catheter beneath Tess' skin. "Sub-q fluids." He patted Cent's face— "You're next"— and stomped on the floor. "She's awake, Stowne!" Aubrey frowned when he saw her cringe. "Sorry." He softened his voice. "They're in the cellar half-buried to recharge, but they wanted to know the moment you woke."

"Can I have a drink?"

"How about some ginger ale?" asked Aubrey. "I ran by Dryler's to get some and to tell Mr. Jones you were too sick to work tomorrow."

"Thanks. What'd he say?"

"Get better. What else could he say?" Aubrey slowly pushed something clear into the catheter, slid a clamp over the tubing, and moved to the other side of the bed to open a new pack. "This is some old-style doctoring, but I decided that toting either one of you to the ER for a proper IV isn't going to help things."

"Dark magic." Cent licked her lips.

"Not quite." Rayne walked into the room holding one of Cent's treasured books open in their arms. "You wrote about this exact thing happening to another witch."

"I did?" Cent struggled to push up on her elbows, but it proved too painful, so she lay back, surprised to feel Stowne behind her.

"I am here, asiule ehu." They adjusted so she propped comfortably against them. "Listen to what Rayne says."

"Wait until Aubrey's finished. I need to see the needle."

"Oh, you're one of those gotta-see-it-go-in patients, are you?" He rubbed hand sanitizer into his palms and felt along her arm for the best spot. "Just under the skin, but it's going to make the area fill a little tight. All right, one, two…"

"Ow." But it didn't hurt nearly as much as her abdomen. "How's Tess?"

"Gan's keeping her energy fed, but she's fading in and out of consciousness." Aubrey set the catheter and pushed in fluid that he pulled from one of the kitchen pots.

"What's that?"

"Homemade saline." He felt around on her right arm. "Survival medicine. It was an optional course in my NP program, and I had the caths stowed away." He shrugged when she raised her brows at him. "No, I didn't steal them. They're technically out of date and were going to the trash anyway."

"I don't care as long as they're clean." She watched him push in a second syringe then lay back to see Stowne's worried face. "All right, Rayne. What did you find?"

"You called it witch nailing." Rayne stood at the foot of the bed. "It's a means of taking revenge on a witch."

"I don't recall the particulars, so what'd I write?"

"'Cricket Jameson came down with something horrid this morning, and his wife asked me to tend him. Not certain what is happening, but it is nothing natural.'" Rayne looked up. "That's your July twelfth, 1822, entry. But there are several here, so I'm going to keep reading.

"'July thirteenth. Cricket is far worse today, and his wife reported seeing a peculiar black mark on his stomach when she removed his nightshirt. I looked at it myself and can honestly say I have no idea what it is. I will search my books after I finish writing this.

"'July fourteenth. Cricket cannot sit up today, and he is sweating and moaning something fierce about his belly. I placed a urine, salt, and green-corn cataplasm on it to draw out whatever is ailing him, said prayers, and burned herbs over him, but it made no immediate change. I hope to see different come tomorrow. Effie claimed Cricket seems better in the evenings, but I do not understand how or why. Most ailments are worse at night. I wish Aggie were here to help. She was always wise about such matters and quick to decipher them.

"'July fifteenth. I went to see Cricket early this morning and passed Jasper Collins along the way. Such a surly, pathetic, weasel of a man, but never mind him. It is Cricket I am worried over. The place on his belly has grown twice as big overnight. It is oozing something black too, but I see no signs of illness in his family. I blessed the four corners of their home, blessed Cricket and his family, hung protections over their dogtrot's doors, and now I am going to search my books for a remedy.

"'July sixteenth. I picked an armful of healing herbs this morning for Cricket and threw half in the river like I learnt from *my granny in Ireland*. Unfortunately, the bundle broke apart in the water, so I threw the rest away. A wasted morning that got worse when I visited Cricket. His wife, Effie, woke early this morning to check on him and said she heard a clanking sound outside. Cricket cannot keep down any food or drink and cannot get himself out of bed to make water or elsewise. He is weak, and I am afraid for his life. I read the good book over him and prayed and recited some older prayers low enough that Effie could not hear over the children. Cricket heard me, though, and thanked me. Magic knows magic, and there is something dark afoot here that I do not understand.

"'July seventeenth. Effie cried in my arms today while her children were outside playing, then she told me a secret. She's expecting her sixth child, but she knows Cricket's dying and so do I. I saw Jasper Collins again too, early in the morning. He thought I did not see him, but I spied him skulking through the woods holding what looked like a hammer. The damn fool has somehow found out about Cricket's magic and is killing him because of it, but why? They do not have any grievances I know of. I am going to stay up all night and catch Jasper in the morning to find out what this is all about.

"'July eighteenth. Jasper somehow got past me, and Cricket died in Effie's arms this morning just after sunup. She claims she heard the clanking again, a heavier sound than the other days. Damn Jasper for what he did, but if I hound him about it he might just do me in too. I will never tell Stowne what happened because they would deal with the Hunter Fairies before they gave Jasper half-a-chance to do me harm. I will say my prayers instead and put a candle in the window tonight to help light Cricket's way across the veil.'

"There's one more entry about this dated September seventeenth." Rayne flipped several pages over. "'I heard tell that Jasper Collins proposed to Effie Jameson. Of course she accepted. A pretty, young widow with five children and another on the way does not have a choice in the matter. Bless her and those children, and damn Jasper for his murderous ways. He witch-nailed Cricket to get Effie to himself, and there is nothing I can do about it.'"

"Witch nailing." Cent patted Jack's head when he shoved his cold, wet nose beneath her hand and whimpered. "How's that work?"

"It's a really old means of killing a witch," said Aubrey. "I had to do some serious online research to find anything on it, but someone takes an image of a witch, drawn, printed, or whatever and nails it to a tree, one whack per day, for seven days. Each day the witch gets sicker until day seven when…" He looked away. "This is late on day three."

Cent felt Stowne's hands tighten on her shoulders. "So me and Tess— there're two clanks every morning." She placed her hands on her stomach. "How do we fight it?"

"The tree has to be on the witch's property," explained Rayne. "Pyre and every lesser elemental residing in this realm are out looking for it."

"This land is mine above all others." Stowne's hands trembled. "I need to look too, but I am afraid to leave your side."

"Go," Cent insisted. "I'm better in the evenings, just like my journal said."

"I'll go with you." Gan appeared in the kitchen doorway. "Let them rest while we pursue."

"Go." Cent reached up to touch Stowne's arm. "Aubrey and Rayne have things under control here." She turned her head to Aubrey. "You mentioned something about ginger ale?"

"I'll get you some." Aubrey packed his bag while Rayne stowed the book, both returning to the room a moment later.

"I am soon to return." Stowne knelt by the bed. "You rest."

"I'll try." With Aubrey's help, Cent was able to sit up enough to drink ginger ale from a half-filled quart jar. "My books."

"What about them?"

"Bring them here."

"Now, you're too…" Aubrey sighed. "Sure. Which should I bring?"

"All of them."

"I'll get them." Rayne carried in the entire lot of books and their bench on a cloud of concentrated water vapor.

"You'll ruin both the ink and the wood." Cent's admonishment didn't come across nearly as angry as she intended.

"No, I won't." Rayne deposited the bench and books beside the bed and bent to kiss Cent's cheek. "You always say that, but it's never happened."

"It might someday."

"I doubt it." Rayne's water-blue eyes twinkled. "Which one's singing to you?'

209

"None of them. That's what worries me."

"Perhaps you're trying too hard." Rayne took the now empty quart jar from her and moved to Tess' side of the bed to smooth back her hair. "She's awake."

"I wish I wasn't." Tess squinted up at Rayne and over to Cent. "You still sick too, girl?"

"Yeah." Cent patted her great aunt's arm. "Almost everyone's out searching down the problem."

"What problem?" Tess licked her lips. "Can I have a drink?"

"Ginger ale?" offered Rayne.

"Eh, no. Nasty…stuff. Water, please."

"As long as you drink." Rayne filled Cent's jar half-full of water from their own form and held it out to Tess. "Tepid, so it will go down better."

"Thank you." Tess choked down three sips then raised her head a bit more to see Cent's books. "If those come out, it's serious." She placed her hand on her abdomen and squinted again. "What's being done to us?"

"You'll be fine." Aubrey sat cross-legged at the end of the bed. "I've heard there's a nasty stomach bug going around."

"Bullshit." Tess pulled up her shirt to show the bandage on her abdomen. "That ain't no boo-boo, and I ain't no child. Tell me the truth."

"We don't know yet," Cent admitted. "But it's only day three, so—"

"What's the number of days got to do with it?" Tess' hands tightened over her blanket. "You three ain't tellin' me somethin'."

"There ain't nothin' to tell. Least nothing you and me can do something about, so let others…" Cent turned her head when something hummed beside the bed. More of a vocal sound, a tune. "My books." She held out her hand to feel the sound in her bones. *I hear you.*

"One of them is finally singing to you?" asked Rayne. "Which one?"

"Now we're to singing books?" Aubrey scratched his head. "Moving here has been the strangest experience of my life."

"Mine too." Cent stretched her fingers toward her books, feeling, seeking. "The little stack. Second from the bottom. Aubrey, will you get it for me?"

"You and Tess should be sleeping, and—"

"Don't get in the way…of witchin', boy." Tess pointed to the stack. "Get her what she needs, or she'll crawl out the bed—"

"Save your breath, I'm going." He held the stack steady, so he could pull the text loose. "This old thing? It's ratty as all get out."

"Stop saying ugly things about my books." Cent caressed the book's peeling, brown leather cover. "What're you trying to tell me?" She placed her hand on its top to feel the song. "Something. Something— Ruleman. Yes. We figured that much out, but what else?"

"Is she serious?" Aubrey's mouth went slack. "'Cause her fever's down right now and—"

"Of course she's serious." Rayne moved closer to Cent. "What're you hearing?"

"Chanting. Tsalagi chanting." Listening proved harder than Cent expected. "I can't quite understand the words."

"I hear it as well. Let me... there." Rayne shoved soft energy into the book, empowering its voice.

"Thank you." Cent turned the book to stroke its collected pages, flipping through their edge, front-to-back, back-to-front. "Speak to me."

"What the— I hear it too." Aubrey scooted closer.

"Hush and listen," said Tess. "Let Cent do what she knows best."

"Yes'm."

Speak to me. Speak... Cent closed her eyes, held the book to her chest then at arm's length, dropping it into her lap so it fell open. *Now the words.* She ran her ring finger over the page until... *there.* She opened her eyes, hoping...

> *Deep, damaged, neglected roots, left to wither, will bring down the*
> *strongest tree with their rot.*

Cent read it twice more before she repeated it aloud. "They need to find an old tree. One that looks sickly."

"I'll let Stowne and the others know." Rayne took the book from her, placing it on top of the same stack it'd come from. "You've done all you can. Now, get some rest."

"More sub-q before you do, though." Aubrey brought the sealed jar from where it sat by the fireplace. "Pyre's keeping it warm so it won't give you the chills going in."

"What is that?" Tess eyed him dubiously.

"He's trying to keep us hydrated." Cent held out her catheterized arm. "Do me first so she can see."

"I can only give you one." He pushed the fluid even slower this time, but it hurt enough for Cent to grit her teeth toward the end. "That'll do you for now. I'm setting my alarm for every two hours overnight to get as much as possible into you both before morning. Speaking of which, does either of you need to pee? What goes in must come out unless things are really going wrong."

"I could go, now that you mention it." Cent tried to flex her arm, but the fluids pushed back, keeping her from moving it much.

"Rayne?" Aubrey moved to Tess' side of the bed. "Can you take her?"

"Certainly."

"He's trying. I promise," said Cent as Rayne carried her from the pallet to the bedside toilet now sitting in the bedroom.

"I know." Rayne sat her carefully down. "I hate that Tess broke her hip year before last, but this has come in quite handy both then and now."

"She what?" Cent grumbled under her breath. "No one told me."

"Aubrey spent a lot of time here then, and we helped her for a while after he returned to work, but that trailer…" They helped Cent pull up her shorts. "You didn't go much."

"There's not much in me. The trailer?"

"Pyre and I managed."

"Thank you for helping her."

"How could we not?" Rayne carried her back to the bed and used a cotton dish towel to hold out the hand sanitizer. "If the bottle were glass, I could lift it without covering it."

"I left a really pretty cut-glass container back in K-Town that'd be perfect for…" Aubrey's expression clouded. "I'll see what I can find next time I'm out."

"Tess?" Rayne held out their arms to her. "Are you next?"

"No. I'm fine." Tess touched around the catheter. "That hurts."

"I know. Sorry." Aubrey pushed her hand gently away. "Can I convince either of you to drink some broth? I've got both chicken and beef down at the trailer I can heat up."

"Chicken," they both said.

"Good." He capped the syringe and slid it into his shirt pocket. "Be back in a flash."

"Tell me about Ethan," insisted Rayne as soon as Aubrey stepped off the porch.

"I only met him once," Tess took a deep breath. "He's a skinny, well-dressed boy. Blond-haired and blue-eyed. He seemed nice enough, but he looked down his nose at everything about this place. He made a couple of jokes about the homestead to Aub when he thought I was out of ear-shot."

"Sounds high maintenance," said Cent. "And two-faced."

"You're being protective." Tess reached over to squeeze her arm. "But, yes, I thought as much myself. Aubrey was with him for five years, so I guess there was somethin' going on there."

"Ethan couldn't keep his hands off his assistant." Cent clutched her stomach when it churned "That's what was going on."

"Jerome?" Tess shook her head. "I warned Aubrey about that happening, but he didn't want to listen. And didn't you have something similar happen yourself?"

"Twice. Don't remind me." Cent pulled up her blanket. "Seems long ago now that I've got Stowne again."

"That's how it should be," confirmed Tess.

"Five years isn't long, but it can feel that way." Rayne rocked on their heels in front of the fireplace. "I'm getting a good feel for Aubrey, but I need some help. Do either of you have anything to offer me?"

"Oh, you're smitten." Tess grinned. "Aubrey's a good man, but he's a skeptic. He always has been. He laughed when I told him about the family magic. So much so that I didn't bother to tell him about his own abilities. But part of him knew, I think, or he wouldn't have chosen the career path he did."

"A physician?" asked Rayne.

"Nurse practitioner," corrected Cent. "He can do almost everything a doctor does, but he likes working with kids best."

"Children?" Rayne's eyes lit a brilliant blue. "He'd be a wonderful father."

"Now, Rayne." Tess gentled her voice. "He ain't ready for anything near that. He's still reelin' from Ethan and…"

"Oh, I know." Rayne smiled ever-so-slightly. "Knowing he likes children gives me ideas on how to reach him when he's ready, but he's coming back this way, so I'll be quiet now."

A water elemental with a crush. Cent found the notion delightful.

Chapter Thirty-Three

Fevered and Empty-Handed
September 11, 2017

Clank! Jack growled and tore off the porch in pursuit of something. Day four had begun.

Stowne immediately rolled Cent onto her side to hold her over the bucket, wavering between prayers and oaths as Gan did the same with Tess.

More sickness. More— Cent bore the pain as best she could, gripping Stowne's hand until the worst had ended.

"Tess is unconscious again." Gan rolled her back onto the bed.

And I'm not far…behind her.

Cent woke late that evening to the burn of Aubrey's fluid injection. "Stowne?"

"They're out looking, honey."

"Oh." It was all she could manage without losing control of her nausea.

"Your fever's down." Aubrey pulled a sheet over her almost naked body. "Rayne drenched you about twenty-minutes ago in case you're wondering why your hair's wet."

Hadn't crossed my mind. But she managed a nod just the same.

"They drenched Tess too." His conversation was more to occupy her than anything else. "But her catheter failed the last time, so I had to use a different method to hydrate her." Aubrey grimaced. "I hate doing that to anyone, but sometimes it's the only way."

Whatever it is, I don't want it. Cent lifted her arm enough to see her own catheter.

"Yours is still holding." He glanced at Tess. "She's a tough old bird, you know?"

"Yeah."

"Do you want some ginger ale?"

"No."

"Rayne let Stowne know you're awake, so they're on their way back."

"Thanks."

"Rest." He kissed her forehead. "When this is over, I want to know all about that four-leaf clover tattooed on your butt."

"Perv."

"You're the one with a Lucky Charms marshmallow forever on her right cheek." Aubrey turned away chuckling.

———————————

"I have searched every tree on this side of the mountain but have found nothing." Stowne's hold on Cent had become desperate.

"You're too emotionally invested in this to search well," claimed Pyre. "And you need to build your energy again."

"After I feed her." Stowne pushed their energy into Cent, but she resisted.

"Go to the cellar." She didn't bother opening her eyes. "Let Pyre feed me."

"Yes, let me."

"But—"

"You're a stubborn ass." Cent opened her eyes enough to narrow them. "Go. Please." She licked her lips and wished for the water she knew she couldn't keep down. "I will need… you later."

"She's got a fever of a hundred-and-four, and she still makes sense," observed Aubrey. "Go, Stowne. I'll yell for you if there's a problem."

"I love you, asiule ehu."

"Love you…too." She felt Stowne fade from beneath her head and Pyre's slimmer, warmer form take their place.

"Keep your burn down." Gan sat beside them holding Tess. "She doesn't need any added heat."

"I know, so keep blowing across the bed but not in my face." Pyre pushed back Cent's hair.

"Like I could blow you out if I tried." Gan laughed.

Cent dozed around listening to their banter, but Pyre slid into her head at some point to tell her about when she had been theirs. *One life, that's all, but it was important to me. You are the reason I can change my form, and that makes you eternally special to me.*

I was your first Human. Huh. Cent pondered this in the silence that followed. *Was I Rayne's too?*

Of course. But not Gan's. They, well, Gan's always had peculiar tastes.

Are you calling my Aunt Tess peculiar?

All witches have eccentricities, but I don't know where Gan found their first Human relationship or when, for that matter. Gan is very romantic with those they're with, but they've never shown much interest in sex.

And you know because...

Why do you think? Pyre sent a pleasurable ripple into her, a laugh in spirit form. *But Gan likes snuggles, long talks, and energy-sharing more than anything, so we didn't work well together at all. Perhaps they see a peer in Tess' quiet wisdom, and that is what attracts them.*

There's nothing wrong with that as long as they're good to Tess. Cent let her thoughts wander again, thinking of her former lives and her short time this one with Stowne. *I don't want it to end so soon.*

You worry too much. Pyre tapered their feeding rate, forcing her body to relax. *Please try to sleep.*

Tomorrow is day five.

Hush, Centenary.

But she could sense Pyre's worry as much as her own.

"What time is it?" She felt Jack pressed against her side.

Save your energy. Use your mind. Stowne was feeding her again.

What time is it? But she knew elementals didn't have the same sense of time as Humans, so she wasn't surprised to hear Stowne ask Aubrey.

"Twenty minutes since you last asked," he said.

"So, what? Three-twenty?"

Three twenty-two in the morning to be exact, reported Stowne when Aubrey grumbled. They pushed back her sheet. *Your fever is rising again.*

No, I'm cold. She tried to draw up the sheet, but Stowne pulled it from her reach.

"Off the bed, Jack. You are making her hotter."

"Rayne?" Aubrey sounded exhausted. "We need more water."

"I refilled the clean bowl after I emptied the other." Rayne's voice drew closer. "We're almost out of dry bedding."

"There's some down in the trailer's dryer."

"I'll get it," said Rayne.

"Not when being in there drains you," insisted Aubrey. "I'll go get it in a few. Hey, Cent?

"Huh?"

"Your friend Betty texted yesterday while you were asleep. Hope you don't get angry, but I told her you were sick with a stomach bug and would text her back as soon as you were feeling better."

"Okay, thanks."

"No problem." Aubrey tweaked her toes. "I'm going to the trailer."

"Then let me feed you for a while when you return. Stowne knows how to do…" Rayne hesitated. "At least they've watched you do it on Tess."

"I can do it," said Stowne.

What're you…talking about? Cent shivered when Stowne rolled her onto her left side and pressed a damp cloth to the back of her neck.

"See if you can get another dose of liquid Tylenol down her." Aubrey pressed his cool hand against Cent's leg. "Tell you what, Rayne. We'll go down to the trailer together. I'll change the loads and you can help me carry."

"I'll pull the blankets from the line too. Gan says they're dry. When we return, I would still like to feed you. Morning is drawing near and…"

"When are *you* going to rest?" asked Aubrey.

"Let them," Cent whispered. "They recover faster… than one of… us."

"You don't even have a dog in this race, sugar." Aubrey snickered. "Sick as hell but still wanting to boss me around."

"This is my… our stupid race." Cent managed a lopsided grin. "Let them. Please."

"Will you quit bitchin' at me?"

"You…wish."

"I'll do it anyway." He kissed her cheek. "Let's go, Rayne, so Stowne can do the deed."

"I'm right behind you." Rayne sounded pleased.

"What…deed?" Cent asked as soon as she heard the front door close.

Use your mind, asiule ehu, and relax. This will lower your fever faster and for longer than any medication or Rayne's drenchings. Stowne stroked her head beneath her hair. *And Aubrey has taught Gan how to do this for Tess as well.*

That doesn't bring me comfort.

It was not meant to.

What followed brought Cent no solace, but she was able to sleep afterward.

———————⟨⟩⟩⟨⟨⟩———————

217

She woke before dawn to listen. *Wonder what time it is.*

"Centenary?" Stowne pressed against her side. "You should not be awake."

"How can I sleep…when I, I…know what's about…to happen?"

"I'm awake too." Tess spoke from Cent's left. "This must be what death row feels like… but we… we ain't done nothing to deserve…this sentence."

"Shh, Tess. You think too much, especially when you need to be calm. Every spirit in the area is searching now." Gan lay on Tess' other side, Cent thought. "We should feed them again, Stowne. The more we can give them— but it fades so quickly."

"This spell or whatever it may be— the intention behind it is insidious." Stowne nuzzled Cent's neck and placed their hand on her chest. "Accept my offering."

"Like I have a choice."

"Same here," said Tess.

"It's like they're related." Gan's laugh rippled through the room. "Quiet, please. This does require our concentration."

Tess grabbed Cent's hand to squeeze it. No words of comfort, because there were none to be had, but they were in this together no matter the outcome.

Chapter Thirty-Four

Haint-Making
September 12-15, 2017

She saw and heard nothing but felt others move around her, stroking her arm, changing her belly bandage. She felt Stowne energy-feeding her, then Pyre, even Rayne, but she couldn't say thanks or even push enough clear thoughts to acknowledge Stowne's presence in her mind.

My beloved Centenary. Stowne kept repeating those words but, as she became weaker, she stopped being able to respond so they could hear.

Go charge. Care for yourself. Please don't bury yourself when I'm gone. I'll be back. I'll be... Stowne rolled her onto her side and lifted her leg. *Oh, God.* She should've been humiliated by where that tube got placed, but she was too thankful for the cool relief it brought, temporary though it was. Cent shivered from her spine outward during the process, and later, from her skin inward when Rayne drenched her.

This land. This place. It needs me. Stowne needs me. The circle must continue. She hummed old church songs in her head. "Amazing Grace," "Little Brown Church in the Vale," "May the Circle be Unbroken." Rock songs too. "Personal Jesus," "Enjoy the Silence." *What the hell? I don't even like Depeche Mode.* Shinedown's "The Crow and the Butterfly." *Nope, I don't care if I like it, that song don't work at all right now.*

Bluegrass, Folk Metal, Punk, and Gospel flowed seamlessly together. Ballads and reels and more chants than she could count. Tsalagi, tribal.

Hail Mary, full of grace.

Gods and goddesses. *Oh, Aradia, Diana's silver daughter.*

"Quit singin' and think!" Birdie rocked on her heels in the front room's corner, twisting her bonnet strings like a whirligig dropping from a nervous Maple. "Half out yer head and crazy to boot. Keep them circlin' ravens off'n the roof by decidin' to live!"

"Don't let your mind wander away, caille." Uncle Kinnon stood facing her, his long hair hanging free about his head as he stroked his gray beard and considered her. "Brownie's sweepin' up for a funeral you won't be needin' if you'll keep yourself in proper order so the rest can come." He slid away and in stepped Granny Sudie.

"Don't you give up so easily, witch child!" Granny Sudie worried her hands in her apron. "You got too much magic built up in ya' to waller 'round like a pig buryin' in slop right afore it's kilt for bacon and chitterlins'. Make use of all them lives! Think!"

But I don't know... don't know.

"Then you're gonna die as soon as that seventh blow lands on that-there coffin nail, and so will my Tessa Jo." Granny Sudie left just as quick as she'd come, leaving Cent alone in the nothing.

Nothing.

Nothing.

No light. The veil hasn't thinned, so I'm not dead... yet.

What time is it? Is it day six? The pain and fever now ran together, making thinking even harder, but she kept trying. *Witches fly. Fly on brooms. Flying ointment. Old ways. Hallucinogens. I'm so sick I don't need an ointment to hallucinate, and— that's it!* She flew from her body, pushing aside pain, fever, and her very flesh to soar above them. The Morrigan. Freyja. Hecate, Bellona. She was fire and energy, and she burned for answers, for her own survival. *Ignore the ache and fly!*

Stowne turned their head toward the door when she flew through it and into the night. "Rayne, take her, please. Keep feeding." Stowne followed Cent's spirit out of the house into the forest behind it. Seeking. Listening. *I see you, asiule ehu.*

She watched in the dark, and Stowne watched her.

Spirits. Elementals. Wee Fairies. She watched them comb the forest for that tree.

Deep, damaged, neglected roots, left to wither, will bring down the strongest tree with their rot.

And a little gust from Gan helps matters. She knew then. *So simple. In our faces.* They'd been able to see it from the kitchen window the entire time.

Cent flew to the toppled tree that rested on the track-hoe's cab, twice circling the portion that crossed onto the property before she saw both coffin nails and the slips of paper they held to the tree.

Don't touch them. She appealed to herself, to her knowledge of Cricket's plight, though she knew the answer. A witch couldn't pull their own nail, nor could an elemental pull it for them, but Aubrey was neither. Healers used energy, not magic. And healers could cure ailments be they magical *or* natural.

She glanced east to see daylight on the horizon then down to see a dark-dressed form creeping up the fence line. *You!* Cent descended on him, screaming her rage, but he paid her no mind. This was a man, nothing more, and he was blind to spirits and their magic. However, Stowne was elemental, magic laced with rock, and sand, and earth, and all of it landed against the dark-dressed man at once, sending him rolling down the hillside.

Rayne! Get Aubrey! Stowne drew up ready to charge again, but they couldn't purposefully kill a Human unless there was no other option. Such things disturbed the Balance and weren't permitted. *Tell him to come armed!*

"What the..." The man climbed the hill again, clutching the hammer that'd seal Cent and Tess' fate. "One more. One— this was an easy payday until now."

Stowne loosened the ground beneath the man before he got half-way up the hill, sending him sliding face-first back down. *Rayne! Now!*

Aubrey appeared on the porch and was down the steps seconds later, holding the high-beam flashlight they used for nighttime outhouse trips in one hand, and—

That's Uncle Kinnon's twelve-gauge pump!

"Where're you at, you son-of-a-bitch?" Aubrey snapped the gun up to load the chamber. "This mother-fuckin' gay boy ain't afraid to blow your trespassin' ass away!"

"He is climbing the hill again!" called Stowne. "He is holding a hammer!"

"Ain't half what I got." Aubrey fired into the air to prove his point then snapped the gun to reload the chamber.

Aubrey! Cent watched and worried and watched and— *Here comes another one!* She screeched when a second figure, taller and broader in the shoulder than the first, began climbing the hill. And he held a handgun close to his body.

"Jack, no!" Aubrey flipped off the flashlight and retreated around the corner of the house before the man fired his first shot. "My dog's sniffing you out, and someone's calling 911, so I'd get outta here if I were you!"

"Then we're gonna make it worth our while!" The second figure fired again, hitting the corner of the house. That was followed by another shot, trailed by Jack's pain-riddled yelp.

You ass! Cent refocused on what she could do, what she could... *Think. Think.* Confusion descended on her in spades, sucking her back into her near-dead body.

Right about the time Cent had convinced herself the light she saw through her eyelids was the veil thinning, she realized it was sunlight.

"We got 'em, honey." Aubrey dangled two coffin nails from his fingers when she opened her eyes.

"Jack?" She tried to sit up, but Aubrey pushed her back down.

"They just grazed him. He'll be fine and so will you, but you ain't going nowhere for a few days." He set the nails aside and held up a picture taken of the homestead from the road. The picture showed her arguing with Ruleman at the fence line, but where her head should be there was a nail hole.

"Here's the one of Tess. Same kind of hole." Aubrey set them both aside. "Six days. You figured it out just before dawn on day seven." He stared at his hands. "Tess is doing better than you. I moved her down to the trailer to get more rest, but she keeps asking about you." Aubrey laced his fingers together in his palms and turned his hands up to wiggle his fingertips. "I've done more critical care nursing this week than I ever did working in the hospital and did better at it. I remembered things too, things that I didn't know I ever could, and maybe that I shouldn't."

"Like?"

"How much I hate guns, for starters." He stared at where the shotgun hung over the front door. "But I'm glad Uncle Kinnon insisted on teaching me how to properly use one, and that Aunt Tess kept it cleaned for all these years. I also recalled just how far I'll go to protect my family." Aubrey wiggled his fingers again. "Stowne and Pyre toted off the bodies, but Gan says we've got a couple of pissed-off haints on our hands."

"The veil didn't thin for them?" *Let the rat-bastards suffer for a while.*

"Not yet. And no one came for them neither." He shrugged. "Haunted by the men I— self-defense. Tess keeps telling me that."

"She's right." Cent placed her hand on his arm. "I'm sorry. I never intended—"

"You and Tess are alive. That matters most." He raised his head until their eyes met. "A sheriff never came, so I did what I had to. That's all. There's nothing in the way of evidence, not even a blurb on the news about anyone missing, so we might never know who they were."

"Do you want to know?"

"Not if I can help it. I want to forget all about it, but I know I can't." Aubrey sniffed and turned to look out the window. "I learned something else too."

"Yeah?"

"Rayne. My God, how I love them."

"Well, that ain't so bad, is it?"

"No, but it scares the shit out of me with it being so soon after Ethan."

"Have you and Rayne talked?"

"Until I was hoarse, and they had to dip in their pool to recharge. We're taking it slow." Aubrey pushed his palms together and unfolded his hands. "Are you up to drinking something? 'Cause I'm over giving you enemas and—"

"I knew it!" Cent snarled at him. "Please tell me Stowne did them."

"Mostly. Now, tell me all about that tattoo."

"College. I wanted the rainbow charm but ended up with the clover. An old girlfriend, booze, and a dare were involved."

"Rainbow charm, huh?" He laughed until he gasped. "Don't you give me grief about my badass unicorn shirt ever again."

"It's worn the hell out."

"'Cause I love it so." Aubrey still chuckled. "You want some chicken broth?"

"And some ginger ale and maybe a couple of crackers?"

"Absolutely." Aubrey's dour expression returned. "I'm bound here now. Just like you. The realtor came to the trailer yesterday with a notary and another woman to serve as a witness while Tess and me signed the papers. The homestead is ours."

"That's wonderful." Cent didn't sound nearly as excited as she felt, but something about Aubrey's tone... "Isn't it?"

"That part is." He stared at his hands again. "It's about your mama."

"What about her?" Cent felt her smile fade.

"She's in the psychiatric hospital in JC. She was in the Med Center first, admitted for what they thought might be a stroke, but as soon as they got her into the CT, she flipped out, I mean, really lost it. She punched two techs and bit a nurse." Aubrey worried his hands harder than ever. "Things went downhill from there."

"Psych hospitals don't tell people those sort of things, even family, unless they have power of attorney." Cent gaped at him. "I've dealt with her being in and out of the hospital all my life, so how'd you get anything from them?"

"I know one of the nurses. Rose. We went to school together. She's a pagan, a natural witch. I think that's what she calls herself. Anyways, she wasn't supposed to, but she tracked me down through Aunt Tess to let me know Nida was there and what'd happened. She asked me about mental illness in the family, about Aunt Nida's schizophrenia diagnosis." Aubrey clenched his hands. "Is it the half-magic?"

"Yeah, it's made her unbalanced."

"I wouldn't have believed you before now. Rose said Aunt Nida was all bruised and scratched-up and screaming about demons and monsters, about a black mass attacking her, about escaping, and…" He raised his head to stare at her. "Who's Dustu?"

"Oh, no." Cent sank into the bed. "Where's Stowne?"

"Down in the cellar, thinking. And they looked just as crestfallen as you. Mind telling me who Dustu is?"

"Our son." Her stomach churned from something besides illness. Long Man had taken Dustu away, but he'd somehow found his way back. *Stowne, please.*

I am here. Stowne materialized beside the bed. "I do not know what to do." They knelt beside her, trembling, frightened as they laid their head in her lap. "Pyre took him to Long Man to drown the half-magic forever."

"Pyre killed him?"

"No." Stowne sat up to wipe the tears from Cent's eyes. "They wrapped Dustu in flame to keep him contained and set him adrift on a wooden raft. Rayne launched a series of waves to send the raft into the rapids, and they left the rest to nature."

"He was half-magic?" Aubrey gritted his teeth. "Like Aunt Nida?"

"Mama doesn't really understand that she's magic, but Dustu knew the second he was born." Cent gulped. "We tried to keep it from him by hiding Stowne's abilities, but Dustu's power grew out of control when his rage did."

"After Long Man took him away, Cent and I spent the rest of her life mourning and trying to heal," said Stowne when she couldn't continue. "We still bear the emotional scars. Have you ever heard the folklore surrounding the Nolichucky's Wailing Woman spirit?"

"Yeah, those are some of the saddest— wait! Cent's the basis?" Aubrey rocked back on his heels. "But she's quarter-magic, so how was Dustu half-magic?"

"Centenary had no magic in her that life but was young and able to see things most children could not, and I took advantage of that, establishing a friendship with her that grew into love when she was old enough to understand and reciprocate." Stowne took Cent's face into their hands. "I am sorry, asiule ehu. Ever so sorry. I did not mean for my love for you to result in this, much less extend across so many lives and…" Stowne's cry shook new dust from the rafters. "This was my greatest fear, what I was warned happened when an elemental loves a Human soul across so many lifetimes, but it had been so long and— I dragged you into my gluttony, took you down the path…" They dropped their hands and cried hard enough to shake the entire homestead.

"Stop it." She lifted Stowne's head to see their face. "I choose my own path, and I choose to walk beside you. Whatever came and whatever comes, I walk with you. I am yours and you are mine."

"That's goddamn romantic." Aubrey had moved to the end of the bed. "But it don't solve our core problem. What're we going to do about Dustu? Aunt Nida managed to get away from him, so he's gotta be pissed. And what does he want with the homestead?"

"Pissed is an understatement." Cent sat up higher in the bed. "Dustu needs Mama's energy back to keep doing damage, so we have to get to her first." She grasped Stowne's hand, bringing them up beside her. "Hand me my Bible, love. We need its wisdom more than ever."

"Anything for you." Stowne placed their hand on Aubrey's shoulder. "Please go get her something to eat and drink, and can Tess come up here? This is going to be a long night."

Chapter Thirty-Five

Spirits in Disguise
September 16-18, 2017

"**Ephesians** Chapter Six, verses one through four. 'Children, obey your parents in the Lord: for this is right. Honor thy father and mother; which is the first commandment with promise; that it may be well with thee, and thou mayest live long on the earth. And, ye fathers, provoke not your children to wrath but bring them up in the nurture and admonition of the Lord.'" Cent closed her Bible and looked back at Stowne who sat behind her in the big rocker. "What does that mean?"

"What was your question?" asked Tess. Aubrey and Rayne had carried her, recliner and all, up from the trailer. It was late evening, so the house was opened to the air, which Gan circulated by swaying their hand every moment or two. It was enough to keep most mosquitos away, but Pyre, who burned heatless and low in the fireplace, flicked out a tiny flame every so often to crisp one that'd still gotten in.

"You're not supposed to do that," Gan gently reminded them.

"They bite our loved ones, so it's in the name of protection." Pyre flicked another fireball into the air.

"Well, I appreciate it." Aubrey stood in the kitchen doorway with Rayne. "The skeeters have always liked me more than they should."

"That's because you're sweet." Rayne kissed his cheek. "Especially when you blush like that."

Pyre snickered and flicked another fireball, this one aimed at Rayne. "Cool down. You're embarrassing him."

"You're just jealous." Rayne slung water that met the fireball mid-air, creating a ball of steam that soon faded.

"Would you stop?" Aubrey glared at them both. "What was your question, Cent?"

"I asked how we can undo Dustu's power." She spread her fingers across the book's faded cover.

"Then I am right to take responsibility." Stowne furrowed their brow. "You were a woman that life too. I presented to Dustu as a male, as his father."

"But you really weren't," she said.

"In a way, yes, I was, am." Stowne placed their hand over hers. "Your bearing Dustu gave me a soul, but it also made me a parent. You do not recall, but I presented myself to you as male the night he was conceived."

"Just because— You did so to please me."

"I did so to seduce you." Stowne dropped their arms to their sides.

"No, you're wrong. I do remember." She pulled Stowne's arms back around her. "We agreed on what we did. I loved you, so you couldn't possibly have seduced me. And the male form— that isn't true either. It was all conscious and deliberate on both our parts. If I was going to return to you, we both had to have souls. Dustu was the product of our choice, so quit trying to take the blame to soften the blow on me. He's *our* child, and we'll handle him together."

"Sounds to me like the boy needs discipline." Aubrey patted Rayne's arm when it wrapped his waist.

"I am the one who set him afloat," said Pyre. "It was my responsibility to see that he never returned."

"Let's quit with the my-fault flow, shall we?" Gan leaned into Tess' hand. "I wasn't there, and even I'm feeling responsible. It sounds like one of two scenarios occurred. Either Dustu didn't die and somehow managed to live for over three thousand years, which I sincerely doubt, or he died but no death elemental bothered to take his spirit through the veil because he was crazed half-magic. With the latter, he's remained in this world so long that he's learned to tap the energies."

"No, his powers were never that well controlled." Cent placed her hand on her Bible when it began to hum. "All right. Tell me. How did Dustu come to have so much power?" She stood the book up and ran her ring finger across the edge until she felt a page hang on her nail. *Yes, that one.* She closed her eyes and let her finger settle on one of the two facing pages, opening her eyes when the page warmed under her touch. "Second Corinthians chapter twelve, verse fourteen, 'And no marvel for Satan himself is transformed into an angel of light.'"

"That child ain't no angel," said Tess. "If anything, he's pure— Ah, I see. He thinks he's been rescued, and that rescuer is controlling him."

"It's the same force that's controlling Ruleman if you ask me." Pyre flicked out another fireball, this one charring a spider that'd swung down from the ceiling. "But who would have rescued Dustu after so long?"

"I would have if I'd known he hadn't crossed," declared Rayne. "And you would have too. Any of us would have. His energy must have been incredibly low for..." Rayne scrunched their face in dismay. "Someone hid him away instead of crossing him, and now they've brought him out."

"You mean the same spirit that's controlling Ruleman and Aunt Nida had Dustu all this time?" Aubrey scrunched his face too. "Why?"

"Energy." Cent flipped her Bible closed. "Power or not, Dustu's still a child and easy to misdirect, just like Mama. He'd also act like a battery to store energy in."

"But who's trying to suck up and store so much power?" asked Pyre. "And why can't any of us sense this?"

"I don't know yet." Cent drummed her fingers on her leg. "But whoever it is wants the greater power that comes from controlling the veil crossing."

"Greed." Gan, along with everyone else, turned toward the front door when it slammed shut. "Them again? I'll handle it."

"The haints?" Aubrey sighed. "When will they be leaving?"

"By Samhain if we can convince them," explained Tess. "And I've gotten real good over the years at convincing spirits to leave the property. Shoo them over the fence, Gan, please? And warn them we'll banish them if they get intrusive."

"Certainly." Gan rose and glided toward the door. "I'll also ask a few of my kind to keep watch on them."

"Thank you," Aubrey called after them then he turned back. "One haint, the taller one, I think, followed me to the outhouse last night, screaming and ranting."

"They'll feed on your guilt if you let it show," said Cent. "You'd best let someone stay close until they're gone."

"That's why I've been following you." Rayne practically purred the words.

"Oh, that's why?" Aubrey blushed again when everyone around them broke into laughter. "The rest of y'all need to hush up."

"If you want them to leave you alone, do this whenever you catch one following you." Cent tried hard to stifle her grin. She'd gone from student to teacher in record time. "Don't run from them. Just walk to wherever you're wanting, but before you go inside, spin deasil three times while you say, 'Haints, ghosts, and them that's dead, turn-around, spin-around, get dizzy in your head.' That'll confuse them, and they'll leave you alone for a while."

"Deasil?" Aubrey scratched his head.

"Clockwise," said Rayne. "To your right."

"So I turn and talk at the same time?" Aubrey repeated Cent's words to commit them to memory. "Awesome. I'll do that next time. Thanks."

"We should get back to the business at hand." Stowne hid their smile against the back of Cent's head.

I felt that.

I am extremely proud of all you have managed to remember in such a short time-span.

Thanks, but I know there's more to that grin.

Your recovered abilities have provoked memories of one of our most satisfying pleasures. Stowne's low rumble vibrated through her. *May I shave the hair that has grown back on your head? It has become rough to the touch. Does it itch?*

Some, but I'm beginning to think my bald-ass head turns you on.

It is part of you so yes, of course, it excites me. But I enjoy kissing every part of you, not just your bald-ass head. Stowne stifled a laugh against her and peered up with a deadpan expression she saw when she looked sidelong at them. "Greed is as deadly for elementals as it is for Humans. Greed throws off the Balance, which means something or someone somewhere suffers as a consequence."

Greed? Cent brought her arm back to nudge Stowne's abdomen. *You should know, greedy gut.*

My greed is for you alone. I have been beside you far too long to stray again. Always remember that.

Oh, I do, but we need to be serious for a minute. Cent folded her hands together and sat straight. "So this *thing* wants the veil, but it can't get it without both Dustu *and* Mama's energy. I've got a plan. Mama's safe where she is right now, but that won't last forever. Will someone please put my Bible up and bring me my big book from the old country? Mabon is tomorrow, so let's celebrate at the circle then I've got some spells to practice, and we've some rehearsing to do."

Cent grinned at herself in Birdie's wardrobe mirror. Hanging by a thread but still there. *That explains a lot of things anymore.* Cent set her phone atop her books and turned back to what she'd been doing. The disguise spell had taken her considerable practice, more than she thought it should, but she was still healing, Stowne had reminded her. They kept her energy up by feeding her often, and Aubrey made her eat more food than she wanted. He brewed her tea too. Healing, herbal concoctions she'd never heard of, but he remembered like he'd last made them yesterday.

"More honey, next time, okay?" Cent followed Aubrey into the kitchen as she choked down the last swallow in her mug, holding it out to him as she spat out a stem. "They make these things called strainers. Can we get one?"

"We'll get a dozen after this is over, so keep practicing. You're taller than Lottie Mae Saddler, so work on being shorter."

"Shorter, right." Cent closed her eyes to concentrate. "How about now?"

"Wrong direction, sugar. You look concave, not shorter."

"Crap." She changed her focus, tapering. The bag of snake bones in her pocket was supposed to help her. Snakes possessed the ability to camouflage and had unstoppable courage, so a person carrying their bones had it too.

"That's better."

"Yeah?" She smiled at him.

"But your entire disguise dropped when you opened your eyes." Aubrey carried her mug to the kitchen. "Better hug those bones and keep working on it."

"Dammit!" She marched to the bedroom to practice in front of the mirror, sculpting her features to match the images of Lottie Mae Saddler Aubrey had captured on his phone. He'd taken a risk to gather pictures outside the church, but no one had seemed the wiser for it.

"How's this?"

Cent raised her fists and pushed her left leg back into a fighting stance the second she turned around. "How the— Rayne?" She dropped her arms when they nodded.

"Good likeness?" Rayne moved to stand beside her. "Slip back into your disguise." They pointed to the mirror.

"Give me a moment. You rattled me." She took a moment to scrutinize Rayne's disguise. Plump body and dark, receding hair, simple black pants and shirt with a black necktie. Yes, Rayne had managed to mimic Ivan Ruleman's physical form to perfection. "Yeah, you've got it right."

"But what about the voice?" Rayne dropped their voice into a baritone that rattled the windows.

"We're going in as a prayer group, remember? No one in there's likely to know his voice, so just speak at a normal Human volume." She shuddered and reshaped her appearance to Lottie Mae Saddler's again. "Hey, Aubrey! Come see!"

"Sure, just a— holy hell!" Aubrey's breath audibly caught in his throat. "You could have told me Rayne was in here too!"

So you haven't gotten to the point of feeling their presence wherever they might be. But Cent knew such things took time.

"I'll take that for a successful trial run." Rayne dropped their disguise and stepped up to Aubrey, drawing him in for a kiss. "I don't like pretending to be that horrid man."

"It ain't him who's bad, honey." Aubrey leaned in for another kiss. "Aunt Tess says Ruleman's actually a nice guy. It's…" He glanced warily at Cent.

"It's whatever's got Dustu and Mama," she spoke for him. "Stowne and I have come to accept what is, concerning Dustu. Not every child turns out well.

Dustu, um…" Cent shook her head. "He was out of control back then and was taken advantage of by something dark. No one deserves that, least of all a little boy, half-magic or not. Same goes for Mama and—"

"How do I look?" Pyre strode into the room in their Mama disguise.

"Great except for your walk," Cent told them. "Most women take smaller strides."

"*You* don't," replied Pyre. "Neither you nor Tess do, so why would Nida?"

"Some women," Rayne tried to explain. "They are taught early how to behave a certain way and—"

"Remember how Mamaw Roslyn died early?" asked Cent. "And how Aunt Tess and Granny Sudie raised Mama? Neither of them is what I'd call delicate."

"But they were always gentle with her," Rayne continued. "Perhaps that's what caused… no, it's too much experience being overshadowed by others, isn't it?"

"Mama ain't what I would call delicate either, but Rayne's correct. It's societal. Just take smaller steps, and you'll be fine." Cent pulled up her disguise and paced the room, gauging her paces to something she thought more applicable. "Does Lottie Mae use a cane?"

"She was when I saw her," said Aubrey. "But they're not going to let you take one back, so be unsteady in your gait."

"Gotcha." *Everything is in place, and tomorrow we act.* But Cent wondered how any of it was going to work.

"No purses, bags, pencils, pens, cell phones, food, drinks, cameras, or anything else that might be used as a weapon. Leave your keys up here." The receptionist held out a large plastic bowl.

"How about my Bible?" Rayne held out Tess' copy. It'd taken time and careful planning to get two elementals inside Aubrey's Camry without draining their energy, but they'd managed with cotton sheets and a wicker basket where Pyre and Rayne had huddled as a puddle and smoke until they reached the hospital.

"The Bible is as welcomed as ever," said the receptionist. "Please have a seat. Someone will be with y'all shortly."

"This place is anything but natural," Rayne looked around. There'd been two pair huaraches waiting for Rayne and Pyre in the Camry's floorboard. "How will this work again?"

"Since we're on Mama's visitor list, we'll be allowed to talk to her in the cafeteria. It'll be supervised, so the change will need to happen fast."

"That means you'll have three spells running at once?" Pyre would be disguised as a blond-haired woman around Mama's age, another church woman, but this disguise didn't need to be as detailed as Mama's would, so they hadn't worked as long or hard on it.

"Only until we reach the car." Cent would have to keep up her Lottie Mae Saddler appearance while she disguised Mama and clamped down on her mouth so she wouldn't object. "I'm hoping they've got her drugged." Cent kept her voice low. "They usually keep patients fairly out of it while they're here."

"That seems cruel." Rayne clutched the Bible in their hands.

"I think so too, but after dealing with Mama, I understand why. One unstable person is more than enough to handle, so I can't imagine a whole building full of them."

"There are children here." Pyre wiggled in their seat. "Several magical children. Two half-magics." They stared at the floor. "This tears at me."

"It tears at us all." Rayne kept their voice baritone. "But we cannot help everyone, so put them aside and refocus before your disguise slips more."

"You're right." Pyre closed their eyes to concentrate.

They look like they're praying. Silence fell between them until a woman wearing a pink-paisley scrub top opened the security door. "Rhodes family?"

"Here." Cent rose as slowly as her disguise warranted.

"Follow me." The nurse waited for them to pass through the door before she pulled it secure. "My name's Joelie, and I'm one of Nida's nurses. We're going down the hall, the last door to the right, but let's talk a moment first." Joelie stepped in front of Cent to block the way. "Nida's rather sedated at present, so don't expect much from her."

"We understand," said Cent in a wavering voice. "We just want to pray with her."

"She might not recognize you," continued Joelie. "But y'all are on her visitor's list from her last hospitalization, so we thought it'd be okay."

"Thank you." Cent patted Joelie's arm. "Can we say a prayer for you while we're at it? You and everyone here have such a difficult job."

"That'd be appreciated." Joelie turned back down the hall, leading them to the cafeteria, where three rows of tables with attached stools overlooked a meditation garden.

"That's pretty," said Pyre as they entered. "Peaceful."

"That's its purpose." Nurse Joelie pointed to a table. "Have a seat, and I'll be back with Miss Rhodes."

"Thank you." Cent settled onto a stool, noting how uncomfortable such a tiny, round seat would be if this were her real form. "So far, so good," she mumbled as soon as Joelie walked away. "Y'all keep doing what you're doing, and we'll be fine."

How goes it? Stowne's voice was no more than a whisper at this distance.

Working hard. Projecting more at once meant she risked dropping her disguise.

Keep me informed, please. And I love you.

Love you too. "Stowne checked in." Cent nodded toward the cafeteria entrance. "And here comes Mama. Game on."

Rayne flipped opened the Bible, and they joined hands, dropping their heads in prayer until Mama stepped into the cafeteria. "Amen." Rayne raised their head and turned around, standing when they all heard the cafeteria door click shut. "Nida." They extended their Ruleman-hand to Mama. "We were just praying for your wellbeing."

Mama kept quiet, but she didn't accept Rayne's hand, and her eyes darted from Rayne to Pyre to Cent where they lingered.

"Sit down, Nida." Joelie guided her to a stool. "She has a group session in twenty minutes, just so you know, and she can't miss that, so the visit will have to be brief."

"Then our prayers will be to the point. Thank you for giving us some time." Rayne waited until Joelie had stepped away. "You look good, Nida."

Mama toyed with her hospital band.

"You sure do." Cent's voice warbled more than she'd intended. "God's seeing that you're being taken good care of."

"Humph." Mama folded her hands on the tabletop and stared at them.

"We know you're hurtin'," said Pyre. "But God—"

"I ain't so drugged that I can't see y'all for who and what you are." Mama peered up with the slightest of smiles. "Get me outta here, Cent, girl. Please."

"Whatever are you talkin' about, Nida?" Rayne remained in character. "We're here to pray with you, to give you the love and support of your church."

"Bullshit." Mama turned her hands palm-down on the table. "Cent's hiding beneath Lottie Mae Saddler, and Ivan and that woman I don't know is coverin' elemental spirits." Her smile spread a little wider. "You found your magic, Cent. I did too once them spells were stripped off'n me, but now they got me too drugged to do much of anything. Use yours to get me outta here, or I'll throw such a conniption ain't none of you gonna be able to keep up those disguises."

"She's got us dead-to-rights." Cent managed to keep up her disguise despite her surprise. "All right, Mama. You want out of here, we'll get you out, but

233

there're ground rules involved."

"Whatever they are, I agree to them." Mama leaned forward to peer into Cent's eyes. "That boy of yours? He makes my crazy look all calm and orderly like." Her eyes widened as she sat back. "You gettin' me outta here or not?"

Cent had almost finished explaining the switch with Pyre when someone stepped into the cafeteria. This person talked to the lone, unarmed security officer, and the man stepped closer to their table. "Something's going on." She closed her eyes to search with her mind, centering on the hospital's entrance. "There's a crowd forming up front. Two police. A couple of doctors. Oh, hell—" Cent opened her eyes and took a deep breath.

"What's happening?" asked Rayne.

"Trouble," said Pyre. "Tell us what you saw."

"The *real* Ruleman and Lottie Mae Saddler are in the waiting room, and they're asking to see Mama." Cent stared at her mother, more worried than ever about her health and sanity. "If that isn't bad enough, Dustu Usdi is squatting inside Ruleman." *Along with someone else.*

Chapter Thirty-Six

Hello, Etsi
September 19, 2017

"Dustu?" Mama's face turned so pale the veins in her temples stood out. "Please, oh, please. I'll do whatever you say, just get me outta here. My being drugged up is the only reason I ain't already screaming bloody murder."

"Let's keep ourselves together." Cent grimaced. Truthfully, she'd never seen Mama act so calm in a stressful situation. *Think.* "Okay, plan B. Mama, you're going to look like Lottie Mae Saddler." She nodded to Rayne. "I'm going to be Ruleman, and you take over the woman Pyre's covering pretending to be." She pointed to Pyre. "When we do, you make a distraction. Nothing major. No real fire, just do something."

"Chaos it is." Pyre pushed away from the table. "Tell me when you're ready."

Cent sat up tall when a police officer followed a second security guard into the cafeteria. "Change *now*." They switched their disguises. "Go, Pyre."

"On it." They sped away in a clear-heat form no one seemed to notice, leaving their huaraches beneath the table.

"Reverend Ruleman?" The police officer approached them with caution. "I thought you were on the other side of the— no matter. Might we have a word with you?"

"Certainly." Cent whispered to Mama and Rayne to stay put then slowly turned and walked to where the officer stood. "We were fixin' to engage in parting prayers, so there'd best be a mighty good reason for this interruption."

"We need to see IDs for you and your companions, sir." The officer shoved his thumbs beneath his belt. "Now, please."

"Our identifications are in our vehicle." Cent held the Bible to her chest. "We are who we say, so why—"

"Where's Miss Rhodes?" The security guard had joined them. "Tyler!" He looked over his right shoulder. "Where's Nida Rhodes?"

"Right there— oh, no." A big man wearing black scrubs approached at a trot. "She was there just a second ago, I swear!" He tore away from them to check every corner then launched into the kitchen area.

"Mister Ruleman?" The police officer's hand drifted to his secured sidearm. "Where's Miss Rhodes gone to?"

"She's flown from this world and into the arms of our Lord and Savior!" Cent waved her Ruleman-arms. "Hallelujah! Praise the Lord!"

"Mister Ruleman." The officer unsnapped the guard from his weapon. "I'm going to ask you again where Miss Rhodes got off to, and you need to answer me truthfully."

"I was merely caught up in the Holy Spirit. She's in the bathroom." Cent pointed to the only door marked as such on the cafeteria's far side.

"Tyler! She's in the can!" The security guard reached the door first, knocking on it. "Miss Rhodes? Are you in there?" He reached for the knob. "Miss Rhodes? What the— It's locked from the inside!"

"It's a patient bathroom, so there's no lock on *either* side!" The police officer kept his eyes on Cent.

Now would be a really good time, Pyre! The harder the security guard pounded and pushed, the more energy it took Cent to keep the door closed.

Hold on! they called.

The overhead lights flicked off as the fire alarm began screeching. The emergency lights flashed, dropping the cafeteria into mayhem.

The security guard spun around when one of the patients shrieked and covered her head while another, a tall, heavy-set man wearing flip-flops and plaid night pants climbed onto the tabletop and screamed at the top of his lungs.

"Ah, shit. Here we go." The police officer secured his sidearm and shoved Cent aside as the tall man began jumping from table to table. "Get down from there!"

"All visitors must exit immediately!" Tyler skidded back into the cafeteria's main space. "Please! Do so as quickly and as safely as possible!"

"Here's our exit." Cent returned to the table. "Let's go!"

"Oh, this is fun." Mama laughed as Rayne took hold of her and Cent, transporting them back to the car.

"The car keys!" Cent pivoted toward the entrance as soon as they touched the ground.

"It's open and your mother's inside!" Rayne dropped their disguise, kicked off their shoes, and slipped into the basket. "The keys are here, too."

"I got them before I set off the alarms," called Pyre from the back seat. "Let's go."

"Hold on!" Cent threw the Camry into reverse as soon as she shut the door, exiting the parking lot just before the fire department and more police arrived, leaving the real Ivan Ruleman and Lottie Mae behind, but Dustu…

"Hello, Etsi!" He appeared in the seat behind Cent, dressed in the same deer-hide pants and shirt he'd been wearing when he'd been taken away, however, his voice was anything but child-like. "Have you missed me?" He stood, wrapping his arm around her neck as he pulled her against the seat.

Can't breathe, can't… Cent fought to maintain control of the car and herself. *Ah, Dustu.* She pulled into an old Food City parking lot and jammed the Camry in park, turning her spirit form around in the seat to face him as her body continued to struggle for air. *The angry, spoiled prodigal returns.* She wasn't about to tip her hand to the spirit controlling Dustu.

Just for you. Dustu leaned over to kiss Cent's cheek, blowing putrid breath across her face. "How's Adadoda?"

Much the same. I'll tell him you asked about him.

"Him?" A leer spread across Dustu's face. "Oh, no, Etsi, Adadoda's not a man. I'd figured that out long before I died… three thousand years ago. You remember that day, don't you? You let one of Adadoda's elemental friends drag me to Long Man to drown. Speaking of which…" Dustu released his hold on Cent's throat and leaned over the basket, growling as Pyre and Rayne rose from inside it.

"You will leave us and these Humans alone!" Rayne dripped with churning water that turned to steam when it fell against Pyre. "Or so help me, I'll—"

"Kill me? Please." Dustu flicked his hand and Pyre and Rayne vanished. "I sent them ahead, so they can tell Adadoda I'm coming home."

Mama managed a whimper but nothing more.

"And you! Wherever did you think you were going when you ran?" Dustu reformed into a black cloud that grabbed Mama's head and pulled it back, forcing open her mouth so he could slide down her throat. "That's better." The same growling voice that'd risen from Dustu now flowed from Mama's mouth. "Nida's an excellent energy source, but surely you've made use of her before."

"Leave my mother…alone," said Cent between coughs.

"Oh, Etsi, look how far you've come. The daughter of half-magic? That makes you, hmmm, quarter? More's the pity, because with Nida, I'm whole magic. That's power you can't imagine, much less defeat."

Enough of the games. "What do you want? Why have you returned?" Try as she might, Cent couldn't feel who hid behind Dustu, but whoever it was had full access to his memories.

"Returned? Why, I never left. No one came to help me cross. No one came for me or my body. Both were left to rot on the riverbank." Dustu tapped Mama's index finger against her double chin. "I languished for millennia, blaming myself. Three thousand years in which to wallow in self-pity and anger until I finally realized that my plight was really my parents' fault. That's a lot of time. And a *lot* of anger." He chuckled low. "Using your mother's energy makes this even sweeter, don't you think?"

"Piss off, you pitiful haint. That form of me died not too many years after you did, or don't you remember setting me on fire? Probably not. Half-magic means you're unstable, so adding half-magic to that doesn't make you whole-magic, it makes you a full-blown nut job!" Cent tried to unbuckle her seatbelt, but Dustu blocked her with his hand.

"Now, now, Etsi. That'd be too easy, wouldn't it?" He reached for the keys, but Cent grabbed them first, throwing them into the back window.

"We're staying put."

Centenary! Stowne's voice echoed in her head. *Fight him!*

Oh, hi, Adadoda. Dustu sneered at Cent. *Etsi and I are having a party. Want to join— Oh, you're stuck in your land body, aren't you? Bound. I'll take care of you later. Right now, I suggest you tell Etsi goodbye.*

Leave my Centenary alone! Stowne's thoughts shook Cent's body so hard they echoed out to shake the Camry too. *Fight him!*

You were never there when I was alive, so don't bother now. Dustu returned his focus to Cent. "I don't need those keys. They were just easier." He flicked Mama's fingers, and the Camry started then slid into drive. "Jump into enough people, and you learn skills." He flicked Mama's hand again, and the Camry surged forward. "Like driving."

"Not happening." Cent stepped on the brakes with both feet, but they pushed to the floor with no effect.

"Ghost in the machine. Do you know the musical reference?" "Spirits in the Material World" blasted through the Camry's speakers as Dustu took control of the steering with one remote finger, moving the car in-and-out of traffic. "Oh, quit fighting, will you? Nida did the same thing when I first stripped the spells from her. That's what landed her in the hospital." Dustu used his non-steering hand to punch Cent's face.

"Jerk." She'd been hit harder in self-defense class, but she'd been wearing headgear and a mouthpiece, so this left her head spinning. She kept fighting regardless, grabbing the wheel even harder and shifting the car into park, putting her entire energy into the brakes until they squealed and began to smoke, breaking loose, one-by-one, from the wheels while the car remained in motion.

"Foolish Etsi. You thought the car had to be in drive?" The Camry blew through the light by Walmart and had almost reached Headtown Road when Dustu pointed ahead. "Oh, there's a good one." He reached down to unbuckle Cent's seatbelt. "I'm taking Nida with me, so this is goodbye. We'll play again your next life." Dustu leaned Mama's body over to kiss Cent's cheek, waved Mama's hand, and they disappeared in a puff of black smoke as the Camry sailed over the median, slamming grill-first into a utility pole across the highway.

Chapter Thirty-Seven

Papaw Death
September 20, 2017

Cent…en…ary! Stowne's voice echoed in Cent's head as another black mass appeared, shattering the window to jerk her from the car before the airbags deployed.

"Down you go." The mass placed her on the ground behind a house a short distance away.

The sound of breaking glass and crushing metal echoed through the area.

"Dear God." Cent lay on her side, panting, her head swimming from what'd just happened. "Thank you, whoever you are." She peered up to see her rescuer, her eyes widening as she came to realize whose presence she was in. "Exan?"

"Yes. But it is not your time." Exan changed their form to that of a tall, pale man of perhaps seventy years in age. Dressed in a black shirt and pants, white hair to their mid-back, they leaned on a silver-tipped cane, managing to somehow look more senior goth than death elemental.

"I never thought you'd be the grandfatherly type." Cent touched her bottom lip when she felt blood ooze from it. "But thanks."

"The correct term is grandparent. And I was not allowed near you until now." Exan peered at the smoke that billowed from the wreck. "I told Stowne you were safe."

I'm okay. She projected. *Tell Aubrey I'm sorry about the car.* It was too much effort to say more from this distance.

Just come home. Now that we know you are safe, Aubrey is calling the authorities to report his car stolen.

She sat with her head in her hands until the cobwebs cleared. "Was anyone hurt?"

"Besides you, no." Exan sat beside her. "I think an explanation is in order."

"Not now. I'm too rattled to listen much." Cent sniffled and scowled. *My nose hurts something fierce.* She could feel it beginning to swell. "No offense intended, but I'd forgotten how much your kind stinks."

"Is that any way to talk to your grandparent?" Exan smiled softly at her. "My kind is no different than other elementals in that regard."

"You smell like what you're made of."

"And you smell quite a lot like your Stowne, like a mountainside." Exan unfolded and rose, leaning heavily on their cane as they held out their hand. "Come along, Centenary. I will fly you home."

"I think I should keep my eyes closed until we're there." She was half-glad when her nose swelled enough to prevent her from smelling anything more.

"Ah, so you remember the process." Exan helped her stand and brought their hand to her face. "Let me ease your pain." Their touch was cool but comforting, and she tried hard to relax beneath it. "Your experience with Demis left you wary of my kind, but I assure you that such rage is not normal." Exan offered her energy next, a gentle feed to stop her nosebleed and steady her on the way home. "My method of transport will take us through the edge of the veil, so you must hold fast to me." They pulled her into their arms. "Tighter, child. And don't open your eyes no matter how intrigued or frightened you are by what you feel and hear."

"That sounds like a warning." But it was one she'd heard before.

"It is. Some things are not meant for the living, so it— Ah, you are descended from me, so you would not be scarred, but you have already endured too much today for it to be helpful. Close your eyes."

Cent did as Exan said, pressing against them as their form changed, and they began to rise. She knew she rested inside their black mass but felt no fear. Elementals like Exan were necessary. They helped the dead cross the veil, comforted those dying alone, and pulled unused energy so it wouldn't go to waste, returning to the earth what they couldn't use for themselves. Demis' vile nature was as unnatural as Dustu's spectral return, but such things happened, like it or not. No god or demigod was a perfectionist, but they all expected their creations to take care of themselves and each other.

Brace for bitter cold. Exan condensed around her. *Calm, child, and remember that you have flown beside me in your past lives.*

It's not you that frightens me. The air around them became so cold that she couldn't inhale without agony.

Hold your breath until I say otherwise. She felt Exan's mass extend over her nose and mouth. *Only to protect you. Even the inner edge of the veil can suck the breath from the living.* They spoke softly to her, comforting, encouraging, assuring her the cold settling into her bones was temporary. *Remind yourself that I am not taking you through the veil. If I were, your body would not be with us.* "There. You may breathe."

She gasped as Exan pulled away from her face, but the bitter cold inside her remained as they descended, even when the surrounding temperature returned to summer heat. "I'm frozen…through."

"That happens when the living fly with my kind. See? Stowne's below us. They can warm you, I am certain."

"Not a very grandparent-like…thing to…say." Her teeth chattered. "I see Aubrey and… Tess too."

"The Humans? You will have to introduce us." Exan slid back into their senior-goth form as they landed. "She is bone-chilled and a bit battered, but she breathes."

"Centenary!" Stowne pulled her into their arms. "You are frigid to the touch."

"Tell me… about it." She shivered against them. "I know Exan's banned, but they saved… me and…"

"Stowne did not ban me from this realm." Exan bowed before Stowne. "My own kind restricted me until I gave reason enough to warrant forgiveness. And you, grandchild, were that reason." They grasped her hand and brought it to their mouth, blowing across it so it'd warm. "Thank you."

"Here. Wrap her good." Aubrey held a quilt out to Stowne, but he kept staring at Exan. "She's…" He lowered his head when Exan returned his gaze.

"You're a death elemental!" Tess exclaimed. "I ain't seen or met one of you, ever, until now. Not even when…" Her eyes grew large. "*You're Exan!* You… you… you're the one what…" Tess sighed and stepped back, releasing the knots her hands had drawn into. "Roslyn died decades ago, but you didn't even appear then. Why?"

"I was not allowed." Exan dropped to their knees before her. "I never intended for her to suffer."

"We've all suffered in some way." Tess wiped her eyes. "Part of me wants to strangle you, but the rest— It was Roslyn's fault. She was the one that conjured you when she shouldn't have. Roslyn told me she compelled you, and she was a powerful witch, more so than me, but not half what Centenary is."

"Yes, I felt that the second I pulled her from the car," said Exan. "Roslyn was as powerful as she was beautiful, but I did nothing to resist her when I should have. I would have stayed by her side, would have— My kind is not supposed to fall in love with Humans. Oh, Tess. I am deeply sorry. I loved Roslyn from the first moment I saw her. I denied my own nature to help create our daughter, and we both suffered as a result." Exan let a wracking sob. "Our child, Nida, Centenary's mother. I could not prevent Dustu's possessor from stealing her away, so I have failed you twice."

"You haven't failed me." Tess brought Exan's face up to see hers. "You loved and created life. That's an amazing feat for a being eternally bound to death and dying. I've seen Roslyn twice since she died, and the second time she told me she was soon to be reborn. Rayne and Pyre helped Kinnon cross, since he died at home, so your absence didn't change as much here as it could've."

"Where *are* Rayne and Pyre?" Cent looked around. "Are they okay?" Her teeth had stopped chattering, and she was finally feeling the stress of going head-to-head with Dustu. *My face feels twice its size.*

"Rayne has returned to their pool with several of their lessers," said Stowne. "And Pyre's gone to their lair where some of their kind are helping them recover."

"Exan!" Gan blew down the hill in a whirlwind of dust and leaves. "It is good to see you again!" They dropped to their knees beside Exan, pulling them into a hug. "Tess and I discussed you at length just the other day."

"They helped me change some of my thinking." Tess glanced from one elemental to the other. "Pick up your chin, Aub. We need to get Cent inside so you can check her out."

"Yeah, I— You." Aubrey pointed to Exan. "I've seen you before."

"At the hospital in Knoxville. Yes, I remember. Few Humans can see my kind's comings and goings."

"I only saw you once when a child I was caring for— Why?"

"It was Charley's time." Exan flexed their hand so their cane returned, using it for support as they rose to their feet. "I witnessed your sympathy and caring, but no amount of love— I did not know then you were related to Centenary."

"Would that have made a difference?"

"No, but I might have approached you in this form to assure you that Charley would be returning." Exan turned to Stowne. "I would like to reclaim my status inside your realm."

"I found no acceptable replacement for you, so I will announce your official return at Samhain. Do you have lessers?"

"That wasn't allowed me either."

"I'll ask for some to be sent from other realms, young ones you can mold as you wish. For tonight, will you go tell Rayne and Pyre of your return?" Stowne wrapped Cent tighter in the quilt. "We will gather tomorrow and plan our next move. Aubrey, will you follow us to the house? I will feel better once you assure me that Centenary is not seriously injured."

"Yeah." Aubrey watched as Exan's form became black smoke that shot up the mountainside. "The rest of you elemental types don't bother me no more, but that one's going to take some serious time to accept."

"That's because we Humans fear death, and you've been stung by seeing it come early so many times," said Tess as Gan took her arm to steady her. "And you're still young, Aub."

"Yeah, maybe, but— all right. Let Gan get you inside so you can rest." He stayed behind with Stowne and Cent, who he began to fuss over. "You got one hell of a shiner coming up, and your nose might be broke."

"I'm feeling both." She turned her face to Stowne's chest. "Just help me to the house, please. I'm tired."

"Aubrey?" asked Stowne as they walked. "Can you give us a few minutes before you come inside? Centenary and I need to talk."

"I'll stay on the porch but not too long. That nose will need set if it's broke."

"Fifteen minutes, no more." Stowne scooped Cent into their arms, carrying her into the house where they placed her on the bed in their room. "Lie down."

"It'll hurt my head."

"Then sit with me." Stowne took her to the front room and sat in their rocker with her in their lap. "Let it out."

"I don't need— don't want..." She shook from her toes up with the terror she hadn't allowed herself earlier, sobbing as she clutched Stowne. "That... him..." She couldn't say Dustu's name.

"I know. I felt everything that happened through you." Stowne rocked her as she cried, shuddering with her, sharing her guilt and misery, hugging her tight and whispering prayers when she screamed into their shoulder. There was nothing more they could say to comfort each other, and nothing but the truth in all its ugliness for them to see and mourn.

The soul-granting love they'd shared so long ago had surpassed anything half-magic had the ability to achieve and was now in the grip of something even darker.

"Demon." Cent looked to Stowne who nodded. That was the only word to describe what held onto Dustu. The only term that applied. This demon had both Mama and Dustu in their grip and the homestead in their line of fire. "Shit, my nose is bleeding again." Cent used her shirt collar to slow the trickle.

"It is definitely broken." Stowne hugged her tight. "But we are not. Neither Dustu nor guilt is going to get in the way of us."

Chapter Thirty-Eight

Long Man
September 23, 2017

"Hold still." Aubrey was careful as he pulled the medical tape from her face, but she still flinched.

"You're pulling my hide off."

"No, I'm not, and it looks better."

"Liar."

"It really does." Aubrey led her to the wardrobe mirror. "See for yourself."

"I guess you're right." Cent rolled her shoulders and sat on the bed, drawing her knees to her chest as she stared out the window. Stowne, Tess, and Rayne were resetting the wards while Exan kept watch above them. They'd already shut down the heavy equipment that morning, and Tess had argued with Ruleman while Mama cackled from the driveway. The constant chaos was slowly draining them, which is what their unseen enemy wanted. Growing weaker as Samhain approached. Growing weaker by the day.

Early that morning, she'd seen a blackbird on the windowsill that'd pulled a splinter from the sill before it'd flown off. Someone was going to die, but you had to be breathing for that to happen, which ruled out the elementals. However, it left Mama, Aubrey, Tess, and… "Me."

To die. To die. She couldn't break the mourning cycle that'd returned when Dustu had revealed himself in the car. A mother's pain. A mother's self-blame. Both were inescapable when a child filled with dark magic.

"You're being oppressed." Aubrey stood in the window to block her stare.

"I know." She avoided his gaze. "Thanks for helping with my face. It does feel some better."

"You've been inside for three days straight except for going to the bathroom. Go take a shower. You're smelling like both Exan and Stowne, and the two don't mix too good."

Cent tucked her legs beneath her. "I'm fine."

"To quote Aunt Tess, 'bullshit.'" Aubrey sat beside her. "You're letting Dustu's possessor get to you, and that's exactly what they want."

"I'm in mourning."

"Over something that happened three-thousand years ago?"

"The other day was like reliving it, and it's all new again."

"Really?" Aubrey folded his arms over his chest. "I don't want to sound callous, but that's not just bullshit, it's flaming, kick it 'cross the holler bullshit to the nth degree."

"Fuck you and that worn-out rainbow unicorn you rode in on." She dropped to her side so her head hit the pillow, shoving Jack away when he put his head on the bed to look at her. "Leave me alone."

"Like that's gonna happen." Aubrey patted Jack's head then pulled her upright. "You're going to have to get past this bad-parent issue. Tonight's the first quarter, and the full moon is right after that. Samhain's getting close."

"Tell me something I don't know." Cent put her hands over her face and—"Ow." She dropped her hands and reached over to pull Stowne's dirt-stained pillow over her head instead.

"Serves you right." Aubrey jerked the pillow away. "Get out of this bed. Aunt Tess wants to cleanse you again. And I need to give you another healing session so those bruises will keep fading."

"Won't neither one do no good." She reached for the pillow, scowling when he wouldn't give it to her.

"I'm calling bullshit again." He smacked at her hand. "You told me they did yesterday."

"Just so y'all would leave me be." She pulled up her legs to get past him and rolled to the other side of the bed. "Leave me the fuck alone!"

"That's it!" Aubrey left the room, returning soon after with Pyre and Exan, both of whom stood over her.

"Time you met Long Man for yourself," said Pyre.

"You worry me, grandchild. A deep cleansing is warranted." Exan's mist swirled so thick no light shined through.

"I've been there before." *And I don't want to go back.*

"Not this lifetime," claimed Pyre. "And you're going whether you want to or not."

"Tess has already cleansed me twice." Cent turned her back to them. "Like I told Aubrey. Leave. Me. Alone."

"Rayne's already gone ahead to ask for an audience." Exan grabbed her by the ankles, dragging her from the bed as their form grew. "Gan is going to blow us there, so we don't have to edge the veil."

"Dammit!" She swatted at their growing smoke-form. "Let me go!"

"The louder the patient objects, the deeper the oppression," Aubrey folded his hands over his chest when Cent glared at him. "I got my own books, and they're coming back even before I find them." He tapped his head. "Stowne said Long Man lives inside their realm, so they'll be there too."

"Put me down!" Cent thrashed in Exan's hold, all but slipping free before Pyre added their energy, suspending her upside down between them.

"Are you coming too?" Pyre extended their hand to Aubrey. "I haven't flown with you since you were my Aggie, so I'd appreciate the nostalgia."

"Sure." Aubrey turned his head to see Cent's face. "Stop fighting, honey. This has to happen for you to get over it." The hateful words that flowed from Cent's mouth were not her own. "They warned me you'd do that." Aubrey accepted Pyre's hand. "All right. Let's go."

They flew just above the ground, Cent shrieking inside Exan's black cloud and Pyre's white smoke as it twisted together.

"Good Lord." Aubrey's face, contorted with worry, hovered close to hers. "You're all screwed up in the head."

Cent screamed something unintelligible even to herself and continued flailing, reaching up to beat on Pyre and Exan's hold, howling spells to make them release her. They almost dropped her twice but recovered, letting her fall when they hovered over a pool just off the Nolichucky. It was hidden among the trees and connected to the river by a stream. A hidden, magical place, she realized as she hit the water to find Rayne waiting for her. They locked their mouth around hers, breathing for her as they pulled her down.

Cold! Cent reached for the surface.

You've been cold for days. Rayne flicked the clothes from Cent and held her naked against them, breathing, countering her struggle with patience until she stopped fighting. *Long Man will rid you of this pain, but I cannot guide you to him.*

Rayne released their hold and spun her around into Stowne's waiting arms.

We do this together, because the pain is ours to share, because our past has returned to haunt us. Stowne placed their mouth over hers and pushed through the water, dragging her into the river.

Sand and silt infused with mica flecks stirred from the bottom until she couldn't see. It hadn't always been this way. She knew that for certain. Humans had almost ruined things, had dammed connecting rivers to control the floods and create electricity, had mined Stowne's mountain and many others in the area, forever altering the Nolichucky.

We should respect Long Man, not fear him. Stowne moved so they both sat on the river bottom among the silt, fish, and bits of trash. *But this location will not cleanse us.* They raised her head from the water, encouraging her to breathe on her own as they floated downriver.

She grimaced when a beer can bounced off her arm. "I'm going to need a Tetanus shot after this is over."

"I do not understand what you said, but the waters are cleaner ahead." Stowne held her when the current became swift, kicking toward a creek mouth where she landed butt-first in the silt. "We go on foot from here."

She kept quiet as they walked but paused when they crossed behind a house.

"No Human can see us." Stowne nudged her ahead.

"What about—"

"Other elementals have volunteered to create distractions, so do not worry."

"I can't help but."

"Hence, your oppression. Long Man will rinse us clean of such things where we are going." Stowne pushed her head down when they crawled through a culvert extending under the highway. "The rest of the way is slippery. I should carry you, but..."

"I need to walk." She pushed away Stowne's helping hand when she almost fell. "Where are the others?"

"Behind us. This ceremony requires us all."

"Even Tess?"

"Gan is assisting her."

At least I won't lack for company. She remembered cleansings when she'd been Tsalagi, remembered the cold winter waters, recalled the daily ritual that she'd ceased partaking in when Dustu was born. Baptism before there were Southern Baptists, teachings about energy within the powerful flow of Long Man's fingers.

Trees hung low over them while great laurels and rhododendrons narrowed the creek bed, creating a tunnel as the woods beyond continued to thicken. They climbed almost vertically in spots, scaling slick, moss-covered rocks surrounding small waterfalls where sunlight bled through in tiny, brilliant shafts. "Are we on park land?"

"Yes. Rayne says it is restricted access."

"All the better." The soles of her feet were becoming bruised, but she kept pushing ahead. The houses were long gone, as was any sign of the road or other civilization. Naked and roaming the untouched wilds. It'd been centuries since she'd felt so frightened and free at once.

The path ended, and the trees opened near the mountaintop, allowing a perfect circle of light to spread across a pond so clear that she could see the bottom was deeper than Rayne's pool above the homestead.

Long Man's home. No one needed to tell her. This water spirit was older than the Appalachian range and filled with cold wisdom that now lapped at her toes.

"Enter my waters and be cleansed of what weighs you." The voice was deep and intimidating but one she knew well, so she stepped into the water, hesitating when she saw it bubbling along the far side. Wee Fairies buzzed her head as she waded, pulling at her hair, one reached beneath her glasses to pluck an eyelash. Minor tests. She kept the fairies at bay with promises of returning someday with a jar of fresh honey and a bowl of homemade biscuits. Beautiful, long-haired dryads, their root-feet tangling together as they dangled in the water, watched and giggled, leaning toward each other to speak in hushed tones. They startled when they heard Stowne rumble behind Cent.

"Show respect for your elders and their eternal loves." Stowne's words rippled the water. This pond rested along the highest ridge in the realm, and Stowne outranked everyone besides Long Man in both age and power, but they gave no sign of the knowledge as they bowed deeply and pulled Cent forward. She slipped when they did so, creating a monumental splash when she landed in the water.

"Clumsy mortal." The dryads laughed so hard they rocked back, tangling their feet even more.

"Hush, children." Long Man rose from the water to shoo the dryads away with a wave of his hand. "This is above your understanding." The dryads turned and fled at his words, leaving Cent and Stowne alone with Long Man, a clear-bodied, glass-eyed form as twisted and slim as the stream they'd followed in. His eyes were wide, his face covered with a long, dripping beard, and his smile as broad as the Nolichucky's widest point. "Welcome to my home."

"Asiule ehu, you must stand on your own." Stowne glanced from Cent to Long Man.

"Oh, please, Stowne. Help her up. She is naked, cold, and afraid, though I am not certain why. Did I not tell you last time that formality is not warranted in a friendship as old as ours?"

"You have told me many times," said Stowne. "But I was taught to respect my elders. Others are following us. Rayne, Pyre—"

"And Gan and…" Long Man's water-beard twitched as he raised his head. "Exan? His kind released him from punishment so soon?"

"Yes. To help us." Stowne lifted Cent to a stand.

"You are going to need that assistance." Water ran down and out of Long Man's clear body as he rose. "And Tess Rhodes. Delightful. I have not seen her in years. And…" Long Man rolled his eyes up in thought. "Another of your Centenary's blood, a healer. Interesting."

"He's new to all this." Cent's voice waivered despite her efforts.

"As are you in this life." Long Man snapped his fingers and pointed from Stowne to Cent. "Warm your eternal, or I will do so myself in ways that will pull her from your side for the rest of her current existence."

"You will not." Stowne pulled Cent against them, warm to the point that fog rose from the water when they touched.

"Still possessive, I see." Long Man rose to stand his full height, his head among the trees as he moved in slow strides to the water's edge, sitting where the dryads had been. "I am teasing them, Centenary."

"No, you're right, sir. Stowne *is* possessive of me."

"As they should be." Long Man laughed long and hard, creating waves that nearly knocked Cent down again. "Bring her here, Stowne. Sit with me while we wait for the others to arrive."

"Father?" One of the dryads stood on her root toes to speak in Long Man's pointed ear.

"Yes, yes, child. I am aware. Return to your trunk like your sisters and await my word to return."

"Your daughters are spoiled," said Stowne as they watched her go. "They think nothing prettier than themselves."

"They look so much like their beautiful mother that I cannot fault them." Long Man shifted on his boulder. "And you are blind with love, Stowne, but rightly so."

They're talking about me like I'm not here. Cent suddenly felt uncomfortable in Stowne's lap, so she returned to the water, swimming out ten feet before she turned around. "And where is their mother?" Stowne's energy had followed to warm the water around her.

"Have you not educated her on such things this time around?" Long Man placed his hands on his gnarled knees.

"We have only just…" Stowne ducked their head and grinned. "Mother Earth has many consorts. Lord Long Man is one of them, but he is not my father."

"Then who is?" Cent treaded water. "No, wait. You told me already. Father Eternity. Right?"

"Ah, she does indeed remember." Long Man slapped his knee as he laughed. "That sharp mind, Stowne, is what I have always appreciated most about your Centenary."

"Mother Earth and Father Eternity. Yes, asiule ehu. I might have told you, but you have recalled the interconnectedness for yourself. I must remain close to my beginnings, more so since you have come to walk beside me and— Ah, Tess!"

"Hello." Tess slid into the water to float on her back. "That's a heck of a walk for someone like me."

"Why did you not fly in like last time?" Long Man folded his arms to flap them like a bird.

"'Cause you won't let no one do nothin' besides walk in for a cleansing." Tess smiled as Gan slipped into the water behind her. "I had help that made the trip enjoyable."

"It was enjoyable for me as well." Gan nodded to Long Man. "My Lord, ever at your service."

"Gan. Yes. I had heard whispers of your return." Long Man's mouth pulled into a frown. "And about Kinnon several years back. I am glad you have found happiness again, Tess."

"Gan makes me smile." She leaned back when Gan wrapped their swirling arms around her. "A different relationship than what I had with Kinnon but no less important." She loosened her hair so it drifted up in Gan's breeze. "My nephew Aubrey's walkin' in too."

"He's right behind you." Cent pointed to where Aubrey, naked and covering himself, stood on the pond's edge.

"Good grief!" Aubrey's teeth chattered. "I'm never going to recover from this chill!" He reeled back then jerked forward, falling face-first into the water when he saw Long Man. "That's neither an elemental nor a haint nor..." He shook from more than cold as he stared up at the Nolichucky's spirit. "Rayne, honey? I, uh—"

"Father! I'd like to introduce Aubrey." Rayne helped Aubrey stand. "He's here—"

"Because he's yours. A fine choice, child. I sensed his healing energies before he ever appeared on my bank."

"That's your *daddy*?" Aubrey fell into the water again. "Hello...sir?" He peered up at Long Man with a weak grin.

"No need for further introduction, Aubrey James Rhodes. I know your history like my own when you step into my waters." Long Man waved his hand toward who next approached. "Ah, Pyre. You brighten my day every time you appear."

"Funny." Pyre stood on the water's edge. "It's always an honor, my Lord. I brought Exan with me." They pointed to where Exan stood in their Human form leaning on their cane.

"Welcome, Exan. It is indeed good to see you again."

"We are all in attendance, Lord Long Man." Exan twirled their cane as they bowed.

"Yes. I am aware. You and Pyre will join your family." Long Man sank into the water until his shoulders dipped below the surface and stretched his arms as soon as Pyre and Exan entered the water, pulling them all together before him. "Float beside the one you are attached to, and if you are not attached, come along anyway. You will all be cleansed in turn." Long Man began to sing in Tsalagi, a water spiritual about how life bubbled from inside Mother Earth, about water's ability to take away grief and pain.

And guilt. Cent relaxed as she and the others slipped beneath the water. Stowne's mouth found hers, and they held each other inside Long Man's arms.

> *For love there must be hatred*
> *For up there must be down*
> *For right there must be wrong*
> *For silence there must be sound*

Long Man spoke about the Balance then preached about water and its healing powers, pulling them deeper into the pond, offering them a feast of energy, forgiveness, and knowledge as he held them.

I will show you the way. His song pushed all other thoughts from Cent's head.

I will show you the means. He pulled Cent and Stowne to his chest, curling their energies like a spring until one's end was the other's beginning, soaking their combined mind, body, and soul with river water and scrubbing away their hurt with river sand. *Enter together, leave apart, but know you must remain one for anything to succeed.*

Cent woke on the moonlit banks of the Nolichucky, her skin as pink and wrinkled as a new baby and her mouth open and gasping like she was taking her first breath. Stowne rocked on their hands and knees beside her, coughing up mouthfuls of water, sand, and glimmering mica. Their form shimmered in the waxing moonlight, clean, their body shined by the river rock they'd tumbled over.

"Stowne?"

"Yes?" They spat a small fish onto the bank that flip-flopped back into the water. "That is the absolute worst part of the process."

"Are we cleansed?" She looked past Stowne to see Rayne, Pyre, Exan, and Gan spitting out mud, fish, and small rocks. Beyond them sat Aubrey, his face to the moon, and Tess who sat up and tilted her head to knock the water out of her ears.

Stowne lurched forward like they were about to vomit then sighed and rolled onto their back beside her. "We are cleansed both inside and out."

"Can we go home now?"

"We have something to find first, remember?" Stowne pulled her to them. "Long Man said you know where it is."

"I do?"

"None of us knows except you."

"Then let's get to it." Cent stumbled along the Nolichucky's banks in the dark, twice taking to the water when there wasn't any bank at all. Stowne followed at a distance, and the others trailed behind, silent as they watched her climb in-and-out of the water. *Not here. Not there.* She didn't know where she was going but knew she was getting close, following the invisible map Long Man had placed in her head.

"Here!" She landed on a rocky stretch of the bank to dig between the river stones. Convinced. Knowing. Aware of what she'd found the second it touched her hand.

"Centenary?" Stowne dropped to their knees beside her and pulled her hands from her chest to reveal what she held. "Oh, oh." They wrapped around her, pressing her to them, absorbing her cries as they set loose their own.

She howled the grief she'd been denied all those lives ago, clutching the remains, the fused topmost bones of a child's skull, stained and fossilized from millennia of exposure, to her chest

She'd found Dustu.

She'd found her child.

Now she could finally lead him home.

Chapter Thirty-Nine

Full Moon of the Redneck Fae
September 24-October 5, 2017

"**You** let her be!" Cent grabbed Ruleman's hand when he reached for Mama, but Dustu turned to smile at her instead, his yellow, rotted teeth bared as he tried to bite her. "Back off!" Cent shoved Dustu away, but he stretched those yellow teeth toward her, gnashing them, dripping acid that stung her flesh. "You'll not!" She screamed those words as she sat up in the bed, no longer afraid or guilty that she'd been part of what'd created Dustu. He'd simply happened. She and Stowne had discussed this until almost dawn. Half-magic didn't mean evil. But Evil sometimes came for half-magic, and Evil had taken Dustu and Mama for itself.

They needed to strain the liquor from the mash, the Evil from Dustu, and lead him across the veil before Evil could claim him again, burying the remains they'd found to complete the process. When that happened, Stowne said, Mama would be released as well.

"Centenary?" Stowne rolled to face her. "This dream, you fought inside it. You resisted. Did you win?"

"I didn't let it get that far before I woke." Cent slid down to snuggle into Stowne's shoulder. "It's still early. No one is awake, so— I need a distraction."

"As do I. We could fly up to Usdagalv and make all the noise we want." Stowne sounded hopeful.

"No, here's fine, and there's something nice about hushed and rushed."

"It can be fun at that." Stowne pulled her closer. "We both smell like the river bank."

"Dirty's what we do best." She smothered a laugh into Stowne's chest. "But nothing magical this time, okay? Just us. I need the tenderness."

"But I am magic and ever so tender." Stowne lowered their head to wrap their mouth around hers. *And so are you.*

"The full moon is end of next week." Aubrey stared down the hillside to where a new company was preparing to assault the land on either side of them. Cent sat with him, tipsy from her early-morning escapades, but she noticed that Aubrey had a similar expression on his face.

"Whatcha been doing this morning?" She nudged him with her elbow.

"The same as you." He blocked her next nudge with his own. "Rayne and I… yeah." Aubrey ran his fingers through his hair. "They definitely aren't a woman. I know that for certain. And I liked it— a lot."

"Makes for a good start to the day." Her smile broadened when Jack leaned into her. She'd been trying to make up with him since she'd returned home, and he was apparently ready to forgive her.

"Yeah, it does at that." Aubrey turned to sit cross-legged facing her. "So, all that stuff we discussed last night, we're seriously going to do that?"

"We don't have a choice." She looked down the hillside like he had. "They have newer equipment than the last company."

"It will fall just as easily," said Pyre from behind them. "I've gotten rather fond of doing this."

"Haint in the hauler." Cent chuckled. "Who's helping you today?"

"Gan says they want to play this time. Exan wanted to as well, but we couldn't figure out exactly what they could do."

"Walk the equipment across the veil after it's dead?" offered Aubrey.

"It'd have to have a soul for that to happen." Pyre laughed. "No, they're off tending someone inside the realm who's dying." Pyre became transparent then flew down the hill to help Gan.

"Wonder who?" Cent stood and pulled onto her ridge-runner toes to see over the trees and down the road.

"No one we know." Tess called to them from the trailer's back porch. "Get yourself around, Aubrey. I need you to take me to Johnson City for a few things."

"Like what?" He uncrossed his legs, jumped from a sitting to a squat position, and stood in one smooth movement.

Flexible little shit. But Aubrey had always been so.

"Pizza," said Tess. "We ate the last of what I had in the freezer last night. I also need a few witchin' things, so take me to Atlantis."

"Smudges." Cent rubbed Jack's belly when he rolled onto his back. "Get all they have in stock. We'll need a lot of them tomorrow."

"I already scalped my sage bushes to burn on the esbat fire." Tess pointed to the herb garden. "They'll grow back next year. Let's get moving, Aub. We're burning daylight."

"You heard the woman." Cent turned toward the homestead's front door. "Can you bring back some Pal's? We should have comfort food while we work."

"Big Pals and Frenchie Fries it is." Aubrey stepped into the house, returning a moment later with his wallet and the keys to the pickup. "As soon as my insurance check clears I'm buying a new car. Maybe a pickup this time."

"I thought you hated Uncle Kinnon's truck," said Cent.

"Yeah, I do, but the new one will be *my* truck."

"Ah, I see. Bring me back a tea?"

"I'm bringing back *two* gallons."

"Even better." Cent watched them drive off then turned her gaze to where Gan and Pyre were complicating an innocent equipment operator's day, grinning when the foreman threw his hard hat with such force it tumbled down the hillside.

"Small victories." She entered the house in search of Stowne, ready to begin the next stage of their plan.

———————

I'm going home next week.
That's great!
It scares me. They cleaned me out the hard way and now
I feel like I'm going right back into the snake pit.
Then come here.
Tennessee? You crazy?
It isn't the snake pit and you've got a friend here.
That's true. I'll think about it. OK?
Think hard, Ms. Betty. Love you.
Love you too.

———————

"You really want me to do this?" Aubrey held Dustu's skull cap between his fingertips. They were alone on Tess' back porch. No one else wanted to be there, including Cent, but Aubrey had insisted she be present in case she changed her mind at the last minute. "You're sure?"

"Well, I can't." Cent was certain she looked as green as she felt. "And neither can Stowne. It'd turn both our stomachs." She held up her hand when Aubrey furrowed his brows. "Figuratively speaking, of course. Elementals don't have stomachs."

"The idea of doing it nearly turns mine." He placed the bone onto the cutting board. "I'll pretend I'm back in grad school and doing a rotation at the coroner's office." Aubrey picked up the Dremel then turned his head to look at her. "You're certain this will work? 'Cause it's going to shatter once I start cutting and—"

"Lord Long Man says it'll work, so I can't think otherwise." She raised her mask and lowered her goggles when he told her to.

They lifted the property wards on October fifth, so anyone and everyone could attend the circle. Cent and Stowne climbed the hillside together, arriving early, taking their seats as Pyre started the ritual bonfire.

"So it begins." Pyre retreated into the flames as others began arriving. The Wee Fairies came first, chirping as they swooped, but midway around the fire they shrieked and flew to the circle's far end, where they huddled behind a stump.

"What's got into them?"

"Their natural enemy." Stowne indicated the group of larger fairies who'd landed along the circle's edge.

"Hunters." Cent felt her upper lip curl with old hatred.

"Yes. Worthy of our caution, but we need not fear them."

"You should've warned me."

"Lord Long Man said they should come, and they, like us, must obey."

"Just what does he expect to happen?"

"It is better to be cautious than caught off-guard." Stowne motioned to one of the Hunters, the only female among them, a hard-faced, plaster-pale woman wearing black work boots, a faded, black denim kilt, and a black, long-sleeved, snap-front Carhart work shirt pocked with welding burn holes. The rainbow print welding cap on her head was turned backward and pulled low to cover her ears, and a gold circlet rested at a tilt on top of that. Her black wings, which were spread behind her, shimmered with blues and purples in the firelight. They were not a thing of beauty but one of power, veined, bony, stretched skin that highlighted her broad shoulders. "Thank you for coming tonight, Dane. I would like you to meet Centenary."

"Centenary this time 'round, you mean." Dane's accent rang pure Southern Appalachia. She was Cent's height and oddly attractive, alabaster Joan Jett with sharper features and long blue-black hair pulled back in a single, tight braid. The leather bracers on her forearms were marked by welding burns like her shirt, but beneath those burns a symbol was cut into the leather.

A sigil. Cent remembered what they were, but not what they were used for, so she drew her eyes back up to Dane's face. Beautiful but angry. Yes, that was the best description.

"What you starin' at, girlie?" Dane gave her a hard, thin-lipped smile. "See somethin' you like?"

"No." Cent turned her head away.

"Yeah, sure. Like I was sayin', I ain't thrilled about being here tonight *and* for the Samhain circle both, but Stowne sparked my interest."

Redneck fae. Cent tried not to laugh when she remembered more. "King Dane Gow." Her name rolled from Cent's mouth like a morning belch after a night of moonshine and Spaghettios. "Your kind arrived in these mountains during one of my earlier lives. You were driven out of your Scottish realm, if memory serves. You hunted Native Americans like the deer until you struck a deal with the major southern tribes."

"We came here from Scotland lookin' for better huntin' grounds, and we don't hunt you Humans no more. There're so many of your sorry asses that it draws too much attention." Dane curled her mouth into a pointed-tooth sneer. "We like feedin' on Human energy better than the meat anyhow."

"Such an improvement." Cent folded her arms across her chest. "Why're you here?"

"Ask your boulder of a beau." Dane stomped her boot against the circle sand when Stowne grumbled. "All right. I'll play along." But Dane still didn't bother to look at her. "We're the darkest amongst you, lil' girl, and we live just over the mountaintop from you. Smithies, welders, and metal workers, and *I'm* their rightful king. We fill our bellies with Wee Fairies, wild game, and the energy from any who go against us." Dane glared at the Wee Fairy who dared to peek from their hiding spot. "You best recollect the order of things, 'cause there're a lotta deep hollers in these here mountains where no one'll ever find your parts."

"Dane, we discussed how you were to address Centenary." Stowne motioned the Hunter King closer. "She is not one of your girlfriends or wives, and I will not tolerate—"

"She's a *Human,* but still worth a gander, I reckon." Dane's eyes drifted to Cent where they stayed, scrutinizing her, judging. Dane drew her finger along the inside of her cheek, flung snuff on the ground just outside the circle sands, and wiped her hand on her kilt. "Like I said, Human." The Hunter King was called king no matter their gender because a few old rules still held from their Scottish days. No queen could lead, so Dane had bent the rules in half and welded new ones over them when she'd taken charge, poisoning her father, brothers, and their supporters with the darkest of magic before seizing the crown to make herself king. "For such a queered-up mess of a mountain girl, you got a passel of loved ones, Centenary Rhodes, but you don't mean diddly-squat to me, queer or not, aside from what I might get outta your livin' or dyin'."

"Do not attempt to intimidate my eternal." Stowne growled low then leaned forward to speak in Dane's ear.

"Yeah, why wouldn't I?" Dane looked at Cent with a grin and returned to her men, a collection of strong-winged good ol' boys dressed in camouflage who kept glancing at Cent.

I don't trust a single— Christ, I've seen some of them at Dryler's minus their wings. Cent raised her brows at Stowne when they sat back. "What was that about?"

"Some very old business."

Others arrived at that moment. The dryads who'd laughed at Cent the day before now bowed before her, placing armfuls of bull thistle, gentian, and heal-all blossoms at her feet in way of apology.

"Father sends his regards," said one of them, and they retreated to the far side of the fire, where they sat close together.

"Well, that's a switch." But Cent was too preoccupied with the other arrivals to think about it long. Gnomes. Water elementals. Fire salamanders. Tess and Aubrey arrived with Gan and Rayne. Exan followed them but seemed reluctant to join the festivities until Rayne grabbed them by the arm, pulling them into the circle.

The ritual proved standard. Stowne called to the four directions, praised Mother Earth and Father Eternity, spoke of life and death and all that rested between, recognized Dane's attendance, then they and Cent danced, slow and close, but the overall tension was palpable.

Do they know what's coming?

Of course. Forewarned is forearmed. Stowne kissed the top of her head. They were in their tallest Human form, the one that was more masculine than any other, and their hair was styled in old Cherokee fashion, much like hers.

This isn't my favorite look for you, but I suppose it's needed.

Stowne peered down at her. *It is one Dustu will immediately recognize.*

He already knows me well enough to try to kill me.

True. Stowne raised their head when Jack howled from inside the homestead where he'd been locked for his own protection. *Someone is coming.*

And we know exactly who. Cent hushed those in attendance when alarmed whispers began to rise. Two Humans were walking up the hillside, and one of them wore a black necktie.

They can see us! The Wee Fairies quivered behind Stowne's seat.

"Shh." Cent reached back to offer them comfort. "We expected this to happen."

"Make them go. Make them go." One of the fairies held fast to her fingers until she shook them loose.

"Those who see this circle and come with good intentions are welcome inside it." Stowne rose when Mama and Ruleman stood outside the circle. Mama's head was down, but Cent could see the bruises on her face.

Son of a bitch. It took every ounce of Cent's energy not to jump from her seat and give Ruleman matching shiners. But he hadn't hit Mama nor had Dustu, so she sat on her hands as she fought for control.

Giving in to anger will infinitely complicate things. Stowne sent calming energy to her. *Breathe and relax. The bruises will heal, and we have larger obstacles in our path this night.*

I know. Cent raised her head to see Ruleman, whose smug expression said everything about his possession. Evil possessed Dustu, Dustu possessed Ruleman, and Evil believed it had control of both. "Mister Ruleman, whatever brings you here? Do you wish to dance with my mother under the full moon?"

"Hardly." Ruleman's eyes burned blacker than his tie. "I came to shame you, to…" His eyes darted around the fire, taking in the attendees. The elementals remained emotionless while Dane glared at him. "Your daughter keeps company with mythical heathens and criminals, Nida. Should I punish you more for her indiscretions?" He hit Mama with the back of his hand hard enough for her to stumble back.

"Please, Ivan." She sank to her knees beside him. "I said I'd come, that I'd…" She cringed when he raised his hand again.

"Enough!" Cent rose to face him. "Come here, Mama. He's not who he says. He's the monster we saw the other day."

"Your daughter brought that evil upon herself." Ruleman pulled Mama behind him. "Right, Nida?"

"That's what you told me." Mama shook her head ever so slightly.

"Your words don't match your actions." Ruleman reached back to grab her, pulling her forward as he twisted her arm behind her back. "Just to make certain we're on the same righteous path."

"Let her go." Cent stepped down to grind her heels into the sand. "She can make her own decisions."

"A psychiatric hospital escapee?" Ruleman's laugh turned bitter. "No. She can't possibly make her own choices." He jerked her arm higher on her back. "Can you, Nida?"

"No, Ivan. I need your direction." Mama stepped back to lessen the pressure on her arm. "I need God's direction in all things."

"That's right, Nida. You need me." Ruleman dropped his hold to wrap the same arm around her, using the other to hold up his Bible for all to see. "This book! This book!"

"It warns us about those like you." Cent crossed the circle sands to stand on the edge facing Ruleman. "We are older. We are wiser. We—"

"You're nothing but the heathen child of a loose woman." Ruleman clutched his Bible tighter. "Your face is bruised. Whatever happened to you? Did you fall prey to your own sins?"

"You'd know, you were there. And I ain't talking to Ruleman or Dustu. I'm calling you out, demon, so you might as well let go of everyone you're hiding behind."

"Ah, Etsi. You know me too well." An adult-sized Dustu rose from Ruleman's body, letting him fall to the ground as he flung the Bible aside. This voice was the same as the one Cent had heard in the Camry. "Why don't you step outside the circle, so I can hug you?" He still held onto Mama.

"No." *This isn't my son speaking.* Cent walked along the circle's edge to draw Dustu away from Mama. "Why don't you step inside? You know you want to."

"I can't, and you know it." Dustu grimaced when his toes hit the circle's edge, sending up a plume of sulfurous smoke. "Your mother is on this side, or do you forget?"

"No, I haven't forgotten." Cent pulled out the bag Aubrey had given her, dangling it so Dustu could see. "But I have something of yours as well."

"What could you possibly have that I—" Dustu curled his mouth into a smile as he sniffed the air. "Ah, rot. A piece of something—" His smile abruptly faded. "A piece of *me!*" He bounced off the circle's edge in his rush to reach her. "All right. We—" Dustu twisted in on himself, warping, pulling inward. "No deal!" He picked Mama up by the throat without touching her. "Open the circle, or I kill her."

"No killing on sacred ground." Cent swung the bag like a pendulum. "Or do you forget the rules?"

"Rules? I'll show you…" Dustu turned his nose to the air, sniffing harder. "You aren't the only one with—" His voice rose in pitch. "Give me my body!"

"Are you missin' it, son?" Cent walked to the fire and held the bag over it low enough for Pyre to smoke the fabric. "We didn't find much of you, but what we did needs burying because that'd be the right and proper thing to do." She swung the bag up into her hand. "Break away from that demon, and you'll get what you desire."

"No, I…" Dustu shook so hard he dropped Mama who crumpled to the ground beside Ruleman. "I don't want— no!" He curled in on himself again, undulating, expanding and contracting until Cent could see black smoke churning inside him.

There you are, you bastard. "Dustu, son. Every bit of you that's left lies within this circle, but you must peel away from what holds you to get it." She returned to the circle's edge still holding the bone bag.

"I can't, I—" Dustu's face darkened as the black inside him fought for control. "They left you to drown!" The voice was Dustu's but not, heavier, darker, and unfiltered by a child spirit.

"We didn't abandon you." Stowne now stood beside Cent on the circle's edge. "We sent you to cross the veil before Evil overtook you, but it gained hold despite our efforts."

"Adadoda?" Dustu whimpered and reached toward the circle only to be pulled back by what lurked inside him. "Please, Adadoda! Help me!" A child's voice, Dustu so distant and distraught that it brought tears to Cent's eyes. "Please!"

My son. Cent couldn't help but sob.

"I am trying to." Stowne pulled another bone bag from their deer-hide shirt. "But you must do as you are told to get what you want."

"You expect obedience?" The evil in Dustu rose so fast it lifted him from the ground. "Oh, no Stowne. We trade." Dustu's voice changed again, becoming as dark and menacing as it'd been. "One Nida Rhodes for control of the veil crossing."

"I speak to my son, not the coward squatting inside him." Stowne placed their hand on Cent's shoulder. "We want to take you across the veil, Dustu. We want to help you find peace."

"Then give me my body!" Dustu howled and tore at his form, ripping it open so the dark within him poured out. "There! They're going! Now please give me what's mine!" His form shrank as the darkness escaped, leaving behind the translucent, skeletal frame of a Tsalagi boy.

"You drive me out after all I've done for you?" The black reformed into a mass that towered over Dustu, lunging forward to encircle his neck. "I cared for you, taught you, fed you with my own energy so you'd strengthen, and you toss me aside for a few fossilized fragments? No, Dustu. It is not that easy."

"They're using you for their own benefit!" Cent fought Stowne's grip on her. "Let him go!"

"You want him, Mother?" The black mass switched into a solid form, landing hard on the ground with cloven hooves to leer at Cent. Evil personified. Death made intentionally terrifying. Death shaped like the Devil down to the horns and flicking tail. "Come get him."

"Demis. You utter fool." Stowne grew their form to stand eye-to-eye with the towering death elemental. "Greedy. Conniving. What could you possibly want with my family?"

"Trade." Demis reached back, dragging both Dustu and Mama up into his hold. "Your son and the half-magic woman. I'll even throw in Ruleman. In return, Centenary. She and I have unfinished business."

"You are banished from my realm, so there is no deal to make." Stowne stepped back. "You may go, but you will leave your victims behind."

"That's not going to happen." Demis reached for Cent, stopping just shy of the circle. "My intent isn't ill. It's about regaining balance. *My* balance."

Your balance is imbalance. "I've beaten you before, Demis." Cent stood on her toes. "What makes you certain you'll win this time?"

"I have your son." Demis dropped Mama at their feet and raised Dustu's translucent form to shake it, slinging water. "He's nothing without my energy feeding him. He'll languish just like he was doing when I found him."

"He became trapped when you didn't come to his aid." Stowne held out their hand. "Give him to me, and I will take him myself."

Demis jerked Dustu away. "That is not part of my offer."

"Then I will take him," offered Exan. "Let me set things right."

"It was before your time in my realm, so you are not responsible." Stowne pulled Cent back when she reached for Dustu. "It was Demis' job to begin with, one that they consciously chose to ignore then hid the evidence of. They hid our child from us. They hid him so he'd never cross."

"What's one rejected haint and such a small one at that?" Demis shook Dustu like a wet rag in Stowne's face, flicking more water from him, but Dustu lifted his arms in response, moving like he was trying to push to the surface. An eternally drowning child. Sinking, choking. Without Demis' energy, Dustu had returned to his death state.

"Etsi! Help me!" Water gushed from Dustu's mouth.

My child. My son. Cent lunged across the circle's edge before she thought, screaming as Demis grabbed her arm to pull her fully across.

"You mothers are predictable." Demis tossed Dustu aside to hold her with both hands, pressing her against their chest to suck her energy from her body.

Stowne. Our son. Cross him. They'd been wrong all those years ago. Half-magic hadn't made Dustu evil. It'd made him vulnerable. The Raven Mocker's pawn. Demis' prey. *Save him.*

"You first!" Stowne bellowed. "You first!"

She felt the protective circle dissolve, the chaos and fighting that ensued. Aubrey pulled Mama and Ruleman to safety beside Tess. But Stowne— they tried to pull her from Demis, but Demis held her too tightly, sucking her will, her drive, her breath.

Me. They only want me. She smothered within Demis' form. *Let me go. Help Dustu instead.* But her pleas were a waste of waning energy.

No! Centenary! Stowne's roar quaked the mountain, sending rock and dirt sliding into the circle's edge, forcing everyone back.

She's mine! Demis took flight, hovering above the circle as they pulled more energy from her.

Not my time. Not my… She saw Uncle Kinnon and heard him yell for her to fight, but he slid back behind the veil when something pierced Demis' shoulder. They fell together, Demis screaming with her energy as they hit the ground.

"Ain't no one leavin' this party 'til I do." Dane tucked her Glock back into her thigh holster and dropped her kilt over it. "Return Stowne's girl, or I'll shoot you again, Demis. This time to kill. You know I can. Hunter weapons are the only thing that'll kill you elemental types, and we got a small arsenal with us tonight." Dane's men pulled handguns and knives from their clothing to emphasize her point.

"But you— We had a deal!" Demis stared up at the Hunter King.

"Stowne made me a better offer." Dane widened her stance and extended one hand. "Give me Centenary."

"She won't survive no matter how much Stowne and those other fools help her." Demis ejected Cent from their form, leaving her at Dane's feet. "I win."

"That'd be a no, Demis. She'll keep her breath with *my* help." Dane lifted Cent to her, careful as she placed her head on her shoulder. "Exan crossed that Tsalagi haint-boy, so you're leavin' tonight with nary a fart for your tryin'."

"Deal or not, why should you care about any of this?" Demis reached for Centenary. "Let me finish her so she can cross. It'll be a mercy, a—"

"I got my reasons." Dane snapped her fingers, and her men lunged forward to surround Demis. "That greed of yours has got to be a skeeter in more than just *my* drawers." Dane's mouth curved into another pointed-tooth smile. "Your kind, even though they smell nastier than a week-old skunk carcass, have come to agree that you gotta die, and they've asked me to do the deed. Fly, Demis, used-to-be resident of Embreeville Mountain. Try 'n hide. 'Cause when my boys find you, they're gonna kill you slow and ugly just for the fun of it."

"But the circle and…"

"The circle's gone." Dane's mouth tightened into a snarl. "But me and my boys ain't."

Demis shrieked as they flew off, a line of Dane's men, screaming Hunter curses, on their tail.

"You're plumb filled with magic, Centenary, even near death, but it ain't the first time I've felt it in you." Dane reached into Cent, pulling out her spirit and almost all her remaining energy, then dropped her body to the ground. "Tell your eternal goodbye."

Stowne. She pushed her energy against Dane's hand in search of an exit.

"You'll live if you mind me." Dane tightened her grip. "Don't and you'll follow Demis to a grave so deep you'll never cross the veil again. That's the deal me and your eternal made."

Centenary. Stowne's presence entered her mind, offering comfort and clarity. *I knew how you would react when Dustu finally broke from Demis, that you would willingly sacrifice yourself so he could cross the veil. Go with Dane. She will heal your spirit while we heal your body, so the two can be rejoined.*

But she—

Hunters are neither our ally nor our enemy. Listen to Dane, be obedient so you may return to my side. Stowne's energy pressed against hers then broke away. "Take her, Dane. Heal her spirit per our agreement and return her to her body."

"Yeah. I'm outta here." Dane's grip on Cent grew cold and distant. "I'll get her back to you by Samhain."

Chapter Forty

Black Jaded Wings
October 6-25, 2017

Stowne *should've let me die.* Cent fought for survival inside Dane's grip.

"Stop feelin' sorry for yourself." Dane landed with the soft thud of work boots touching the ground. "Welcome to my world again, girlie. Come right in and make yourself at home at *my* convenience." She shoved her sweaty fist into her pocket, smothering Cent even more. "Quit your bitchin'." Dane pulled out her fist and shook it until Cent stopped trying to escape. "That's better. Hold still, and you'll be breathin' easy in no time."

The Hunters lived on the other side of Embreeville Mountain. "We're hidden up here." Dane separated her fingers enough for Cent to see the collection of parted-out luxury vehicles and heavy equipment setting in the broad, shallow gully earlier hydraulic mining had created. "You can't see much from above, and what you can, we've covered with some real good camouflage spells."

You're running… a chop-shop up here.

"You can call it that, but I prefer forced recycling. My kind don't need no sleep so it's a twenty-four-seven operation." Dane squeezed her fingers together to keep Cent from seeing more. "You can't get by in this modern world without money." She took Cent inside the gully the Hunters had covered and made into a home, showing her how the interior of her kingdom was nothing like the metal-cluttered, oil-leaking exterior. The main hall was wide, well-lit, marble-tiled, and mica removed from other local mines covered the walls until they shimmered. There were animal heads by the hundreds along those walls too. Wild boars, small game, nearly extinct Wood Buffalo, and deer with the largest racks Cent had ever seen. Dane liked luxury, weapons, and taxidermy, in that order, and displayed all three in her spacious underground bedchamber. She liked women too, but she yelled for her wives to fly elsewhere the minute she entered with Cent in her hand.

"Git!" Dane folded back her fingers as soon as they'd fled, holding Cent's waning energy between her fingertips, encasing her in a gold-wire ball and tethering her to her wrist with a heavy gold chain. "Now I can keep a good eye on you." She dangled Cent before her face. "I'm gonna teach you a thing or two while I got you, girlie, first one bein' don't piss me off by pullin' like that!" Dane hung her circlet and welding cap on a deer antler then ran her hand over her head to smooth down the wayward hairs, smiling as she dragged Cent into her hand to squeeze hard. "You gonna listen now?"

If I didn't want to live…I'd have already…pissed you off…even more. Cent grew quiet when Dane laughed at her.

I'd hush up if I were you, 'cause I'm the only one what's keepin' you alive right now. Dane was even rougher in her means of energy-feeding. She'd reel Cent in to gorge her, then jerk most of it away. Binge and purge. Bloated to hollow. Afterward, she'd quiz Cent on her spell knowledge, taking delight when Cent became almost too tired to reply, chastising her for loving an elemental when she was capable of so much more.

"What a waste. I might just hafta enchant you and make you my bride, a Human bitch worthy of doin' my laundry." Dane tucked her wings beneath her shoulders and drove to her welding shop, minimally tolerant of her Human customers until she couldn't stand it, then she retreated to her office where she quizzed Cent about business. "While you're here, you might as well learn me some about runnin' my recyclin' profits through this shop." Cent complied only because she had no other choice, and the next day they went bow hunting deep inside the National Forest, though it wasn't deer season. "Food you won't be eatin', girlie." She laughed when Cent lunged at her. "Guess I'll hafta have your part too so I can feed you later." Lavish meals took place every night inside the Hunter's Great Hall, a throwback to their earlier days. Appetizers of Wee Fairies cooked different ways were followed by a feast of illegal game, fried potatoes, fresh greens, cornbread, cheap beer, and moonshine. Cent was forced to watch the revelry and its resulting debauchery when Dane dragged her wives into her bed.

I'll have to gouge my eyes to unsee that. Cent worked at escaping her tether whenever Dane wasn't looking, but the welds of her circular prison were Dane's magic and, therefore, inescapable.

During her sober hours, Dane tempted Cent with promises of wealth and eternal life, teaching her how to fight unfair, sneak, and deceive like a Hunter. *You were mine once a few hundred years ago. I was huntin', had my bow drawn on you for a kill, but you were so goddamn cute in that deer-hide dress that I couldn't do it, so I netted you instead, and Daddy let me keep you for a pet.*

How kind.

Hey, I kept you off the dinner table. That's somethin', but Daddy and Stowne had a nasty-ass fight over you, and I had to give you back. A peculiar sadness dropped into Dane's voice. *Nah, just kiddin'. Daddy gave you back in pieces.* She laughed, but something in her tone said there was a truth to the story. *Had you goin' for a minute, didn't I?* Dane sent her wives away after that, ate her dinner with only Cent as a witness, and drank heavily afterward, her head to her chest as she became lost in a moonshine-fueled fugue. "I loved you." She mumbled at one point. "Still do. I could never forgive Daddy for what he did. You're the whole reason I'm king now."

Cent didn't know if Dane was serious or not, so she kept silent and was relieved when Dane's mood lifted, and the conversation turned.

Careful what you wish for. Hunters don't give nary a lick more than you ask, unless it gives us somethin' back, or we think it's funny. Dane put her jar aside and placed Cent in her bed to wrap powerful energy around her, showering her with magic-laden temptations designed to make her forget, but Cent refused the Hunter King as often as she refused to set Stowne aside. *Forget that dirty ol' bag of gravel.*

I can't, and I won't. Cent pulled away from Dane and curled to save her energy. Dane raged when she did, returning to her body to pull Cent from the bed, squeezing her inside her fist until the gold of Cent's prison folded in, and she nearly extinguished. Cent still rose before the Hunter King the second she released her hold, guarded in her hatred as she pulled on her tether.

Not enough, girlie. You gotta hate me even more than I hate you. Dane dangled Cent before the tall mirror in the room's corner, showing her death-pale, battered body where it barely breathed in her homestead bed. "Leave it behind, give yourself to me, and I'll make you a new one. Dark-winged beauty slid into a pair of tight-fittin' jeans. You'll be one of us. Wild Hunter. Eternal and more temptin' than a NASCAR race, fresh deer roast, and a quart of smooth-ass moonshine all on the same night. I'll marry you then, make you my queen who knows the world like only my men and me usually do. You'll work magic on my books and be able to come and go as you please, but you'll always come home at night, so I won't hafta come huntin' you." Dane pointed to the weapons lining her bedchamber wall. "No one wants me out lookin' for them after dark."

Don't threaten me. I'm not going to cower like your shallow, magic-dabbling wives.

No, you're a back-talkin', hard-ass bitch of a witch who takes risks and knows her way 'round numbers. You'd be as good in bed as you'd be for my business. Dane waved her hand to place Cent inside a new body, showing the power that came with it. Raven-haired, curvaceous, dark-eyed, and pale-skinned. A perpetual creature of the night. She wasn't dressed in a short skirt or tight jeans but in hunting clothes— camouflage coveralls opened down the front, clod-hopper boots, and a polished circlet identical to Dane's mounted over a Carhart ballcap.

She's shaping me into what she wants, an equal and a business partner, a better-educated version of herself. Cent smothered her laugh when she realized King Redneck-Junkyard-Fairy thought she was both hot *and* smart.

"Fly with me." Dane released Cent's tether, and they soared out of the mine tunnel and into the darkness, flying side-by-side, flitting among the trees, sailing toward the moon until Dane captured Cent in her arms. She kissed Cent as they hung in the air, long and desperate, hissing as she dragged her teeth across Cent's bottom lip. "I agreed to save you, that you'd return, not that you'd stay."

"You ain't so bad after all, and smart too. Catch me, and you can have me." Cent slipped from the Hunter king's hold and flew between the trees, laughing as Dane pursued her. She hid amid a pond's tall grasses then among the top branches of an old-growth Oak. Dane found her both times, but Cent slipped from her grasp, hiding until Dane called to her.

"Come back to me. It's high time we made things official."

Cent settled to the ground beside Dane, grinning as she ran her tongue over her pointed teeth. "You called, Great King?"

"You're gonna be my favorite queen and huntin' partner." Dane held out her hand.

"But what if I don't want to share you with them other women?" Cent batted her eyes.

"We can talk about them later." Dane spat her snuff from her mouth. "Slip outta them coveralls and share your brand-spankin'-new janey with me. We'll fly together 'til dawn, and you can tell me how you're gonna be mine forever."

"But I'm ready to speak my decision now." Cent sidled up to Dane, leaning in to kiss her cheek and rub against her, unzipping her coveralls even lower, curling her wings against her back in a Hunter sign of submission. "I am a witch. I am Hunter blood." She took the Hunter King's hand and let herself be drawn in, sighing, relaxing into Dane's touch as her spirit broke free, floating just outside Dane's reach as she laughed. "But more than that I am Human, and I am Stowne's. Now, *send me home*."

"You straight-up fooled me." Dane's tone became admiring. "All right, I'll send you home, but not without a little somethin' to remember me by." She slammed Cent back into her Hunter body, kissed her hard, then shoved her away. Cent tore backward through the air, streaking over the mountaintop and toward the homestead, scraping the treetops and burning the grass as she flew, her new skin tearing as rock and twigs embedded into it.

Exquisite agony. A will to live. A will to love who and how she wished. She returned to her Human body with this knowledge intact, but her Hunter form remained with her too, melding her into something new.

"Stowne." She opened her eyes to see their face hovering over hers.

"You have returned to me." Stowne pulled her into their arms. "We have all missed you so, and—"

"Let's not." She nearly fell from the bed in her drive to put distance between them. "How dare you deal with that black-winged, redneck bitch without my knowledge!"

"There was no other way." Stowne pulled back to sit on the edge of their bed. "I could not prevent what I knew you were going to do, so I dealt with Dane to save you. But I knew the risks when I did so. The Hunters came here because the Seelie and Unseelie were working together to drive them to extinction."

"I thought they were immortal."

"They can be defined as such, but fae can kill each other, and Hunters can kill elementals as well. They can remain here only because Mother Earth and Long Man see a purpose in their presence."

"Like what?"

"Those like Demis."

"Huh. I guess they did come in handy there." Cent pulled the quilt over her body and rolled to her side away from Stowne. She hurt inside and out, her body still beaten and bruised, possessor of both Human and Hunter wounds. "Dane told me a story."

"The one about you coming back to me in pieces?"

"It's true?"

"Yes, it is. And it is the reason I knew Dane would not kill you."

"That's not a memory I want to recover." But she still wondered what had happened between them. "She said I'm the reason she killed her father and brothers."

"You are, and dealing with her is easier than it was to deal with any of them."

"That says a lot." Cent glanced back at Stowne. "She wasn't kind."

"No Hunter is kind."

"She tried to make me hers, tried to seduce me with wings, with power and wealth."

"Yet, here you are. You chose to come back to me." Stowne's voice remained neutral, but she felt their pain.

"What would you have done if I hadn't made the choice I did?"

"I'd have buried deeper than ever because you had rejected me," they murmured. "It would have been the end of us."

"You risked losing me entirely to save me?" She turned to stare at Stowne, trying to decipher their reasons. "I would have returned sooner or later." *I can't help but.*

"I could not stand by and let you die so early again. I could not accept the intervening time, the wait for you to be reborn and become aware. I have endured it too many times."

"You arranged this without my consent." Cent rolled her shoulders as she sat up. "And you lied when you said Long Man had asked Dane to attend."

"Yes, I did, but if you are expecting an apology—"

"I expect nothing from you anymore." She pulled up her legs and set her face against her thighs, fighting off both emotional and physical pain.

"You have no reason to trust me." Stowne turned their head to look sidelong at her. "Did my desire to keep you forever end our relationship instead?"

"I'm pissed, that's for certain." She wrapped her arms around her calves to squeeze them, but they burned so much that she dropped her arms. "I'm not walking away. We've been together too long for me to let you go that easily."

"That is good to hear." Stowne lifted their mouth in a slow smile. "Our path together has never been a simple one."

"We've got a long walk before we're good again."

"Yes, I know, but we can walk side-by-side."

"Or drag each other along kickin' and screamin'. I expect both." Cent cringed as she rolled her shoulders again. "Ow, what's wrong with my…" She glanced back, gasping. "Oh, no." Her wings had followed her, wet with newness and partially rolled against her back. "*You* did this to me."

"No. That was not part of my deal with Dane. You were to become part Hunter, to become immortal like I am, but now I see I wasn't specific enough."

"Careful what you wish for." Cent flexed her back as the urge to unfurl her wings became overwhelming. They opened behind her, dark gossamer threaded with veins that throbbed with her heartbeat. A part of her. A permanent portion of her now eternal life. "Damn." She rose from the bed to flap them, finding odd acceptance in the very thing that pulled her from humanity.

"I heard you two talking and— dear Lord!" Aubrey closed the door to knock tentatively on it. "May I come in?"

"You've already seen, so why stand on ceremony?" She lifted herself from the floor with her wings, settling by the door to open it, covering her chest with her arms. "Come on."

"I saw them folded against you early this morning but, shit! They're huge when they're open!" Aubrey couldn't or wouldn't look at her, but she wasn't certain which. "Please tell me you can put them away, so we can at least go to the Walmart together."

"Hunters can, so let me try." She closed her eyes to concentrate, flexing muscles she never knew she had, until her wings folded beneath her shoulder blades. "Better?" She went to the wardrobe to put out a t-shirt, pulling it and a pair of sweatpants over her body, pushing the sweats to her knees when they rubbed against her calves.

"Yeah, but you've got a bunch of road rash I need to clean." He held out a Mason jar filled with tea when she turned around

"That'd better be Pal's." She snatched it from him and returned to the bed.

"Like I'd bring you anything else after what's happened." He held out a brown paper bag. "Burger?"

An offering? Cent found this absurdly amusing. "And fries?" She glanced at Stowne who'd turned to face her on the bed. "You and me, we got some serious issues to work through, but right now, all I want to do is eat."

"Then eat before you argue more." Aubrey turned to the door. "Yell for me when you're ready to clean up those legs."

She didn't say much to Stowne as she ate but offered them occasional glares they returned with emotionless gazes. "You know…" She washed down her last bite of burger with tea. "You could've at least clued me in."

"I had no idea Dane was going to do what she did."

Stowne showed no intention of apologizing, so she let the subject drop, sipping on her tea as she looked around. "Where're my glasses?"

"They broke during the chaos. Aubrey wants to take you for an eye exam before you get new ones."

"I don't think I need them." She pondered this as she set her tea aside to draw her knees to her chest. "You got me forever now. Is that what you wanted?"

"I will not lie. It is." Stowne raised one side of their mouth in a smirk. "You get me in your preferred form. I get you forever. It seems an equal trade."

"You're an ass for saying that." She nudged them with her toe.

"You have called me much worse for lesser indiscretions."

"Ain't half what I want to call you. These wings itch!" She took off her shirt and unfurled her wings again as she stood before the mirror, turning left then right to better see them. They weren't the only thing about her that'd changed. Her hair was now coal black, and her eyes were dark brown, but neither was as prominent as her wings. "They're not as pretty as when Dane showed them to me."

"Dane exaggerates for her own interests." Stowne moved to stand behind her. "Your wings will grow larger as you learn to use them."

"Spec-frackin'-tacular." She arched her back. "Scratch the right one for me. No, the other right."

"You could at least say please."

"I'm part Hunter Fairy, so you're lucky I don't command you." She sighed when Stowne found the right spot.

"I will be your humble servant if you ever do." Stowne stepped back so she could tuck her wings then turned her around. "Your mother is on the porch with everyone else. The evening is warm and pleasant for the season it is."

"I know. I feel Mama, the weather, and every rock and stem that's worked into my legs. Ruleman too. What the hell is he doing here?"

"He is every bit the kind and patient man your Aunt Tess described, so please give him a chance."

"Yeah, maybe, but does he know about— he saw it all, didn't he?"

"Possessed or not such things cannot be unseen, so we had to be honest with him. He knows everything aside from your newest condition."

"He's going to think me an angel or a demon. I'm not certain which." She flexed her back as the itch returned. "I hope Aubrey has some cortisone cream in that backpack of his."

"Neither angels nor demons exist." Stowne stopped when she frowned at him.

"Dane's Satan in a Dale Junior ballcap."

"Very well, perhaps they do exist, but not in the manner they are often referred to in. Ivan will come to understand in time."

"I wasn't wanting to pull the rug out from under the man's faith." Cent turned to face Stowne, admiring the way they'd perfected their androgynous form. "You don't have to stay like that all the time."

"But it is what you like."

"Just because I'm stuck with these wings—"

"Let me. It is self-penance for forcing them upon you."

"You said yourself you didn't— all right. Then will you surprise me with what's under those clothes every now and again?"

"I will enjoy doing so." Stowne extended their hand to her. "After Aubrey treats you, shall we join our family for an evening on the porch? Warm or not, it is still a fall evening, so I suggest we bring the quilt from our bed."

"Yeah. Sounds nice." Cent folded her wings and pulled down her shirt, grimacing as the itchy tip of her right wing poked through the back. "Yep, I'm going to freak Ivan Ruleman's shit for certain."

"Then let him be freaked." Stowne draped the blanket over her shoulders. "There is someone else waiting outside for you too."

"Who could possibly— Betty?" Cent's eyes filled with tears. "When did she get here?"

"While you were with Dane. Aubrey paid for her bus ticket and picked her up in Greeneville. You said she needed to come, and she agreed. She could not return to her former life and hope to survive."

"Why didn't you tell me earlier?" She'd felt Betty's presence but had convinced herself Dane had thrown her senses off to keep her subdued. "Is she okay?" Cent still felt fear and sympathy, both of which Hunters saw as weaknesses. *Maybe I'm not so much like them after all.*

"Betty is not the person you once knew." Stowne pulled her blanket higher on her shoulders. "But, then again, neither are you."

"What does she know, what does…" Cent shook as her nerves threatened to overwhelm her.

"More than you think. I will retrieve both her and Aubrey, so you can ask for yourself."

"Weird shit, but it explains a whole lot." Betty sat beside Cent, their feet dangling over the porch's edge so Cent's legs, now bandaged, wouldn't ache as much as they had been. "It's late October, and I'm drinking iced tea while I sit on the front porch of a log cabin in Tennessee. If you'd told me this in June, I'd have laughed." She turned her face toward the setting sun. "It's beautiful here but strange. Surreal and peaceful in a way I never expected."

"You're finally figuring things out." Cent nudged Betty's foot with hers. "So how long have you been able to see spirits?"

"I remember seeing them standing over my crib." Betty stared down the hill to where Aubrey's haints huddled at the driveway's edge. "The drugs and alcohol drowned out most of them. If I didn't see them, they weren't real." She brought up her hands to pick at her nails. "Pyre says I'm a physical medium. I feel, see, and hear whatever spirits want me to. Oh, hell, Cent. I've been waking up every night of my life until I got here. Every. Night. Three AM. Same shit. Spirits lined up to talk to me. I tried to kill myself twice over it, but that only made it worse. Suicide cases came at me then, and I absorbed their angst until I thought I'd explode. That's when I turned to heroin." Betty wiped her eyes with the back of her hand. No mascara and she was prettier for it. "I start therapy in three days. This woman, Darla, she's not a regular counselor. I don't know how, but Aubrey found her. She's a medium too, and an addict, so she's going to teach me how to better handle both."

"I'm glad for it, and you— what a crap way to have lived for so long. But you're sleeping now, and the haints are staying away, so you can." Cent offered to share her blanket when Betty shivered, and she accepted it, scooting closer.

Jack sat on the porch's far end, watching. He'd not come when Cent called to him but neither had he growled. *He's trying to figure me out, too.*

"Everyone here is helping me." Betty slid her hand into Cent's. "You and this backwater hole are the best things that ever happened to me." She kissed Cent's cheek and rested her head on her shoulder. "I was right about your cousin. He's cute, but he's only got eyes for Rayne." Betty laughed. "Stowne's incredible, by the way, but that's what you deserve."

"You deserve someone too." Cent kissed her forehead. "And you'll eventually find them. You and me, we're not on that downhill slide anymore. We're on our way back up. Not stuck. There's no pharmaceutical plant or fish stand stinking up the air. No pavement, dealers, or drugs getting in the way. The sky's the limit."

"Especially for you with those wings." Betty sat up when Cent tensed. "Oh, relax. You're still my cute little cuttah. That's all I care about. Your aura's different now, a little darker, but that's not necessarily a bad thing."

"I guess not. You really had this ability up in Chicago?" Cent rolled her shoulders when her wing-tips renewed their itch. "I had no idea."

"Yeah, me either. I just thought I was nuts, but you…" Betty grinned. "I knew you were something bigger when we first met, but you were unsettled up north. Not like here at all."

"Unsettled is one way to put it." Cent raised her hand in a hex sign when the haints moved closer. *Outside the fence, or I'll wrap you in a spell and send you floating down the Nolichucky, so Long Man can deal with you.*

All right! We're going! They retreated across the road where they stood watching. Evil men reduced to fading haints who begged to be crossed. She couldn't help but feel the smallest of sympathies— until she recalled they'd almost killed her and Aunt Tess.

Jack snorted in agreement and scooted closer to Cent but still stayed out of her reach.

"They'll cross at Samhain if they do what Exan told them."

"I haven't heard them apologize yet. The bastards tried to kill my Cent and her great aunt." Betty scooted back to draw her knees to her chest. "Aubrey's taking me to Knoxville tomorrow to see the same doctor his ex does."

"Aub used to work there. That's where he and Ethan met."

"Really? That explains how he managed such a fast appointment. Small world. Afterward, he's taking me clothes shopping. Aubrey says there's a tall women's store near there where I can get a couple of decent outfits to go job hunting in. Rayne's going too. That pickup of his is massive inside. I got all the leg room in the world." She tugged at her high-water sweatpants. "Short skirts aren't the real me any more than these stupid sweats are."

"Those are mine." Cent laughed nonetheless. "And Aub lives to do such things for people." She rubbed her hands together. "I owe him a lot."

"That's funny. He said the exact same thing about you." Betty grabbed her hand to examine the nails. "You've got to let me give you a manicure."

"Ick. No." Cent pulled her hand back.

"Then how about some black polish to match your hair and eyes?"

Dear God, I'm turning Goth. A Goth Hunter fairy. She liked the sound but knew Dane might well be repulsed. *More the reason.* "Yeah, black polish would work, but only natural products can come into this house."

"Aubrey had me throw most of my cosmetics out at McDonald's. Better stuff for a better life." Betty snatched Cent's hand again, turning it over to see the palm. "Your lifeline still runs past your wrist. I told you before I wasn't certain what it meant, but I think I do now."

"Yeah." Cent closed her hand and leaned against Betty. "I'm glad you're here."

"So am I, baby doll, so am I."

Chapter Forty-One

The Fine Print
Samhain (Halloween) 2017

So *this is a Samhain circle.* Everyone had made a great effort to decorate the area with harvest vegetables, glowing jack-o'-lanterns, and fall flowers, a welcomed distraction since they'd buried Dustu's remains that morning. *I hope he soon moves to his next life.* She wished him well and hoped he didn't remember the pain of the life and afterlife he'd left behind. Cent had spoken a Tsalagi prayer in his honor and cried in Stowne's arms afterward.

It is finished, asiule ehu. Your Uncle Kinnon said our son is playing with other children who are waiting for their turn at being reborn.

That makes me as happy as can be.

Me too. Our son is finally being a child. Maybe he will learn digadayosdi.

Yeah, I hope so. Cent pressed her forehead against Stowne's shoulder. *Sounds like Uncle Kinnon's been making the rounds. He came to Aunt Tess last night to talk to her about Gan.* She wiped her eyes and lifted her head to smile at her eternal. *He gave her his blessing.*

That is very good. Stowne kissed the top of her head. *Did she also tell you that Dane sent you a gift?*

Tess was so pleased about Uncle Kinnon she must've forgot, but I thought I smelled Dane's reek somewhere around midnight.

Play nice. She sent your gift via one of her men.

Whatever it is, I don't want it.

A fully processed and wrapped deer? That would be a waste of good venison considering Tess has already placed it in her deep freezer.

Did she check it for spells and poisons?

It was a clean kill and so fresh it was warm to the touch.

Which means it was poached. Cent sighed. *I fucking hate Dane, do you know that?*

I am aware. Stowne raised one brow when they looked down at her. *But Dane finds you highly attractive, a fact we can use to our advantage.*

Especially if we want cheap car parts.

Centenary!

Poached deer, illegal parts. What's the difference? She'd come to realize she was more Hunter than she'd initially thought. Her teeth were sharper, her tongue even more so, but she still possessed patience, especially where Mama was concerned. And she had lots of help in that regard. Ivan Ruleman, she'd discovered, found Mama's craziness endearing. *Well, someone needs to.* When he'd found out she was half-magic, he'd marched her back to the hospital, insisting that she be re-admitted so she could be stabilized. He had taken control of her meds after she'd been discharged and had escorted her to every doctor and therapy appointment since.

Ivan had pulled Cent aside earlier in the day. "I've lost my church and most of my family's money, but I love Nida with all my heart and believe the Lord put her in my life so I can take care of her." He folded his hands together. "She knows she has to take her medications. No cheeking or skipping, I have the key to her medications box, and I dish them out each-and-every time. If we're going to be together, she's got to follow her treatment plan. She can be dangerous if she don't."

Tell me something I don't know. "You're biting off a big chunk by taking her on." Cent rolled her shoulders to still their perpetual itch. "But if she's who you want, I say go for it."

"I need to ask something of you too." Ivan pulled his ballcap from his head to worry it in his hands. He'd set aside his suits and ties in favor of faded blue jeans and t-shirts, a working man's look, and one Cent believed suited him better. "I've seen too much to preach the gospel without doubt, so I'm needing work to keep myself busy while I sort things out. This place needs a lot of fixin', and your mama needs constant supervision."

"You noticed."

"I can't help but, so I'd like to help you around here and… I ain't asking for pay besides food, shelter, and Nida's medicines beyond what her Social Security pays." He worried his cap even harder. "She's transferring her share of the homestead proceeds back to Aubrey, so it won't complicate her disability payments or Medicare, and I've got enough stowed away to take care of other issues if they come up. Not nearly as much as Aubrey seems to, but— I'd like to sell the land on either side of the property if y'all want it."

That's interesting. The idea had taken in his head quicker than she'd anticipated when she'd created the spell to plant it. "And here I figured you'd be running for the hills as soon as it all came out." Cent chuckled. "But, yes to the land. We can discuss price later, however, until then I need you to help Stowne stabilize both hillsides before winter hits. Those hired men—"

"Did long-term damage, I know. I'm sorry." He gazed down the hillside at the trailer. "I've lived in this area most of my life and, while I ain't got no magic in my blood, I grew up with my granny and learned to read the signs and about water witchin' from my papaw. I reckon it shouldn't have surprised me as much as it did." He shrugged and grinned at her. "I want to marry your mama if she'll have me and you'll allow it."

She's a grown-ass woman and— No, I get it. "You have my blessing, but you'll have to have Mama's agreement too."

"I pray she does." He'd walked away happy, and Cent had been relieved, but now she sat dressed in a long, black tunic and leggings, beside Stowne, welcoming others into the Samhain circle. There was just as much ceremony as there'd been for their first dance, more so in some regards. Water, Air, Fire, and Earth followed by Exan, who'd crossed Aubrey's haints just before the festivities began. All were welcomed as were the fae, the Wee Fairies first, so they could dance around the fire a few times before they hid from their larger, meaner relations.

They didn't hide behind me this time. This vexed Cent even though she understood. The Wee Fairies feared The Hunters, but they weren't alone in their unease. Dane and her followers unsettled Cent too with their beautiful redneck cruelty. She was more than quarter-magic now, over three-quarters Stowne said, but she was still part Human and a witch besides, making her a force to contend with.

She waited until the Wee Fairies had hidden and Dane appeared in the sky before she pulled back the flaps Betty had cut in her tunic and unfurled her wings, ignoring the gasps along the circle's edges as she flapped them to stretch and exercise the muscles. *Swimmer's back.* Aubrey had meant it as a compliment, but she thought it made her shoulders appear even broader than they naturally were.

Aubrey turned from the circle when Charley rushed into his arms. She was a curly-haired, cute-as-a-button kid, even in haint form, and was drowning Aubrey in kisses to thank him for his efforts. *Aub needs that.* She wanted to meet Charley, but Dane was already landing, her two queens immediately behind her, all three of them decked-out for Samhain. Dane wore a kilt of black and blue Hunter tartan, new work boots, and a polished circlet while her queens wore glistening tiaras and tight denim dresses that looked as though they'd been ravaged by a BeDazzler. The taller queen held a quart of moonshine in a blue glass jar, and the shorter one swayed like she was already drunk.

What a pair.

"Dane, you honor us with your presence." Stowne rose from their seat to bow before the Hunter king. "You are welcome here anytime."

"Oh, save it. You got her, I don't." Dane flexed her wings in a sign of power. "But it's Samhain, and I wanted to see how our girl's doin'."

Our girl? "I'm well, thank you, but I'm not, nor will I ever be *yours*." She glanced toward Dane's wives, both of whom scowled at her. "Your positions are safe, trust me."

"That's sounds stupid comin' from a Hunter." Dane rolled her eyes, but Cent saw her smirk before she hid it. "Hangin' around with me will solve that lil' problem. I'll pick you up at the Brigid circle and deliver you back at Beltane. Wear somethin' sexy." Dane nodded to Stowne. "Per our agreement, of course."

"Fine print," mumbled Cent. "Yes, I was told, but certainly not by you. I'm bringing two escorts with me." Yes, Stowne had told her, and she'd told them it'd be a cold day in hell before she went, but she knew it'd been a meaningless retort. Dane wanted guaranteed protection for her illegal operations, so she'd given a bit when it'd come to Cent, more so when she'd reminded Dane who'd be updating her accounting system next year. What'd been six months was now three, a favorable compromise in their direction.

"That's not…" Dane flexed her back again when her wives snickered. "Who're you bringin' along?"

Stowne's right. She must still love me to accept without argument. Cent made a note to think of ways to take advantage of this, starting with purchasing a pair of black coveralls, a deer hide dress too, if she could find one. "Pyre and my grandparent."

"I ain't lettin' no goddam Human—"

"She means me." Exan stepped forward. "And I plan to keep a careful watch on her."

"*Two* elementals." Dane's hand drifted to where her empty holster rested under her kilt. Samhain meant peace and transition, Stowne had said, and weapons were never, ever allowed. "Why should I?"

"They're coming along if you want me to figure a permanent means of funneling cash from your chop-shop through your welding business without raising red flags."

"You're a smart one, Cent." Dane narrowed her eyes. "All right, I'll abide as long as you guarantee what you figure out works."

"There'll be no trail whatsoever when I'm done." She rose from her seat to face Dane. "But no one will be allowed to torture, be unkind, or kill me or my family or friends for *any* reason. No Wee Fairies can be eaten while we're there either. Stowne has a letter addressed to the IRS and FBI stamped and ready to mail, and we've got backup copies stowed elsewhere that'll be sent out the moment any of us goes missing or is found dead."

"I save your life, and this is the…" Dane lashed out, but Cent was quicker, retreating to Stowne's side before the Hunter king's pale fist could reach her. "You bitch! I shoulda glommed down on you until you damn-well extinguished!" Dane snarled and threw her circlet across the ritual sands.

"I'm as much a bitch as I am a witch, and I'll do magic for your bottom line if you take care of me and mine." Cent smiled when Stowne wrapped their arm around her. "It's called the fine print, my darling Dane, my way of tethering you so you'll behave. You made me a Hunter, so you're the only one to blame for my being underhanded. Now take my offer or leave it. Oh, and thanks for the deer meat. I placed protection spells over it to keep you from tainting it later."

"I ain't— argh! So be it!" Dane bellowed for her queens to retrieve her headwear and stomped to her seat alongside the elemental groups, but Cent could see the fury behind the Hunter king's eyes. They'd bested Dane this time, and she'd face the consequences come Brigid. However, that was still months away, and she had Stowne every moment until then.

Mama came up to her before the evening progressed much further. "We're still going to celebrate Christmas and New Year's, ain't we?"

"Christmas, yes, because I've still got a tender spot for it, but New Year's? Tonight marks the new year for magical beings in most realms, especially witches."

"I know but—"

"Come on, Nida. You can talk to her about it tomorrow." Ivan led her back to Tess, who offered her a jar of mead. Special mead, Tess called it, which meant it didn't contain a drop of alcohol. But Cent's mead— She took a long draw from her quart jar. She'd mixed in a double shot of peach moonshine that made Dane tolerable and helped her to see Mama as sweet and innocent as Ivan did.

Stowne cast the circle, calling to the quarters, recognizing each major elemental group in their watchtower call. Earth. Air. Fire. Water. Stowne held their hand out to Cent. "Spirit."

She accepted their hand, stepping onto the circle sands and into Stowne's arms, placing her feet atop theirs as drums began to beat. The first dance. Their dance. Stowne would dance with no other while she was gone.

"New year, asiule ehu."

"New life." Cent stretched up to kiss Stowne's cheek. Other dancers joined them on the sand as the music shifted time. Couples of various mixes. A drunken triad of Dane and her giggling wives. *Shit, she's staring at me.*

Dane does not forget the things she wants. Stowne's hold on Cent tightened.

Well, she can't have me. Cent watched as Dane's wives moved their heads back to share a wicked smile Dane couldn't see. *Those two are up to no good.*

There is always something dubious happening within the Hunter ranks. Stowne spun Cent away from the scene. *But it is more the thrill of pursuit than the catching for Dane. She knows that anything more would be a losing battle where you are concerned.* They rumbled low to punctuate their assertion.

Ain't that the truth. Cent startled when Mama and Ivan passed them.

"Do they understand what it means to dance in my presence?" Stowne asked as they spun away.

"Mama, no. But it wouldn't surprise me if Ivan did. He's been a fast learner."

"Yes, but he clings to his Bible."

"There's nothing wrong with that," Cent replied. "As long as he clings to the right parts. Besides, I'm rather fond of mine."

"Then why did you order two new copies this morning?"

"Because King James used poetic lies as a means of control, and the Greek translation I ordered will be as helpful as the New International Version." She flapped her wings, rising from Stowne's feet to look them in the eyes. "These things do have their good points."

"Yes, I can see that." Stowne grabbed her by the waist, supporting her weight as they kissed her, their want seeping through until Cent's bare toes curled.

"Wow." She'd leaned in to kiss them again when a familiar form crossed the corner of her vision. "Aubrey?" She gaped as she looked down at him.

"That's my name." He lifted his head from Rayne's shoulder to beam at Cent.

"Et tu, Aub?"

"I decided it wasn't a rebound after all." He peered into Rayne's smiling eyes.

"Isn't love grand?" Rayne held tight to Aubrey, their water robes swirling around his legs as they swung away.

Yeah, it is.

"A delightful night indeed." Stowne pointed to where Gan sat with Tess in their lap. Jack sat at Gan's feet. This was Jack number fifteen or maybe sixteen. They couldn't be certain, but there should always be a dog or two on the homestead.

And cats too. "As soon as we get the new barn up, I want some cats." Shelter cats. Fixed, furry, fluffy ferocious mouse hunters who like to lie on the front porch in the sun next to Jack. "I want one for the house too."

"So it can sleep in our laps during cold winter evenings." Stowne smiled down at her. "Perhaps Gan and Tess will be dancing in my presence someday soon."

"Maybe. Tess deserves happiness."

"I think so too, and did you see our newest pairing?" Stowne nodded toward Betty who was running her finger down the back of Pyre's fiery hand. There was no mead in Betty's jar either, just iced tea, but she didn't need anything to enhance her joy. She'd found a home and family in Hare Creek. Sure, temptation was everywhere. Opioid abuse ran rampant in Appalachia. But strength came from a good support system, and Betty had that if nothing else.

Cent chuckled when she saw Pyre push Betty's cigarettes away with their free hand.

"You have a wonderful, magical family, Centenary Rhodes." Stowne pulled her in for another toe-curling kiss.

"And a history and an eternal future I never expected, but it's all good." She flapped her wings, moving forward to press against Stowne. "It's all so very good."

Epilogue

December 1, 2017

"Did you use the bank card again?" Cent held out her phone for Stowne to see. Dark came early this time of year, so her phone lit the bedroom but no more than Stowne's contented glow.

"Yes, Aubrey printed a receipt for me, and I placed it in the basket where you asked me to put such things. The book arrived this afternoon before you returned home." Stowne looked up from the paperback in their hands. They served as their own reading light and often Cent's night light, a fact that amused her to an unreasonable degree.

"Yeah, but you do understand that I make crap wages working at Dryler's, even as a manager, right?"

"You have told me as much, yes, but it is a good book." Stowne pushed their hair behind their ears when it curtained their face.

"Cheap romance novels are never *good* books."

"They are widely read, and I find their predictable content calming. Hence, good." Stowne lowered their eyes to the page again.

"Stowne? Honey?"

"Yes?" They peered up at her with a weak smile.

"If you order any more books this month, we're going to overdraw the account again. And we need most of my next check to make the property payment to Aubrey."

"Then I will refrain." They closed the book and set it on their lap. "But I am almost finished with this one, so I will need more reading material. Nights are long, and your Human portion still needs sleep."

"I'm going to buy you an e-reader next month then we're going to discuss a book allowance for you, but tomorrow I'll stop by Mr. K's and buy you a stack of used paperbacks."

"And you will drop by Pal's for a tea, I am certain."

"That goes without saying."

"Will buying more books not overdraw the account?"

"No, comparatively speaking. I'll use cash at Mr. K's."

"Thank you for doing so." Stowne patted the bed beside them. "Come sit with me."

"I've got things to do."

"Ivan and Nida have finished repairing the cellar stairs, and I completed the trench for the line to the trailer's septic tank. Aubrey also placed dinner in the slow cooker down in the trailer before he left for work this morning. The architect is scheduled to be here next week to discuss changes to the house." Stowne furrowed their brow. "And the electrician is scheduled for the day after tomorrow. You and Aubrey are both off work that day, if memory serves."

"That's nice, since the solar panels are ready to go, but I still need—"

"Rayne fed and watered the chickens and goats, Pyre stacked more than enough wood on the porch for the next week, and Betty helped Tess pack the trailer all afternoon."

"Well then." Cent kicked off her clodhoppers, collapsed onto the bed beside Stowne, and rolled onto her stomach. "Scratch?"

"Gladly." Stowne set their book aside and rolled to press against her. "You must unfurl so I can."

"Yeah, hold on." She pulled off her shirt and undershirt then flexed her back to flip out her wings, narrowly missing Stowne's head as they spread. "Sorry. The tips are sore."

"You've been rubbing on door facings again." Stowne scratched around the raw spots then took the jar of cortisone cream from the bedside table, rubbing the cream over her wing tips until she sighed. "Better?"

"Yes. Thank you. You know what I've decided?"

"What is that?"

"I've decided Hunters are always cranky because they itch." She grinned over her shoulder at Stowne.

"It is certainly the center of your discomfort." Stowne waited until she'd tucked her wings then rolled her onto her back, straddling her waist. "I love you. Witchy, itchy, or otherwise."

"And I love you too, you big hunk of rock. You can say I'm being bitchy, because I sometimes am."

"You said it for me." Stowne leaned in to kiss her, their mouth warm, soft as fine sand and still smiling. "And I love the Hunter in you too."

"Glad someone does." She pulled them down to kiss their nose. "Any and all."

"Newlyweds. Going at it like…" Birdie's orb drifted out the bedroom door. "I'm gonna move my wardrobe. I swear I am!"

"Any and all," repeated Stowne as they moved to cover Cent's mouth with theirs again. *And forevermore.*

Mountain Gap Books sincerely hopes you enjoyed reading this book as much as we did. If so, we would greatly appreciate a short review on your favorite book website. Reviews are crucial for any author, and even just a line or two can make a huge difference.

About the Author

Born and raised in the foothills of the Appalachian Mountains, Science Fiction and Fantasy author Jeanne G'Fellers has taught on both the secondary and collegiate levels, but she now devotes her time to writing. Her early memories include watching the original Star Trek series with her father and reading the stacks of books her librarian mother brought home. Jeanne's influences include authors Anne McCaffrey, Ursula K. Le Guin, Octavia Butler, Isaac Asimov, and Frank Herbert.

Author website: http://jeannegfellersauthor.com/
Twitter: http://twitter.com/jlgfellers
Facebook Author Page: https://www.facebook.com/Jeannegfellersauthor/

Other Titles by Jeanne G'Fellers:

The Appalachian Elementals Series (Mountain Gap Books)
Cleaning House
Keeping House (2019)

The Surrogate Series
Surrogate (Supposed Crimes Publisher)
Surrogate: Hunted (Supposed Crimes Publisher)
Surrogate: Traditions (Mountain Gap Books 2019)

The Sisters Series (Bella Books)
No Sister of Mine
Sister Lost Sister Found
Sisters Flight
No Sisters Keeper

Appalachian Elementals Series Glossary and Word Primer

Adadoda – [Tsalagi] father

Agayvli Itseiyusdi Nvya – [Tsalagi] Old Green Stone (Embreeville Mountain, also Stowne's full name)

Asgayaninela – [Tsalagi] husband

Asiule Ehu – [Tsalagi] lover

Aubrey James Rhodes – [character] human healer and empath

Ayoli Invigati Saquu – [Tsalagi] Young Tall One (Mount Mitchell)

Centenary Irene Rhodes (Cent) – [character] quarter-magic Human witch

Dane Gow – [character] Hunter Fairy King

Demis – [character] death elemental

Digadayosdi – [Tsalagi] game similar to billiards or marbles

Dustu Usdi – [Tsalagi] small spring green frog (also the name of Cent and Stowne's son)

Embreeville Mountain – [geographical feature] mountain in the Appalachian chain located in Northeast Tennessee, (see also: Stowne)

Etsi – [Tsalagi] ma, mama

Exan – [character] death elemental

Ganolesgi (Gan) – [character] air elemental

Hunters – [group/species] human-sized fae known for their deceit, illegal activities, and metal-working skills, can be either benevolent or malevolent depending on the profit to be had

Invigati – [Tsalagi] tall

Itseiyusdi – [Tsalagi] green

Itseiyusdi Odlav – [Tsalagi] alternative name for Embreeville Mountain

Ivan Ruleman – [character] human Christian preacher

Kinnon Byrne – [character] Tess Rhodes' husband

Long Man – [character] spirit of the Nolichucky river

Mount Mitchell – mountain in the Appalachian chain located in North Carolina, the tallest mountain in the Appalachian chain

Nida Rhodes – [character] Centenary Rhodes' mother, half-magic Human

Nolichucky – [geographical feature] river that runs through Northeast Tennessee and Western North Carolina

Odlav – [Tsalagi] mountain

Pyre – [character] fire elemental

Raven Mocker – the most feared of Cherokee witches, sometimes said to appear as a sasquatch/bigfoot

Rayne – [character] water elemental

Stowne – [character] earth elemental

Tessa Jo Rhodes (Aunt Tess) – [character] Human witch

Tsalagi – Cherokee people

Ududu – [Tsalagi] grandfather

Unitsi – [Tsalagi] mother

Usdagalv – [Tsalagi] cavern (also the name of Stowne's underground home)

Usdayvhsgi – [Tsalagi] wife

Wee Fairies – [group/species] small fae who are mischievous but benevolent

Yvwitsunastiga – [Tsalagi] Little People

Mountain Gap Books

www.mountaingapbooks.com

CPSIA information can be obtained
at www.ICGtesting.com
Printed in the USA
LVHW08s0540060718
582738LV00001B/3/P